FRIENDLY FIRE

BOOK TWO OF THE BASTARD LEGION

FRIENDLY FIRE

BOOK TWO OF THE BASTARD LEGION

GAVIN G. SMITH

This edition first published in Great Britain in 2018 by Gollancz

First published in Great Britain in 2017 by Gollancz
an imprint of the Orion Publishing Group Ltd
Carmelite House, 50 Victoria Embankment
London EC4Y 0DZ

An Hachette UK Company

1 3 5 7 9 10 8 6 4 2

A CIP catalogue record for this book
is available from the British Library.

ISBN 978 1 473 21727 0

Typeset by Deltatype Ltd, Birkenhead, Merseyside

Printed in Great Britain by Clays Ltd, St Ives plc

www.gavingsmith.com
www.orionbooks.co.uk
www.gollancz.co.uk

For Julian, Rita & Noah

CHAPTER 1

Miska was a ghost in the blue and violet foliage of the jungle undergrowth. She was moving just a little too fast for her reactive camouflage ghillie suit to keep up. It left fractal images in the air, as though the undergrowth was flowing over her heavily obscured shape. She could feel the humidity and smell the sweet, fetid rot in the jungle air, but the inertial armour suit she wore under the ghillie regulated her temperature, helping to mask her heat signature. Miska had her SIG GP-992 in one hand, the combat knife her dad had given her in the other, and a big grin on her face. She was in her element.

The narco-insurgents' supply depot was in a gulley covered by camouflage netting and partially obscured by the jungle canopy. It was a great place to hide but a lousy place to defend. The insurgents had pickets in fighting holes out in the jungle but Miska had been able to murder a path wide enough for the support squad element of the attack to move through stealthily. It would only be a matter of time before the pickets' comms silence was noticed, though. Biometric monitoring hooked up to a central command net would have scuppered her plan but these were gangsters playing at being soldiers, not the real thing.

She slid under a gap in the camo net and found herself on a loose dirt slope overlooking the hive of activity that was the supply depot. There were stacks and stacks of the packed metacoke, which had been refined from the genetically engineered coca plants that had been introduced as a result of the hacked terraforming process. The bundles were being loaded onto robot mules in preparation to be moved to waiting shuttles, or snuck into aerodynamic containers and fired into orbit by the only electromagnetic cargo catapult on the moon. There were caves on the opposite side of the gulley. Judging by the jury-rigged ventilation embedded in the rock, Miska guessed they refined the coke in the caves. There were also two lean-to plastic shacks on the other side of the gulley, close to the entrance to the cave structure. According to the intel these were dormitories; the larger one was for the workers in the refinery, the smaller one for the gunmen and women who guarded them. Her job was to destroy the hacked printer that the insurgents were using to make their weapons and ammunition. She knew it was on the same side of the gulley as she was but intelligence had been sketchy as to its exact location, which was why she was going in alone ahead of the main assault.

Miska was moving down the slope towards a smartcrete gun emplacement on an outcrop that overlooked the gulley. There were four of the insurgents in the emplacement. They were looking inward rather than up the slope. She guessed they were there to protect the drugs from within rather than without. Still, if they'd had motion sensors she wouldn't have been able to sneak up on them like this. Even trip wires would have made her life more difficult. This was a pretty rudimentary operation. She was starting to think that she wouldn't even need the two squads of Bastards she had with her when she slipped, just keeping her footing as she made her way towards the gun emplacement. Loose dirt rolled down the slope in front of her.

Overconfident. Funny how her inner voice sounded like her dad.

One of the gunwomen turned to look her way. That was fine, Miska decided, she could die first. A three-round burst, the gauss pistol's recoil negligible. The velocity was dialled down to subsonic. The only noise the pistol made was the slight metal-on-metal clicking from the movement of its components. It still sounded loud to Miska. The three rounds hit the woman almost dead centre in the triangle formed by her forehead and upper cheeks, exactly where the crosshairs from the smartlinked pistol were overlaid in Miska's internal visual display. The woman's nose and one of her eyes ceased to exist, replaced by a red mess. Miska kept moving. The second insurgent died before any of the others had even realised what was happening. The third was turning when a three-round burst from the gauss pistol caught him in the side of the head. Again, if they'd been wearing helmets instead of bandannas, which were, to be fair, more comfortable in the heat and humidity, he might have survived a little longer. The fourth and final insurgent almost pulled the trigger, he almost managed to shout a warning. Miska's fourth burst was hurried, the caseless, electromagnetically driven, thorn-shaped rounds catching the gunman in the mouth and throat. He slumped back and slid to the ground, leaving a red smear on the smartcrete. He was almost certainly dead but Miska put two in his head because it was better to be safe than sorry.

Sloppy. Again the voice in her head sounded like her dad as she crouched down behind the smartcrete and reloaded. She kept her knife in her left hand, fingers reaching around the hilt to pull a magazine from a quick release pouch at the front of her inertial armour. The magazine she removed from the pistol wasn't even half empty but it was better to have ammunition and not need it than the other way around.

Miska was moving more slowly as she slid over the smartcrete and onto the steep narrow path that ran down the side of the gun emplacement to the floor of the gulley. She was giving the reactive camouflage time to adapt to her surroundings, letting her blend in like a chameleon. She reached the gulley floor and peeked round the edge of the outcrop, checking her surroundings. Further down the valley she could see the workers loading the bales of metacoke onto robot mules under the watchful eyes of the drone rigger who'd be running the team. She checked the dormitories and saw very little movement in either of them. Miska knew the refinery ran 24–7, so the workers were either in the refinery or sleeping. Further up, the gulley narrowed until it met the rock wall. What she couldn't see was anything that looked like it contained a printer big enough to make weapons. Unless it was in the refinery, and she didn't really want to have to go in there – too much chance of discovery. She was all but invisible, but she found that people tended to know someone was there when you got really close to them.

Process of elimination, she thought as she leaned against the outcrop. Despite the ghillie suit and her inertial armour she felt the thrum of power through the rock. She moved out slowly into the gulley, feeling exposed despite her camouflage. It looked like someone had taken a laser torch to the rock and hollowed it out. She suspected the rock had then been rendered down and used to form the smartcrete. Miska followed the heavy gauge

4

power cables that ran into the mouth of the artificial cave and walked straight into two of the insurgents.

Both of them looked very similar: hugely muscled, tattoos, hair shaved around a topknot. Miska wasn't sure if they were brother and sister or it was just 'a look'. She'd bumped into the male insurgent. He'd grabbed at her blindly but, more through luck than judgement, had managed to snag the wrist of her gun-hand. Even boosted there was only so much muscle that Miska could fit in the wiry build of her small frame. It was the reason she favoured use of force multipliers like her knife. She didn't bother resisting with her gun-hand. She was never going to win a contest of strength with the musclehead in front of her. Instead she lashed out at his face with her knife, cutting through his cheeks, filling his mouth with blood. He staggered back, dragging Miska with him. The female insurgent was trying to get round Miska's attacker. Miska pushed the male insurgent, guiding his stagger into the female before ramming the blade up into his chin and through his mouth. She felt resistance from subcutaneous armour but the point of the diamond edge penetrated, reaching his brain. Miska could see the black titanium of the blade in his mouth. The male insurgent shook for a moment and then started to fall back. Miska pushed with all her might, knocking him into the female who went down underneath both of them. Miska wrenched her knife free. The male insurgent still had her wrist in a death-grip. Miska slithered over his body and then hammered the bloody knife down. The tip bit into the female insurgent's skull. She had a surprised look on her face for just a moment and then she was still.

Really fucking sloppy! Except her dad tried not to swear in her presence. He failed a lot, though.

She wrenched her gun-hand free and rolled off the bodies

into a crouch. Only then did she have the time to take in her surroundings.

The printer looked not unlike an ancient printing press. The large machine had seen better days but the conveyor was still churning out slug-throwing weapons made from patent-hacked templates. The only light was from the sun streaming in through the cave mouth, but even the shadowed parts of the cave were bright as day to Miska as her realistic-looking cybernetic eyes amplified the existing light. Other than the printer, the slugthrower rifles and the plastic crates of ammunition, the cave was empty. She turned her attention back to the cave mouth, surprised that nobody had heard the scuffle. Satisfied that the alarm hadn't been raised, Miska holstered her gauss pistol, then flicked the blood off the stayclean finish of her knife and sheathed that as well. The dead male insurgent's boot was lying across the terminator between light and shadow, on show for anyone who happened past the cave mouth. She sighed and reached down for him.

Moving the bodies felt exactly like dragging two hundred-and-fifty-pound sacks of growth hormones, steroids and boosted muscles across bare rock. Satisfied that the bodies were out of sight for the casual passer-by, she started attaching the charges to the printer. Blowing up the printer was the bullshit side of strategic planning to Miska's mind, though she'd always been more of a tactician (it was why she lost to her dad when they played chess). Yes, she could see the strategic gain in denying the enemy a resource like the printer, but it wasn't going to make the slightest bit of difference in the oncoming fight, so she felt it could have been done after the fact. But no, the military thinking was *printer equals weapons, and we don't want the enemy to have them.*

Miska worked slowly with the charges even though she knew it was only a matter of time before someone found one of the bodies she'd dropped. *Slow is smooth, smooth is fast*, she thought. Get it right now, save time, fuck ups and lives later. She had studied the schematics of the printer. The charges weren't large, there would be no spectacular explosion, she hoped, but she knew where to put them to make sure the printer was permanently out of action. She was placing the fourth charge when she heard the shouting. It came from above. They'd found the bodies in the gun emplacement.

'Hangman-One-Actual to all Hangman call signs, are you in position?' Miska subvocalised over the comms link.

'Hangman-Two-Actual, affirmative,' Nyukuti replied. Even over the comms Miska could hear the eagerness in his voice.

'Hangman-Three-Actual, we are ready for dust-off on your go,' Mass answered. The Mafioso was stood in the belly of one of the Bastard's two recently-acquired Pegasus assault shuttles a little over twenty miles away.

Miska finished setting the final charge and shifted the M-187 laser carbine that she'd slung across her back so it was ready in her hands. She moved to crouch by the entrance to the cave. Insurgents were pouring out of the smaller of the two dormitories. There seemed to be little actual organisation, just a lot of running around and shouting. Miska smiled. She was going to introduce real chaos into their already disorganised lives.

'Hangman-One-Actual to all Hangman call signs, I'm about to make some noise,' she subvocalised across the comms.

'Hangman-Two-Actual, understood,' Nyukuti said.

'Hangman-Three-Actual, we are inbound,' Mass informed them. That gave them two minutes. Two minutes to stay alive. They were into the first contingency plan now as their initial

1

plan had been to wait for the assault shuttle and Mass's squad to arrive, but she'd dropped too many bodies. She might not have been found yet but they were effectively compromised.

She raised the laser carbine to her shoulder, switched the hybrid weapon from laser to its under-barrel mounted grenade launcher via the smartlink, and fired. There was a popping noise and then the smaller dormitory exploded. The blast knocked over a number of the insurgents who had been too close to the dormitory. As the roof caved in Miska knew that the shrapnel from the fragmentation grenade would have torn apart any-body inside the flimsy structure. With a thought Miska sent the detonation commands through her neural interface to the charges in the printer. The dull crumps of the explosions came almost in unison. Miska barely felt the pressure waves from the blast but she grunted as something hit her in the back causing her inertial armour to harden.

The insurgents were taking fire from two of Nyukuti's four-man fireteams from the ridge overlooking the gulley behind Miska's position. Her audio filters cut out the hypersonic screaming as automatic weapon gunners in each fireteam poured suppressing fire down into the gulley. Miska saw stone turned to powder where the 6.3mm penetrators, fired by Nyukuti's squad, hit the cliff-side. The squad's riflemen cut down insurgents still out in the open. Miska was pleased. It was disciplined. They weren't just going wild. Her Bastards almost resembled a military force, though they still had a way to go before they were comparable to her beloved Marine Corps.

'Hangman-Two-Actual to Hangman-Two-Nine, take your team down into the gulley,' Nyukuti told his squad's third fireteam. Miska wanted to add that they weren't to advance forward of the bottom of the slope. They all had carefully designated fields of fire. She forced herself to stay quiet; she had to trust them to follow the plan. Instead she risked moving out of the cave mouth and looking down the gulley towards the bundles of metacoke and the robot mule train, controlled by the drone rigger, which was making its way rapidly down the gulley towards the treeline. Miska raised the carbine to her shoulder and the crosshairs appeared in her IVD over the back of the rigger's head. He was wearing a hard helmet but she doubted it would be enough protection to stop a laser. She squeezed the trigger. Unforgiving, hard, red light connected her carbine to the back of the rigger's head. The superheated hardened ceramic composite material of his helmet blew out and his head was turned into a hollowed, red, steaming bowl.

Miska was aware of movement above her in the gun emplacement. She ducked back into the cave just as an explosion shook it. Powdered rock and smartcrete rained down, along with a smoking body. Miska assumed that someone had hit the gun emplacement with a grenade from a launcher.

'Hangman-One-Actual to Hangman-Two call signs, please be advised I am in the cave beneath the gun emplacement.' She left unsaid that they had to be careful she didn't get killed, as her death would trigger the explosives in the lowjack collars that each of the convict-mercenaries wore.

'Hangman-Two-Actual to Hangman-One-Actual, acknowledged,' Nyukuti said over comms. He sounded like he was concentrating. Fleetingly Miska wondered if he was enjoying his promotion to sergeant and squad leader. Somehow she doubted it. He would resent the responsibility.

As she hunkered down in the cave mouth there wasn't much for her to do other than take the odd opportunistic shot with her laser. Any insurgents left alive in the gulley were keeping their heads down and presumably had no interest in drawing attention to themselves. Nyukuti's support squad, Hangman-Two, were keeping the insurgents left in the refinery pinned down. She thought about opening up the feeds from the convict-mercenaries' gun and helmcams in her IVD but she always found that a little distracting when she was operational. Besides which, part of the point of this action was for Mass and Nyukuti's squads to prove that they could operate without close supervision and as part of an integrated force.

The hypersonic screaming was closer this time. Hangman-Two's advanced fireteam had moved down into the smartcrete gun emplacement on the outcrop above the cave and started laying down fire. Stolen Martian Military Industries *Kopis* gauss rifles and a *Xiphos* gauss squad automatic weapon fired across the gulley, forcing the gunmen in the cave refinery to keep their heads down.

'Mech! Mech! Mech!' someone yelled over the comms link. It was the cry that all infantry feared. A flashing icon in Miska's IVD identified the voice as belonging to Hangman-Two-Nine, who was in charge of the forward fireteam. Then Miska was moving out of the cave mouth, counting on the ghillie suit to keep her hidden among all the chaos. She glanced down the gulley and saw the ancient Bismarck-class quad mech crawl out of the jungle, knocking down trees with each of its four legs.

She barely had time to recognise the mech before she was in the air in a cloud of powdered rock. She hardly registered the impact as she hit the ground some twenty feet away from where she'd been standing. In the moment before her internal air supply kicked in and reflated her lungs, it felt like she would never be able to breathe again. Still enveloped in the cloud of rock dust, it took a moment for her to work out what had happened. She had been hit by an enormous pressure wave that had battered her diaphragm despite her hardened bone structure and subdermal armour. Even through the thinning cloud of rock dust she could see that the cave and the gun emplacement no longer existed. What little rock remained was glowing red from the heat of the friction from the impact of the Bismarck's 500mm mass driver main gun. Miska knew that if she checked the biometric feeds from Hangman-Two-Nine through to Two-Twelve she'd see four flat lines.

She shrugged off the ghillie suit. The reactive camouflage had been destroyed in the impact. It would just get in the way now. The rock cloud was keeping her hidden for the moment. The Bismarck would have thermographic sensors but it was an old design, and the coolant system in her battered but still functional inertial armour should keep her hidden.

IVD full of red warning icons, Miska pushed herself up onto one knee. She could hear again. Her audio dampeners had presumably switched off her hearing when the mass driver had fired. She could hear a hypersonic ripping noise. The mech's ball-mounted rotary railguns were tearing up the top of the ridge where the rest of Hangman-Two had been.

'This is Hangman-Two actual,' Nyukuti said over the comms. 'Taking heavy fire. I've pulled my fireteam back into the treeline. We're moving up the valley, looking for another position.' Now Nyukuti sounded like he was enjoying himself, though Miska knew there wasn't much they could do while the mech was still in the gulley.

Miska felt the ground shake. She could just about make out the squat shape of the mech, its armoured main body cradled by its four spider-like legs. She tried to get a lock on it with her smartlink but her optics just weren't good enough. She needed thermal and she hadn't brought her helmet with her. She lifted the carbine into a firing position.

'Hangman-One-Actual to Daughter-One-Actual,' she sub-vocalised as she upped the power on the carbine with a thought. 'I'm sending you a targeting package.' She squeezed the trigger on the carbine. Superheated air molecules and rock dust particles exploded in a line between the barrel of her carbine and the squat shape of the mech stalking through the cloud. She painted the target. Sent the information over the comms to the rapidly approaching assault shuttle. She watched the battery icon's energy bar in her IVD disappear but she tried to keep the diffuse beams of hard light on the mech for as long as possible.

'Daughter-One-Actual to Hangman-One-Actual, received, Harpies inbound,' the co-pilot in the assault shuttle said over the comms link. Daughter was the call sign for the air element of the assault. Miska threw herself to one side as she heard the hypersonic ripping noise, the report of each railgun round merging with the next as they were fired rapidly from the Bismarck's rotary belly guns. There was a trench where Miska had been knelt moments before but the mech was still firing blind, though the cloud of rock dust was starting to settle. Miska needed cover quickly but she was blinder than the Bismarck; she was only able to see the mech because of its bulk. She replaced the empty battery in her carbine, hoping the dust wasn't going to foul the delicate weapon. She was very aware of the countdown running in her IVD showing the time until the assault shuttle's estimated arrival. She needed to stay alive for another thirty seconds.

The assault shuttle was fast but the multi-role Harpy missiles were faster. The joint-mounted ball lasers of the Bismarck's point defences cast the dust-filled gulley into hellish red light. One of the inbound missiles exploded in the air, hit by an angry red beam. Miska was running. She needed to find cover or religion quickly, and she preferred the former option. She actually heard the clank of the missile's impact, the shaped warhead going off as it penetrated the Bismarck's thick armour. Then the mech exploded.

Miska opened her eyes. Her head was ringing and she was covered in dirt. She checked her IVD, she'd been unconscious for a little over twenty seconds. The force of the blast had blown the rock dust away but the air was thick with smoke and the sky was on fire. She had no idea why she was still alive. It took a moment to realise it wasn't the sky that was on fire. The camo netting that covered the gulley was being systematically burned away by Hangman-Three. Mass's squad, the assault element of the operation, had mounted flamethrowers under the barrels of some of the Dory railguns carried on the flight-capable Machimoi power armour suits they were wearing. Bits of the burning netting were falling from the sky like rain. It was quite beautiful to watch, Miska decided.

Get up and move or you are dead! This time it was her own voice she heard screaming at her. She rolled to her feet. She was almost on the other side of the gulley now, close to the darkened entrance of the cave network that contained the drugs refinery. She was looking straight at one of the narco-insurgent gunmen. Bulging veins and wild bloodshot eyes suggested he was high on his own supply. The crosshairs from the carbine's smartlink were already in the centre of his face. Miska squeezed the trigger. Nothing happened. The rock dust must have damaged the weapon's delicate optics. It was a problem with lasers. Miska swept her carbine to one side with her left hand, reaching for the gauss pistol in her drop holster with the right. She already knew that she was going to be too slow. Again, something hit her in the back. Again, the air exploded out of her. There was an odd burning sensation and she was sure she felt something moving through her body. Part of her chest, a red part that was best kept inside her skin, exploded onto the ground in front of her. Even the gunman who had been about to kill her looked surprised. The shot had come from behind.

Miska sank to her knees. Friendly fire. She fell backwards and looked up at the sky again. Except the sleek, armoured shape of the assault shuttle visible above the burning netting obscured the sky. Hangman-Three flew into the tracer fire that crisscrossed over her head. The Machimoi combat exoskeletons the squad wore made them look like giant, high tech knights.

From an opening higher up the cliff face an insurgent fired a missile from a portable launcher at the assault shuttle. The Pegasus banked sharply, shedding chaff and firing point defence lasers. The missile exploded before it reached the assault shuttle and then it looked liked the entire cliff face exploded as the Pegasus poured railgun fire down onto it.

Well, it seems to be going okay, Miska thought surprisingly calmly and then watched her own biometrics flatline. Despite her apparent death, she was still aware of all the explosive collars the Bastards wore detonating. It was a ripple effect, the signal reaching the closest first and then very quickly spreading out. She could hear the pop of the explosions. It was an oddly innocuous noise. Combat exoskeletons fell from the sky and then the assault shuttle nosed forward and hit the ground with an almighty crash, accompanied by a sound of shrieking metal that shook the earth. Dead-Miska reckoned she was lucky it hadn't landed on her, or exploded.

Something hit the ground nearby. She somehow managed

14

to turn the neck of her corpse to look at it. It was Nyukuti's severed head. She could make out the printed circuit tattoos. His eyes were still open. He had a surprised look on his face.

'I'm not sure if I'm dreaming or not,' Nyukuti's severed head said.

'You're not,' Dead-Miska reassured him. He was convinced that his dreams were his real life and his waking existence was unimportant. It was how he had justified most of his crimes. At Miska's words there was a look of relief on his face.

'Well, that was a total fucking clusterfuck!' Miska's dad's voice echoed down the gulley. She could just about make out Gunnery Sergeant Jonathan Corbin, United States Marine Corps, deceased, silhouetted against the sun. She would have sighed, or at least shaded her eyes from the sun, but she was dead now.

CHAPTER 2

They were back in the briefing room in the command post at Camp Reisman. Her father had left them 'dead' in the gulley and the surrounding jungle for a good long while to think about what they had done before triggering the resurrection function in the virtual training construct. The sophisticated VR program strived for verisimilitude as much as possible – if the brain thought it was real then it learned the lessons that it was being taught. The exception to this was death. The only time the verisimilitude dropped out was when people's virtual representations died. This was because the brain needed to realise that you weren't actually dead so it didn't psychosomatically shut itself down. It was also to try and minimise the psychological damage. People needed to learn from their mistakes, not get post traumatic stress disorder from them. That was why death in the construct was no worse than death in a particularly harsh sense-game. It didn't stop some people from developing PTSD as a result of their training. Miska had heard about vets struggling to separate combat experience from the VR simulations. She'd

16

always enjoyed them – but then again, she enjoyed combat. Though getting shot in the chest had kind of sucked.

Sucked, sucking chest wound, she thought, smiling at her own joke.

'Something funny?' her dad asked. He was pissed, his flinty eyes staring at her like two gun barrels.

The briefing room was a featureless poured smartcrete cube. The support and assault squads were crowded around a table in the centre of the room. Most of them were still in their combat gear, the construct's full sensory immersion allowing her to smell their sweat. Sometimes she wondered if the construct took the whole verisimilitude thing too far. A holographic model of the gulley and the surrounding jungle hovered in the air over the table.

Miska shook her head. 'No, Gunny,' she said to her dad. She commanded the Bastard Legion, the six-thousand-strong mercenary company made up of the convict inmates aboard the *Hangman's Daughter*, the space-going prison barge she had stolen. The virtual ghost of her murdered dad had total authority in the training construct, however. Command was a fine line. It was difficult sometimes, having her father subordinate to her, particularly as she had never reached a rank higher than corporal in the Marine Corps. Most of the time, particularly in front of the virtual representations of the prisoners, her father toed the line, but today he wasn't happy.

'Where'd you go wrong?' he asked her. Miska forced herself to focus on the hologram. She knew she had to learn from this, or else she risked falling into bad habits. She'd only just got back to working as hard as she should on her fitness. Now she needed to work on the tactical side of things as well.

'Well, SOP suggests that we shouldn't have left anyone

17

behind us in the jungle,' Miska started. SOP stood for standard operating procedure. Leaving some of the pickets still operating after they had penetrated the narco-insurgents' outer perimeter, strictly speaking, went against SOP. 'But I judged that worth the risk to maintain stealth.' A rifleman from each fireteam had been acting as rear security. 'Me getting compromised early was a bummer but we handled that. I still don't think that the printer deserved the priority it was assigned. And we had bad intel on the mech.' The expression on her dad's craggy features suggested that he was far from impressed by her explanation.

'Begging the gunnery sergeant's pardon,' Mass said. 'But explosive decapitation tends to limit the combat effectiveness of any force, in this legionnaire's opinion.' Massimo Prola had a bodybuilder's physique, tan skin, and his once-blonde hair was turning grey as he had little access to hair dye in prison. He'd been a 'button man' for the mob in New Verona City on Barnard's Prime. Nicknamed 'the Fisherman' due to his penchant for gutting people with a hooked fishing knife. He was mostly using the military jargon ironically but Miska still found it somewhat gratifying. Now all twenty-five men in the room were staring at her and, once again, she found herself reminded of how much shorter than everyone else she was. She wondered about bringing a box to stand on to these things.

'That's a hard reality of the situation,' her dad told Mass.

'I can't see you doing what we tell you just for the asking,' Miska pointed out. Each member of the Bastard Legion wore an explosive collar to help encourage their obedience. As far as the convicts knew, if anything happened to her the collars went off.

'I get that,' Mass said. 'But maybe you should stay further back rather than running round where the bullets are flying.' There was lots of nodding from the two squads. The very idea sat badly with Miska. She liked the action, she hadn't wanted to end up some bullshit rear-echelon-motherfucker, or REMF. Still, she knew he had a point. She could feel her dad watching her without having to look.

'Okay, listen up,' her dad said. 'You should always act as though your intel is bad. When it's not it will come as a pleasant surprise.' He pointed at Miska. 'Your recce should have been more thorough. Camouflaged or not, you should have found that heavy ass. You don't like the mission priorities then you query them, make your case. Perhaps operational security means the reason for the priority is above your pay grade.'

Miska nodded and her dad turned to Nyukuti.

'The support team should have stayed back in the jungle. The air element destroying the mech should have been your signal to go forward. You should have engaged the pickets, then the extreme violence of your actions would have carried you through to the edge of the gulley to provide support for your assault team,' he told the support team leader.

Miska frowned at this. Nyukuti gave it some thought. He glanced over at Miska. More than any of the other prisoners, the tall, powerfully built Aboriginal Australian appeared loyal to her. He seemed to enjoy being a member of the Bastard Legion. On the other hand, you could never be sure of the sincerity of a career criminal, and as a standover man he had been a particularly vicious one. Miska kept her face impassive and Nyukuti turned back towards her dad and nodded, accepting the criticism.

'And you,' her father said to a young Japanese man who looked as though he was trying hard not to appear intimidated. 'You were doing good work, Private Kaneda. What made you decide to shoot your CO?'

Miska turned to stare at him. At the same time she used her neural interface back in her real body to hook up to the *Hangman's Daughter*'s systems and get a look at Kaneda's file. Kaneda, Atsushi. Armed robbery had sent him to prison and a series of assaults and drug offences had seen him transferred to an Ultra Max. He was finally sent to the *Hangman's Daughter* after the attempted murder of a member of a rival gang. Kaneda was one of the Bethlehem Milliners, a powerful *bōsōzoku* gang or Speed Tribe in the Lalande system. The Milliners, like other *bōsōzoku* gangs, were used as a proving ground for the Yakuza organised crime syndicates that existed among many of the colonies. Reading between the lines, he was another kid who'd been institutionalised by higher-ranking members of his own gang and the Yakuza. Required to prove himself in prison, each further criminal act had increased the length of his sentence. Somehow he still looked too young and innocent to have the rap sheet he did. His looks meant he must have been popular inside. He would have needed the protection of the older gang members. Miska would have felt a bit sorry for him if the little fucker hadn't shot her. Kaneda looked stuck between his deference to authority and the need to look tough and never show weakness that was so important in prison.

'I thought she was one of the enemy,' he finally managed. There was muttering and shaking of heads among the assembled men. Mass in particular was glaring at the young gang member. There was no love lost between the Mafia contingent and the Yakuza or their *bōsōzoku* proxies. This was the result of Teramoto Shigeru, the leader of the Scorpion Rain Society Yakuza contingent on board, arranging for the death of one of the Mafia *soldatos*. Miska and her father were trying to break up the gangs, while simultaneously trying to keep those with a beef away from each other. It had been a risk putting Kaneda on the same exercise as Mass but Miska and her dad had deemed it worthwhile because of Kaneda's burgeoning ability as a sniper. They had put him in Nyukuti's squad because, while Mass wasn't exactly scared of the strange Aborigine, he couldn't get a handle on him – which made the button man wary.

'You were the designated marksman, your smartlink should have told you that you were aiming at a friendly, but more than that you always check your target,' the gunnery sergeant told Kaneda. Miska could feel her father's frustration. With modern smartlink systems you had to put some work in these days to create a friendly-fire incident.

'I was squeezing the trigger as the warning came up.' Kaneda looked as though he was trying hard to suppress any outward signs of guilt. He kept glancing at Miska. Her dad was giving the poor kid the hard eye. Miska did wonder if Kaneda had done this on purpose, perhaps on orders from Teramoto, to see what would happen. To see if it would really kill everyone? If so, good, she decided. It would reinforce the consequences of turning on her.

'Just out of interest, Gunny,' Mass said, turning away from Kaneda. 'Would the attack have succeeded if our heads hadn't been blown off? The mech had been dealt with. Nyukuti's squad had established control of the gulley. Maybe some hard fighting in the caves where the refinery was, but I think we could have cleared them out.'

Gunnery Sergeant Corbin gave the question some thought. He didn't look happy.

'There were a couple of surprises waiting for you in the cave. You might have lost one of the combat exoskeletons, maybe two if you really screwed up, but you would have pulled it off.'

Mass was nodding thoughtfully. He looked over at Miska.
'That's what I thought.'

'Okay, dismissed!' her dad barked.

'I was a little reckless,' Miska admitted once the others had
gone. She had pulled a chair out and was leaning back on it, feet
up on the table, her muddy boots obscured by the hologram.

'A little,' her dad muttered. He was leaning on the table
with both hands as he glared at her. 'Why the hell was your
scout element also your command element? Was that just your
commitment to doing both things badly?'

'Expedience,' she told him. After all, as an ex-Marine Raider
– the USMC's elite special forces unit – and an operator for the
CIA's Special Affairs Division, she had the experience.

'Oh bullshit!' her dad snapped. He pushed himself upright,
all six-foot-two of his rangy, muscled frame. He pointed at her.
'You were there for the action.'

'Okay, fine!' Miska snapped, swinging her feet off the table.
She didn't really want to think too much about his accusation,
probably because she knew it was true. 'What was that bullshit
about the pickets? We were through. The risk was acceptable,
each fireteam had rear security.'

'The risk was acceptable for special forces,' her dad said
and then pointed at the wall. 'They're not even trained to the
standard of rank and file marines yet.' He crossed his arms and
stared at her. He was right. She knew he was right. If he'd been
anybody other than a family member then she probably would
have admitted it by now. 'And Prola is right about the collars,'
he continued. 'Every one of them dies when you get taken out?'

'It's not that simple,' Miska replied. 'There are parameters
for the kill switch. My death doesn't automatically set all the

collars off.' The kill switch program stored in the integral computer implanted in her brain was basically a dumb AI program capable of making split second decisions with regards to the collars if something was to happen to her.

'I know that, but being killed by one of the Legion does cause the kill switch to trigger all the collars, right?' her dad asked. Miska nodded, looking down. 'Bit problematic for friendly-fire situations, don't you think?'

He was right of course, but as sophisticated as the kill switch program was, it wasn't sophisticated enough to differentiate between friendly fire and one of her convict soldiers intentionally fragging her.

'I think they understand why they've got to do what we tell them to do, and the incentives were a good idea to encourage them, but you'll lose them if they don't trust you to command,' he told her. She didn't really have much in the way of a response. The deceleration warning in her IVD came as something of a relief.

Miska opened her eyes as the stars went from fractals to points of light. She was slumped on the throne-like captain's chair at the top of the *Hangman's Daughter*'s split-level bridge. She sat up straight watching the huge sail arrays folding down and sliding into their armoured sheaths on the outside of the ship. The bridge was high up in the conning tower that looked down over the roughly rectangular-shaped main body of the ship. Whatever else you could say about the *Hangman's Daughter,* it wasn't a pretty ship. A converted troop carrier that had seen action in the war with the alien Them more than a hundred years ago, the prison barge was a mass of industrial superstructure and scarred armoured plate interspersed with weapons and countermeasures, batteries and communications and sensor arrays. By no means a warship, it had managed to pull its weight against two cruisers and a frigate during the first, and so far only, job the Bastard Legion had worked in the Tau Ceti system.

One of the cruisers in question was currently securely anchored to the *Hangman's Daughter* like a sleek, hi-tech parasite. With a little bit of help, Miska and her Bastard Legion had captured it from Stirling Security Systems, a military contractor also hired by their erstwhile employers, the system-controlling Tau City Company, to double-cross her Bastards. The double-cross hadn't gone quite according to plan. The captured frigate, the *Excelsior*, was the main reason she had returned to the Sirius system, the closest thing she had to a home.

The ship's AI autopilot had brought them in subjectively above the Dog's Teeth. For an asteroid belt the Teeth were surprisingly dense. It was theorised that this was due to their presence in some kind of 'sweet spot' between the binary stars of Sirius A and Sirius B. From Miska's perspective, looking down at the asteroid field through the view-screen that ran around the top level of the bridge, the Dog's Teeth looked like a wall of asteroids stretching as far as the eye could see.

She wasn't sure how she felt about being so close to her home world of Sirius 4. The planet where her father had been murdered. Miska knew that the killers were on board the *Hangman's Daughter*, serving with the Bastards, but their tracks had been covered so well by whomever they worked for she still had no idea who they were.

She felt a slight tug towards home but that wasn't the reason they had come here. They had come because of the frigate. They were going to take it to one of the most notorious freeports in the colonies: Maw City. The current Maw City had sprung up in the location of the main base of Them, the genocidal aliens that had attacked humanity just over a hundred and fifty years ago. The current Maw City had started life as a research station attempting to find out more about Their mysterious biotech. The aliens, however, had left little behind when they had fled the sphere of human space. When the notorious Crimson Sisterhood pirate fleet had moved into the Dog's Teeth, the research station had become a pirate den, and more to the point for Miska, it had become the centre of trade for stolen ships in the system. The Triple-S frigate was top of the line Martian military technology and should net the Bastards a good price. Even after they had managed to get paid, the Bastards had lost money on their first job through resource expenditure. Selling the frigate should make up for that and bring the previous job into profit.

'What's the plan?' her dad asked, appearing in hologram in front of her face. Miska could tell he was being short with her. It wasn't so much that he was angry, she knew, more that he was worried. He wasn't sure about the whole Bastards idea in general, particularly as a significant part of the reason for their existence was for Miska to discover who had murdered him. He was also worried she was becoming sloppy. If she was being honest, Miska knew that his worries weren't without foundation, and she was compounding the problem with her stubbornness.

She had been a bad marine. Her independence and capability had been enough to follow in her father's footsteps into the Marine Raider Regiment but even then she had never been a team player. She was on the cusp of being drummed out of the Corps when the CIA had recruited her. She was just too used to

25

operating on her own, and, again if she was honest, she resented authority, military or parental. It had caused a lot of friction between her and her dad when she'd been growing up.

'Are you going to take *Little Jimmy* in first and recon the area?' he asked. '*Little Jimmy*' or the U.S.S.S. *Jimmy Carter* was a stealth ship designed as a covert electronics warfare platform. Like the frigate, the *Little Jimmy* was attached to the hull, though it was hidden on the underside of the *Hangman's Daughter* among the superstructure. Miska had stolen the ship from the National Security Agency, the intelligence organisation responsible for electronic security and information gathering for the US government and its colonies.

'I don't want to risk exposing the *Little Jimmy* to these people,' she told her dad. If/when things got FUBARed, the stealth ship was her get out of jail free card. Only one of the prisoners knew about the stealth ship and he was in solitary.

Don't think about the Ultra, she commanded herself. She wasn't ready to examine too closely how she felt about the beautiful but prolifically deadly serial killer.

Well, aren't you just living in denial?

'We're criminals doing criminal things, it'll be fine,' she said. Her dad looked less than convinced.

'Personnel?' he asked.

'Shore leave for everyone who was at Faigroe Station,' she said.

'QRF as well?'

'Yes.' She could tell her father wasn't happy with this. Circumstances had forced her dad to put together a Quick Reaction Force on the fly. He had chosen to create it from a group of people who were used to working together. This meant sending out one of the gangs en masse. It was exactly the sort of thing that they had been trying to avoid because they wanted the Bastards loyal to each other, not their old criminal associations. Miska knew it had been the right call for the situation, however. The gang he had chosen had been the Bethlehem Milliners.

Teramoto, the *shatei gashira* or second lieutenant of the Scorpion Rain Society Yakuza clan, had led the QRF. Miska had begrudgingly promoted him to corporal even though he'd effectively led a company, which in the marines would have meant the rank of captain. Her dad was right though; given the murder of the Mafia-associate Jimmy 'Beans' Bennini, which had presumably been committed at Teramoto's behest just to prove a point, it did seem like rewarding bad behaviour.

'They won't have as much money in their pockets as those who got combat pay.' To incentivise the Bastards, and encourage them to volunteer for missions, Miska and her dad had decided to put aside a quarter of any of the money they made to split up among those who'd gone on the mission. They could spend it on 'shore leave'. If they acted up on shore leave, hurt or stole from innocents, tried to escape or generally did anything that Miska disapproved of, then they knew it would result in them suddenly becoming a head shorter. Still, she wasn't looking forward to seeing if they were still frightened of explosive decapitation once they'd had a skin full of booze.

'Armed?' her dad asked. Miska was shaking her head. She drew the line at arming drunken, violent, combat-trained convicts. This her dad seemed to approve of, at least.

'I'll take a security element with me, sidearms and PDWs for them.'

'Who?'

Miska smiled.

'Teramoto, two of his guys and Vido?'

'Vido? You sure?'

Miska could understand her dad's reticence. Vido Cofino was just about managing to keep up in both the physical and virtual aspects of the training but he had been trained as a lawyer and was in his sixties. He would hardly be anyone's first choice for the member of close protection team. He had been *consigliere*, or adviser, to the Cofino family on Barnard's Prime. The leader of the family, Antonio Cofino, was a distant cousin of Vido's.

'Yeah, I kinda want his eyes on this. Also I've got something special in mind for Kaneda.'

'Pissed off that he shot you?' her dad asked.

'It wasn't ideal, but no.'

Her dad gave this some thought and then nodded. Miska was also of the opinion that it might be a good idea to put Teramoto and Vido in the same place under her supervision. There was bad blood between the Mafia and Yakuza contingents. Vido, however, was a reasonable person. If peace could be found without loss of face or any further bloodshed then the *consigliere* would find a way.

'What about the Sisterhood?' her dad asked. Miska grimaced. They had a number of the pirate organisation's menfolk on board.

'Well, they're not in charge and I'm not going to walk in there waving flags,' she said.

'They're going to know who you are,' he said, and she knew he was right, 'and they're going to want their menfolk back, aren't they?'

The aliens had cored a lot of the asteroids in the Dog's Teeth, breaking them down into raw materials for their war effort throughout the Sirius system. Conveniently, this allowed Miska to pull the same trick they had used over above Tau Ceti G. They found an asteroid with a hole in it big enough to hide the *Hangman's Daughter*.

Miska had taken the *Excelsior*. She was sat in the dark, ergonomically designed bridge in the centre of the sleek frigate. She was peeking into the ship's net representation, just keeping an eye on the autopilot. Her CP team had stationed themselves around the bridge and she was somewhat gratified that they seemed to be taking their close protection training seriously, though Vido looked a little out of place, snubby gauss personal defence weapon in hand.

They were accompanied by one of the two Pegasus assault shuttles that had originally been part of the *Excelsior*'s complement. Miska had had the frigate stripped down by the *Daughter*'s ageing droids. They had taken anything that could possibly be of use. The Machimoi combat exoskeletons, armour, small arms, heavy weapons, ammunition, drones and droids, both the assault shuttles, missiles to replace those used by the *Hangman's Daughter* over Tau Ceti G. There had even been two Centaurs, wheeled armoured personnel carriers, one of which had been fitted out as a mobile command post; a Satyr scout mech; and a couple of wo/man-portable plasma weapons. The majority of the gear was designed by Martian Military Industries and therefore considered the best that money could buy.

The real prize, however, had been a military grade printer loaded with MMI templates. It had taken Miska a while to crack the encryption on the printer, and she wasn't sure when she would have been able to without the stolen NSA software that had come with the *Little Jimmy*, but it was worth it. She'd had the printer moved to the *Hangman's Daughter*'s hangar deck. It gave her the capacity to microfacture equipment, armour and weapons up to and including railguns and wo/man-portable mass drivers. Sadly there were no templates for laser or plasma weapons, and the printer wasn't big enough for combat exoskeletons. With the raw material stocks they had taken from the *Excelsior*, she could probably equip two whole companies, or about three hundred and twenty men, to a reasonable degree. This would include a combat exoskeleton squad. The printer had enabled her to upgrade a lot of the old kit that had belonged to the *Hangman's Daughter*'s guards. This would mean maybe another two platoons, or eighty or so men, at a push. The *Daughter*'s Wraith combat exoskeletons had definitely seen better days, though at least Miska could now provide them with real ammunition instead of rubber bullets. In short, her Legion still wasn't really a Legion in terms of the size of force she could field, but it was looking a lot better than it had. It worried her that she was still very short of vehicles, though.

The shuttle was piloted by two of the Hard Luck Comancheroes, a road gang who'd originated back on Earth. They were both excellent shuttle pilots but Miska could have done with the skill set of some of the Crimson Sisterhood she had on board, many of whom were excellent pilots. She couldn't take the risk. If someone jumped the frigate on the way in, they were pretty much helpless. She was approaching the city broadcasting the intent to dock, trade and spend some money as the autopilot brought them in very slowly, manoeuvring engines burning, steering the ship through the labyrinth of asteroids. The city's drone ships found them first. Little more than weapon platforms with large engines, the drones fell in around the frigate and the assault shuttle. The *Excelsior*'s systems fed warnings to Miska's IVD as the drones locked weapons onto the frigate. The assault shuttle's co-pilot let her know that something similar was happening to them.

The feed from the *Excelsior*'s sensors showed Miska the sentry drones scuttling across the bare rock of the asteroids, their weapons tracking the frigate and the shuttle as well. Finally they saw the heavier embedded weapon emplacements. It seemed that Maw City took its defence very seriously.

'Careful, people,' Vido muttered. Miska said nothing, she just checked the Escape and Evasion plan she'd plugged into the autopilot. If things went bad it would just be a case of hanging on while the frigate ran to the best of the autopilot's ability. Miska was a fair pilot but the ship was too large and complex for her to manage on her own.

They received a simple set of coordinates in answer to their hail. Miska isolated the message, checked it for hacks, and then plugged it into the autopilot. The frigate changed direction, the assault shuttle following suit. They hugged an asteroid spotted with laser, mass driver and missile batteries, and coming over the rocky horizon they saw the city. Miska's first impression was of diseased rock. The clustered asteroids had all been cored. They were filled with superstructure, or hive-like stacked habitats. Some were glass-fronted and she could make out plants, even trees inside them. Others were sealed over with smartcrete and had the look of ugly utilitarian bunkers. The rock skins of the asteroids were crawling with drones, vacuum-capable mechs and exoskeletons, and that was what had made her think of an infected wound. Her second impression was of a vast construction site. There seemed to be building work going on everywhere, illuminated by the strobing light of laser torches. This was not the cobbled-together, jury-rigged mess that Miska had come to expect from many free ports. There was clearly a lot of money at work here. This looked more like a hypercorp operation than a criminal one.

There were ships everywhere. Many of them looked like fast, well-armed cargo ships, presumably belonging to smugglers. She saw little in the way of military ships, apart from a couple of ageing but still fast-looking corvettes. There was certainly no sign of the *Queen Eleanor's Revenge*, the light cruiser that was purported to be the Crimson Sisterhood's flagship. Nevertheless, Miska ran a search for the bloody skull and crossed bloody scythes insignia of the Sisterhood. The image identification software found that the two corvettes and a small but heavily armed converted freighter all bore the design. It could have been a lot worse, Miska decided, but suddenly her dad's caution didn't seem so bad.

'Where do you want us, boss?' the assault shuttle pilot asked over the comms link. 'They're telling us to dock.'

'Hold off. Tell them to take it up with me, explain the situation,' Miska replied, meaning the collars. 'Keep an eye on our whereabouts.' She wanted to trance in and check out the net architecture of the place. She opened a window in her IVD to 'peek sideways' into the net. It was a mess, lots of different aesthetics, which meant different designers, which in turn meant that different factions controlled the city's net. She looked for anything that stood out as belonging to the Sisterhood. She couldn't see anything but that didn't mean it wasn't there. She didn't have time to trance in and delve deeper.

The autopilot brought the frigate in over the skeletal superstructure of what looked like a shipyard. On closer inspection it didn't look as though any ships were being built, though a number were being modified and one of the ships, a bulk freighter, was being stripped down. The drones doing the work looked like termites consuming the huge ship.

The docking arm and clamps extending out of the rock looked modern and well maintained, as the *Excelsior*'s manoeuvring engines made final tiny adjustments to bring the frigate into position. Miska felt the arm and the clamp attach themselves to the frigate. She checked the feed from the airlock's external camera. She could see the welcoming committee. Eight well-armed men and women, many of them sporting obvious cybernetic enhancements. She ran the feed through the image recognition software looking for obvious Crimson Sisterhood gang colours or ink but found nothing. Again, that didn't mean it wasn't there.

'Everyone on their best behaviour,' Miska muttered as she pushed herself out of the obscenely comfortable command couch.

'Does that mean you as well?' Vido asked. Miska just smiled.

Teramoto hadn't said much during their short journey, instead commanding the two members of the Bethlehem Milliners, also part of the CP team, with simple gestures and movement of his head. The wiry Yakuza lieutenant sported a goatee. It was the most stand-out thing about his appearance. Dressed in civilian clothes, there was something of the pedantic accountant about him. Only the two missing fingers on his left hand and the hint of tattoos at his cuffs and neckline gave him away. Vido and Teramoto had pretty much ignored each other throughout the short journey.

They made their way through the *Excelsior* to the forward airlock. She had listened in on the one-sided conversation between the assault shuttle and Maw City traffic control. The shuttle's pilot had apologetically explained that he couldn't dock. Traffic control hadn't answered. She doubted the Maw City authorities were worried, they had enough ordnance aimed at the shuttle to ensure it would cease to exist the moment it made a wrong move.

Miska checked the feed once more. The welcoming committee were in the docking arm on the other side of the airlock. They all looked quite casual. It was in the moment between Miska ordering the airlock doors to open and the doors actually opening that the welcoming committee raised their weapons so that Miska, Teramoto, Vido and the two Bethlehem Milliners in her CP team found themselves looking down the barrels of eight weapons wielded by people who looked as though they knew what they were doing.

'Put your weapons down,' a dreadlocked man with metalled skin demanded. 'Then lace your fingers behind your head.'

'Miska-sama?' Teramoto asked, tensing. She heard Vido sigh.

CHAPTER 3

'Well shit,' Miska said staring down the barrel of eight assorted carbines. She supposed it came down to the choices that she'd made in life, but every so often it would be nice to meet reasonable people.

'What we doing here?' Vido asked. Miska suspected that the nervousness might have just as much to do with how he thought she might react to this as the eight guns pointed at them. She was aware of Teramoto tensing. He seemed ready to go but she knew it was futile. The gunmen and women had them cold.

'Do what they ask,' she said. 'These guys seem insecure.' Vido's chuckle sounded somewhat relieved. She noticed the gunman with the dreads and the metalled face had cracked a smile. Teramoto looked less than happy, however.

They were searched thoroughly and expertly. The gunmen and women even used chemical sniffers, looking for explosives. Then they were cuffed with memory cable and marched through the docking area. It was a weird mix, Miska thought. The place looked like any other modern spaceport in the more civilised and well-established colonies but the people hanging around all looked like well-armed scum. Many of them turned to watch as Miska and the others were marched through a commercial area filled with autobars, vending machines and even real bars, restaurants and shops. Teramoto bristled as a few people spat on the floor in front of them. A wiry, weasel-faced punk tried to spit in Miska's face and got the butt of one of the guard's carbines in his own.

'Thanks,' Miska said. The gunwoman just smiled.

'Your reputation seems to have preceded you,' Vido told her.

'I'm a popular gal.'

Miska spotted a statuesque woman, with long, straight, blood-red hair down past her ass. She had had some kind of implants in her hair that made it move with a life of its own. It looked agitated, somehow. She wore thigh-high boots over a red sleeveless one-piece. A large pistol rode her hip, both her eyes were obvious cybernetic replacements, and her arms were tattooed sleeves. She was making no secret of watching Miska and her CP team. She was surrounded by a group of armed men and women. All of them wore at least one piece of clothing that was dark red in colour and most of them were visibly tattooed. Miska met her eyes, smiled, and nodded a greeting.

'Reckon she's got a bloodied skull and crossed scythes on her back?' Miska asked. 'Her whole outfit just screams pirate.' Vido chuckled and nodded.

'Trying too hard,' he added.

Teramoto had noticed the group of Crimson Sisterhood pirates as well. He said something in Japanese, pointing them out to the two Milliners with him.

*

They were marched into what looked like an executive lounge of some sort. An impressively fat man, wearing a velvet suit and a padded waistcoat, his ensemble completed by a ridiculous porkpie hat, was waiting for them. He was puffing on a huge and absurdly phallic cigar.

'Really?' The word seemed to burst out of Vido unbidden, as though the *consigliere* was offended by something. The fat man nodded. Four of the guards slung their carbines, drew their sidearms and forced the CP team to their knees before stepping back, covering them with their pistols.

Stood just to the right and behind the fat guy was a pale, thin man. He wore smart trousers and a more subdued waistcoat; his suit jacket thrown over the back of a nearby chair. Hair parted in the middle, he wore spectacles over pale blue eyes. He looked like a banker. Miska could make out figures cascading down the inside of his glasses. She tried something, opening a window in her IVD to look at the net representation of the room. It looked like a very old-fashioned bank vault. Very heavy duty security isolated it from the rest of Maw City's net. While she was doing this she watched the banker. He concentrated for a moment. Miska was sure that he had an integral computer hardwired into the meat of his brain, just like she did. She suspected he was some slumming ex-corporate hacker.

'Don't do that again,' the fat man told her.

'That really necessary?' she asked and nodded towards where her CP team were down on their knees. They'd pretty much let her roam free. 'We're here to talk, make a deal. This makes you look frightened.'

The fat man frowned and then seemed to brighten up.

'Why would we deal,' he asked her, 'when we can just take?'

'Well then, you'll need to refit all the frigate's systems

because I can just junk them with a thought,' she said, turning away from him and looking out through the porthole over the whole docking area. She tried subvocalising a message to the assault shuttle but wasn't surprised when the data vault blocked the signal. The shuttle pilots would have been able to track them until they stepped into the vault. Hopefully that would be enough for them to work out where she was.

'From this room?' the fat man asked. He had a point but something about this wasn't ringing true. There was something wrong with the fat man. She turned back and looked out of the porthole again. She was gratified to see the assault shuttle rise into view about five hundred feet away from where she stood. The external doors of the shuttle's forward airlock were open, and she could make out the space-suited figure sat in the airlock. She performed a small piece of sleight of hand as she reached out to touch the porthole as if she was testing its strength.

'Shit, you got me,' she said. 'I guess you outmanoeuvred me.' She stepped out of the way of the porthole. 'Except for the marksman in the assault shuttle with a high-powered sniper railgun pointed at you. No muzzle flash, no sound, your scanners won't even pick it up,' she said, and smiled. This job was Kaneda's penance for shooting her during the training exercise. The fat man's face fell. Just for a moment he looked unsure, then the smile was back. He sucked on the cigar and exhaled a cloud of actual carcinogens.

'Even a railgun's not going to get through that,' he said.

'Look closer,' Miska said, stepping aside and pointing at the putty she'd stuck to the window. 'Concentrated plastique.' She threw a small plastic sac down in front of the fat man. 'Got it past your chemical sniffers in that. It's a musk sac.' She pointed at herself and the CP team. 'We're all wearing stikpads and are augmented to survive in vacuum for short amounts of time. How about you?'

'Where'd you hide the musk pad?' the fat man asked, but his voice was faltering. She just raised an eyebrow. She'd hidden it in her armpit but she didn't see any reason to tell him that. Something definitely wasn't right here. The fat man seemed too much like a mob boss, while simultaneously coming across as unsure of himself.

'Doesn't matter,' Vido said. 'He's not the boss.' He pointed at the banker. 'He is.' The fat man looked up.

'You are an actor,' Teramoto said to the fat man.

'Yeah, he looks familiar,' Vido said.

'He was in Yinglaze's *Tarnished Soul*,' Teramoto added.

'I love Yinglaze's early work,' Vido said.

'That was a long time ago,' the fat man said. 'I'm surprised anyone remembers.'

Miska was watching the banker. He had the slightest smile on his face.

'It was a good viz,' Vido said. Teramoto was nodding.

'Okay, thank you, Paul,' the banker said.

Vido snapped his fingers.

'That's it, Paul Ferman, you were in that show about the hermaphroditic detective ...'

'*The Empress of Capital City*,' Ferman supplied.

'Loved that show.' Vido glanced behind him at the gun-woman covering him and then at the banker. 'I'm getting up now, okay?' The banker nodded and motioned for the guards to un-cuff the CP team. Vido stood up and shook Ferman's hand.

'You can go now, Paul,' the banker said. Miska found his voice strangely without accent. Ferman nodded, pushed his bulk out of the seat, and waddled to the door.

39

'Boss?' the gunman with the dreads and the metalled face asked. Teramoto was retrieving his weapons from the table they had been placed on.

'That's fine, Terrance,' the banker said. He leaned over and picked up the plastic sac. 'A musk sac?' he asked. Miska shrugged.

'It's a thing,' she told him.

Then he walked over to the porthole and looked at the putty. Miska was aware of Vido tensing as the banker reached up and pulled it off.

'Plumber's putty?' he asked.

'You'd be surprised how much it does look like concentrate,' she told him. He threw it back to her. Miska caught the putty, pocketing it as she crossed to the table. She tried not to look too eager as she retrieved her gauss pistol and knife.

'Terrance, would you mind sticking your head out of the door and asking them to bring in extra chairs and take our drink orders,' the banker asked before turning to Miska and the others. 'Have you eaten?'

'I could eat,' Vido told him.

Miska had stepped outside the executive lounge/data vault and told Kaneda to stand down over the comms link. She hadn't told the assault shuttle to dock just yet, however. If the shuttle was making Maw City traffic control nervous then she certainly saw no sign of it from the banker.

Teramoto and the two Milliners refused food and drink and went back to guarding Miska, once they had rearmed. Miska had ordered a beer and then tried to order a burger to go with it – after all, somebody must have boosted some decent beef coming out of Sirius 4's cattle country. Vido had stopped her and instead asked the banker if there was a good Italian restaurant on board. The banker had replied in the positive and Vido had ordered a number of dishes and some wine. Miska had been content to let him order for her. He seemed to know what he was talking about.

'So what do we call you?' Miska asked. She was sitting on the table, sipping a beer.

'You may call me Nicholas,' the banker said. Vido offered him his hand, which Nicholas shook, though he seemed a little surprised by the gesture.

'I'm Vido—'

'I know who you are, Mr Cofino,' he turned to Miska, 'Miss Corbin, and of course, Mr Teramoto.' The Yakuza lieutenant inclined his head in a slight bow. Nicholas sat down in the comfortable-looking chair that the actor had vacated.

'And you run this place?' Vido asked, also sitting down in one of the chairs that had been brought in. The gunmen and women who had marched them in had all left, with the exception of the metal-faced Terrance, though he seemed very relaxed, and his carbine was on the table next to Vido's personal defence weapon.

'I administer it. I am paid well by various concerns to ensure that Maw City runs smoothly and profitably for all,' Nicholas told them. Miska suspected that running Maw City wasn't a long-term plan for Nicholas. She reckoned the administrator had come in with specialists like Terrance, offered his services, would make himself rich and then move on.

'Corporate life not suit you?' Miska asked.

'I enjoy a challenge, Miss Corbin,' he said.

'If you're Nicholas, then I'm Miska,' she told him and he nodded. Miska found herself warming to him and corporate types weren't normally her sort of people. This was mostly because they saw a scruffy, pierced, purple-haired (today) punk when they looked at her. There was no doubt in her mind that Nicholas was smart, but so far he hadn't behaved in a condescending manner. She guessed that running this place was something of a balancing act and he couldn't afford to underestimate anyone. 'So what was with the charade?' she asked.

'I wouldn't try playing poker with him,' Vido said and took a sip from a glass of Chianti.

'The charade ended earlier than it was supposed to, Miss ... Miska. My information did not include Mr Cofino ...'

'Vido,' the *consigliere* insisted.

'Vido and Mr Teramoto's love of film. However, I know that you will bluff, or offer violence. Vido will negotiate and—' he turned to look at Teramoto. 'I did not get a reading on Mr Teramoto.' Miska glanced at the Yakuza lieutenant. His face was an expressionless mask. He hadn't shown the slightest reaction to Nicholas's words. More than anything this drove home to Miska that Teramoto could be really useful to her if she could somehow get him to stop playing his games.

'Yep, he's like a sphinx. So you're open for business then?' Miska asked. Nicholas didn't answer immediately.

'Problem?' Vido asked. Nicholas spent some time considering the question.

'Don't worry about being diplomatic,' Miska told him.

'Well, you have baggage. We pride ourselves on not turning anyone away but you have enslaved six thousand men who were engaged in the same criminal activities that many of us are involved in. I'm sure you can imagine why that wouldn't make you popular here,' Nicholas told her.

'C'mon, guys, tell him how much fun it is working for me,'

Miska said, grinning. The two Milliners wouldn't meet her eyes. Teramoto gave nothing away, and Vido just looked at her ruefully before turning back to Nicholas.

'Hence the charade of parading us through the habitat in cuffs?' Vido asked.

Nicholas nodded. 'Though it will be apparent by now that that's all it was: a charade.'

Now Vido was nodding. He seemed to sympathise with Nicholas's perspective.

'Pressure coming from the Crimson Sisterhood?' Miska asked.

'They are significant shareholders in the Maw City venture.'

She suspected it was as close to an affirmative as she was going to get.

'So where does that leave us?' Vido asked.

'The articles of the city say that we pretty much have to offer you a place to dock and a market for your goods. However, defence of the city remains the paramount concern.'

'If we bring down too much heat?' Vido asked and Nicholas nodded again.

'We have already received veiled threats from the Sirius 4 offices of Triple-S. They were demanding the return of a frigate they claim was stolen from them in the Tau Ceti system.'

'We don't know anything about that,' Vido said. Miska warmed to Nicholas even more when he dropped his professional demeanour, just for a moment, to laugh.

'Frankly, I don't think they fully understand the concept of piracy,' Nicholas told them and it was Vido and Miska's turn to laugh.

'You worried about them?' Vido asked. Nicholas just shook his head.

'They have some serious people in their employ,' Miska pointed out.

'They are a commercial outfit. I've done a cost analysis of the situation. Their insurance premiums will go up but not enough to justify an operation in the Teeth.'

'Not everyone makes decisions that way,' Vido pointed out.

'Indeed, but my intelligence suggest that they do and if not' —he gestured at Terrance— 'I have tremendous faith in our head of security.'

'And I have a great deal of faith in the vast pirate fleet that calls this place home,' Terrance told them. Miska raised her bottle to the metal-faced gunman and he nodded back at her, smiling.

'So, we got other heat?' Vido asked.

'You mean aside from the bounty?' Nicholas asked. Vido looked over at Miska, she shrugged. She'd known it was coming. Even so, it made her feel cold hearing it out loud.

'Five million, dead or alive, for Miska,' Nicholas told them. 'Fifteen million from Group 13 for the return of the *Hangman's Daughter* with its cargo intact.'

Vido let out a whistle.

'Never popular in high school. Steal a prison barge and suddenly everyone wants to know me,' Miska said. Her voice didn't shake but the sums involved had still come as a shock.

'That's going to get every gun tramp in the colonies looking for you,' Vido told her. She'd worked that out herself. She forced her mouth to form a smile.

'Part of the plan; practice for you guys,' she told the *consigliere*. He didn't smile. He just looked at her. Miska couldn't quite read his expression. Sympathy?

'Bounty hunters aren't an issue in Maw City. This, however,

is ...' Nicholas concentrated for a moment. A hologram appeared in the air in front of his chair. It looked like footage shot from a sentry drone stationed on one of the outlying asteroids in the Dog's Teeth. The footage showed a destroyer hanging in space a little way off the asteroid belt. 'That's an FBI ship,' the administrator told them.

'Now you're in trouble,' Vido said, smiling. The FBI had been instrumental in his RICO investigation. This didn't come as a shock; Raff, her CIA handler, had said as much would happen. She was pretty sure that it was part of a joint FBI/Marshal Service task force. Even though the FBI ship was a lot smaller than the *Hangman's Daughter*, Miska knew it was more than capable of making mincemeat of the prison barge in a straight-up fight.

'Jeez, you'd think they'd be pleased. I took all these anti-social types off their hands,' she muttered. Vido was shaking his head, Nicholas's smile looked a little pained. 'One ship isn't much of a threat to Maw City.'

'Nobody really wants to talk about it, but effectively we are *allowed* to exist. With a concerted effort from one of the larger government forces, or a coalition of the smaller ones, they could destroy the city and scatter the pirates. That is why we avoid atrocity and try not to draw too much attention to ourselves, despite the boasts you'll hear in the bars.'

'But we could tip the balance?' Vido asked.

'You compound our own law enforcement scrutiny. You're too loud.'

'So you're turning us away?' Vido asked. Miska felt her heart sink. If she couldn't offload the frigate here then she was really going to struggle with things like fuel and feeding her legion.

'Nothing would give me more pleasure than to make Maw

45

City the *Hangman Daughter*'s home port. We would happily buy any goods from you, provide entertainment for your people. We could refit the ship. Make it quite formidable. Fence any goods that happen to come your way. I'm sure it would be mutually profitable for both parties ...'

'But?' Miska asked and leaned against the wall, pulling her boots up onto the table.

'Not while you hold members of the Crimson Sisterhood,' he told her, and the thing of it was she knew that he wasn't being unreasonable. 'And that's just a door you can't open, isn't it?' Nicholas asked and he was right.

'I notice you condone slavery for the rest of us,' Vido said.

'More that we would look at Maw City as respite for your otherwise cruel circumstances.'

Vido laughed and pointed at Nicholas. 'Smooth, I can see why they employed you.'

'So what now?' Miska asked, feeling a little despondent.

'I'm guessing you wish to sell the Triton-class frigate you arrived in?' he asked.

Miska nodded.

'Or you could take it and call it quits,' Vido suggested. 'Just run.' Miska let her head drop until she was looking at Vido.

'You gonna claim the fifteen million?' she asked. Vido laughed. 'Nah, you'd miss me.'

'We're happy to accommodate you during this visit but it's a one-time deal,' Nicholas told her.

It wasn't quite what Miska had hoped for but she understood their reasoning and it was better than nothing.

'Fair enough,' she told him. 'I've also got a damaged old surplus prison transport to sell.' It was the shuttle that had been damaged during the first disastrous assault on Faigroe Station.

46

She'd hoped to get it repaired here but it didn't sound like that was going to be an option.

'Send me a list. I'm assuming you're here for shore leave and to buy supplies?' Nicholas asked as Miska sent over the specs on the two ships and a list of the supplies they wanted. Figures came back surprisingly quickly. They were going to pay her slightly less than she had hoped for the frigate and the shuttle, and charge her slightly more than she had hoped for the supplies, but it still meant that the Bastards had come out way ahead on their first job.

'Two days in the city to conduct your business and use our facilities. I'll guarantee your safe passage bar the inevitable brawling. Then you need to leave. I can't offer you safe passage beyond our city limits. The Sisterhood are going to come and speak to you. I suggest you listen to them.'

'That's fair,' Miska said. Though she wasn't looking forward to a conversation with some pirate queen. Vido stood up and offered his hand. Miska had to smile at the fake-it-till-you-make-it pretence of power from the *consigliere*. Nevertheless, Nicholas was gracious enough to shake the proffered hand.

The door opened and the food was wheeled in. Miska realised that she was famished. Vido inspected the contents as though he was at some swanky restaurant in New Verona Beach. He looked over at Teramoto and the two Milliners.

'You guys sure you're not hungry? This is good Italian food.'

Miska had eaten too much. It was the best food that she had eaten in a very long time, certainly since before she had stolen the *Hangman's Daughter*. The assault shuttle had gone back to the *Daughter*, returning to Maw City with the damaged prison shuttle, the Bastards that had been involved in the Faigroe

Station job onboard. They had some money in their pockets and were let loose in Maw City's recreational areas. Teramoto had tried to remain on duty watching over her but she had insisted that he take his shore leave. She had faith in Nicholas's promise of safety in the station. Besides, she was more than capable of looking after herself. Though she had to admit that what Nicholas had told her had driven home the sheer size of the target on her back. She had liked the administrator. He had dealt fairly with them.

She was searching through her dead letter drops, though the closest relay point was in orbit around Sirius 4, so there was a sixteen-minute lag. She saw there was a heavily encoded message from Raff. It was pretty recent. He was in Maw City. Miska was surprised that he'd managed to keep up with her.

She'd taken a zero-G tunnel from the asteroid they had docked at onto a collared terrarium – a hollowed out asteroid with a terraformed environment that had been spun for gravity. She peeked sideways into the net. The terrarium's virtual representation was of a fantastical hollow world. She requested information on the asteroid habitat and discovered that it had actually been hollowed out by Them, the aliens that had initially inhabited Maw City. The interior walls of the asteroid had been sculpted into extensive parkland interspersed with some magnificent hotels. Miska guessed that this was where the wealthier pirates retired. Given what Nicholas had said about the precariousness of Maw City's position within the system, the terrarium seemed somewhat grandiose and optimistic.

Miska took a maglev through the rock skin of the asteroid to the hotel that Raff was staying in. It was a huge edifice on a hill overlooking a lake with bright blue water. According to the net it was based on a hotel in some place called Switzerland. The original hotel had been built in the nineteenth century. It looked nice and all, but straight away Miska felt like it wasn't the sort of place that she would be welcome in her big boots, jeans, T-shirt and leather jacket.

She ignored the front desk and snuck into one of the ancient and disturbingly rickety-looking elevators. Raff had given her a room number. She suspected a CIA slush fund had taken a pounding for Raff to get a room here. She was also wondering just how much piracy paid.

She knocked on the door to Raff's room. There was no answer. She checked around for the biometric reader that would provide access but saw nothing. It seemed like the lock was mechanical and worked when a key was put in it and turned. She had to do a net search to work this out. It was weirdly anachronistic. She tried the handle and found the door was unlocked. She was starting not to like this, so as she opened the door she palmed the SIG GP-992 from its holster. She pushed her way into the room. There was a figure reaching for her. She reacted. Raff was lying on the floor, a gun in his face, before she'd even really recognised him. He had his hands up and looked terrified.

'Fuck, Raff!' she spat, and kicked the door closed behind her before holstering the gauss pistol. 'I nearly shot you.' He was wet and had a towel wrapped around his waist, his dark brown skin and gym muscles on display. She looked around the room. Dark wood panelling, pictures on the wall, huge four-poster bed that was larger than some apartments she'd lived in, a balcony overlooking the lake. Out on the balcony was a table with an ice bucket on it. A bottle of champagne stuck out of the bucket and there were two glasses next to it. It was all very ... romantic.

Miska looked back down at Raff as he wriggled away from her and sat up on the floor.

'I was in the shower, I didn't hear you,' he told her.

Miska pointed at the champagne.

'Tell me I've interrupted some James Bond-style spy shit here,' she said. Raff just looked a little sheepish. 'At least tell me you're romancing some high-priced call girl or rent boy on the company buck?'

Raff held up his hands.

'Okay, I think I may have misjudged the situation a little,' he said.

'A little? A little!' Miska demanded. She looked over at the champagne, the four-poster bed. 'Where do I fucking start? First of all, have you ever even met me? Do I really strike you as the sort of girl who's interested in all this shit?'

'Oh, I'm sorry, it's just difficult to arrange dates around blowing shit up or CQB these days,' he said, meaning close quarters battle.

'Shut up! Secondly, how could you possibly misjudge this when I made it abundantly fucking clear the last time you tried this shit that we don't do this?' *Y'know, except for the one time we did*. She told her inner voice to shut the fuck up. She had been grieving for her father. Raff had been there. She crossed her arms and leaned closer to him. 'I want a new handler. What we're doing is far too fucking dangerous for this bullshit. Do you know how much they've put on my head?'

'You can't have a new handler, we're in too deep. This is too classified,' he told her. He was still sat on the floor, looking up at her.

Miska narrowed her eyes. She didn't like the sound of 'too classified' at all.

'What the fuck's that supposed to mean?' she demanded.

'Exactly what it sounds like,' he told her. He was sounding less sheepish and more pissed off now. Something about him reminded her of the inner churlish teenager that many men seemed to have inside them.

'Stand up,' she told him. Raff started to get up and then sat back down on the thick carpet.

'You're going to hit me, aren't you?' he said.

'It seems that me telling you that it was a one-time thing wasn't emphatic enough, so every time you try this I'm going to fucking hit you. It's called negative reinforcement. Jesus Christ, I should get you one of the fucking collars.'

'I'm not getting up so you can hit me,' he told her.

'Then I'm going to kick you in the face.'

'Has it ever occurred to you that I may actually have feelings for you, real actual feelings, y'know, like people do?'

In some ways Miska was surprised that his words actually hurt.

'Stand up, Raff, I'm not going to tell you again.'

'You know violence isn't always the answer,' Raff said as he stood up. Miska hit him. Raff sat back down again. Hard.

'No, but it's a useful fallback when people aren't fucking listening!' Miska pointed out before turning and making for the door.

'I've got a job for you,' he told her as he tried to stem the flow of blood from his broken nose.

CHAPTER 4

'That it?' Miska asked. She was sitting on the bed, her legs up, still wearing her boots, drinking from the bottle of champagne.

'We know it's there,' Raff said. He was sitting on a chair, still in his towel. He had wrapped some of the ice from the bucket in a washcloth and was holding it to his newly broken nose. 'Can I have some champagne?'

Miska shook her head and took another pull from the bottle of bubbly liquid.

'So a small team?' she asked.

'We'll drop you in from a commercial carrier; there's no orbital elevator on Barney Prime.' Raff was studying the pattern of blood and snot on the washcloth. Miska didn't like the sound of this at all. Barney Prime – or Barnard's Prime – was the main colony in the Barnard's Star system. It was an established world and one of the few success stories in attempting to terraform tidally-locked worlds orbiting red dwarf stars. New Verona City, on the sun side of Barney Prime, a popular holiday resort, was also deemed to be one of the most criminally corrupt cities in human space. It was practically owned by the Mafia. Among the various Mafia families vying for power on Barney Prime, the Cofino family were considered by many to be the strongest. They ruled New Verona. Vido was a member of the family and Mass had served them as a *caporegime*, or street captain. Torricone was from New Verona as well, but the Mafia were the city's aristocracy.

'It's American soil,' she pointed out. 'Just confiscate the item.'

'We've no legal reason to take it. We're sending you because you're the most deniable of deniable operators.'

'The whole point of Operation Lee Marvin was to bring a military force to bear in parts of the colonies where America couldn't be seen to be operating. Part of the deal, I had assumed, was that we didn't put ourselves into the path of the authorities,' Miska said. Lee Marvin was the CIA operation behind setting up the Bastard Legion. 'For fuck's sake, I'm wanted in every colony that had a prisoner on the *Hangman's Daughter*. We'll be making it easy for the Feds and the bounty hunters.' And she would be operating without the support of the rest of the Legion and the ship.

'Not if you're careful. I think you underestimate just how corrupt that place is. Everything's for sale and we'll be giving you a lot of money to spread around,' he told her. That, at least, was right. She had operated on Barney Prime before, most of her experience with la Cosa Nostra, or LCN, the Mafia's term for itself, had been on that planet. Raff had put the washcloth down. Miska wasn't sure if he was looking longingly at her, or the rapidly disappearing bottle of champagne. 'Besides, you've got people who know their way around.'

Miska actually gaped at him.

'Are you fucking crazy?' she demanded. 'I can't take them

back there. They're completely hooked into that city. At best I'd never see them again.'

Raff looked unconvinced, but he didn't understand the situation. He didn't understand just how cunning and manipulative even the dumbest convict could be, let alone master criminals like Uncle Vido.

'This is important, Miska,' Raff said. 'We'll pay you a lot.'

I'm not in it for the money! she almost snapped, and she wouldn't be able to find her father's killers if some LCN thug put two in the back of her head because she'd enslaved some of their men. Nor could she do it from federal custody.

'You haven't even told me what the item is, what you want me to steal,' she pointed out. Raff looked down and didn't say anything. Miska narrowed her eyes. She was supposed to erase the brief from her internal memory having read it. She didn't think that would be an issue, the brief had contained very little information beyond some vague idea that the CIA wanted her to steal an 'item'. 'Raff, look at me, do you know what this item is?' Raff looked up at her and squirmed in his seat. Her eyes were pretty much just tight slits as she glared at her case officer. 'Raff, is this an alien artefact?' He looked down again. Miska resisted the urge to throw the nearly empty bottle at his head. 'For fuck's sake Raff! Do you know how many times I've been tasked to track down alien artefacts? These are always wild goose chases! Barney Prime was settled before the war. Had there been anything there it would have been found years ago. Who are we supposed to be stealing it from?' Again Raff didn't answer. 'You don't know?'

'We suspect Martian interests,' Raff finally said. Even he didn't sound as though he believed it. It took a moment for Miska to recover.

'Martians under the bed, really? If that's the case then have the Feds arrest them as spies and confiscate the bullshit artefact.'

'If it is Mars they'll be using proxies and the artefact would be covered under the colonial prospecting laws.'

'Viva la free market,' Miska muttered. Prospecting was one thing, but if the Company was interested then it was because they thought that whatever was there was either powerful or dangerous. If that was the case then the federal government was more than within its rights to confiscate it in the name of public safety. So if the Company were prepared to send Miska in then they wanted control of whatever the artefact was. 'Sure there's not anything else you'd like me to do? Maybe assassinate Mars himself with an exploding cigar?'

'If it wasn't important I wouldn't be asking,' he told her.

'In terms of equipment we'll only be able to take what we can carry,' she said, but Raff was already shaking his head.

'You'll be jumping from a commercial operator but we need to smuggle you on board first. Sidearms, nothing more. Weapons, vehicles, everything else you have to source locally. Like I said, we'll give you a lot of money.'

'Exfil plan?' she asked.

'Local resources. You smuggle the artefact out. Which is why I strongly suggest that you utilise the assets you have with local knowledge.' Miska was just shaking her head.

'Are you trying to get me caught or killed because I won't sleep with you?' she asked. Raff didn't answer but she noticed a blinking message icon in her IVD. She checked it and then opened it. There were two figures in the message.

'The first is your expenses. The second is your fee,' Raff told her.

'You're taking this pretty seriously, aren't you?' Miska said.

The first figure was large. The second was obscene. She focused on Raff. 'If, and I mean if, we check this out then we get paid even if it's bullshit.'

Raff considered this.

'As long as you supply solid intel to that end,' he said.

'And if we do it you hook us up with some of that sweet slush fund money we discussed the last time we met, so I can properly fund the op. Enough of this hand-to-mouth shit.'

'I'll see what I can do.'

'One other thing. When we infiltrated Faigroe Station the lowjack collars hugely increased the risk of exposure. All anyone had to do was check one of my guys' necks and we were blown. If we're going covert, especially to a beach resort ...'

'Check under the bed,' Raff told her. Miska dropped the now-empty bottle onto the huge bed and rolled over the edge to look underneath. She pulled out a case of hardened plastic and placed her palm against the biometric lock. The case clicked open. She found herself looking at a jet injector and a number of vials.

'Toxin or nano-explosive?' she asked.

'I thought you'd prefer explosive,' Raff said. Miska closed the case and headed for the door with it.

'We'll think it over,' she told him.

'Are you going talk to your dad about it?' he asked.

Miska stopped by the door.

'That's none of your business.' Then she left the room.

Miska was pissed off and more than a little light-headed from having consumed a bottle of champagne as she took the maglev to the terrarium's collar, before making her way back to the docking area via the walkway. She knew that Raff hadn't approved of her using her dad's backup as part of the Bastard's training programme but that didn't give him the right to question her operational decisions. He wasn't on a ship with six thousand dangerous criminals who would like nothing more than to tear her apart.

She almost groaned as she saw an incoming message from her father. She opened the comms link and his craggy features appeared in a little window in her IVD.

'More than half of those on shore leave have been arrested by Maw City's security,' he told her.

'What for?' she asked. She was hoping it was nothing serious. She didn't really want to blow any more collars.

'Mostly brawling and property damage,' he told her.

Miska shrugged and then felt foolish because her dad couldn't see it.

'Didn't you used to get into trouble when you were on leave?' she asked. 'This is exactly what they're supposed to be doing.'

'Aren't you keeping an eye on them?' he asked.

'If I was do you think the situation would be better or worse?' she asked. Her dad considered the question.

'Good point,' he said. 'Where were you?'

'I'll tell you later. Vido report to you about the situation?' she asked.

'We're going to need a friendly port or two in the long run.'

'A problem for another day,' she told him. 'Now I'm going to get drunk and arrested.'

'Miska—' he started but she cut the comms link. She was still smarting a bit from the post-exercise debrief, though she knew he had been right. She wasn't looking forward to discussing the New Verona job with her dad either. That and Raff trying it on again had left her in a particularly foul mood.

Miska had returned to the assault shuttle and locked away the case with the injectors and the nano-explosives before heading to the bars and the clubs of the recreational area. She saw a number of her Bastards, mainly members of the Bethlehem Milliners who'd formed the QRF, staggering from bar to bar. Most of them seemed just drunk enough to think well of her at the moment. She returned their nods, waves and shouted comments. She wondered if any would get drunk enough to go for her later. She didn't really care. She saw Vido and Mass having a drink together, deep in conversation.

Miska found the sleaziest looking dive that was playing real music and went in. It was a lap dancing club, but that didn't really bother her as the band was decent enough and playing some stripped down retro blues-rock. She ordered a beer and whisky and found a seat at the back.

She watched the strippers for a while, unimpressed by the gyrations of the variously gendered dancers.

Why didn't you give the Ultra shore leave? Her thoughts had strayed. After all, he had been involved in the operation. He had killed the woman who had hired them and then double-crossed them, and he had done so in a way that had made her feel like an abject amateur. *That's not how he made you feel.* Her inner voice seemed particularly keen on honesty, whereas Miska just wanted to get properly drunk in peace and quiet. She found herself thinking about the beautiful serial killer in solitary with the other two members of the Trinity. The prisoners too dangerous for GenPop, or general population. Skirov, the mostly dismantled uncontrollable-psychotic warewolf, and Red, the thoroughly institutionalised unstoppable killing machine. The Ultra was just a crush. She knew that. A ridiculous and utterly unrealistic crush. He might be beautiful but even by her standards he wasn't wired right, assuming he was even human. When he had been captured there had been some speculation that he was one of the Small Gods, an AI given form by nano-technology – illegal outside of Small Gods-controlled territory back in the Sol system. *He's so pretty, though!* She had to resist the urge to trance in, send her consciousness back to the *Hangman's Daughter* and go and look at the lens feed of the Trinity's three cryo pods hanging on their own. Of course she'd have to do it sneakily so her dad didn't know.

'Hey boss.'

Broken out of her Ultra-based reverie she suddenly felt absurdly guilty. She looked up to see Torricone standing over her, his lean muscled body covered by a sleeveless vest that showed off his jailhouse tattoos. There was a tattooed tear on his cheek and a crown of thorns around his shaved head. She couldn't make out the colour of his eyes under the blue steel lighting in the bar but she knew from memory that they were brown. Maybe it was because he had interrupted her thinking about the Ultra, but she was suddenly reminded of kissing him on Faigroe Station. *Cut yourself a break,* she told herself, *you were starved of oxygen at the time.*

'Oh great, it's my conscience,' she muttered. *The best defence is …*

'If that was the case I think I'd look guiltier,' he retorted, the smile gone from his face.

'Oh good comeback, and you are guilty, you're in prison!'

Torricone turned to walk away. A group of the Bethlehem Milliners walked into the bar.

'Wait, I'm sorry,' Miska told him. She could see the edge of the tattoo of the crucifixion that covered Torricone's back. He turned round to face her. 'It's been a day,' she told him. 'Let me get you a drink.' With a thought she ordered two more beers and two more whiskies. The Milliners were ordering drinks as well. They looked ridiculous as far as Miska was concerned. Other than their prison overalls and battle dress uniforms, the only clothes the Bastards had on board were the clothes that they had been delivered to prison wearing. Torricone was wearing smart chinos and the vest he had presumably worn under a shirt for his court appearance. The Milliners had apparently gone to court in gang colours. The colours were based on some ancient kids' story. They wore frock coats, elaborate waistcoats, button-down spats over high-heeled boots, and a ridiculous amount of accessories. They even wore brightly coloured wigs and had used some of their allotted money to buy grotesque make-up that they had caked on their faces. The most important part of their costumes, however, were their top hats.

'These guys were the scourge of Lalande 2's tunnels?' Miska asked as Torricone sat down and looked over at the Milliners. A droid delivered their drinks.

'Yep. Difficult to believe, right?'

On second thoughts, the distorted child-like costumes seemed somehow sinister in their grotesqueness. Kids' stories were weird, she decided. Torricone knocked back his bourbon and Miska did the same and then followed it up with a mouthful of beer. She realised that some of the other clientele were barking at the Milliners. The clientele mostly looked like crewmembers from independent ships. They were tough-looking, and openly carried weapons, but she suspected they were mostly smugglers, as the harder core pirate crews all tended to have their own colours, like the Crimson Sisterhood. Miska's face screwed up in confusion.

'What's the barking about?' she asked. Torricone just tugged at his collar. 'Oh, I get it!' Miska said cheerfully. She was definitely drunk. The beers she'd had while negotiating with Nicholas, followed by the champagne she'd drunk too quickly (and largely out of spite, if she was being honest) had been enough. The Milliners were exchanging insults with the other crews, though there didn't seem to be much in the way of a common language. A bottle was thrown and it kicked off.

'Watch the barman,' Torricone said and drained his beer before concentrating, presumably ordering another drink with his combat pay. Miska looked at the barman behind his see-through mesh. He didn't seem particularly bothered by the fight. The dancers, who were not fight adjacent, kept dancing, and the band kept playing. It was only when furniture started getting thrown around and things were getting broken that she saw the barman subvocalising. 'See it?' Torricone asked.

'Sure,' Miska said. 'So what?' She drained her beer, watching the serving droid with their drinks order take a circuitous route around the fight.

The security droids that answered the barman's summons were similar to the ones that Miska used on the *Hangman's Daughter*, only much more modern. Torricone was watching her.

'What?' she asked. He nodded towards the fight. The problem with droids was that they couldn't be negotiated with or intimidated. The brawlers got a warning and if they didn't desist then they got tasered and/or beaten down and dragged out. 'Efficient,' she admitted.

'Response time of under a minute,' Torricone said as he watched one of the Milliners break his foot kicking a droid in the face. The droid clubbed him to the ground and tasered him until he was a drooling mess on the beer-sodden floor. 'For a criminal enterprise they take their law enforcement very seriously. Bit like you.' Miska turned to find him looking at her, smiling. She was half impressed at his situational awareness, but only half.

'What are you doing?' she asked suspiciously.

'I thought maybe I'd teach you how to drink tequila, *mamacita*.'

'I know how to drink teq— wait, did you just call me mom? Torricone, are you drunk?' Then she mock-gasped. 'Oh my god! Are you actually having fun?'

'Fuck it, forget it,' he snapped and stood up.

'Torricone, were you flirting with me?' she called after him. She was laughing now. 'You know you're still wearing a collar right!' She called just as the band finished their song. Her shouted voice carried. Heads turned. 'Shit,' she muttered. The security droids were just dragging the last of the Milliners out of the bar. Torricone turned angrily around to face her. In doing so he bumped into a huge, heavily muscled figure of indeterminate gender. He/she was carrying a tray of drinks that went crashing to the floor.

'I'm really sorry,' Torricone said straight away. 'Let me get you another round.' The huge man/woman looked down at the soaked front of her flight suit.

'What. The. Actual fuck?' he/she growled. His/her voice didn't help Miska with pinning down the gender, not that it really mattered. Then he/she saw the collar. 'I think your bitch queen needs to keep you on a tighter leash.'

'Hey!' Miska said aggrieved. A lot of eyes turned her way.

'You're her, aren't you?' he/she said. Miska hated being famous. She stood up, a trifle unsteadily for her liking, as he/she pushed Torricone to one side and lumbered towards Miska.

62

Miska almost hurt her neck looking up at him/her. Again she was forced to reflect that everyone was bigger than her.

'I've got friends on that ship,' he/she spat, literally, Miska had to wipe flecks of drool off her face.

'Okay, let's just calm down,' Torricone said.

'Excuse me,' Miska said to the person looming over her. Then Miska leaned around their bulk to look at Torricone. 'You really are so boring, you need to loosen up.' The man/woman chuckled at this and turned to look at Torricone.

'Yeah, why don't you run along and get me my drinks while I beat the—' That was when Miska hit him/her and it kicked off again.

'Ah!' Miska sat bolt upright on the bench in the cell. She'd been dreaming that she'd been involved in a polyamorous relationship with Torricone and the Ultra. The dream had at times been incredibly erotic but had descended into appallingly complicated domestic drudgery that Miska didn't have anything like the patience for. 'Ow!' Her own internal repair systems notwithstanding, the security droids had played her ribs like a xylophone they were particularly angry with. Then the pain in her head hit her, hard.

As drunk tanks went it was quite a nice cell. Torricone was on the bench opposite her, stripped to the waist, using his vest as a pillow. She narrowed her eyes trying to remember if anything had happened but she had pretty much been unconscious since her extensive tasering.

There was a groaning sound from the other bunk and Torricone pushed himself up, and swung around to put his back to the wall, pulling his knees up to his chin and hugging his legs. Miska took some pleasure in how utterly wretched he looked.

She wondered how much he'd drunk before they had bumped into each other.

'Oh shit!' he muttered seeing her. 'Did we ...?'

Miska stared at him.

'Yeah, you were really disappointing,' she finally told him, trying not to laugh at the bewildered and hurt expression on his face. He opened his mouth to retort and the door to the cell slid open. Terrance was standing there holding coffee, some painkillers and a pair of sunglasses.

'There's somebody here to see you,' the metal-faced head of security told her. Miska was too hungover to really care. She stood up, put the sunglasses on and took the painkillers, washing them down with the coffee.

'Thank you, Terrance,' Miska said. 'I'm going to recommend this drunk tank to all my friends.'

'You have friends?' Torricone asked. Miska gave him the finger and walked out of the cell. She heard Torricone try to follow and fail.

The drunk tank was in a small security tower in the middle of the dockside recreation area. She suspected it was normally automated and that Terrance had visited specifically to let her out. The tower had storage for the security droids on the ground floor, with stackable modular cells that moved round on rails above that. The doors opened out onto a small green, surrounded on three sides by a food court that seemed to specialise in hangover-worthy food. It struck Miska as clever business placement. The fourth side was the asteroid's transparent frontage that looked out over the bustling docks.

She sighed when she saw the woman with the living red hair sat at one of the tables. She was smoking a cigarette, nursing a beer, and looking out at the docks as a heavily armed, medium-sized freighter was towed down towards the pulsing lights of the shipyard. Miska contacted one of the food court franchises and ordered a breakfast burrito, then she ordered a Bloody Mary from an autobar called Hair of the Dog. The pirate woman turned to look at her as she approached. Terrance had returned the holster with the SIG and the pouch with the spare magazines, which Miska clipped on to her belt, and her knife, which she sheathed. She wanted the other woman to know she was armed. Miska sat down opposite the member of the Crimson Sisterhood. The pirate didn't say anything. She just studied Miska for a while. Miska was pretty sure it wasn't an attempt at intimidation. The pirate was trying to work out which tack to take.

'My name is Captain Gosia Tesselaar of the *Sneaky Bitch*,' the woman said. Her voice was deep and throaty, Miska suspected the results of too many cigarettes and screamed orders. Her hair was swaying as though caught in some gentle breeze.

'Good name,' Miska said after a few moments' thought. 'I'm guessing you know who I am?'

Captain Tesselaar nodded. 'We're not going to be friends, are we?' she asked.

'I suspect we're at an impasse,' Miska said. It was a shame, she thought that the captain was probably the kind of person she wouldn't mind having a drink with.

'We need our people back. You keeping them as slaves makes us look weak,' she said, and stubbed out her cigarette. She lit another and took a sip of her beer. 'And just the thought of them ...'

'I'm sorry, I can't do that,' Miska said. The captain nodded as if she understood and then Miska watched her face harden.

It was like watching water flash-freeze. Her hair was suddenly very still.

'My man's on that ship,' she said.

'I'm sorry,' Miska said. Captain Tesselaar spent some time staring at her. This time it was about intimidation. Then she stood up and walked away. Miska's burrito and Bloody Mary turned up. Miska lay face down on the table. She sent texts to Mass, Nyukuti, Torricone and Teramoto, telling them to round everyone up. They had to cut their losses, take what supplies were ready and head back to the *Hangman's Daughter*. Then she sent a message to her dad back on the prison barge. It wasn't a huge surprise but it was something she had hoped to avoid. The Crimson Sisterhood were going to attack the moment they left Maw City.

'Hello Miska,' a very familiar voice said. Miska froze. She hoped it was a horrible joke, someone using a voice modulator to mimic speech patterns.

She looked up. It wasn't a joke.

'Where's my ship?' her sister demanded.

CHAPTER 5

Angela was slender, athletic, had her mother's looks and her father's height, whereas Miska had got it the other way around. Cold blue artificial eyes that had, very accurately, been modelled on the originals, stared at her from the other side of the table. Miska glanced over at the window looking out over the cold space of Maw City's docks.

'Don't worry, I'm not going to defenestrate you,' Angela said, still standing. The last time Miska had seen her sister had been at their dad's funeral and Angela had kicked her through a window.

'Defenestrate?' Miska asked. She didn't look straight at her sister. Instead she was checking her surroundings. Her sister was dangerous, no doubt about it; with a gun to her head Miska might even admit that she was more dangerous than herself. An ex-member of Delta Force, she now worked for the NSA, who were probably keen to get the *Little Jimmy* back. The ship had originally belonged to her sister. Its loss would have hugely damaged the other Corbin girl's career. 'You forget you're the daughter of a marine gunnery sergeant?' Then she turned and looked at her sister. Angela stared back at her. She was a control freak, so you had to look hard to see the sibling rage, but Miska knew what to watch for. Angela forced herself to swallow and sat down.

'I said ...' she started. Miska was looking around again. Dangerous or not it was a ballsy move walking into a place like this without backup.

'I heard what you said. Why don't you do something useful? Something family oriented.'

'Is that what you think you're doing?' Angela asked. Miska ignored her. 'I'm looking into Dad's death,' she said more softly. 'But what you're doing now ...'

Miska looked away again, then she found the backup. It wasn't quite what she'd expected. A grizzled African American man in his fifties. Salt and pepper beard, he looked like someone who'd been carved out of rock by a hard life in the frontier colonies. Jeans, faded combat jacket, probably both armoured, a plaid shirt and an actual real Stetson and cowboy boots. He also had a shotgun hanging from a sling, his finger curled around the trigger guard. He just screamed law enforcement. He was in the corner where the huge window met the asteroid's rock, next to one of the autobars. Miska pointed at him.

'Nice. I see you've got a daddy replacement already,' Miska said. She almost smiled when she saw Angela's hands bunch up into fists.

'That's Chief Deputy Mac Castro—' Angela started.

'Mac Castro!' Miska said, laughing. 'Seriously? Does he have his own action figure?'

Angela rolled her eyes.

'He's a marshal, he's here to take you back.'

'Back where?' Miska asked. 'There's nowhere to go back to, Angie.' Her sister hated the contraction of her name. 'Besides, if I'm going to spend the rest of my life on a prison barge, it may as well be the *Hangman's Daughter*.' Miska couldn't quite make out the expression on her sister's face. The older Corbin girl almost looked sad. 'Besides, I can't see your current employers being all that gentle with me.'

'I can protect you,' Angela told her. She almost sounded as though she believed it.

'No, you can't,' Miska told her. 'Good talk, we should do this again.' Miska stood up. Angela reached for her. Miska moved back, hand to her SIG.

'Whoa!' she told her sister. She was aware of Chief Deputy Castro pushing himself off the rock, changing the grip on his shotgun.

'Don't make us do this the hard way,' Angela said.

Miska looked between her sister and the marshal. Her sister was dressed in casual, dark clothes, loose enough not to hinder her movement, tight enough to not flap around too much. The clothes were almost certainly armoured and it wouldn't be Angela if she wasn't armed.

'Are you out of your fucking mind?' Miska demanded. Heads were starting to turn their way at the sound of raised voices. 'You going to start on me here? With just your daddy surrogate as backup?' Angela actually flinched at this. There was just a momentary feeling of guilt. Miska didn't want to think too hard about her father's electronic ghost back in the training construct.

Angela pushed herself up, hands still on the table.

'Of all the stupid, childish shit you've pulled in your life, this is by far the most irresponsible, and it's just going to get worse.

Have you any idea how many people you killed on Tau Ceti E?' she demanded. Miska had attacked the arcology headquarters of the company that had double-crossed the Bastards with a massive mining robot that she had hacked. Miska looked her sister straight in the eyes.

'You know I don't care,' she told her. It was mostly true. The Tau City Company appeared to practise a recruitment policy of positive discrimination for assholes and besides, remorse wasn't really her thing. 'This ends with me dead, incarcerated, or getting away with it. Coming with you, now, really narrows my options, doesn't it?' Miska noticed Torricone coming out of the security station. Vido, Mass and the remaining members of Mass's assault team had just walked out of one of the open, mall-like corridors. Many of them looked the worse for wear after a night of drinking, and strictly speaking, they were disobeying her orders but she was still pleased to see them. Teramoto, Nyukuti, and one of her Bethlehem Milliner 'body-guards' had emerged from another corridor. She saw looks exchanged between the two groups and Torricone.

'Your toy soldiers?' her sister asked. 'Wow, Stockholm Syndrome set in quick.' Miska glanced at Chief Deputy Castro, who was aware of the Bastards as well. If he was worried it didn't show on his face. 'You know you're going to get them all killed?'

'Yeah, well they're not exactly nice people,' Miska said.

'Grow up!' her sister screamed at her. 'This is obscene!'

A number of the Bastards started towards her at the sound of Angela's raised voice. Miska held up her hand and they stopped. Training, and even combat experience notwithstanding, Angela would tear through them like paper, and she suspected that the Chief Deputy knew what he was doing as well. When she next had time she was going to ask Raff to look into Castro. She was willing to bet that he was ex-Military and a member of the Marshal Service's Special Operations Group.

'You all right, Angela?' Castro asked. Deep voice, southern drawl, it was straight out of one of her dad's westerns. Some of the other people in the food court were starting to take an interest in the obvious confrontation. Hard-looking men and women, crewmembers from criminal ships. Angela opened her mouth to answer Castro.

'Oh, she's just fine thank you, Marshal's Deputy Castro!' Miska shouted, emphasising the words 'Marshal's' and 'Deputy'. People were starting to look his way now. Angela stared at her, appalled. It was a huge taboo among intelligence operatives. You never burned somebody's cover. 'Oh, come on!' Miska protested. 'I'm not on his side. Besides, look at him! He screams law enforcement!' Angela just shook her head, looking at Miska with distaste. It was a look Miska had got used to growing up.

'You a marshal?' some overly augmented half-metal gorilla asked as he stood up. Now Castro looked nervous. He brought the butt of his shotgun to his shoulder but didn't point it at anyone yet.

'Now why doesn't everyone just calm down?' he suggested. 'This can be resolved with a conversation.'

'I asked you a goddamned question,' the gorilla snapped. He had a thick German accent. Miska turned back to her sister.

'So what do you want to do?' she asked. 'Fight me or help your new daddy?' Angela glared at her. Miska smiled as sweetly as she could manage before turning and walking towards Teramoto. Mass, Vido and the others fell in with them. Teramoto and the Milliner 'bodyguard' were still armed, so they covered the rear.

Miska sent a message to the shuttle as Torricone caught up with them at a jog. He looked as though he was going to throw up at any moment.

'Who's that?' Torricone asked.

'My sister,' Miska muttered as she heard the fight start in the food hall behind them.

'She seemed angry.'

'Always.'

'That seems to happen around you a lot.'

Miska just turned to glare at him.

'What's the plan, boss?' Vido asked. She caught him looking at Torricone and shaking his head. Miska was reviewing the supply situation. The *Hangman's Daughter* had rendezvoused with the supply and tanker shuttles that Nicholas had sent and he had transferred the balance of the sum from the sale of the *Excelsior* and the damaged shuttle. The only things missing were a few of the harder to find items she had asked for, nothing too crucial. More to the point they had raw material to feed the printer, and enough food and water for at least six months. That was the good news. She received a reply from the shuttle. The bad news was that two of the Crimson Sisterhood ships, one of the corsairs and the converted freighter, had left Maw City almost immediately after Miska's conversation with Captain Tesselaar.

'We're getting out of here,' Miska told Vido. She just wasn't sure how, yet. She wondered if the Bastard Legion's motto should be *nothing's ever easy*.

'I'm getting tired of living in rock and breathing bottled air anyway,' Mass muttered from behind her. Miska could relate. It sounded like a full-on riot had broken out in the food court behind them but she hadn't heard any gunshots yet.

The assault shuttle's pilot met her at the end of the docking arm. Perez, Joseph; fifteen to life for second-degree murder stemming from a fight in a bar in the Gliese system. He'd stabbed a member of a rival gang to death while high on crystal. He was in his mid-twenties, with a prison muscle build, and a surprisingly neatly trimmed beard for a member of the Hard Luck Comancheros. He wore a military style flight suit that had come out of the printer Miska had taken from the stolen frigate. His flight suit still had the Aces and Eights of his gang colours. He was by far and away the best shuttle pilot on board the *Hangman's Daughter*. He also had actual military experience.

'Boss?' he said as Miska approached. Her entourage had grown bigger as she had made her way through the recreational area adjacent to the docks. She'd sent a message to Nicholas asking for her people to be released and paid the requisite fines/bribes to facilitate this. 'Don't want me flying this one?' he asked. Miska shook her head.

'Naw, you know the plan, right?' she asked. He smiled.

'Such as it is,' he said. He wasn't wrong, she was cobbling it together on the fly while trying to ignore a mild but still aggravating hangover that had been compounded by her sister.

'Want us to come with you?' Torricone asked. Miska turned to face him, and noticed some of the other Bastards looking at him. At some point she should probably put him out of his misery and make it clear that they hadn't slept together.

'Not unless you fancy spending some quality time with me throwing up,' she said. Nyukuti clapped one of his big hands on Torricone's shoulder, making him wince.

'This one is not for us, I think,' Nyukuti told the car thief.

73

Torricone looked between the standover man and Miska and then nodded.

'Look after them,' Miska said in Nyukuti and Mass's general direction before turning and walking into the docking arm. She would be interested to see if Mass and Teramoto could keep their egos in check without supervision.

McWilliams, Ralph, was twenty-five years into a thirty-year bid for good old-fashioned drug trafficking, also in the Gliese system. He had constantly failed parole hearings due to gang activity. Miska climbed into the pilot seat of the assault shuttle next to her new co-pilot. McWilliams turned and gave her a gap-toothed grin. His face was a mass of beard and prison tattoos. He looked every inch the Hard Luck Comanchero Original Gangster he most obviously was. His flight suit was ostensibly the same as Perez's, except McWilliams's had been more extensively customised. She waved away an offered hip flask as her systems wirelessly connected to the Martian Military Industries' Pegasus assault shuttle and began a very rapid pre-flight check.

'How you doin', Ralphy?' Miska asked.

'Good, boss, head's still on my shoulders.'

Miska glanced sideways at him as the ship's diagnostics played down her IVD. Everything looked to be in the green. McWilliams favoured her with another grin.

'Ready to do some flying?' she asked.

'Sure,' he said. Miska reckoned McWilliams was her target audience. He was pleased to be a member of the Bastard Legion just to get out of his cryo pod. 'You got some moves? Because the kid's pretty good.'

Miska reckoned the kid was Perez. She didn't answer him, instead she checked that the final Crimson Sisterhood corsair

74

was still docked and opened a comms link to Maw City traffic control.

'Maw City this is Daughter-Two-Actual, I'm afraid we're going to have to ask forgiveness rather than permission.'

'Maw City traffic control to Daughter-Two-Actual, I know I'm going to regret asking, but for what?'

Miska hit the emergency dock release and umbilicals sprang away from the Pegasus and the dock clamp released its hold on the shuttle. Miska was barely aware of the flashing red lights from the docking area, the cockpit's warning klaxon and the icons appearing in her IVD. The manoeuvring engines flipped the shuttle so it was nose down, belly to the asteroid. Miska triggered full burn, the main engine's torch narrowly missing the rapidly retracting docking arm. The acceleration rammed Miska back into her seat hard enough to bruise as they rocketed straight down, subjectively, accompanied by McWilliams's rebel yell.

'Multiple missile locks,' her co-pilot warned as Miska weaved the assault shuttle through the various docked ships and down into Maw City's shipyard. The manoeuvring engines squirted out light and force as she weaved in and out of the vast super-structures surrounding the ships that were being worked on. It was no way to fly, Miska knew – safety protocols switched off, seat-of-the-pants stuff, and all that was keeping them alive was her boosted reactions and the performance of Martian military technology.

'It's just traffic control,' Miska managed through gritted teeth. 'Stall them. Watch that corsair at seven o'clock.'

She heard McWilliams over the comms link trying to placate a furious traffic control. She was pretty sure they wouldn't fire but if they did then she wouldn't have to worry about anything any more.

'Corsair's launching,' McWilliams said. 'What do you want from me? Weapons?' He didn't sound enthused by the idea of fighting the corsair. Presumably he knew that even a top of the line shuttle like the Pegasus was no match for even an old corsair.

'This is where we're going,' she told him and transferred the coordinates over the comms link.

'Oh,' McWilliams said. She didn't think that the coordinates had been what he was expecting.

The shuttle was out of the city main now. Miska curved the Pegasus under one of the asteroids, the rock close enough for her to reach through the cockpit and touch.

'Between here and there we're looking for small places,' Miska told him.

'Small places?' McWilliams asked as Miska banked hard and twisted the shuttle round another asteroid.

'We can't outrun them, we can't outfight them but we are smaller ... whoa!' Miska triggered the manoeuvring engines, narrowly avoiding a small asteroid about the size of a truck but putting the shuttle in a spin. She corrected and banked hard again, just as the lidar picked up the armoured, angular wedge that was the *Sneaky Bitch*, Captain Tesselaar's corsair, hoving into view behind them. Miska curved the shuttle into a tight gap between two huge asteroids. If she wanted to live she needed to keep a lot of rock between her and the *Sneaky Bitch*.

'Don't they know this area pretty well?' McWilliams asked. He didn't sound scared, despite the fact that they were a few feet away from a high speed rocky death.

'Give me solutions, not problems,' Miska muttered. 'And don't put me in a fucking cave. I need passages, and ideally shortcuts. I don't want them getting there before me, okay?'

McWilliams didn't answer. Instead he just concentrated as his neural interface forged a link between the soft meat of his brain and the shuttle's navigation system. Information started appearing in her IVD, graphics overlaying the possible routes. 'Okay, which one is fast but not too obvious?' she asked. She needed something counterintuitive and could only hope that Tesselaar didn't out-think her. The routes disappeared until only one remained. It wasn't for the faint-hearted but the old drug smuggler's instincts were still good. The manoeuvring engines lit up the front of the ship as they forced the shuttle to bleed off speed. Engines burning just as brightly, the *Sneaky Bitch* hove into view behind them again. With a thought Miska triggered the manoeuvring engines on top of the shuttle and sunk rapidly towards a big cave mouth in one of the asteroids. Red light lit up the night as the corsair fired at where the Pegasus had been moments before.

'Four, six – no, eight missiles inbound,' McWilliams announced as the cave swallowed them. The problem was that the corsair might be too big to follow them into the passages but missiles weren't. 'Activating countermeasures and point defences.' *The old coot sounds as though he's enjoying himself*, Miska thought as she cut the aft roof manoeuvring engines, flipping the shuttle nose-down as it spored chaff and launched tiny decoy drones. She triggered the main engine again, the torch burning the rock to slag behind them.

'Yes! Two have gone after the drones,' McWilliams announced, unable to contain his excitement. Miska felt the shock wave through the shuttle as the missiles exploded, destroying the decoy drones. The Pegasus's sensors were now her senses as a result of the neural interface. The shuttle's point defence lasers strobed out aft as the missiles pursued them through the winding tunnel. Miska jinked the shuttle hard to starboard, narrowly missing a rock formation bisecting the tunnel as an explosion blossomed behind them and another missile was gone.

'See if you can use our missiles against the rock, bring the roof down on them,' Miska suggested. 'And if you have a moment see if you can open a link to the *Sneaky Bitch*.'

'Who?' McWilliams asked as the hardpoint that the missiles were mounted on reversed.

'The corsair, the fucking ship shooting at us!'

The ship rocked as the point defence lasers took out another missile, this one much closer. Miska fought to control the ship. She knew the problem wasn't just the missiles hitting them. At the speeds she would have to move at to outrun the corsair, even a near miss from a missile could bounce the shuttle into the wall. She compensated for the force of the missiles firing as they launched into the rock wall just behind them. Miska risked another squirt of speed from the main engine, burning harder with the manoeuvring engines to steer them as the force wave from their own missiles kicked them around a bit.

They shot out of the planetoid's passages and into open space between the rocks. Miska pulled up, subjectively climbing hard over another large asteroid. Moments later there was more red light and the shuttle lost some of its paint and armour to one of the *Sneaky Bitch*'s laser batteries.

'I've got Captain Tesselaar on comms for you,' McWilliams said and transferred the link. 'Oh, and they've launched another four missiles.'

'Find me another shortcut!' Miska tried not to scream and opened the comms link, audio only. 'Are you out of your fucking mind?' she demanded. 'Do some research. I've got a dead woman's switch. You kill me and your man, all your men, die. Stop shooting at me!'

'Live free or die, bitch,' Captain Tesselaar snarled, and then severed the link.

'She seems nice,' McWilliams said.

'Should have called her ship the *Unreasonable Bitch*,' Miska muttered as she poured on the speed, the four missiles appearing over the rock horizon behind them. Point defence lasers stabbed out again and again, destroying the missiles.

'She sounded a bit like a grumpy you,' McWilliams said.

'Imagine me glaring at you right now,' Miska said, trying not to smile. 'Any more shortcuts?' She knew any moment the corsair was going to catch up with them.

'Sorry, boss,' McWilliams said. He did sound sorry as well. 'Want me to send some missiles their way?' he asked as Miska starting weaving the shuttle, trying to make it at least a slightly more difficult target.

'Naw, waste of money; when they come into view launch some more chaff, they're going to hit us with their lasers, see if we can break them up a bit.'

'Sure, boss.' It was practically busy work and McWilliams knew it. 'Uh, boss, we seem to be heading into open space.'

'Yeah, we do, don't we. I want you to start broadcasting a mayday, any old shit, but make sure you include that we're under attack from pirates, our transponder's down, and don't use our call sign.' Before McWilliams could respond, the corsair came into view behind them. Eschewing missiles, its laser batteries turned local space a hellish red. The shuttle shook as superheated armour exploded on its hull. Plumes of superheated rock shot up from the surface of the asteroid they were skimming. Chaff blooms filled the cold vacuum behind the shuttle, refracting the lasers in a dazzling lightshow, but it wasn't enough. Despite how heavily armoured the shuttle was, it couldn't take much more of this abuse and the corsair was closing. McWilliams made his panicked sounding mayday call and then put it on repeat.

'This is Captain Jennings of the U.S.S.S. *Teten*. I am ordering the two craft in the asteroid field to immediately cease all hostilities, heave to, and prepare to be boarded.'

Miska knew that McWilliams was staring at her.

'The space force?' he asked her.

'FBI,' Miska told him. She could practically smell his dismay. Spaceship sensor systems were pretty sophisticated but at the end of the day a huge lump of rock was a huge lump of rock, and it was more than enough to hide the FBI destroyer from the *Sneaky Bitch*. But Nicholas had told Miska where it was. She had run for the Feds instead of the *Daughter*. The Crimson Sisterhood weren't stupid enough to start a shooting war with the FBI who were, along with Air & Space Force, one of the agencies with an anti-piracy remit. The destroyer had caught the pirate corsair red-handed firing on the shuttle. The *Sneaky Bitch* burned hard, and banked harder, curving round the asteroid and back into the Dog's Teeth. The *Teten* took the bait and followed. Now the corsair could play cat-and-mouse, though Miska had a bad feeling she knew where the *Sneaky Bitch* would run to, if they couldn't lose the destroyer.

'The Feds are launching tracker drones,' McWilliams told her. The drones would be faster than the corsair but they were designed to keep back to try and avoid weapons fire. They would stick just close enough to keep the pirate ship in sensor range and relay its position back to the slower moving frigate as it made its way through the thick asteroid field.

Miska dipped the shuttle back into the Dog's Teeth. She didn't want the *Teten* taking too close a look at the Pegasus.

'Okay, I need the most direct route for this vector,' Miska told McWilliams and transferred the vector. She didn't have exact coordinates because the parties involved would be moving at some speed. She popped back out of the Dog's Teeth and into open space, burning hard, skimming the wall of asteroids.

A few moments later the *Daughter*'s remaining prison transport shuttle popped out of the Teeth and Miska had to bleed off speed so the ancient shuttle could keep up.

'Daughter-Three-Actual to Daughter-Two-Actual, good to see you, looks like you've lost some paint,' Perez said over the comms link. The Pegasus was subjectively above and behind the transport shuttle, flying in escort. Daughter-Three-Actual was carrying the hundred-and-twenty-plus members of the Bastards who had been on shore leave. With the Pegasus drawing the *Sneaky Bitch* away, the transport shuttle had been able to make its own way to the rendezvous.

Miska checked the transport shuttle's passenger manifest. She noticed one was missing. She opened the comms link to Mass.

'Where's Hinton?' she asked. Mass didn't answer. It meant he wasn't going to snitch. It meant that Hinton, a member of Mass's assault team back on Faigroe Station, was making a run for it. He hadn't accidentally been left behind. Miska sent the code. The code might take some time to work its way through Maw City's net and find the escapee. Hinton was probably in some tech workshop trying to get his collar removed, but if he hadn't triggered the tamper mechanism already then the signal would catch up with him and blow the collar.

'Understood,' Miska said and cut the link. She had other

things to worry about but an example had to be made. Though after a certain amount of time the collar would have blown anyway.

There were flashes of light subjectively below them, inside the Dog's Teeth. It was like watching a thunderstorm from above, if lightning were red.

'Okay, Ralphy,' Miska said. 'We're going to be providing cover for the transport shuttle. You are weapons free. I don't want any missiles left in the rack when we dock, okay?'

'Sure, boss,' McWilliams said.

'Use the lasers to target their point defences and then—'

'I know how to do this,' he told her.

The *Hangman's Daughter* emerged from the Dog's Teeth like a moray eel shooting out of its lair. It was bathed in hot, red light and wreathed in explosions as its point defence lasers destroyed incoming missiles. Miska could see the glow of the prison barge's engines between the rocks before it had fully emerged into open space. It was burning hard, but not so hard that the two shuttles wouldn't be able to catch it. The *Daughter* was firing her batteries back into the Dog's Teeth at her pursuers. Miska tried not to think too much about the cost of all the missiles the prison barge was launching.

'Easy come, easy go,' she muttered. The *Hangman's Daughter* emerged fully from the asteroid field. Moments later the *Sneaky Bitch*, the other corsair, and the converted freighter emerged from the field too. They were firing at the *Daughter* and back into the field as well, and in turn being fired at.

Both the shuttles changed course, burning hard to rendezvous with the *Daughter*. The *Teten* emerged from the asteroid field, firing its own weapons at the three Crimson Sisterhood ships. The *Daughter* wasn't firing on the FBI destroyer, so they weren't firing on the prison barge. Miska could hear them ordering the *Daughter* to surrender, however.

'First weapons lock on Daughter-Three-Actual and you cut loose, okay?' Miska asked.

'Understood,' McWilliams told her. Miska used her smart-link to target the railguns on the closest Crimson Sisterhood ship, the other corsair, for all the good it would do. It would be less than hard rain against the pirate ship's armour. McWilliams didn't even warn her of the weapons lock. He just launched half the Pegasus's payload of missiles at the corsair and then started firing the laser. Hard red light connected the assault shuttle to the corsair's surviving point defence lasers. Miska banked the assault shuttle, putting it between the incoming missiles and Daughter-Three-Actual, lending the Pegasus's own point defence lasers to the transport shuttle. Meanwhile the destroyer was calling for everyone to surrender but mainly pouring fire into the three pirate ships.

Missiles made it through the corsair's defences and plasma fire blossomed across its hull. The ageing warship exploded, coming apart in silence, turning into a fast moving debris field.

'Holy shit!' McWilliams cried. 'We killed a corsair with a shuttle.'

I think we had help, Miska thought, but she didn't want to spoil the old drug smuggler's moment.

'Split your missiles and laser fire between the other two pirate ships,' Miska told McWilliams as they launched chaff to further confuse the incoming missiles. They were inside the *Hangman's Daughter*'s defence perimeter now and the prison barge's point defence was helping protect them as well. They were still getting kicked around as shockwave after shockwave from laser-detonated missiles buffeted the assault shuttle but the transport shuttle was matching speed with the *Daughter*. Perez was using the manoeuvring engines to inch the shuttle into the dock. Miska had been a passenger on a shuttle coming in under fire before. She knew how helpless the men on board the transport would be feeling.

The *Sneaky Bitch* and the other Crimson Sisterhood ship turned and ran.

Now you have a choice, Miska thought. *Do you chase the clear and present danger the pirate ships present, or do you prosecute your standing orders to capture the* Hangman's Daughter? Miska was pretty sure she knew what Captain Jennings was going to do.

Her flight path took her over the *Daughter*. She knew that beneath her more than six thousand men, the men that made up her convict legion, were sleeping in their cryogenic pods, presumably oblivious to the storm out here in the real world. Glancing to starboard she was close enough to see into the bridge. It was eerily empty, as though the *Daughter* was a ghost ship.

She banked towards the prison barge's forward starboard shuttle dock. She could hear the threats that the *Teten* was broadcasting. She matched speed, the manoeuvring engines burning all over the shuttle as she made the incremental changes to push the craft into the socket-like shuttle port. Behind her the *Daughter*'s sails unfurled like dirty industrial moth wings as the prison barge prepared to accelerate to FTL. The frigate opened fire. She knew they would target the sails. It was a messy docking. Miska all but crashed into the shuttle port. McWilliams turned to stare at her. The *Daughter* accelerated. Miska sagged in her seat. She wasn't looking forward to any of the conversations she was going to have to have with her dad.

'Does anyone like you?' McWilliams asked.

CHAPTER 6

'Are you out of your mind?' Miska's dad demanded.

Miska gave the question some thought.

'I pirated a prison barge and enslaved six thousand hardened convicts into a mercenary legion, so I'm sure some people would think so,' she told her very angry dad. She was sat on the throne-like captain's chair up in the bridge. Her dad's craggy features were staring at her from the hologram floating in front of the chair.

'You want to operate without support on US colonial soil when you've certainly made the FBI's top-ten most wanted list?'

'Operating without support is sort of the definition of black ops, Dad,' she said, fidgeting in the chair.

'Miska!' She looked up at the hologram. 'We're already burning through our expensive missiles, we're exchanging shots with the FBI ...'

'It was kind of one-sided; we didn't shoot at them,' Miska pointed out. The FBI were, at the end of the day, just doing their job. She was feeling a little bad about what she had done to the marshal but Angela had really got under her skin.

'They've damaged the sails. We can still accelerate but they will need to be repaired before too long and we're running out of friendly ports.'

Again Miska found herself looking away from her dad and out through the viewport that ran all the way around the bridge, at the total blackness, the result of travelling at superluminal speeds.

'Give me solutions, not—' she started.

'Disappear. Leave the *Daughter* somewhere the authorities can find it, take the stealth ship, fake ID, change your face, go and live somewhere quietly and in peace, maybe have a fam—'

Miska looked up at the hologram sharply.

'You serious? Does any of that sound like me?'

Sadness and anger warred on her dad's face.

'No. I think you've been looking for a war since your mom died.'

Miska leaned back in the captain's chair.

'Yeah, well, *Semper Fi*,' she muttered. 'Thanks for the pep talk, Dad. I thought you were going to support me.'

'Sometimes support means trying to prevent your youngest daughter from dying chasing alien pipe dreams. I've played this game. It's always bullshit.'

Miska frowned and turned to look at her dad. There had been just a moment's hesitation there, as if he wasn't entirely sure of himself.

'I'm doing this, Dad. The money's good and the risk is no different from the work I did for the CIA. Besides I'm more likely to get arrested than dead.' She didn't mention that she had no intention of ever being locked down like her Bastards.

'I heard some of the guys talking. They said Angela was there?'

'Brilliant,' Miska said. She was wondering how this had gone from a discussion of the mission at hand to her being made to feel like a scolded little girl. Her dad crossed his arms.

'And what did she have to say about this?' he demanded.

'What do you think she had to say?' Miska asked. 'Little Miss Judgemental was in her element!'

'You know your sister loves you, right?' her dad said. That stopped Miska dead. She was astonished to find herself feeling the ache behind her eyes that meant she wanted to cry but couldn't. Because her eyes weren't real any more.

'Dad, I just want to talk about the practicalities of the mission,' she pleaded.

'There aren't any.'

'Oh for fuck's sake! Thanks for your contribution.'

'Massimo Prola? Vido Cofino? His family run that city!'

'Which is why—'

'Teramoto? He practically declared war on the Mafia up here.'

'Teramoto, Kaneda and the other Bethlehem Milliners have the skill set ...'

'Torricone? Which organ are you thinking with?' he demanded. Miska stared at him, furious. 'About the only members of your team that aren't suffering from suicidal ideation are the two Comancheros and Nyukuti, and you can't have him.'

'What! Why?' she demanded.

'He's still recovering from all the shot he got on Faigroe Station,' he snapped. In this, at least, she had to admit he was right. It had been wishful thinking to add him to the list. It was a shame. Nyukuti was fearless, competent and at least appeared loyal. 'The others are going to hook up with their old contacts the moment they get boots on the ground. They'll find the expertise to remove the collars ...'

'They won't be—'

'And that's assuming the Yakuza versus the Mafia thing doesn't blow up first and they kill each other. And this Jarrod Sykes character, the hacker. I thought we were being careful of hackers? Not only is he competent, he is a straight-up psychopath with a game-playing personality.'

'So am I,' Miska pointed out.

'You have a *risk*-taking personality, it's different. The moment you hit the ground these guys are going to be looking for an advantage, looking for a way to slip the leash, like Hinton ...'

'Hinton's dead.'

'You don't know that, and if they do get free they'll cut your throat. At best.'

'They're criminals—' Miska started.

'But you're operating without backup. As half-assed as it was, even at Faigroe Station we had contingencies and we got lucky. If it hadn't been for the Guevara Virus we would have been screwed.'

'That's enough!' Miska snapped. 'We're doing this and all you're doing right now is messing with my head. Look, the vast majority of soldiers are decent people, even in special forces, you know that. The things they do mess them up. The CIA, on the other hand, are looking for the supremely morally flexible, understand me?' Her dad crossed his arms again. 'I've lost count of the number of times I've been trapped in tight confines with full-blood, apex predator, alpha-psychopaths.' Her dad was glaring at her. 'People like me, you understand? I can handle them. Not one of them is capable of going toe-to-toe with me.'

'Teramoto's dangerous. If Cofino gets free, he'll probably just walk away, leave you be. Yes, he can be ruthless, but he's also a sentimental old man. Massimo, however, is a fucking snake!'

Miska sighed.

'Yes, it'll be dangerous. Yes, it might fuck up. That's no different from any other day.'

'I don't want anything to do with this clusterfuck!' he spat.

'Do I need to pull rank?'

Gunnery Sergeant Jonathan Corbin, deceased, looked as though he had just been slapped.

'I can do this. Can you do your fucking job?' she demanded. The hologram blinked off. 'Shit,' she muttered.

He wasn't wrong about anything he had said. She was going to be facing the same problem in New Verona City that she had in Maw City with the Crimson Sisterhood, only more pronounced. She was also right, however. She would need to keep Mass and Uncle Vido – and Torricone, to a lesser extent – away from their contacts, but their knowledge would be invaluable. She had chosen the rest of the team because she needed people who were capable of mobility. The Comancheros were a road gang. The Milliners and Teramoto had all come up racing bikes in the Lalande 2 tunnels. They were all capable wheelmen with experience in armed robbery. She had to admit Jarrod Sykes was a worry. There was no doubt about it, he was a stone-cold psychopath, utterly ruthless, but he had experience in running net support for sophisticated robberies. He had only been caught when someone had cut a deal and rolled on him. She needed a hacker, though. She couldn't work the net and lead at the same time.

The other thing she agreed with her dad about was the alien artefact bullshit.

'Doesn't matter if we get paid,' she said quietly. It didn't matter if it took her one step closer to finding her dad's murderer. And for that she needed money.

She pushed herself back into the throne-like chair, only the glow from the empty bridge's screens and holograms for company. *A throne can be a lonely place to sit*, she decided.

Camp Reisman was like a ghost town. She knew there were exercises going on in the training construct somewhere but she guessed it was field training out in one of the virtual environments beyond the camp. Unlike real world military bases the virtual Camp Reisman didn't need any support staff. It felt odd to see a place that was normally bustling with activity so empty and still. Eerie. The rain was a bit strange as well. Normally she would have expected to see at least one of her father's ghosts but he wasn't present. That wasn't good. Gunnery Sergeant Jonathan Corbin, deceased, was used to tackling his problems head-on. If he didn't want to see her it wasn't because he was sulking, it was because he was trying to calm down.

Uncle Vido, Mass and Torricone were sat at a table under an awning just outside the ugly smartcrete bunker that was the base command post. Like her, each of them wore their marine-issue battle dress uniform. Unlike hers, theirs were in jungle pattern camouflage and soaked in sweat. Their beers were virtual but their brains couldn't tell the difference. Miska sat down at the table. They all looked too tired to even wave at her.

'Still jungle training?' she asked. It seemed her dad felt that the next big colonial conflict was going to be jungle based. That made sense given the situation in the narco-insurgency in Gliese system and the independence movement in the Epsilon Eridani system.

'Your dad angry with us?' Vido asked. Even in the virtual environment he looked tired to the point of haggard.

'My dad's just angry,' Miska told them.

'Bullshit, guy's got a problem with Italians, you ask me,' Mass muttered and took a sip of his drink. Torricone just watched, toying with his beer. He seemed to have got over any residual embarrassment. She wondered if he'd worked out that they hadn't slept together yet. She should put him out of his misery, though he wasn't the sort of guy who'd go bragging to the other cons. Still, if he thought it was true it could complicate things in the long run. 'I get him being pissed at Mikey-T here,' Mass nodded towards Torricone. Torricone rolled his eyes. 'What with him spending the night in a cell with his daughter.' *Or it could just complicate things in the short run*, Miska thought. She opened her mouth to say something.

'It's all right,' Uncle Vido said. 'We're pretty sure that nobody else knows where you both spent the night. We only know because one of Terry's security guys let it slip.'

So Terrance, the head of the security on Maw City, was Terry to Uncle Vido now, it seemed, and Miska was being made to feel that she was just that little bit more in debt to the *consigliere*. If this got out it could undermine her leadership and make life very tricky for Torricone. *Well played, guys*, she thought. She couldn't shake the feeling they were creeping into her life the way a fungus infection creeps into a toenail.

You need to convince them that nothing happened, she thought, but the conversation moved on before she had the time to say anything.

'So you want the three of us,' Uncle Vido said. 'You're going to Barney Prime.' Miska was impressed. It wasn't much information to go on.

'Just looking for some advice, information. I need places to lie low, people who can get me gear.'

Mass leaned back on the chair, put his legs up on the table and crossed his arms with an air of finality.

'What?' Miska asked, confused. Vido shrugged and Torricone had a smile on his face.

'We're not snitches,' Vido explained, almost apologetically. It didn't really matter to the op but Miska was a little taken aback.

'What the fuck are you talking about?' she demanded.

'You're the man,' Mass explained. Miska stared at him and then burst out laughing.

'I've got purple hair,' she said, still laughing.

'And a leash around our throats,' Torricone said quietly. Miska stopped laughing.

'I'm looking for contacts to do business with.'

'Sorry, we can't help,' Uncle Vido said, and he too crossed his arms.

'I can but I won't,' Torricone said. 'I'm not putting anyone in your firing line.'

Asshole! Miska thought. The night before last he'd been trying to get in her pants.

'Torricone's got a point,' Vido said. 'Whatever you may think of how we do business it's our home, and you seem to have a penchant for automatic weapons fire and explosions.'

'You were a fucking mobster!' Miska exploded.

'Hey,' Mass said, shaking his head. 'C'mon now, there's no need for that.' Torricone seemed to be finding this all quite amusing. Miska felt like kicking him off his chair.

'Fuck it,' Miska said. 'I'll do it without you. You ain't the only cons from New Verona, place seemed to breed criminals.' She put her hand on the arms of the chair to push herself up.

'Now hold on,' Vido said. Miska had to work hard not to give the game away by smiling. 'We've got a proposition.'

Miska couldn't help herself. 'You guys really say that?'

'They really do,' Torricone said.

'Hey,' Mass warned. Miska wondered if Mass realised just how unafraid of him Torricone really was.

'A proposition?' Miska said. 'Didn't we discuss this last time? There is no proposition.'

Vido eyed her for a moment.

'Yeah, your dad can be pretty uncompromising,' Mass said. 'Surprised he's not here for this little chat.'

It was clear who the good cop and the bad cop was, now. She wasn't sure who Torricone was chuckling at but it seemed to irritate Mass, who glared at the car thief, as much as it irritated her.

'Look, despite the situation, we like you,' Vido said.

'Yeah, you got some balls on you,' Mass agreed.

'But you've got to compromise, let us breathe,' Vido added.

'The military doesn't run on compromise,' Miska told them. 'Negotiating every order is exhausting and it'll get us killed.'

She made to get up again.

'You've showed us the bait, now let us taste the hook,' Torricone said. Miska decided that she liked drunk Torricone better. *Because you want to fuck him?* Her inner voice seemed pretty uncompromising today. She told it to shut up.

'We want to come with you,' Vido told her. Miska spent some time watching the rain pour down on the parade ground.

'You're all smart guys,' she finally said, turning back to the table. 'Tell me why that won't work.'

Torricone got up and walked over to the beer vending machine and looked at her. She nodded and allowed the machine to dispense.

'Get me one as well,' she said. Nobody said anything until Torricone returned with four more bottles.

'You think that we'll try and get the collars off, and with the resources we have in our home territory we might just manage it,' Vido said.

'It's my plan,' Torricone admitted.

'And?' Miska asked. Nobody said anything for a moment.

'And then Mass cuts you up for fish bait,' Torricone said. Miska looked at Mass. He shrugged.

'It is what it is,' he admitted.

'Jesus Christ, women have been trafficked for thousands of years, traffic a few men and suddenly everyone loses their mind,' Miska said to stony silence. 'So my best case scenario is the three of you dead due to radical cranial weight-loss. My worst case scenario is a slow agonising death.'

'We meant what we said. We like you,' Mass told her. 'I'll make it quick, I'm not a monster.'

Miska smiled ruefully at Vido.

'We give you our word ...' Vido started.

'Oh well, why didn't you just say? I mean, if you're going to give me your word.' Miska made no effort to hide her sarcasm.

'Hey, that ain't right. Vido's word's been good in New Verona City since before you were born. Hell, even Mikey-T here is a stand up guy.'

Torricone looked a little surprised at Mass's words.

'I thought he was chickenshit?' Miska asked before she could stop herself.

'I just don't think violence is his thing,' Mass said. Torricone had proven himself more than capable of violence but Miska let it pass.

'You'd be surprised at how much trust is involved in the work we do,' Torricone pointed out.

'Yeah, but not for the gal who put you all in chains, huh? As you pointed out: "I am the man." Besides, that's just you guys. We hit the ground and I've got your friends and families to worry about.' She pointed at Vido. 'In your case, the scariest of scary-ass families. I'd have to keep you locked down. You wouldn't see anyone or anything. Sorry, guys, but no dice. If you help me I can promise you shore leave and a few extra bucks in your commissary accounts when we do the job.' Mass was staring at her, and he didn't look happy. Torricone's eyes were narrowed. Vido was studying her like he was looking for a poker tell. 'No takers?' She actually got up and walked away this time.

'Miska,' Vido called after her. She turned around, crossing her arms. The rain was cold. 'Guys, will you give me a couple of moments?'

'What, and go and stand in the rain?' Torricone asked.

'C'mon,' Mass said to him as he stood up. For a moment Miska thought Torricone was going to argue. Then she saw him take the path of least resistance and get up and walk away. Miska moved back under the awning. Vido gestured for her to sit down. She ignored him.

'Okay, you've showed us the stick. Want to show us the carrot?' he asked.

'The carrot's shore leave and a share of the money,' Miska told him. 'And you damn well know it. Neither of which you would have got in here.'

'You have to admit that you've radically increased the mortality rate.'

'Not for you, not yet.'

'Darlin', your dad is going to PT me to death,' he said, referring to the limited physical training they were able to do out of the pods under the watchful eye of the guard droids.

'Oh bullshit, you're in excellent shape for a man of your age.'

'I am now,' he muttered. 'Look, I know you want us down there but your worries are valid, so how about offering us something of more value?'

'You get that this is a slippery slope for me, right? Sooner or later I've got a ship full of special snowflakes who want to argue the toss every time I give them an order and then, guess what?'

'We're all dead?' he asked. Miska just nodded. 'At least hear me out.' Miska crossed her arms. 'I know what you must think of us …'

'You'd be surprised how judgemental I'm not—'

'But that doesn't mean you're not cognisant of what we're capable of, who we are. Some of the guys complain about how hard done by they are when they get caught. Like they're some heroic counter culture. We're greedy criminals. Cause and effect. Risk versus reward. We get caught, we do time, but we ain't monsters.'

'Mass did some pretty bad stuff, and you're complicit in that, but seriously, I'm in no position to discuss ethics. What's your point?'

'My point is we're not monsters all the time. We have people we care about, people we miss.'

'A family visit? Are you fucking serious?' she asked. Though she had to admit what he wanted wasn't as bad as it could have been.

'Look, even Mass isn't going to fuck around with his family on the line. He loves his kids.' He gave this some more thought.

'His wife too. You do this, you get our undivided cooperation right down the line.'

'And the other guys? What happens when they come back and tell everyone that I'm open for negotiation?'

'Maybe you should be,' he suggested.

'What're you, a union boss?'

He made placating gestures with his hands.

'I'll come up with something.'

That was when she realised how desperate he was. She sat down opposite him.

'Vido, you've been very complimentary about me, and I'll be honest I like you as well, but I think you know what Mass is, and therefore I think you know what I am. I won't hesitate to kill you if you try and screw me over, okay?' she told him. He nodded and she could see it in his guarded expression. He understood, he believed. 'I'll talk this over with my dad, see what he thinks, but there is something you will have to reconcile. Teramoto and two of the Milliners are joining us. You need to cooperate, you need to get Mass squared away, because I don't have any time for your Mafia/Yakuza bullshit, okay?'

Vido nodded. He almost looked relieved. Miska stood up again, drained her virtual beer and walked away.

'Miska Corbin,' he called after her. She stopped in the rain and turned to look at the *consigliere*. 'Well played,' he told her. She resisted the urge to smile. She was, however, feeling a little smug. A message icon was blinking in her IVD. She opened it.

'Oh,' she said. She hadn't been expecting this at all.

Miska strode along the metal walkway, her boot steps lost under the clank of the eight guard droids following her. Unusually their automatic shotguns were carrying recently printed lethal explosive rounds. Cell block 6 was actually the top level of general population. There was another five levels beneath her, and at the base was the rectangular exercise yard which, along with the hangar deck, was used for physical training now. Each of the levels contained twelve hundred cryopods, the majority of them with a hardened criminal inside. Her Bastard Legion.

Her father's face started appearing on the screens on the pillars interspersed along the walkway as she approached them.

'Yes Dad, I am out of my mind. Let's leave it at that,' she said as he opened his mouth to speak.

'Why aren't you doing this in the construct?' he demanded. She had to admit, it was a good question. She didn't know. Part of her couldn't shake the feeling that the training construct, somehow, wouldn't have made her any safer, though she knew this was absurd. *Do you just want to see him again?* she wondered.

'I'm just not,' she told him. 'Seriously, Dad, if you've got nothing to contribute ...' Her dad's face disappeared from the screens on the pillars and then appeared again, six storeys high, on the back wall of general population. He looked furious and at that size there was something mythical about his anger. Just for a moment Miska felt like a child again, when her dad had always seemed like such a big man. He looked as though he was about to shout at her but then he disappeared and the screen was blank. Somehow that was worse. *It's worse because you know what you're doing is idiotic*, she told herself. It didn't stop her.

She reached the end of the cellblock and looked up at solitary. Three pods hanging on their own, close to the ceiling at the end of a retracted robot arm.

Skirov, the dismantled cybrid warewolf. She had started

98

putting aside a little money to assemble the components she needed to rebuild him. She wasn't sure how she was going to control the psychotic killing machine. A few of the cons on board had worked in black clinics and there was at least one doctor among the prisoners who could help reassemble him when she had the resources. If nothing else it would be interesting.

Red, the huge red-bearded professional convict who hadn't started killing until he had been incarcerated but had since racked up an impressive body count. Again, the problem with using him on a job would be controlling him. She didn't think he would fear the collar, regardless of the form it took, and she didn't want to waste a talent like his.

And the Ultra. The sleeping angel. *Sleeping god?* His alabaster skin glowed with the blue neon light permeating the gel that filled the capsule. With a thought she extended the robot arm down to the catwalk. Umbilical hoses sucked the gel from the pod. The guard droids lifted their shotguns to cover the pod as the front hinged open.

The Ultra stepped out through the freezing mist. He was like some classical statue from ancient Earth. It irritated Miska that she had to look up at him, but then she had to look up at most people.

Get your game face on, she practically howled at herself. She reminded herself that it was all artifice. This was a designed being. He hadn't had to work for his physique. Even his mannerisms, his voice, his mind, were all either products of, or augmented significantly by, intelligent design. She reminded herself that he wasn't real. *Not like Torricone*. She banished that thought as well. The Ultra was, however, very, very pretty. *Get a fucking grip!* She was wondering if this would have been easier in the training construct. *Well, he wouldn't have been naked*. He appeared about as bothered by his nudity as Adam had been before the serpent's intervention.

'Thank you for agreeing to see me,' he said. His voice was a deep, modulated bass. She knew it was her imagination that his voice caused vibrations that made her feel funny. 'I didn't think you would see me in this world.' He seemed utterly oblivious to the eight fully automatic shotguns levelled at him.

'I'm a little busy,' she said. 'What do you want?' *That's it, stay cool*, she tried to convince herself.

'I ... have limitations,' he looked down as though ashamed. *No, not ashamed. Surprised, maybe.* She was coming to the conclusion that she just wasn't set up to read this guy, but at least a relationship wouldn't be boring. *Stop it!*

'Uh, okay,' Miska said.

'I want to help,' he added. Miska wondered if he was working from some kind of algorithm designed to make him say the things that she least expected him to say.

'Okay ...' she managed.

'I don't wish to be uncooperative, but teamwork ...'

'Not really your thing?'

'I am sorry.'

'Well, I'm sure we will still be able to find a use for you.'

'Hmm,' he said and nodded. 'I have been considering war.' It was the kind of thing that people who had never been in one said but somehow she didn't mind the contrivance coming from the Ultra. He had gravitas. She saw another message icon had appeared in her IVD. She ran very thorough diagnostics on the message before opening it. She wasn't sure why, since it had come through the ship's isolated system and the Ultra had been thoroughly declawed when he had been incarcerated, but still, it didn't hurt to check. There shouldn't be any way he could have access to anything nasty.

The scan came up clean. She opened the message. It was a short list of names. Prisoners. Skirov was on there, though Red wasn't. The doctor was on there as well. With one exception it was the worst of the worst. It read like an atrocity waiting to happen. The letter U, though made to look a little like the Ancient Greek symbol for Omega, was at the top of the list.

'Your own squad?' she asked. Even Miska was a little horrified.

'For the absolute, most extreme situations,' he told her.

'Rufus Grig is a vigilante.'

'Rufus has a lust for murder that would put most in here to shame, regardless of how he chooses to justify it to himself. He would take careful handling but I could ... motivate him,' he told her. Miska closed the list and looked back up at the angelic monster in front of her. 'You are, of course, thinking that I am empire-building like Teramoto, like Prola.' Miska narrowed her eyes. It was interesting that he had mentioned Mass, rather than Vido. 'I assure you I am just seeking sensation.' This last he made sound almost intimate. It sent a chill through Miska.

'I'll be honest, I don't like it,' Miska told him. 'For a number of different reasons, and it's of no use to me now, but I promise I'll give it some thought.' He considered this and then nodded.

'I can ask no more. And thank you. I have enjoyed our time together.' Without being asked he stepped back into the pod. The front shut and he closed his eyes as it started to fill up with the gel. The comms link icon in her IVD was blinking. She sighed and opened it.

'Tell me you're not really thinking about that?' her dad demanded.

'I'd really have to hate someone before I did,' she muttered.

CHAPTER 7

Barnard's Star. Another red dwarf system. They always seemed faintly lit to Miska, these fading suns. She had her legs stretched out across several seats in the prison transport and was looking out through the porthole at the lights of the *Hangman's Daughter* in the distance. She could make out the glow of the shuttle's engine torch. Feel the tug as the ageing craft accelerated. Her dad had barely spoken to her during the journey from Sirius to Barnard's Star. Just the bare minimum to allow them to complete the limited prep for the mission.

The remaining prison transport shuttle had been redecorated to look like a civilian craft. Miska had hacked the transponder herself and given the shuttle a false ident. It would pass casual scrutiny, and in orbit around a place as corrupt as Barnard's Prime nobody wanted to look too hard.

Colonial manifest destiny was supposed to have been a new start for many Americans, far away from the Small Gods-dominated politics of the Sol system. Colonial ventures, public and private, had allowed organised crime a foothold in the colonies, however. Nowhere more so than Barnard's Prime. This had its good and bad points. The colonists and authorities were used to criminals doing criminal things, but they didn't want that particular boat rocked too much. With the amount of money that Raff had provided access to, Miska could buy cooperation, influence, and possibly a degree of protection – but so could the other guys. That was assuming that they didn't work out who she was. If that happened then the people she would have to deal with would be very insistent about getting Uncle Vido and Mass and the rest of them released.

'I don't see why we have to dress like fucking citizens,' Enchi groused. Information on the *bōsōzoku* gang member cascaded down Miska's IVD. Tsuyoshi, Enchi: a twenty-five year sentence for armed robbery, assault with a deadly weapon and attempted murder. The result of a series of hijackings on Lalande 2. Enchi was still somewhat podgy, but she'd seen his file and he had been fat before her dad's physical training regime. The image in his file had made her think about the kids she'd known at school who had been bullied, though unlike Sirius 4, she was pretty sure that Lalande 2 had a virtual school system. The expression of contemptuous hatred on the image gave lie to the idea of Enchi as a victim. She had read the hate in his eyes. Enchi had grown his straight, black hair down to his neckline. The style made his face look like it was framed by a pair of curtains.

'I believe, my young friend, it is because we are supposed to be incognito,' Sykes told the young Milliner. Miska had to concentrate on what he was saying. Earthborn, from London in England, he had something called a Cockney accent that caused him to mush up his words and made him difficult to understand at times. He was using a printed mirror to adjust his slicked-back sandy blonde hair. In his suit trousers, shirt, tie, braces and vest, Sykes dressed like banker and reminded Miska a little of Nicholas back in Maw City. He had a neatly trimmed beard and strangely pale green eyes. According to his file his eyes were real. Most of his other cybernetics came down to the integral computer and neural interface implanted into the meat of his brain, which Miska had reactivated. With some misgivings, she had allowed him to update his software. His reactions were also wired pretty high. High enough to be close to her own. The difference was Miska's implants were top of the line military cyberware. His were overcooked street-tech. He had to be suffering from nerve damage. She'd wondered if the dodgy cyberware had created any psychological issues.

Sykes, Jarrod: life sentence for murder and accessory to armed robbery. He had been providing net support for a crew of armed robbers. After a series of successful jobs he had turned on his compatriots for a larger share. One of them, badly injured, had survived the trap that Sykes had laid for him. The police had caught up with the robber in hospital and he had turned Sykes in for revenge and as part of a plea bargain deal. Her dad was right, dealing with Sykes was like putting your hand in a basket with a snake in it and hoping the snake didn't bite.

They were wearing inertial armour that had been printed to look like real clothes. Other than that they were running light. They could only take with them what they could carry on the HALO jump. As they would be getting dropped in by a commercial carrier Raff had suggested not being too overtly armed, so they were only carrying handguns. Though there were more than a few edged weapons hidden away as well.

'Yeah, I'm not sure a bright orange wig is as subtle as you think it is, dude. Do you guys have any idea how fucking ridiculous you look in that get up?' Hradisky asked. One of the two Hard

Luck Comancheros they had with them, whip thin, Hradisky had what Miska had come to think of as the 'junkie physique'. He looked taut, somehow, as if he was always straining. He was one of the violent new breed of Comancheros, his beard little more than a braided goatee, his hair shaved close to his skull, five tattooed tears on his cheek, one for each of the bodies he'd dropped. Unlike Torricone's tear, Miska didn't think there was much remorse behind the tattoos on Hradisky's face. He had the Aces & Eights of the Comancheros Dead Man's Hand tattooed on his back, and Born to Lose in gothic script across his chest. He either didn't give a shit, or really wanted people to think that was the case.

Hradisky, Peter: life sentence for murder and armed robbery to support a crystal habit.

Enchi was up and striding towards Hradisky. The Comanchero was on his feet. Miska sighed inwardly and wondered if arming them had been a good idea. She would make an example and kill the first one who went for a weapon by triggering the nanobomb she'd had the guard droids implant in each of them, replacing the bulky and obvious explosive collars.

'Youngblood.' The voice was a low drawl, a collision of accents that Miska'd heard before in documentaries, games and vizzes set in Crawling Town back on Earth. Goodluck, Sherman: life sentence, also for armed robbery and murder, again exacerbated by drugs. Though his crimes had been committed a long time before Hradisky's. He was Comanchero OG, or Original Gangster, and judging by his prison record, he had been looking for a quiet life. While all the convicts on board the *Hangman's Daughter* had to train now, Miska was only taking volunteers for jobs. A surprising amount of the prison population wanted the chance to get out and about and commit acts of violence for money and the possibility of shore leave, so she had no shortage of volunteers. She had been surprised that Goodluck had been one of them.

The OG was clearly a traditionalist. His face was hard to see under his dreadlocked hair and beard. Goodluck was third generation Crawling Town. His mother had been a Comanchero, his father a member of Big Neon Voodoo, the ruling council/gang of Crawling Town. The Comanchero OG had grown up in the mobile drug factories of the vast convoy community.

Hradisky looked down at Goodluck. The OG just shook his head.

'Pack it in, both of you!' Mass snapped. He was sat next to Vido. The pair of them had been deep in conversation since they had boarded the shuttle. Given where they were going, Miska couldn't imagine that boded well. Miska was pleased that Mass seemed to be taking his NCO duties at least seriously enough that she wouldn't have to intervene. Enchi was inches away from Hradisky's face, glaring at him. Goodluck leaned out of his seat far enough to catch Teramoto's eye.

'Enchi.' It was all Teramoto had to say. With one last glare the Milliner turned around and stomped back to his seat next to Kaneda.

Well, it's good they're all bonding as a team, Miska thought. Not for the first time she wondered if it was really difficult being a boy, all the macho bullshit getting in the way of actual thought processes. She could feel Torricone staring at her. She tried to ignore it. She was studying Kaneda instead. The kid didn't look happy. He looked shaky and he was dripping with sweat. She had initially put it down to nerves but now she was wondering if it was something more. He hadn't taken his left hand out of his pocket since they had got onto the ship.

She felt another pair of eyes on her. She shifted her head slightly to find Teramoto watching her. He leaned to one side and whispered something to Kaneda that she couldn't hear. She wasn't sure if Kaneda nodded or bowed slightly, but he stood up and walked across the shuttle's passenger area, moving up the rows of seating to where Miska was. He produced a small composite box from inside his leather jacket and offered it to her. Miska looked at the box and then Kaneda's left hand, hidden in his pocket. She had a sinking feeling she knew what was in the box.

'Miska-*sama*, I made a terrible mistake and must make amends,' he told her. With mounting anger she took the box.

'This your idea?' she asked quietly, dangerously. Kaneda didn't answer. 'Take your hand out of your pocket.' Kaneda didn't move. 'Right now.' Kaneda produced his left hand. The stump of his pinkie had been tied off with a tourniquet. A red-stained handkerchief covered the wound. A Yakuza apology.

'Mass!' Miska snapped.

'Yes boss?'

Miska threw him the box. The Mafia button man opened it without thinking.

'Jesus Christ!'

'Put that on ice, we'll reattach it when we get back to the *Daughter*. In the meantime, dress Kaneda's wound.'

Kaneda glanced back at Teramoto.

'No, Miska-*sama*,' he started. 'That would—'

'Shut up!' Miska told him, standing up and pushing past the young *bōsōzoku* gang member as she stomped across the deck to where Teramoto sat, watching her approach.

'Another power-play, Teramoto?' she demanded. 'You want to mutilate my sniper before we even start?' She punched him, his head flying back into the moulded plastic seat. Then she punched him again. The give of his flesh under her knuckles felt deeply satisfying. 'You want to learn about power, you nothing street-punk?' She kicked him back against the seat and sent a command to the shuttle's systems to lock him in place. 'That feel good, you fucking sadist?' She swung a punch into his stomach. He spat blood down his nice white faux-linen suit. She hit him with a cross. Enchi was on his feet reaching for a weapon but he found Miska's SIG in his face instead.

'You try it and I'll trigger the nanobomb,' she told him and then shifted her gun round to aim it at Teramoto's face. He was grinning up at her, savage and bloody.

'What seems to be the problem, Miska-*sama*?' he asked.

'It was training, virtual, it wasn't even real, you stupid bastard! If we cut off our fingers every time we screwed up in training we wouldn't have any left.'

'Kaneda judged his mistake of sufficient severity to require a traditional apology. It is not just for you but for all who were on the exercise.'

'Kaneda decided, did he?' Miska demanded. She was angry enough to pull the trigger. Teramoto's bloody grin wasn't helping.

'Just so,' the Yakuza lieutenant told her.

'I decide what gets punished and what doesn't. And self-mutilation isn't on the menu, do you understand me?'

'Of course. Self-mutilation is not allowed, but slavery is. What strange morals you have.'

Miska stared at him for a moment. Then she broke his nose with the butt of her pistol. She raised the pistol to hit him again, and again. Somebody grabbed her and pulled her off him. They got an elbow in the throat and then back-fisted in the nose for

108

their trouble. She swung on Torricone as he stumbled back, levelling her bloodied SIG at the car thief. She wanted to squeeze the trigger. She wanted to kill something. Everyone was staring at her. Torricone had his hands up now, eyeing her warily.

'Shit!' she hissed and lowered the weapon, storming out of the passenger area.

She was curled up in the passageway leading to the engine maintenance area, ever so gently knocking her skull against the bulkhead. Her bloodied SIG was on the deck next to her. She'd lost it, and she knew it. Maybe that was what Teramoto had intended, or perhaps he just wanted to make it clear to her who owned who. He was careful not to push her hard enough to justify blowing his head off.

'Boss?' She had half expected Torricone to come after her. She wasn't sure if she was surprised or disappointed that it was Mass. Though strictly speaking he was the second in command, with Teramoto supposed to be third in command.

'What is it?' she asked. Mass didn't reply. She looked up at him. He looked as though he was struggling to find the words for what he wanted to say.

'Spit it out,' she told him.

'I can deal with your problem when we hit the ground.'

'He see you come out here?' she asked. Mass nodded. 'Then he knows what we're talking about.'

'Guy's a fucking snake. That kid's hand ...'

'I think it's too late to start pretending we're nice people,' she told him. Mass leaned against the bulkhead.

'It just seems a waste is all, what with him being a sniper.'

'It shouldn't affect his shooting but yeah,' she agreed. She turned to look back up at him. 'Get everybody squared away, no more bullshit, okay?'

'And Teramoto?'

She was tempted to tell Mass to throw him out of an airlock. Solve one problem but create others. She knew the button man wouldn't hesitate. He had his own beef with the Yakuza lieutenant.

'Leave him secured. He can clean himself up when we get closer to the entrepôt.'

Mass gave this some thought and then nodded. He pushed himself off the bulkhead and headed back towards the passenger area. Then he stopped.

'Wheelmen, robbers. You're planning a hijacking, right?' he asked. Miska didn't say anything. 'I think you've got the right crew, if they'll work together.'

Miska turned to look at him. 'Hey, you guys wanted to empire-build. You're senior NCO, make it work.'

Mass smiled. 'But I can't kill Teramoto?' he asked. Miska shook her head. 'Interesting.' He walked away. 'Torricone wants to speak to you,' he called before he disappeared round the corner.

Brilliant, she thought. She did, however, really need to tell him that they hadn't slept together.

'You okay?'

Miska decided to bang her head off the bulkhead one last time before turning to look at Torricone standing in the passage a little way off. She could hear Mass shouting from the passenger compartment.

'Sure,' she told him. Torricone looked at the bloody pistol lying nearby. 'Seriously, if it's more of your hippy "I'm not going to kill anyone" bullshit then I'm not in the mood.'

Torricone moved a little closer and then crouched down next to her.

'Look, we're a little bit worried about you—' he started.

'We?' she asked. 'You and the other murderers and thieves?'

'Uh no ...' he said. He looked absurdly guilty.

'Who've you been ...' Then it hit her. 'Did my dad talk to you?'

'You're getting more and more reckless, taking risks. Maw City, the Ultra ...' he started but she wasn't listening. His voice was a distant drone against the white noise of rage. She couldn't believe it. She tried to force herself to be calm before she reached out and snapped something.

'Torricone,' she said cutting him off mid-sentence. She turned to look at him. 'Go back to the passenger compartment and lock yourself in a chair.' He opened his mouth to say something. 'Do it now before I kill you.' He must have seen something in her eyes because he straightened up and walked away.

She felt like she was having a panic attack. Her heart was an amphetamine-dosed moth in the cage of her ribs. Except it wasn't panic, it was rage. The level of betrayal was staggering.

She pushed herself to her feet and moved to the engine maintenance compartment. She sat down on the deck, wedging herself between some of the machinery, closing the door and locking it behind her with a thought and then she tranced in.

Hot rage had been replaced with a cold fury as she rode the light of a comms link from the net representation of the shuttle to the prison hulk/mythological funeral barge hybrid that was the net representation of the *Hangman's Daughter*. The representations of the ship's systems were flickering ghost lights deep within the hulk.

'Father!' her summoning signal was a scream. Normally

111

when she was in the net she used an icon that was her as a cartoon. She was far too angry for something so cutesy. She was using the naturalistic icon that she used in the training construct. If her father didn't answer then she would tear him out of the construct, she thought, as she touched down on the deck. Space was a black glass ocean against a black sky with neon stars, themselves distant communications networks within the system. 'I mean it! Get out here now!' Her dad appeared in front of her. She couldn't read the expression on his face. Resolve, maybe. 'You fucking talked to Torricone?'

'Well, you weren't going to listen to me ...'

'Have you any idea how much that undermines me!' she screamed at him.

'That boy's not going to—'

'That boy? That fucking boy!'

'Miska don't use—'

'Don't you dare lecture me about my language!' she snapped, stabbing her finger at him. 'You've put this mission—'

'The mission?' he demanded. Now he was getting angry. 'You're not thinking straight. It's a suicide mission on the end of a wild goose chase and you're trying to sabotage it with the decisions you're making. Your team's a powder keg waiting to blow, and meanwhile you're taking face-to-face meetings with one of the most dangerous serial killers who ever lived. You're sailing far too close to the edge, young lady. You're damn right I spoke to Torricone. I'm desperate, Miska, because from where I'm standing it looks like you're trying to kill yourself!'

She hated it when he called her young lady.

'What's it to you?' she demanded. He stared at her.

'What the f— what's that supposed to mean?'

'It means that you're a goddamned computer program

112

designed to do one thing, and that's train my people, you fucking understand me?'

His mask slipped. Just for a moment she saw the damage she had done with her words. Then it was back in place. He snapped to attention and saluted her.

'Permission to return to duty, sir?'

'You go behind my back one more time and I will wipe you, understand me?'

He narrowed his eyes. As a child that had meant that she was really in a lot of trouble.

'I'll give that some thought.'

'You are fucking dismissed.'

And then he was gone. She snapped back to her body hard enough to hurt.

'Shit,' she said, curled up on the deck among the machinery.

The morphic solution hurt. Miska had never liked using it. She had dyed her previously bright purple hair back to a colour that actually occurred in nature and had taken out her nose piercing again before injecting her face and sculpting it just enough to confuse image recognition programs. The others were doing the same. They'd had to remove the medgels from Teramoto's face to do it. It must have hurt. Miska was struggling to generate any sympathy for him. She'd also demoted him back down to private. She suspected it wouldn't make much difference to his authority. Enchi seemed pathetically eager to please the Yakuza lieutenant. She couldn't quite make out Teramoto's relationship with Kaneda, however. She suspected the young *bōsōzoku* gang member felt he owed Teramoto fealty, or was just plain scared of him.

Miska had been studiously ignoring Torricone.

She had given contact lenses to each of the Bastards with her. They acted as cameras and transmitted their footage over the comms link, allowing her to see what they were seeing via one of the nine windows minimised in her IVD. There had been more than a little complaining about this but it allowed Miska to keep tabs on them, for tactical purposes and otherwise.

She had checked her feed from the shuttle's nose lens. They were approaching Barney Prime's nightside. The colonists had been able to terraform the planet so successfully because the tidally locked world's surface was mostly water. The vast ocean that covered ninety per cent of the planet's surface helped regulate the temperature. The ocean on the nightside was a vast icecap, much of it sculpted into mountainous sky resorts. The temperature was kept from dropping too far by the arcology-sized atmosphere processors, which were actually little more than vast heat exchangers. Huge orbital sun mirrors, and the warm air and ocean currents from the ocean of steam on the sunside of the planet, likewise helped control the temperature. Because of the relative weakness of red dwarfs like Barnard's, the Goldilocks Zone, where habitable planets could exist, was a lot nearer the star than usual. To Miska's eye, the sun – even though the planet mostly eclipsed it – looked far too close to the world.

Because it was tidally locked, Barney Prime was not suitable for an orbital elevator. Surface to orbit transport was handled by shuttle, or for suitably robust cargo, one of several electro-magnetic mass driver catapults. Vido had told her that there had been a number of skyhook projects that had never made it into production due to 'labour problems'. Miska assumed that labour problems meant corruption among the colonial administration.

They were approaching Pinto Station, one of the vast entrepôt space stations, used as an exchange point for the export and import of goods and people. Through the feed from the shuttle's nose lens she could make out starliners and vast bulk freighters all docked with the multiple interlocking rings of the station. It looked busy. Huge passenger shuttles and even larger cargo shuttles were rising up from the surface on powerful rocket motors, while others were wreathed in fire as they dropped towards the snow-covered ice of nightside.

'Can you see my world?' Vido asked. She had stopped to watch one of the huge sun mirrors shift, catching the rays of a false, red, sunrise over the planetary horizon. They had checked their printed parachutes and the rest of their High Altitude Low Opening gear. They were in the process of packing them into civilian-looking luggage. She reckoned Vido was making conversation because he was nervous. She'd seen the way he looked at the HALO gear. She could understand why a man in his sixties wasn't especially eager to jump out of a perfectly serviceable shuttle just moments after atmospheric entry.

'Yeah, it's pretty,' she said.

'Only if you've got the money,' Torricone muttered to himself, but everyone ignored him. He was wearing a beanie hat that covered his crown of thorns tattoo. He'd used make-up to cover the tear on his cheek. The morphic compound had changed his features but Miska was worried that he was still recognisable.

'We're coming into dock,' McWilliams told her over the comms link. Miska thanked him.

'Vido, we going to be okay carrying guns on the station?' Miska asked. It was time for the natives to start earning their keep.

'It's not the cops' favourite thing but we've got quite a liberal approach to gun laws up here,' he told her. 'You can't just walk onto a shuttle carrying one but I guess as we've got these stupid fucking parachutes that's less of an issue, right?'

Miska could feel the shuttle bleeding off speed. They all heard the heavy metallic click as it connected to the docking arm. Miska checked the lens feed from the airlock. She was relieved to see there wasn't a hostage rescue team – the FBI's version of a SWAT team – waiting in the airlock to take her down. The station's system was trying to contact her. She checked the signal and then opened the message. It was just a set of instructions and some codes. The path they needed to take was superimposed over her IVD.

'C'mon,' she told them.

Their simple robot luggage followed them through the bowels of the station. It was mostly automated and they saw very few people. They had come in at a service vehicle dock, rather than one of the commercial airlocks. They wove their way through the baggage area past loading robots and into the cargo hold of a big Lockheed passenger shuttle. They moved through stacks of luggage and Miska opened the avionics compartment with one of the codes she had been given. The compartment was pretty cramped for all of them. Miska opened her mouth to tell them to suit up but Mass beat her to it. There then followed a comedy of errors as they all tried to squeeze into their jumpsuits, parachutes, air masks and helmets in the cramped compartment. They eventually managed it just before they felt the shuttle disengage and push itself away from the station.

'Even for Barney Prime this is a real violation of flight security,' Vido said. 'Whoever we're working for must have some pull.'

Miska didn't answer. Instead she reached up to check her mask was snug under her helmet. Teramoto was staring at her. Under his mask she could make out the reapplied medgels still fixing the wounds from the beating she had administered. His smile was predatory. Miska gritted her teeth and didn't set off the nanobomb in his skull. Instead she opened up a direct comms link to him.

'You'd better make yourself fucking useful when we reach the surface, understand me? We ain't carrying dead weight.' He didn't reply. She felt the shuttle lurch and then they were plummeting towards the surface.

CHAPTER 8

Miska felt the heat of the passenger shuttle's atmospheric entry through the fuselage, the insulation turning the inferno the hull was experiencing into pleasant warmth. The shuttle would cool as soon as it hit the upper atmosphere but they would still have to be wary exiting the craft. All nine of her Bastards were suited up and strapped into their chutes. She touched the chemical reaction wands to the luggage they had carried their gear in, rendering it down to carbon dust. She was constantly checking the altimeter read-out in her IVD as she looked around at the squad. Teramoto's face was as inexpressive as ever, he certainly didn't look as though he was worried about the jump. Miska couldn't make out Kaneda's expression either, and she was starting to worry a little about his inclusion on the job. Enchi looked psyched. Sykes had his near-omnipresent cat-got-the-cream expression on his face. Miska only had the slightest urge to slap him every time she saw it.

Both the Comancheros looked as psyched as Enchi, even Torricone looked as though he was looking forward to the jump. Whatever his feelings might be, Mass projected total confidence. Only Vido looked less than happy. Miska couldn't say she blamed him. His good health notwithstanding, he was quite old to be doing his first parachute jump. Never mind plummeting more than twenty-five-thousand feet before opening the canopy. The *consigliere* had enough neuralware in his head to accept skillsofts for parachute operations, and he'd done a number of simulated drops during training, but that wasn't the same as real life experience, no matter how realistic the VR was. She wanted to ask him how he was doing but she knew that would make him look bad. She checked his hands. They weren't shaking. Whatever Vido Cofino was, he wasn't a coward.

'Buddy check,' Miska announced. 'Uncle V, will you check me?' They partnered up, checking each other's gear. Miska caught Vido's eye. He smiled and nodded. She checked his gear, tightened a few straps, and they were ready. She felt eyes on her and turned around to see Mass looking at her. Miska checked the altimeter again and then nodded to Teramoto who worked the manual hatch lever. Immediately the shuttle started to buck as its aerodynamics were altered, a hurricane filled the avionics compartment and the pile of carbon that had been their luggage was blown away.

Torricone was out first. Then a grinning Goodluck. Hradisky leapt out with a rebel yell that made the covert operator in her cringe, though she could appreciate the sentiment and knew it would make no difference. Mass went through with the hesitant competence of someone having electronic information downloaded into the meat of their brain. Next was Vido. Just a moment's reluctance but then he seemed to take the tearing-the-medgel-off approach and he leapt with an unconvincing rebel yell of his own. Enchi couldn't wait to get out, a huge grin on his face as well. Teramoto and Kaneda jumped without a fuss. She was left in the compartment with Sykes. He spent just a second smiling at her. Miska spent a moment wondering what had been going through the hacker's head, then she jumped and all thoughts were banished in the rush.

She was out in the faint glow of Barnard's Star, a smoky orange ball huge in the sky. On the dayside of the tidally locked planet, the light was a never-ending summer sunset to Miska, who had grown up under a white main-sequence star and a white dwarf in a binary system. A smile on her face, Miska turned over in the air to look up at the huge passenger shuttle overhead. She magnified her vision to make sure that the hatch was shutting automatically, then she rolled over again, facing the surface. She found herself looking down at huge banks of vapour rising from the Steam Sea, part of the vast ocean that made up the majority of Barney Prime's surface. Through the sweating clouds she could just about make out the Barack Archipelago that made up the American colony on the planet. They were making for the coast of the largest island, New Roanoke. From this altitude the islands looked like the crested spine of a great sea serpent making its way through the ocean's steam.

Miska checked on Vido. He had his arms and legs outstretched and his face towards the ground. It was difficult to tell from this altitude but he seemed to be roughly on target. Miska closed her legs and tucked her arms in at her sides, gliding through the sky to get closer to him. She thought about opening a private comms link but then decided against it. She noticed that Mass was sticking close to Vido as well. Hradisky and Goodluck were performing all sorts of acrobatics that would have angered her dad but made Miska smile. They had either done this before or had practised a lot in VR. Enchi was doing his own acrobatics but separate from the two Comancheros. She was even a little surprised to see Torricone enjoying himself. She hadn't really spoken to him since he had tried to act as her father's messenger boy. Miska wanted to play as well but knew that she had to try and lead by example. Teramoto, Kaneda and finally Sykes joined the very rough formation with Mass, Vido and herself.

Tendrils of steam reached up for the skydivers as the huge humid clouds engulfed them. Now it would get tricky. She checked on the GPS positioning of the separated jumpers. A 3D display overlaid her vision in her IVD. It looked like Enchi had stopped mucking around, but Torricone and the two Comancheros were still engaging in acrobatics. She considered saying something but decided against it. She would chew them out if they screwed up, otherwise they could have their fun. Then suddenly one of the jumpers was heading straight towards her. Sykes appeared out of the humid cloud, his masked face suddenly filling her vision. She tried to twist out of the way but he caught her a glancing blow and sent her spinning. Miska managed to control the spin and moved back into formation.

'Sorry,' he said over the group comms link. He didn't sound very sorry. 'Are you okay?'

'Get control of yourself,' Miska told him. Judging by the 3D GPS model in her IVD he was now back in formation.

'Still getting used to it, skillsofts and all that.'

Then they were out of the clouds and into the pocket of clear sky over New Roanoke provided by the atmosphere processor. It dominated the landscape. The processor was basically a huge heat exchanger that aided the ocean in moving the heat around the planet to regulate the temperature to liveable levels on the day and nightside. The genetically modified flora growing all over the atmosphere processor, also part of the terraforming process, did little to disguise the technological mountain that sat atop the terraced hills surrounding the coastal city of New Verona. They were just north of the city, aiming for a supposedly deserted part of the coastline. Even if they were spotted skydiving it was a reasonably common activity in this part of the world.

Miska could feel the humidity now, despite the temperature regulators in the printed, armoured clothes she wore under the jumpsuit. She wanted to tear her mask off; she was sick of breathing bottled, recycled air on ships, stations and habitats. She could make out the bright lights reflecting on the wet streets of the city. She was able to pick out some of the larger houses, many of them lit up in an ostentatious demonstration of wealth. Magnifying her vision she could make out the vineyards on the rock terraces surrounding the city. The vines, modified with symbiotic bacterial growths that allowed them to feed on the infrared energy from the comparatively weak red dwarf star, produced some of the finest Sauvignon Blanc in the colonies.

Along the beaches she could see fires and make out the tiny forms of surfers riding the artificially generated waves. New Verona was, after all, considered one of the party capitals of human space, even welcoming visitors from the Sol system – including, some said, the scions of the Small Gods.

Just below her parachute canopies bloomed and automated navigation programs steered the chutes towards the landing co-ordinates. Miska dropped through them and saw that Torricone and the two Comancheros hadn't opened theirs yet and were still dropping. Miska had nothing to prove. She just wanted to get to the ground before Vido, whom she had passed. Miska deployed her chute and felt it yank her upwards. By the time she had checked her canopy had properly deployed and looked down again she saw the three canopies open beneath her. She all but tore her mask off. The air felt thick but there was breeze, presumably from the atmosphere processor, blowing down from the hills and pushing the mist-like banks of steam further out into the hot sea. She could hear laughing below her. She had a big grin on her face, too. Miska checked the GPS model; the other five Bastards were all above her and all heading for roughly the same point. They were outside the range of the wave generators so Miska hoped there wouldn't be too many people around.

Below her she saw one of the chutes catch a thermal, rise up and get blown out over the sea.

'Shit,' Miska muttered as her chute caught the thermal as well and she had to fight it. According to her IVD it was Goodluck who'd been caught, though he was trying to angle the chute back in towards a small beach between two bluffs.

'Goodluck, you okay?' she asked over the comms link.

'I'm fine but it's going to be a wet landing,' he answered. He sounded pretty relaxed about it.

'Understood, I recommend hitting the quick release when you're—' she started as the ground accelerated up to meet her, though more slowly than she was used to in the .75G of Barney Prime. Goodluck had hit the quick release and dropped sixty-odd feet into the ocean. '—a bit lower,' she finished. She wasn't too worried. Their jumpsuits were waterproof and could supply buoyancy.

She dropped through the covering of tall, tendril-like plants reaching towards Barnard's Star and felt her boots touch earth.

*

A grinning Goodluck had been helped from the surf and they gathered on the bluff overlooking the red-reflecting waters of the ocean. The chemical catalyst wand had reduced the printed skydiving gear to so much carbon powder blowing in the artificial winds. Miska was pleased that they were stood in a rough circle, close enough to hear each other, while looking outwards at their surroundings and simultaneously trying not to look too suspicious. Arguably they were failing at the latter but atop the bluff, about a quarter mile from the coastal highway, there didn't seem to be anybody around. It was late in the early hours of the morning but that didn't mean too much on the sunside of a tidally locked planet. Night and day were largely arbitrary constructs.

'Time to start earning your money, gentlemen – we need a base of operations,' Miska told Mass and Vido. She didn't like the silence that answered her and she had to resist the urge to look round at them. They needed some place they could live, plan, work and run their recces from. 'Gentlemen?'

'Okay, we've been having a little chat about that …' Mass started. Sykes irritated her by chuckling.

'You told me you could get everything we needed,' Miska said, not liking where this was going.

'And we can,' Mass told her. 'But there's a problem.'

'Anything we do is going to show up on someone's lidar,' Vido explained.

'Which I told you we can't do,' Miska said, with mounting irritation. 'In fact avoiding that was one of the conditions for you being allowed to come.'

'I am shocked, nay appalled, to find that criminal elements can't be trusted,' Sykes said.

'Shut the fuck up, limey,' Mass spat.

'That's enough,' Miska told them, resisting the urge to turn and look at the two Mafiosi. 'Sykes, trance in. I want you to hire two four-wheel-drives to come out and pick us up, cover our tracks, understand me?'

'You want me to sit down in the dirt? You must—' he started.

'Fucking now!' Miska spat.

'You cannot trust your own organisation?' Teramoto asked Mass. She heard the button man's sharp intake of breath at being addressed directly by the Yakuza lieutenant.

'We can trust our organisation.' It was Vido who answered. 'That's the problem. They'll want us back.'

Miska turned to face Mass and Vido.

'Torricone, join us. Kaneda, you're on hacker guard, stand over Sykes. The rest of you spread out and form a perimeter. I just want a quiet warning if you see anyone coming.'

'Has it occurred to you that we look a bit susp—?' Vido started as people shifted position. Miska silenced him with a look. He held up his hands and took a step back.

'I swear to god if you guys are of no use you'll spend the entire trip sedated, assuming I don't just blow your N-bombs,' she told them. What was irritating her most was that the voice saying 'I told you so' in the back of her head sounded a lot like her dad.

'We will be useful,' Vido promised. 'Even if we find a workshop to use as a base of operations, nine people up to no good, it rings alarm bells.'

'You mean everyone wants their cut,' Torricone said with just the slightest tone of amusement.

'Basically,' Vido admitted after a moment's hesitation. The *consigliere* seemed no worse for his first HALO jump.

'Way the world works,' Mass said.

'This one anyway,' Torricone said.

'So what use are you?' Miska demanded.

'We'll be able to point you in the right direction – guns, people to speak to to get things done, that sort of thing,' Vido promised. 'But anything on this big a scale ...'

'What have you got?' Miska asked Torricone. The car thief shrugged.

'For what you've got in mind, they're right. You need a garage where you can do illegal stuff. That means a chop shop. They're all affiliated, either sets or wise guys.'

'Sets?' Miska asked.

'Subdivisions of the gangs,' Vido explained. Torricone nodded.

'A set sounds like a better idea,' Miska said. Mass started laughing.

'Trust some crystalled-up homeboy?' Mass asked. 'We might not be cheap but at least we're professional?' Now it was Torricone's turn to shake his head. 'Besides, I don't think Mikey-T here is as close to the Disciples as he once was.' Torricone shrugged.

'He's not wrong,' the car thief agreed. 'But we've all been away a while.'

'Solutions?' Miska almost screamed at them.

'Hire a commercial property?' Kaneda asked from where he stood over Sykes. The hacker was slumped against something that looked like a very tall palm tree with a network of tendril-like leaves reaching towards the huge, smoking orange ball that dominated the sky.

'Still need to get all the equipment from somewhere,' Vido pointed out. Miska knew it would slow them down but it might yet come to that.

'I might know someone,' Torricone said reluctantly.

'Who?' Vido asked.

'Hector Manon,' Torricone told them. 'But we're going to need some serious money.' Vido shook his head and looked at Mass.

'The Fourth Street Reaper?' Mass asked. Torricone looked a little exasperated.

'He ain't like that no more.'

'Yeah, I heard he'd gone straight.'

'That's why we're going to need the money,' Torricone explained.

Miska was in the front of the second of the two Dodge SUVs that Sykes had hired, which had driven out on autopilot from the city to pick them up. Miska peeked sideways into the net, opening a window into Barney Prime's virtual world to check on Sykes's work. The SUVs' information reflections were ghosts, as much realer-seeming, spoofed versions of the vehicles were giving off false locational information somewhere down in the central strip of New Verona City. In the net, the mostly translucent vehicles looked like hundreds of years old, classically styled, retro versions of themselves. They had headed away from the coast, skirting the vineyard terraces, looking down at the lights of the city, then headed towards the hills and canyons that lay in the shadow of the atmosphere processor. In the real world the central strip of the city that ran from the foothills in the east down to the ocean in the west was all garish neon and bright lights; the hotels, clubs, restaurants, bars, casinos and other amusements competing with each other. The net feed window in her IVD showed the virtual representations of those same establishments – they were brighter, more garish and a little vulgar even for Miska's reasonably unsophisticated tastes. They also looked very retro.

That was the thing that struck her whenever she came to Barney Prime. The whole colony seemed like an exercise in reliving halcyon glory days from Earth's past that had probably never existed anyway. She wondered how much of it was historically inspired and how much of it was manufactured from various fictional media. She glanced briefly in the rear viewer at Mass and Vido in the back seat, a still tranced-in Sykes wedged between them. She wondered how much of their behaviour was influenced by sense games, and before that vizzes.

They snaked into the canyons of Pueblo Town, mostly low-tract housing originally printed for the construction crews who had built the processor. The houses clung to the sides of the hills, the streets forming a tangled warren. Miska tried to follow their route out of habit. Her dad, and then the marines, had taught her the importance of being able to navigate without the help of machines. She was soon lost, though, and had to resort to GPS and the maps stored in her neuralware, though even they didn't seem entirely accurate.

It was clear that Pueblo Town was a poor area from the sheer number of gun and liquor stores that always seemed present in such places. She recognised the territorial markers of the gangs sprayed on the walls. She assumed that Torricone could read the rest of the not-so-secret language. She saw the scratch-built rotor-drone couriers flitting between kerb-crawling vehicles to deal drugs on behalf of their unseen riggers. In the net the drones looked like anything from winged monkeys to bat-like demons to tiny clown homunculi. The net in this area was mostly hive colonies of branded commercial nodes for communications and entertainment in the houses and apartments, interspersed with various automat concessions and the occasional stylised data fortress, which she assumed were for criminal purposes. Much of the stylising seemed to involve skulls and bones.

A low-riding car cruised past them on the other side of the road. UV lights lit the inside of the vehicle, making the skull-tattooed faces of the occupants glow. In the net the car was made of bone with skeletal spider legs. It was also quite heavily protected, for a civilian vehicle. The drivers were eyeballing their SUVs. Miska was pleased that she had tinted the windows at Torricone's behest.

'What's with all the death stuff?' she asked. Tendrils of neon rot seeped out from the bone car in the net. A tentative probing of the SUVs' electronic defences with a view to a possible hijacking. Sykes's net icon was a masked highwayman from Earth's past that he swore blind was based on an ancestor who'd been hanged. The rot was met by burning lines of gunpowder as Sykes protected the hired SUVs' systems.

'Wannabe badasses,' Mass muttered. He clearly wasn't impressed.

'They're a death cult,' Vido said.

'Santa Muerte worshippers,' Torricone said quietly.

'Who?' Miska asked.

'Heathens,' Mass spat and made the sign of the cross. Torricone glanced at the button man but didn't say anything. 'Patron saint of assholes.'

'She's the patron saint of drug dealers and killers,' Vido told her.

'Among other things,' Torricone added.

'You worship that pagan bullshit?' Mass demanded. Torricone turned around in the front seat to face Mass. The button

129

man looked faintly ridiculous with Sykes lolling around on his shoulder.

'I'm a good Catholic, Massimo, just like you.'

Mass opened his mouth to retort.

'Mass,' Vido said.

Mass closed his mouth again.

Torricone just went back to looking out the window.

They turned onto an incredibly steep canyon street that Miska wasn't sure she would have liked to attempt without four-wheel-drive. As they made their way down the hill lined with terraced houses in gaps carved out of the canyon walls, they were offered a tantalising glimpse of downtown and the ocean.

'I take it we're in Disciples' territory?' Miska asked. Torricone just nodded.

The two SUVs came to a halt at the bottom of the steep street where it curved back onto another, wider through-road. The garage had an armoured, concertinaed frontage with a faded, and much tagged, graffiti mural showing customised cars, pickups and SUVs on the front. It looked like there was an apartment above the garage. Torricone stared at the door. There were lights on in the apartment despite the earliness of the hour.

'You up for this?' Miska asked after a few moments. Torricone didn't answer. Instead he put up his hoodie and climbed out of the car.

'Vido, you're with me, Mass, stay and babysit Sykes.' She glanced behind her and Mass nodded, though he shrugged Sykes off his shoulder. Miska wondered how long ago Mass had drawn his sidearm. He held the SIG GP-692 against his leg. It seemed that this part of town even made Mafiosi button men nervous.

Miska climbed out of the SUV and into the humid night. Torricone was already talking into the apartment's vizcom. The door was open by the time Vido and Miska had reached it, revealing a flight of stairs with threadbare carpet.

Hector Manon was a big man, heavily muscled but with a belly that suggested he enjoyed his food and beer. His gang past was written on his skin in ink and scar tissue. The apartment itself looked old and worn, the furnishings looked old and worn, the tech looked old and worn, but everything was clean and functional. They were stood in an open plan lounge, dining and kitchen area. Aside from Hector there were another two people present. One was a short, olive-skinned woman with extensive face tattoos and long black hair that was tied back. The other was a taller feminine person of a more indeterminate gender. He/she had a wet collar that, presumably, covered and provided oxygenated water to his/her implanted gills. Torricone had told them that one of Hector's partners was a cybrid mer who spent a lot of time working offshore in the underwater aqua-farms. Both of Hector's partners looked tough-as-nails and less than pleased to see them. She suspected that was because there were at least three kids in the house, according to Torricone.

'You won't need that shotgun there, friend,' Vido said to the mer. Normally civilians with guns made Miska nervous but the mer looked comfortable with the shotgun, which made Miska nervous for a different reason. She also noticed that the woman had a pistol in the waistband of her cut-offs.

'Any weapons, put them on the table and back away from them,' the woman said.

'We don't do that,' Miska told her. She was optimistic that Hector wasn't armed.

'You've been away for a while, and now you bring trouble to my home?' Hector asked. Torricone put his hood down. He opened his mouth to say something and then thought the better of it and just shook his head.

'I'm sorry, *ese*,' he finally managed.

'In which case you need to turn around and leave, T,' the mer said. He/she had a deep and strangely sonorous voice, though heavily accented.

'Lira, look we've got a proposition ...' Torricone started.

'Our children are here,' Lira told him. Miska could hear the anger in his/her tone.

'If I had another choice ...' Torricone started.

'You had all sorts of choices, and you made a wrong one and now you need to get the fuck out of my house,' the woman started. Hector turned around to look ruefully at his girlfriend. Miska didn't like the way this was going down. The woman had her hand on the butt of the slug-throwing pistol in her waist-band. Miska was sure she could get the woman and Lira before they could fire, and probably Hector before he could react, but she wasn't sure what Torricone would do, which didn't please her. Nor did she particularly want to have a gunfight in an apartment full of children.

'It's the bitch off the news vizzes,' the woman said, nodding at Miska. *Well shit,* Miska thought. 'The slaver.'

'Slaver's a strong term,' Miska said.

'But accurate,' Vido said. Hector glanced at the *consigliere*, then looked away before taking a second longer look. 'I'm going to take my pistol out very slowly and lay it on the table.' The woman nodded, but drew her pistol and held it downwards against her leg. Vido, very slowly, put his gauss pistol on the dining room table.

'Now the rest of you,' Lira demanded. Torricone did the same. Vido turned to look at Miska.

'But I don't wanna!' Miska complained – and it was true, she really didn't.

'Miska,' Torricone said quietly. She sighed and put the SIG on the table. 'And the knife.' Miska turned to look at him.

'Whose side are you on?' she demanded.

'Theirs,' Torricone said. Miska glared at him and then put her knife on the table.

'Nice knife,' Lira told her.

'Thanks,' Miska said.

'Now, can we maybe just sit down, have a discussion? And if you don't like what we say then we'll leave and never bother you again,' Vido said. Recognition dawned across Hector's face.

'Holy shit, you're Vido Cofino,' he said.

'You've got to be insane coming back here,' Hector said. He was sat on the sofa with Lira lying across his lap. Tina, the woman with the tattooed face, was leaning against the wall staring at Miska, who was leaning against another wall, smiling back.

'It wasn't by choice, *ese*,' Torricone said.

'You know we could make some money selling his ass to the Disciples,' Tina said. Torricone turned to look up at her.

'Tina, I respect you and this is your house and all, but you threaten me and I've gotta react.'

Miska had noticed that the rhythm and pattern of Torricone's speech had changed since he had started talking to Hector, Lira and Tina.

'Just out of interest, we put a gun to your head and tell you to let them go, what happens?' Hector asked Miska. She suspected his question was designed to head off the brewing confrontation between Torricone and Tina.

'I kill you with my bare hands; in the unlikely event you tag me, it kills these two and six thousand other badasses,' Miska told him matter-of-factly. Hector gave this some thought and then nodded.

'Cool,' he said.

'How you been, man?' Torricone asked.

'You care?' Hector asked. Hector had been the least hostile. He had hugged Torricone once all the guns had been put away but he still wasn't pleased to see him. Miska couldn't shake the feeling that it was Vido's celebrity status that had helped calm the confrontation, which was great but presented a whole new set of problems.

'Yeah, *mano*, I do,' Torricone said and Miska believed him.

'The business isn't doing so bad but two lots of protection is killing us.'

'Two lots?' Vido asked. He was sat in the other seat in the lounge. Hector turned to look at him. He seemed to be deciding whether or not to explain.

'This is Disciple turf. Disciples used to kick up to your lot but they decided to go their own way.'

'You're fucking kidding me!' Vido said.

'Keep your voice down,' Tina hissed.

'I'm very sorry,' Vido apologised. He looked a little shaken by the news. 'Just took me by ... I'm surprised it's being tolerated.'

'It's not,' Hector told him. 'Open warfare in the street but ... well ...'

'The Cofinos?' Vido prompted.

'Not what they used to be,' Tina muttered.

'So now we pay to the Disciples and the Mob,' Lira growled.

'Who takes your payments?' Vido asked.

'Don Teduzzi,' Hector told him.

'You know him?' Miska asked.

'I know him,' Vido said. He didn't sound happy.

'Tough motherfucker,' Hector said and Lira punched him gently.

'Needs to be,' Tina said. 'He's basically taking payments behind enemy lines. The Disciples have even put a bounty on his head.'

'That's Don,' Vido muttered. 'Well, we can help you with your payments.'

'We want to give you some money,' Miska said.

'A lot of money,' Vido added.

'Really a lot of money,' Torricone finished off and Miska rolled her eyes.

'What for?' Hector asked.

'We need to use your place for a few weeks,' Miska told them. 'A month at the most.'

'To do illegal shit,' Tina snapped and then turned to Hector. 'We made a decision, remember?'

'I'm sorry, *mano*, we're clean now. We're not doing any more time,' he said, but didn't look Torricone in the eyes. 'We've got the kids to think of.'

'I understand,' Vido said. Miska saw she had a message from him in her IVD. 'But we're talking about the sort of money that could help change their lives.' Miska opened the message and read it. 'You get caught you say we – and by we, I mean the evil pirate queen there,' he nodded towards Miska, 'threatened the kids.' Tina came off the wall. Vido held up his hands. 'We're

135

not actually threatening the kids, that's just in case it bounces back on you.'

The message contained a very large number. Miska sighed and sent him back an affirmative. Vido told them the number. Six eyes stared back at him. Even Torricone turned to look. It was certainly going to make a dent in their expenses. 'Needless to say this also buys confidentiality. We can't have anyone knowing we're here.'

'That's a lot of money,' Hector said. He sounded a little dazed.

CHAPTER 9

'Well shit,' Miska said looking out over the Steam Sea. They were north of the city now, beyond the wave generators, just off the coastal highway. She still hadn't quite got used to the warm winds carrying the steam salt mists in off the ocean. Her mood wasn't improved by Teramoto's chuckle. He had removed the medgels from his face and the only sign of the beating he had received at her hands were a few fading bruises.

'Our employer did not mention this?' Teramoto asked.

No he fucking didn't, Miska thought. She'd got the co-ordinates of the facility where the alien artefact was supposedly being kept after she had arrived on Barney Prime. Raff had left them for her in one of their electronic dead letter drops. *He kept the fact that facility was underwater pretty fucking quiet.* She was looking at a glow emanating from the water about half a mile offshore. It was difficult to tell purely from the sub-surface light, but it looked like quite a substantial facility. There were a few patrol drones on the surface.

'This suggests to me it will require a different skill set to what we expected,' Teramoto suggested. Miska forced her face into a smile and turned to look up at him. He was still wearing his white suit. She was wondering if it had been a mistake, letting her crew choose their own clothes. At least the two Bethlehem Milliners had had the common sense to eschew their fairy tale gang colours.

'What, don't like a challenge?' she asked. 'The plan stays basically the same. We just need to force them to move the package.'

'They'll take it out by air,' Teramoto said.

'That means either a beach or water landing, possibly a pontoon out there—' Miska stopped talking as she noticed one of her search routines had returned. Upon receiving the coordinates and realising where they were, she had sent out a number of reasonably subtle programs to find out what the official story for the underwater facility was. As a matter of course she isolated the program and then ran a diagnostic check on it.

In the open window in her IVD, the search program was one of her colour-coded furry worms. The isolation program looked like a cross between a pet carrier and an idealised version of the gatehouse in a medieval castle. The diagnostics program was depicted as an automated pet grooming apparatus within the pet carrier/gatehouse. All of it was done in the style of her favourite retro cartoons that her dad had shown her when she was a child. It only took a matter of seconds, and only that long because she was being thorough. Even so, she almost missed the trace. Miska felt herself fall as she tranced in.

In the net she was a humorously angry and spikier cartoon version of herself wielding a club. A neon liquid represented the sea. The landscape was a crystal copy interspersed with animated adverts. Blinking lines of more neon represented the various communications links.

A window showing her a view of the real world, captured through her artificial eyes, showed Teramoto catching her and carrying her back towards the pickup truck they'd hired to replace the SUVs.

The isolation program became transparent as cartoon waldos turned over the captive fuzzy worm of the search program and revealed the corruption. Her worm had caught the trace like a disease.

'Clever,' Miska muttered. She had only caught it because of the NSA software that she had stolen with the *Little Jimmy*. It was a *very* sophisticated trace program. She isolated it. Released it from isolation and then hit the tiny little black slug it made with her club, which represented her attack programs. That good a trace meant a hacker at the top of their game, with top of the line software that had almost beaten augmented NSA intrusion countermeasures. That in turn suggested government-level resources.

Mars? she wondered. Raff had said that they were also interested in the 'artefact' but she hadn't been happy with that. How could Mars act with impunity in such a staunchly American colony? She considered trying to trace the trace, but she was already unhappy about how much attention they had garnered. The fact that she had caught and destroyed the trace would tell whoever had sent it that there was another hacker involved, one with a certain amount of skill. If she had been thinking quickly enough, she would have spoofed it and sent it back with false information about her identity. There would have been no guarantee, however, that they would have bought it. She scanned her local net environment. There was nothing that suggested they had been further compromised. Having added another, paranoia-induced, layer of security to the already secure integral computer melded to the meat of her brain, she dropped out of the net and back into the real world.

She was lying across the back seat of the pickup. Teramoto was stood outside the vehicle, checking the surrounding area. He glanced back at her.

'Are we compromised?' he asked. Miska shook her head and sat up. She knew he must be curious about what had just happened. He was more than smart enough to work out that there had been some kind of net incursion.

Miska checked the information that the search program had discovered. According to public record the offshore site was an exploratory dig looking for geothermal energy sources.

'Bullshit,' she muttered. What she couldn't work out was what it actually was. If they were just storing something there, say for example, an alien artefact, why was it lit up like a Christmas tree? Underwater warehouses were far from unheard of but there was no need to advertise their presence.

Miska turned to look at Teramoto. 'Can you dive?' she asked. Teramoto just raised an eyebrow.

There was not much in the way of recreational dive interest in the area of the 'facility'. As part of the terraforming process, the Steam Sea had been seeded with genetically modified flora and fauna from Earth – but most of it was centred on the aquaculture kelp forests. The submarine farms were located on the shallow oceanic shelf that surrounded the Barack Archipelago. The 'facility' was on the same shelf but in a relatively low traffic area.

As they put on their hired scuba gear, Miska was in no doubt that they were under surveillance. She couldn't see any drones but if they were good enough to almost successfully run a trace on her search program then they would either have bought or hacked time on one of the satellites that watched the surface. Miska was hoping that they looked like a practice shore dive. Miska and Teramoto pulled on their ultra-thin, thermally regulated, buoyancy-controlling wetsuits. They had locked their clothes in the hire pickup's strong box. Miska used a jet injector for the nitrogen stabiliser and then handed the device to Teramoto. The Yakuza lieutenant injected himself and they picked up their lung-masks, propulsion scooters and kinetic fins, and made for the surf. Miska was wondering if whoever was running the facility had already been notified, despite the fact they were more than two and half miles away.

Miska loved diving. The Recon Marines had trained her in the deep inland rift-seas and lakes of Sirius 4. She had loved the tranquillity of the deep dives. She had explored the bored-out caves that had once acted as submarine bases for the alien Them. Shallow diving off the shore of New Roanoke Island was, by comparison, very boring. Other than microscopic life, the oceans of Barney Prime had been pretty inert until the colonists had started terraforming them. Even at this depth, where the weak red light managed to penetrate the water, there was little to see without the support of genetically modified life. This part of the shallow shelf that surrounded the archipelago was a rocky, sand-coloured submarine wasteland. The sea scooters pulled them through the bath-hot water. They were in contact by comms link but Teramoto was so still and quiet that Miska was of the opinion that she might as well have been alone.

The underwater landscape, red from the water-muted light of Barnard's Star, was so samey that without her internal systems counting the distance it would have been difficult to tell how far they had travelled. Miska could, however, now see the steel-blue light from the underwater facility in the distance. She sent Teramoto a message and then slaved her sea scooter to his and magnified her vision. The facility was still pretty far away but what she could make out wasn't quite what she had expected. There was no heavily defended submarine warehouse. Instead she found an area surrounded by floodlights. There was a structure anchored to the seabed but it looked like a machine shed to her, which made sense as what she could see was a series of excavators eating into the shelf rock. The excavators had long umbilical tubes attached to them that were sucking the chewed rock away and depositing it in collection bladders. It was strange, the robot excavators seemed to be set up for delicacy rather than volume. Their excavations were measured and careful. The machinery itself was state of the art.

The whole area was patrolled by the same drone craft they had seen on the surface. It seemed that they were more than capable of submarine as well as surface operations. Two of them were already heading their way at some speed. What Miska didn't see was any sign of human life. There was no cybrid drone rigger in view, or piloted submersible. The whole operation appeared to be completely automated. Miska adjusted the magnification on her eyes and glanced back at Teramoto. As far as she could tell through the lung mask, his face wore his normal lack of expression.

'This is a restricted area. Use of force is authorised. You must turn back immediately.' The patrol drones speeding through the water to intercept them were broadcasting the message. Miska sent a message protesting the drones' actions but then both she and Teramoto turned around and headed back the way they had come. The Barack Archipelago was nominally subject to

US law. In reality the law was what people could afford it to be. Regardless of that, Miska knew there was no arguing with drones.

The drones shadowed them most of the way back until they went ashore. Miska removed her mask as they carried the fins and scooters back towards the pickup parked up next to the coastal highway.

'What did that look like to you?' Miska asked Teramoto. The Yakuza lieutenant did not answer immediately.

'A marine archaeological dig,' he finally said. Miska nodded. She had thought the same thing,

Curiouser and curiouser. Any dig would pretty much have to be looking for something that had been here before the human colonists. She wasn't sure she bought Raff's alien artefact idea, but the dig would suggest that at least one other person believed the same thing.

'Miska-*sama*,' Teramoto said. She heard the warning in his tone but she had already seen the smooth, curved, aerodynamic shape of the black sports car with tinted windows, parked by their pickup. She didn't recognise the make or model but something about its sleek lines made it look as though it was breaking the sound barrier while it was parked. The strange thing was, she couldn't shake the feeling that the car was watching her somehow. She and Teramoto didn't stop, just kept moving towards the pickup. Both of them were armed but their sidearms were zipped up in carry bags they had taken under with them. As they mounted the sand and scrub incline that led to the roadside, the sports car started up silently and, accelerating incredibly quickly, hit the regolith blacktop at speed, leaving a cloud of dust behind it. Miska had recorded some footage of the vehicle through her eyes. She didn't want to run a search on it because of the earlier trace but she decided to look into it. She sent the image of the car to a heavily encrypted electronic dead letter drop to see if Raff had any idea who it belonged to.

Teramoto was staring after the car. It took a moment for Miska to identify the expression. Concern. It looked out of place on the Yakuza lieutenant's face.

'Problem?' she asked.

There were a few more moments of silence before Teramoto just shook his head and climbed into the SUV. Miska stared at the empty space where Teramoto had been, before rolling her eyes and climbing into the vehicle after him.

Miska already knew what to expect before she got back. She had watched the little drama play out on the viz feed from the contact lens in the windows of her IVD. Hradisky and Enchi seemed to be the main antagonists. Kaneda was supporting Enchi, though even through the point-of-view lens footage Miska got the feeling that Kaneda was only doing so out of gang loyalty. Goodluck was trying to keep Hradisky calm, without giving an inch to the Milliners. Prison yard politics. Mass appeared to be trying to keep the peace, but in a not very partisan fashion – he still, after all, had an issue with the Milliners. Torricone was watching on despairingly but keeping out of it. Sykes appeared to be egging both sides on and enjoying the spectacle. Vido was nowhere to be seen.

'Is there anything wrong, Miska-*sama*?' Teramoto asked from the other front seat. They were letting the pickup drive itself, though the controls were on Miska's side of the vehicle. It was entirely possible that Teramoto had picked up on her body language but it was just as possible that Teramoto had sown the seeds of discord to create a problem that he could solve.

Miska chose to ignore the Yakuza lieutenant, though she had to admit he had radiated competence on the dive and seemed unflappable.

The truck pulled up outside Hector's garage. Hector and his family had used the money that Miska had given them to pay off some debts, as well as the protection money they owed to both Teduzzi and the Disciples. Then they had booked a snow-boarding holiday in New Erebus on the nightside and still had some money left over. Miska sent the entry codes and the door rolled up. She could already hear the shouting and it looked like none of the really rudimentary things she had tasked them with had been done. Miska tried not to grind her teeth, though she was really missing working alone. Enchi and Hradisky were nose to nose, screaming at each other. The pickup moved into the garage and the shutters rolled down behind them. Enchi and Hradisky didn't seem to notice. In some ways the most annoying thing about the whole situation was the smile on Sykes's face.

Miska got out of the truck and stared at the pair of them. They ignored her.

'Guys. Guys!' Torricone shouted. Hradisky looked at him and Torricone nodded over at Miska. Now both of them turned to look at her.

'He—!' Enchi began. Miska held up her finger and he went quiet.

'Corporal Prola,' Miska said, looking over at Mass. He was clearly angry, fists bunched at his side.

'Yes, boss?' Mass asked.

'We appear to have had a breakdown in discipline, here. Why is that?'

'This piece of shit—' Hradisky started.

'Quiet!' Miska snapped. Mass looked as though he was

shaking with rage. Teramoto was half in and out of the pickup looking on with an expression betraying only slightly less humour than Sykes's. 'Corporal Prola, I asked you a question.'

'I have no explanation, boss,' Mass finally said.

'Private Torricone, in your experience how do I handle lapses in discipline?' Miska asked. She hated playing the mean NCO. That was her dad's job. She suppressed the spike of anger as she thought about what her dad would make of this particular situation.

'Normally you blow someone's head off,' Torricone said grimly. Miska was watching Enchi and Hradisky to see if they would take her seriously. Enchi blanched somewhat. Hradisky was still seething with anger. He might be clean as a result of his time in prison but it was clear to Miska that he was still too much the angry street junkie at heart to back down.

'Corporal Prola,' Miska said. 'Have you seen people executed during a mission for breaches of discipline?'

'Yes, I have,' Mass said. Whatever else, she had everybody's attention now.

'Perhaps the problem is that Private Hradisky and Private Tsuyoshi do not believe that I would do this. Perhaps a demonstration of my resolve in this matter is called for?' Miska asked Enchi. Mass didn't say anything. Neither did Enchi or Hradisky, though both of them were looking at her warily.

'Miska—' Torricone started. Miska silenced him with a look.

'Which one?' Miska asked Mass. The button man stared at her. He glanced over at Hradisky and Enchi. Enchi would be the best choice. It would go some way towards redressing the balance for the dead Mafioso one of the Milliners had left on the hangar deck floor on Teramoto's orders. Fortunately Mass made the correct decision.

'I guess it has to be me,' Mass said. 'You left me in charge.' He looked her straight in the eyes.

'Yes I did,' Miska said.

'Perhaps if someone else was in—' Teramoto said. To Miska's mind he was overplaying his hand a little.

'Shut up,' Miska told him. 'Is this going to happen again?'

'No, boss,' Mass told her.

'I wanted the garage tidied and swept. I wanted a sleeping area set aside and a supply run done for food and camping gear. Instead I come back to schoolyard dick measuring. Imagine my incredible boredom. Do I like being bored, Corporal Prola?'

'You really don't,' Torricone muttered, earning himself a glare.

Sykes clapped his hands together and started laughing. Miska turned to face him.

'Something funny, Private?' Miska asked.

'I'm not a private in anything, and I think you know that,' Sykes said.

'*Mano*—' Torricone started but Miska held up her hand. Sykes looked over at the car thief.

'It's a fucking pantomime, mate.' He grabbed at his groin. 'Grow some *cojones*. She can't do shit without us, so I think it's time to renegotiate, yeah?'

Torricone looked down and was shaking his head. Mass's face was impassive.

'I think maybe he's right,' Hradisky said.

'Me too,' Enchi added. Miska was pleased that they had found some common ground.

'No you don't,' Teramoto told the Milliner. Miska glanced over at Kaneda. He was keeping well back, though his hand was close to his holstered SIG.

147

'So we do this for you, what do we get?' Hradisky asked. 'For a start you're letting us go.'

'Youngblood, no,' Goodluck said quietly to Hradisky from where he was leaning against a car lift. Sykes sneered in the Comanchero OG's general direction.

'Original Gangster, my ass,' Sykes scoffed. 'Fucking pussy septic.'

Miska frowned.

'Septic?' she asked.

'Septic tank, yank,' Sykes said. 'Now what about it? Maybe a little redistribution of the tasks, a more even split.'

'You need to drop this now,' Torricone told Sykes.

'Yeah? And you need to man up,' Sykes told him.

'Shut the fuck up and get on with what you've been told to do,' Mass snapped. Sykes looked pained as he turned to face Mass.

'You don't get it, do you? I'm not in no fucking army and if we stand together she can't do nothing. What's she going to do? Kill us all?' he demanded. Torricone and Mass nodded. The arrogant expression on Sykes's face faltered for a moment. 'Oh, bullshit.' In some ways Miska was fascinated by the sense of delusion going on here.

'Listen to them, boy,' Goodluck told him. 'They're trying to keep you alive.'

'Fucking cowards, the lot of you,' Sykes snapped. 'Not a man among you.'

'I need a volunteer,' Miska said.

'I told you I'm not in the fucking—' Sykes started. Then he toppled forward.

Miska frowned. 'It really lacks the visceral impact of the collars, doesn't it?' she said.

148

'Wasn't a hacker pretty important to the plan?' Mass asked.

'Plans change,' Miska told him. She crossed the distance to Sykes's body and turned him over with the tip of her boot. His eyes were turning black and half his face looked like an enormous bruise, the results of the N-bomb he'd been implanted with being detonated.

'You know where to get rid of bodies on this planet, right?' she asked Mass. He just nodded. Miska turned around to look at Enchi and Hradisky.

'Questions, comments?' she asked. They just stared at her.

I wonder if it's because I'm short? Miska wondered. She had often found that people didn't seem to take her seriously until she did something really violent.

Enchi was shaking his head. Hradisky was staring at her with undisguised hatred in his eyes.

'What?' she asked.

'This would be a very different conversation if I didn't have a bomb in my head,' he spat.

'You think so?' she asked. 'But you do. So come to terms with the situation.' She pointed at the two original antagonists. 'Why don't you both bond over your hatred of me while you're helping Mass get rid of the body?' Hradisky was still glaring at her. Goodluck moved across the dirty floor of the garage to put a hand on the younger Comanchero's shoulder.

'We're off the *Daughter*. We're going to get to play with cars,' he told him. 'All else is for another day.' Hradisky continued to glare at Miska a moment or two longer and then turned to look at Goodluck. The OG was just shaking his head.

'Corporal Prola,' Miska said. 'I'm about to execute Private Cofino unless there's an extremely good reason as to why he's not here.'

149

'Ah—' Mass started. It was clear he had no idea where Vido was. Then the garage door started to slide up. Uncle V was stood on the other side with a bag of groceries. Goodluck and Mass moved to stand in front of Sykes's body.

'You went shopping in this neighbourhood?' Torricone asked. Vido shrugged.

'I wasn't always a lawyer, kid,' Vido told him. 'I found this amazing *bodega* two streets over, mom and pop operation. Miguel and Rose, lovely couple. I thought I'd make steak *parmigiana*. Hey, what's up with Sykes?'

Enchi and a still-angry Hradisky had gone with Mass to dump Sykes's body. Miska had told Mass to make sure that it didn't get found, as it would be proof of the Bastards operating on the planet. Miska had sent Teramoto out for the rest of the supplies but kept a close eye on him through his contact lens feed. She helped the rest of them tidy up, sweep and then wash down the floor of the garage. They had agreed to stay out of Hector's family's apartment other than to use the shower. She had taken Vido aside while they had been cleaning. She hadn't really had to say anything, just raise her eyebrow.

'I know, I know,' he said. 'But they were all arguing. Mass was wise enough to know that if he got involved the Milliners wouldn't back down and that just would have made matters worse. They're not going to listen to an old guy like me.'

'So you thought you'd make everyone dinner?' Miska asked.

'Judge me after you've tasted my steak *parmigiana*?' he asked. It really was difficult to stay angry with Uncle V for long. That was one of the reasons he was so dangerous. *When did I start thinking of him as Uncle V?* she wondered.

'You really get talking to the couple that run the bodega?'

'They didn't recognise me,' he reassured her. 'They were worried about an old guy like me wandering around on his own. Real shame, they've got a nice little store but it's all locked away behind armoured glass.'

'Maybe if you hadn't worked so hard to make this city a playground for criminals?' Miska asked. Just for a moment his face fell.

'That has occurred to me,' he said. He looked sad but Miska couldn't tell if he was playing her or not.

Torricone approached Miska while she was on her own a little while later.

'I don't want to get my brain blown up or anything ...' he started.

'Oh my god, what is it?'

'Look, Hector is renting you his place ...'

'For a lot of money.'

'Doing illegal shit is one thing, dropping bodies is another.'

Miska narrowed her eyes.

'But is also illegal shit,' she said. He opened his mouth to retort. 'Okay, I get the point. I'll try not to kill any more people here but you guys have to be a lot less annoying! You could start by not bothering me any more.'

'I'll see what I can do,' he said and walked away again.

'This was one of the nicest things I have ever put in my mouth!' Miska exclaimed through a mouthful of steak *parmigiana*. It was all the more impressive because the *consigliere* had cooked it on a camp stove.

'This is almost worth having a nanobomb in your head,' Goodluck said. Miska rolled her eyes. 'Almost.' He raised a glass of the red wine that Uncle V had also come back with.

'*Salute*!' Vido said, raising his glass in return.

They were all sat on folding chairs around several camping tables that had been slid together, piled high with the veritable feast that Uncle V had cooked. Miska wasn't sure what it said about them that despite the death of one of their own, the food seemed to be easing the tension. She guessed the wine helped. They were all criminals at the end of the day. She had wanted to ask Mass what he had done with the body but she knew she had to trust him to do his job. To a certain degree.

'So are we going to stick up an underwater habitat?' Torricone asked. Miska had been explaining what she had seen at the coordinates that Raff had provided.

'It's not impossible, but we've got the wrong skill set here,' Miska said.

'The plan was to take them by the road, I'm guessing?' Goodluck said, looking round the table.

'In so far as we had a plan,' Miska said. 'We were always going to be coming into this intel-blind.'

'I love an honest-to-goodness hijacking,' Mass said as he tore himself off another bit of bread to mop up the juices on his plate.

'So you need to force them onto the road,' Vido said. Miska nodded. 'Which means you need to keep them out of the sky.'

'Wow, wouldn't a hacker have been good for that?' Hradisky pointed out.

'Don't spoil my dinner, son,' Vido told him before turning to Mass. 'What was the name of that guy who used to work at the spaceport?'

Mass's face furrowed in concentration. 'Trimble?' he finally suggested.

'Trimble!' Vido scoffed. 'Trimble was a chick.' He turned to Miska. 'Sorry, a woman.' Miska held her hands up to indicate she didn't care. 'No. Customs guy, degenerate gambler. Used to turn a blind eye for Mickey's crew.'

'Jodor? A customs guy's not going to do us any good.'

'No, but I wonder if he knows anyone.' Vido turned Hradisky. 'See, this is how you hack people in this city.'

'Assuming you can bring enough influence to bear to prevent them taking whatever the cargo is out by shuttle, then what? What's to stop them taking it out by ship, or even submarine?' Teramoto asked. He hadn't looked impressed by Uncle V's 'hacking'.

'Yeah, that's trickier,' Uncle V admitted. 'It's a big old sea.'

'We know people at the docks, but it would mean dealing with … friends,' Mass said.

'You guys never say Mafia, do you?' Goodluck asked, smiling. 'We know who you are, you know.'

'Hey!' Mass said, offended.

'After I made you dinner?' Vido protested. Goodluck just laughed.

'Okay, I need people I can approach whose appetite for cash will outweigh their unwillingness to deal with strangers,' Miska told them.

'This would be easier if—' Mass started.

'Not going to happen,' Miska cut him off. 'We need eyes on the facility at all times, which means hard times on a cold observation post,' Miska said. 'That's Kaneda, Enchi, Teramoto and Hradisky on rotation.'

'What?' Hradisky protested. 'Why don't these old fucks—'

'Because rank has its privileges,' Mass said. 'Now stop fucking whining and don't call me an "old fuck" ever again.'

'And this old fuck' —Teramoto enunciated 'old' and 'fuck' very clearly— 'will be with you.' Hradisky lapsed into quiet. Miska noticed that Goodluck didn't look too happy. She guessed it was the prospect of the younger Comanchero being stuck out on the beach with the Milliners that he had worked so hard to antagonise.

'We're going to need gear, including crab drones. I want to get eyes on the dig. We also need guns, cutting gear, lock burners and some other bits and pieces of intrusion tech.' She really wished that she had access to the *Daughter*'s resources.

Mass and Vido looked at each other.

'We can do that,' Mass said. Vido nodded.

'Fine,' Miska said. 'That means you and Goodluck get the cars,' she told Torricone.

Torricone looked over at Goodluck, who nodded.

'What do you want?' Goodluck asked. She noticed that Hradisky had perked up.

'Two cars, fast but not delicate, not sports cars.'

'Muscle cars?' Goodluck asked, trying unsuccessfully to mask his eagerness.

'Sure, as well as something with a bit of grunt to it, a bit of weight.'

'Truck?' Torricone asked.

'Pickup,' Miska suggested.

'Just one?' Goodluck asked.

'Two of each,' she said. 'Redundancies.'

'Bikes?' Teramoto asked. 'You've got some of the best tunnel racers out of Shirow City here.'

'Bit delicate in a hijacking,' Mass pointed out.

'When was the last time you jacked something, old man?'

Enchi demanded. Teramoto put a hand on the young Milliner's shoulder. Mass turned to fix Enchi with a glare.

'Call me old man once more,' he told him.

'Get some bikes,' Miska said. 'Four.' It was all but a whim. She was pretty much making this up as she went along. She was aware of Torricone looking at her but she avoided his eyes. Instead she was watching Kaneda. The handsome young gang member was normally pretty quiet but he had become almost silent since they had reached Verona City. Miska had almost forgotten he was with them. She noticed that Goodluck was watching Kaneda as well.

'Can you steal bikes?' Enchi asked Torricone with more than a little sarcasm in his voice.

'Yeah, I used to be a kid too,' Torricone said without taking his eyes off Miska. It took Miska a moment to realise that the ringing noise she could hear was somebody on the apartment's buzzer. They had set up the table so they could see the screen for the intercom. All of them looked up at it.

'Shit,' Mass said. 'That's Don Teduzzi.'

CHAPTER 10

'Okay, you guys get out of sight,' Miska told Mass and Vido.

'Who's doing the talking?' Vido asked.

'I am,' Miska told him.

'Seriously?' Vido and Torricone said at the same time. Miska took a moment to glare at them both. 'Now!' she snapped at Vido and Mass. Both of them headed up the stairs to the garage's office. 'Everyone else on best behaviour, I want gang ink hidden, okay?' She noticed that Torricone had faded into the background. Everyone else kept eating, though most of them were doing so one-handed, gauss pistols held under the table.

Miska walked towards the armoured concertina door. She used her neuralware to access the outside security lens. Teduzzi, the street boss who did the collections for the Mafia in this neighbourhood, had three other people with him. They carried gauss carbines and looked for all the world like military contractors. She had seen the type before. Probably high-end skillsofts, possibly some virtual paramilitary training, boosted reflexes and muscles. It wasn't a substitute for actual training and experience but they at least looked capable. There was an SUV parked on the street. It looked like a civilian version of a military vehicle and Miska suspected it was armoured. The Mafia didn't seem to be taking any risks in this part of town. They looked like they were on patrol in a demilitarised zone. She hadn't realised from Hector's description that the gang war was quite that bad. No wonder he and his family had gone snowboarding.

With a thought Miska started the door cranking up. The only woman with Teduzzi was immediately under the door and into the garage, carbine up at the ready, scanning the area. The other three let the concertinaed door reveal them. Miska reckoned that Don Teduzzi was in his mid-forties. She suspected he had been a good-looking guy in his younger years but he had let himself go just a little. His slicked-back, possibly dyed, hair was starting to recede and his belly flopped over his belt. His suit was just a little too loud and he wore just a bit too much gold for Miska's taste.

'Whoa!' Miska said. 'What's with all the firepower?'

Teduzzi cocked his head to one side.

'Sirius?' he asked. Miska was impressed despite herself.

'Good ear,' she told him.

'You here for all our cattle?' he asked. Miska just smiled. She'd heard all the *Siriusians are cow-fuckers* jokes a long time ago. 'And you are?'

'Angela,' Miska told him.

'Got any ID?' He walked over to the manual button for the garage and pressed it. The armoured door started to drop behind him. Miska could practically feel the tension from the remaining five of her convict legion sat at the table behind her.

'You cops?' she asked.

'Where's Hector?'

'Snowboarding in New Erebus,' Miska said. 'He said we could use the place. And who are you?'

'Everybody calls me Teddy, I'm a friend of Hector's.'

'You seem a bit heavily armed for a social visit,' Miska pointed out.

'The natives are restless,' he said examining a laser torch before putting it down and turning to look at Miska. 'What are you doing here?'

'I told you, Hector said—'

'That doesn't answer my question.'

Miska regarded him for a moment or two and then put her hands on her hips.

'You're right, it doesn't,' she admitted. 'What I am in fact doing is minding my own business and fielding some pretty fucking rude questions from Teddy-I-don't-know-who-the-fuck.'

The two gunmen with him exchanged a glance. Teddy just nodded.

'Well, let's start off with the fact that I'm not someone you can talk to like that,' he said.

'No, let's start off with who the fuck are you, and what the fuck do you want?' *Easy*, she told herself, *this guy is coming across as someone with a fragile ego*. She knew she was pushing him too hard but one of the problems with the lower echelon criminal was that they were made to feel powerless so often that they had to take it out on someone.

'Maybe watch the mouth, huh?' he suggested, eyes narrowing. 'My friend Hector pays off a business arrangement early …'

'You mean the protection money you extort out of him.' Miska was practically internally screaming at herself to stop but this guy was really rubbing her up the wrong way.

'Next I hear he's gone on holiday and there's some people up to no good in his garage.'

'Up to no good?' Goodluck asked. 'We're eating dinner.' Teduzzi looked around Miska at the five Bastards sat at the table as if just noticing them for the first time. Whether the ink was on display or not he must have known what they were.

'I see. So you rented the garage to eat dinner,' he said.

'Experimental dining,' Hradisky said from behind her. Even Enchi laughed.

'Look, pal,' Miska said. 'Hector's paid up. Who and what we are is none of your business. Leave us in peace and we'll soon be on our merry way.'

He sniffed the air.

'Smells good,' he said. 'I guess you were about to invite me to sit down and have a bite.'

'We really weren't,' Miska told him but he walked past her and helped himself to food and wine.

'See, it's obvious what you are, and therein lies my problem. You come around here, pull a job, maybe it upsets some of our friends. Even if you don't, it's rude to show up in somebody's town and not announce yourself, not pay your dues.'

Well at least he's finally got round to the shakedown, Miska thought.

'I thought this was the Disciples' territory,' Teramoto said. Miska felt the two gunmen and the gunwoman tense up behind her. Even Miska raised an eyebrow. More to the point, she was trying to work out Teramoto's angle in antagonising Teduzzi. Teduzzi looked the Yakuza lieutenant dead in the eyes.

'You were mistaken,' the street boss told Teramoto. Teramoto held the other man's stare and Teduzzi looked away first.

Tch, boys, Miska thought.

'Okay, this is really boring; you seem busy and important, well, self-important. Can we get to the point?' Miska asked.

'This is really good *parmigiana*,' he told her.

'Thank you,' Miska said slowly.

Teduzzi was shaking his head. 'You didn't cook this,' he told her.

'Okay,' she said, slowly again, wondering where this was going.

'You're not Italian.' He pointed at the *parmigiana*. 'An Italian cooked this, and see, we've all got our own recipes, and I've tasted this before.'

'I'm Italian,' Goodluck told him. 'Half. The other half is Haitian.' Teduzzi looked Goodluck over in a way that suggested the Comanchero had somehow insulted him.

'I don't think so, my friend. Now why don't you tell me what you're really doing here?' His voice was full of menace. 'And I won't ask again.' Miska didn't say anything. 'Well?' he demanded.

'I was embracing the "won't ask again" part of your statement,' Miska told him.

'Draw down on these motherfuckers,' Teduzzi told his people. Carbines started to move to shoulders but it was what Miska and the others had been waiting for. Miska fast-drew her SIG, levelling it at the gunwoman before she could bring her carbine to bear. She was only peripherally aware of just how fast Teramoto was. He was on his feet, a SIG in each hand, moving sideways to cover the two gunmen. Kaneda, and finally Enchi, were doing the same thing. Torricone advanced out of the shadows, his gauss pistol levelled at one of the gunmen.

Hradisky, also surprisingly fast, had his SIG at Teduzzi's head. Goodluck just kept eating.

'Are you out of your fucking mind?' Teduzzi demanded and took another sip of wine. 'Pulling a gun on me in this town?'

'Yeah, we thought we'd just stand still and let you kill us out of respect,' Hradisky spat and slapped the wine out of a furious Teduzzi's hands.

'Kill these motherfuckers!' Teduzzi snapped.

'Erm ... boss,' one of the gunmen said.

'Reality not your boss's friend?' Miska asked. 'I've an idea. Why don't you all put your guns down and we' —she raised her voice— 'who very clearly have the drop on you, won't kill you all. Okay?'

'It sounds like the starting point to a negotiation to me,' the gunman said.

'You seem reasonable, maybe you should be in charge?' Miska suggested. She couldn't shake the feeling that the gunman agreed with the suggestion, at least at this moment.

'I gave you a fucking order!' Teduzzi screamed. Through the feed from Hradisky's contact lens, Miska could see the drool hanging off Teduzzi's lip. It seemed he was used to getting his way.

'You know your order is to commit suicide in a really point-less way, right?' Miska pointed out to the gunmen and woman.

'No wonder they're getting their ass handed to them by the Disciples,' Torricone said. Through the window showing the lens feed from Hradisky she saw Teduzzi turn to look at Torricone again.

'She's Sirius but you, you're Verona born and bred,' the street boss said. Miska felt her heart sink. 'I know you?' Torricone didn't answer. 'Joking apart, you've gotta know better than to draw down on guys like us in this town.'

'We're really slow learners,' Miska told him, thinking back to what her dad had told her before they had come here.

'You bet you are, getting yourself into a stand-off like this.'

'You're not in a fucking stand-off!' Enchi shouted in heavily accented English. 'We're pointing guns at you!'

'All we're really trying to do is keep your people alive. You we're not so worried about,' Miska added. Cursing inwardly. This guy was too stupid to live. He was too used to being king of the city. With this level of entitlement he was clearly a made man and he was right. She didn't want to start killing them.

'Hello, Teddy.'

Miska's heart sank. Through Goodluck's lens footage she saw Vido standing at the top of the stairs. Mass was halfway down them looking at 'Teddy'. This was pretty much the last situation she wanted to be in. Vido and Mass making contact with their old friends. Teduzzi smiled. He pointed at the food.

'It was the *parmigiana*, I knew I recognised it.'

'Seriously? You guys can recognise each other by your recipes?' Miska asked.

'It's like a fingerprint,' Teduzzi told her. 'It was your dad's recipe, right?' he asked Vido.

'Passed down,' Vido told him. It was difficult to tell through the grainy lens footage but Vido didn't look too happy to see Teduzzi. 'There a need for everyone to be pointing guns?'

'Not at all. You have this lot put theirs down, we can get them on their knees and decide what the appropriate action is,' Teduzzi said.

'Seriously, can I shoot this fucking moron?' Hradisky asked.

Miska gave the question some serious thought. Then she gave it some more thought.

'Angela?' Vido said. Miska was pleased that he'd heard that.

'No,' she relented. 'Well, not yet anyway. Vido, don't you horribly outrank these people? I mean, this is Vido Cofino. You guys have heard the name Cofino, right?'

'Oh Jesus Christ,' one of the gunmen said. None of them looked happy.

'I heard you got into a spot of trouble,' Teduzzi said. 'Something about you getting kidnapped?'

'It's complicated,' Vido said.

'Maybe you'd better explain it to me,' Teduzzi told him.

Miska made sure that the gunwoman she had drawn down on was covered and then turned around to face the conversation.

'There's some question over your loyalties,' Teduzzi continued.

Vido actually flinched. He did a good job of covering his anger, however. Mass, less so.

'Who the fuck do you think you're talking to? You always were a little punk, Teddy!'

'Go fuck yourself, Mass,' Teddy told the button man.

'Wow,' Miska said. It was now clear to her that Teduzzi wanted to die. Mass was down the stairs, hooked fishing knife in hand. 'Hold on,' Miska told him. He didn't listen. He was going to gut Teduzzi. The psychopath that Mass managed to keep so well hidden was written all over his face.

'Mass,' Vido said and the button man stopped, though Miska noticed he was breathing funny. 'Maybe this is something I should take up with my cousin,' Vido said to Teduzzi. Vido was a distant cousin to Antonio 'Old Man' Cofino, the head of the Cofino family, the prince of New Verona.

'Things have changed while you've been working for someone else,' Teduzzi said. Mass bristled.

'How is my cousin?' Vido asked.

'He's not well,' Teduzzi said. 'He's been spending more time with his family, leaving the business to younger guys.'

Miska saw Vido's eyes narrow as Teduzzi said 'guys'.

'Blanca?' Mass asked. Vido held a hand up to forestall the question but it was too late.

'What about her?' Teduzzi replied.

'She step up?' Mass asked. Teduzzi just stared at him, a sneer on his face that made Miska want to shoot him. 'I asked you a fucking question, you little punk.' Teduzzi still didn't answer.

Hradisky pistol-whipped him so hard it knocked him off his chair and onto all fours, spitting out blood and teeth onto the concrete floor.

'Whoa!' Mass said. 'You can't fucking do that!' Hradisky shrugged and stepped back. Mass looked up at Vido, who nodded. The button man yanked Teduzzi to his feet.

'Who's running the family, you little fuck?' he demanded, shaking Teduzzi. The gunmen and woman looked like they would rather be anywhere else but where they were. Teduzzi was quiet until Mass pressed the hooked fishing knife a little too hard into the street captain's groin.

'Dominic! Dominic's running the family!' he squealed. Mass looked up at Vido. Neither of them were happy.

'Okay,' Miska said. 'I've had enough of this. Get this asshole out of here.'

Mass started dragging Teduzzi towards the door.

'Mass,' Miska said as he passed her. The button man stopped and turned around, still holding on to Teduzzi. Miska hit the street boss in the throat. Not as hard as she wanted to.

'Really?' Mass demanded. Teduzzi's eyes went wide as he tried to draw breath in through his newly damaged windpipe. Miska turned to the three that had come with the street boss.

'When he can speak again, he's going to order you to come back here and try and kill us. Don't,' she told them, and then thought for a moment. 'In fact, you guys need a new boss, this one is a fucking idiot.' One of the men caught himself nodding. Mass helped Teduzzi through the door and the gunmen and woman backed out with as much dignity as they could manage.

Miska turned back to find everyone looking at her.

'You can't do that to people like him—' Mass started. Miska held up her hand.

'I find out you had anything to do with Teduzzi turning up and I'll trigger the N-bomb, understand me?' she told Vido. He had come down the steps.

'We wouldn't call Teddy,' Vido assured her.

'He always was an asshole,' Mass added.

'Is it me, or was he suicidal?' Goodluck asked.

'No, he's just very dumb,' Mass explained.

And entitled, Miska thought.

'We're compromised,' she said.

'Well, that was quick,' Torricone muttered. 'Have you ever considered being nice to people?'

'How was that my fault?' she demanded. Torricone just shrugged.

'We're out of here, personal gear only, we leave the rest and we are gone, *now*,' Miska told them.

'The meal,' Vido said. Miska just glared at him.

'We taking the pickups?' Hradisky asked hopefully.

'No, he's seen them. Tint the windows, lower the suspension

165

so it looks like they're carrying people and send them back. If anyone is watching hopefully they'll follow them.'

'What are we doing?' Teramoto asked.

I'm open to suggestions, Miska thought.

'Contingency one escape and evasion. We split into two groups. We go to a public place but keep a low profile until we've decided on another base. Understood?' They nodded. Splitting in two was going to be a nightmare. She would have to watch them through their lens feed. Even groups of four-to-five were too big, but a group of nine looked outright suspicious. She noticed Torricone shaking his head.

'What?' she groaned.

'This isn't a good neighbourhood for being a pedestrian,' he said.

'Have you actually got anything to contribute?' she asked. He was right but it had all happened too fast for them to sort out clean cars.

'We have to warn Hector.'

'Agreed,' she told him.

They were out on the street a couple of minutes later. Torricone was having a subvocal conversation with Hector. He didn't look as though he was enjoying it. They had developed contingency one during the rushed planning stages of this mission and Miska had stuck with the original groups. She had Torricone, Teramoto, Kaneda and Goodluck with her. Vido and Mass had gone with Hradisky and Enchi. The setup had been designed to mix experienced with less experienced and for both groups to have people who knew the city. It was also meant to split up the Comancheros and the Milliners. Too late, Miska realised that given the change in circumstances perhaps it wasn't the best idea to put Vido and Mass in the same group.

Dad was right, she decided miserably as they moved quickly down a steep canyon pathway littered with refuse behind some of the low tract housing, *this is a chickenshit operation.* She checked on the other team, enlarging the contact lens feed from Hradsiky, who was bringing up the rear of the group. They were following the curve of the street away from the garage, making their way back to Pueblo Town's main strip. Hradisky glanced up at something and Miska saw grainy footage of the foliage-enshrouded pyramid that was the atmosphere processor. She could make out the fast-moving angular shape of an assault shuttle against the monolithic building. Moments later she heard the shuttle's engines as it roared past overhead.

'Shit!' Mass swore over the open link. From his feed she could see the assault shuttle hovering over Hector's garage. Its cargo ramp was extended. Flight-capable Honey Badger combat exoskeletons were leaping out of the back of the shuttle into the night air, the engines on their flight fins burning brightly. Two pairs of the bulky power-armoured suits took off after the pickups. Four more dropped out of view but even from where they were Miska could hear breaching charges exploding, armoured glass breaking, doors being blown off their hinges as the garage was assaulted. All the combat exoskeletons had the Marshal Service's star painted on them. She assumed members of the Marshal's Special Operations Group would be piloting the Honey Badgers. She saw conventionally armoured members of the FBI's Hostage Rescue Team sliding down ropes flung out of the back of the assault shuttle onto the roof of the garage and into the surrounding streets.

'Jesus Christ,' Goodluck said.

'Keep moving,' Miska told him, pushing him ahead of her. Angrily he shook her off but kept going. Miska checked the footage from the other team. They were hustling, moving quickly away from the garage. Perhaps too quickly. They would draw attention to themselves. Enchi glanced back and in his lens feed Miska saw discs about the size of hubcaps drop out of the back of the shuttle.

'Rotor drones,' she told everyone over the group comms link. 'Vido, Mass, slow your group down, make it look casual.' She could see through Vido's feed that they were getting close to the blinking fluorescent lights of a dilapidated strip mall.

On Mass's feed the button man was continually glancing behind him. One thing all criminals had in common was that they hated the snoops in the sky that were surveillance drones.

'We're not going to make it,' Mass said. As he said this she saw from Enchi's feed that the Milliner had turned around and started walking back towards the garage, towards the drones.

'Enchi, what are you doing?' Miska subvocalised over a private link. Teramoto wasn't receiving the contact lens feed but he still turned and looked at Miska as if he knew something was wrong. There were two drones heading towards Enchi, their steel blue searchlights illuminating the Milliner, demanding to see ID. Enchi had fake ID, part of the package that Raff had provided for them, but instead of showing it he drew his SIG. The rotor drones both fired their belly mounted dart guns. Taser darts hit Enchi in the chest, hooked into the inertial armour hoodie he wore, and delivered their voltage. His armour provided a degree of insulation but he was still receiving some of the shock. He was screaming, tears blurring the lens, but he still managed to raise the gauss pistol. He fired the electromagnetically driven, thorn-like tungsten penetrators in two long, undisciplined bursts.

One of the rotor drones flipped in mid-air and tumbled to the ground. The other stayed in the air even though it was bouncing back from the impacts. Enchi staggered back but didn't go down. He raised the gauss pistol and fired another more controlled burst. Miska knew the smartlink would be telling him where to place his shots. This time the second rotor drone fell from the sky. Enchi turned to follow the rest of the group but he was suddenly in the centre of two more spotlights. Through the glare in Enchi's lens feed it took Miska a moment to work out what was going on. Then she saw the power-assisted armoured arms of the Honey Badger combat exoskeleton reach out for Enchi. He emptied the rest of the SIG's magazine into the marshal's power armour. All he did was create sparks and ricochets. Enchi was lifted up off the ground. Miska caught a glimpse of another Honey Badger covering his partner from the air.

'Shit,' Miska cursed quietly. This wasn't good, Enchi knew too much.

'Problem?' Torricone asked.

'They're going to have thermal sensors. Our clothes will mask our heat signature to a degree,' Miska said. 'But not enough.'

'There's a culvert going through the hill just ahead, that'll have to do,' Torricone told her. It was the closest thing she'd heard to good news all day.

'Drone,' Teramoto said behind her.

Enchi would have to wait.

'Wait until it's down, then head into the culvert,' Miska subvocalised over the group comms link so the drone's microphone wouldn't pick her up. She was already turning around, her smartgrip holster relinquishing its hold on her pistol. She was moving to the side, taser darts crackling through the air past her. She had the pistol in a two-handed grip, the crosshairs

169

in her IVD showing where the rounds would hit. She breathed out, squeezed, firing a three-round burst. The drone plummeted out of the sky. 'Go!' she hissed over the comms link. Kaneda, Teramoto and Goodluck followed Torricone.

Miska raced back up the narrow, rubbish-strewn gulley and found the wreckage of the drone. She peeked sideways into the net. She couldn't see its net representation. It was an isolated system. The drone was basically a ring of cameras and long-range microphones surrounding an impeller. There was a dart gun mounted beneath the drone, a receiver, and a tight beam comms laser on top. It had to be semi-autonomous, receiving instructions from a rigger or dumb AI expert system, presumably aboard the shuttle. She used her knife to quickly cut and prise the drone open. She took out a small electronics tool kit and attached two data clamps to exposed wires leading from the solid state CPU to the comms laser. The clamps were attached to a wireless transmitter. The system wasn't isolated any more. Miska could hear the back-mounted flight fins of the incoming combat exoskeletons. She turned and ran back down the gulley. She almost attacked Torricone as he grabbed her when she was running by and dragged her into the culvert. Outside, the Honey Badgers' spotlight stabbed down from the sky searching for them. Miska's eyes amplified the ambient light as she followed Torricone deeper in.

'Avoid the water and, er, the rats,' he told her. She was hopeful that the Honey Badgers wouldn't fit in the culvert. That didn't mean they couldn't fly over the hill and be waiting for them. It didn't mean they couldn't fire their belt-fed auto shotguns into the culvert. It didn't mean they couldn't send the conventionally armoured HRT members in after them. All of this was going through Miska's mind as they caught up with the others.

'Hold me,' Miska told Torricone. He grabbed her and she tranced in. There was no net where she stood in the void as her angry cartoon icon. That didn't matter. She reached out for the wireless transmitter she had attached to the rotor drone. Like a lot of the FBI web architecture it was designed to look as though it had come from the heyday of their foundation era. It looked like an art deco Frisbee. It was well protected. Miska went looking for a back door. She was pleased when she found one. She loaded one of her most annoying viruses through it and then sent it to the assault shuttle via the comms laser. The FBI were going to be chasing cartoon-shaped ghosts for a while. It wouldn't stop them looking the old-fashioned way with their eyes, but the drones, at least, were going to be worse than useless. She tranced out of the net.

'Did you faint?' Goodluck asked.

'Well?' Teramoto said.

'I've bought us some time,' she told them and then turned to Torricone. 'Where?' she asked.

'I know a place,' he told her.

171

CHAPTER 11

When they came out of the culvert on the other side of the hill Miska reconnected to Enchi's contact lens feed. He was in the back of the assault shuttle now. She was catching grainy glimpses of the orange and red sky as one of the Honey Badgers knelt on Enchi's back and he was smart-cuffed. She was less than pleased when she caught a glimpse of her sister strapped into one of the benches in the shuttle's cargo bay. *This could complicate things*, she thought. Angela was wearing combat gear but her eyes were closed, head hanging limp. Miska assumed that her sister was tranced in, probably due to the chaos Miska had wrought by hacking the rotor drone.

Sorry, Enchi, you were a pain in the ass but you didn't deserve this, and with a thought Miska sent the kill signal. The microscopic nanobomb went off in the young Bethlehem Milliner's brain and Enchi was still. Suddenly the shuttle banked sharply and Enchi slid limply across the deck. Miska caught the bright red flashes of laser light, then the flash of an explosion. Moments later she heard it. She glanced back over the hill to see a fireball rising above it. She checked the feed from Enchi's still transmitting contact lens. The shuttle was intact. She guessed that someone had just fired a surface-to-air missile at the craft.

'What the hell's going on?' Miska asked. She could hear gunfire echoing through Pueblo Town's canyons.

'It's the Disciples,' Torricone told her. Miska and the others were making their way through another narrow canyon street. It wasn't quite what she had expected from what she had thought of as a *barrio*. The housing was cheap, low quality, rammed together in a way that would make it easy to leap from roof to roof, but the houses looked well maintained. Most of them had gardens on the roof, growing tendril-like genetically modified vegetables.

'A street gang in a shooting war with the FBI?' she asked. They were coming up to a junction with the Cypress Road, the main drag that ran through Pueblo Town. She saw extensively customised low riders, SUVs and muscle cars roaring by. Many of the vehicles bore the stylised skull motif of the Disciples. Torricone stepped into an alley, turning his back to the road as the convoy passed.

Teramoto, Kaneda and Goodluck joined them. Miska wasn't sure if it was her dad's military training or criminal instincts, but she was gratified to see the other three keeping a watch all around them.

'It's our neighbourhood,' Torricone told her.

'Our?' she asked.

'I grew up around here,' he told her. 'Look, it's not as simple as gangs are just mindless thugs, or fledgling organised crime. They protect and police the neighbourhood. Sometimes badly, sometimes well. They're a surrogate family for some of the most desperate kids, and frankly they're one of the few job providers around here. I'm not trying to justify what they do, I'm just saying there's more to it than meets the eye.'

'So why are you trying to avoid them?' Teramoto asked.

'I'm not popular with them any more,' Torricone explained. Miska knew he had ended up on the *Hangman's Daughter* because he had killed a Disciple who had tried to make Torricone his bitch.

Miska saw an open-topped SUV with murals of Santa Muerte painted on the side of it. There was a raised throne-like seat in the back of the vehicle. A hugely muscled figure with a shaved head, his torso tattooed to look like a black skeleton, his head a blackened skull, sat on the throne cradling a staff of bone. Loudspeakers were broadcasting in English and Spanish, telling people to get off the street. Even Teramoto raised an eyebrow.

'Shit,' Torricone muttered and then turned away from the Cypress Road again.

'Who's that?' Kaneda asked. Miska wasn't sure if the surviving Milliner was frightened but it was one of the few things he'd said since they had landed on Barney Prime. He had been very subdued.

'That's King Skinny,' Torricone told them. It sounded like all hell was breaking loose on the other side of the hill.

'He didn't look skinny,' Goodluck pointed out.

'He almost starved to death as a kid ...' Torricone said. It sounded like he was going to say more but thought the better of it.

Miska glanced up the street again.

'I think we need to move,' she told them.

They were out on the Cypress Road now. The neighbourhood fitted her preconceptions of a *barrio* better. Crumbling tenements all but stacked one on top of the other running up the canyon walls. A number of the buildings were clearly fortified drug dens. She could see Disciple soldiers, openly wielding assault rifles, standing guard, most of them looking to the south where the sounds of gunfire and the occasional explosion were coming from.

'The police stopped coming here,' Torricone started. 'The gangs had a choice. Either scavenge from the corpse of the neighbourhood, or try and help it.'

'Makes good economic sense,' Teramoto said. Miska couldn't shake the feeling there were hypercorps that hadn't learned that lesson.

There was another convoy heading towards them. Four large sedans with an eight-wheeled armoured personnel carrier sandwiched in the middle, eight Honey Badgers in the air above them providing an escort.

'The local FBI,' Teramoto said. Miska magnified her vision. She could see FBI HRT stencilled on the combat exoskeletons. Then she put her head down. The FBI had other things to worry about than her group right now. The Disciples had probably saved them from arrest.

'Where are we going?' Goodluck asked.

'I've lost contact with Enchi,' Teramoto said. Miska could feel his eyes on her.

'A bar,' Torricone told them.

'The FBI would have shut down his comms as soon as they got him. Stop trying, they'll trace you,' Miska told Teramoto.

'Why a bar?' Goodluck asked Torricone. 'I'm not challenging you, man, just want to know what I'm walking into.'

'Are we going after him?' Teramoto asked. Miska glanced back at the Yakuza lieutenant. Kaneda was looking at her as well.

'He's not a priority,' she told them. Teramoto stared at her but said nothing.

They had come to another narrow alley that branched off the Cypress Road. The bar was a squat, rectangular, bunker-like building. Miska suspected that it had once been more colourfully decorated but that had been a long time ago. Torricone started walking purposefully towards the bar. Miska and the others followed.

'Because the Disciples don't drink here,' the car thief told Goodluck.

About twenty skull faces of various genders turned to look at them as they entered.

'Or didn't use to,' Torricone whispered just loud enough for the five of them to hear.

'Keep going,' Miska subvocalised. They would just make it worse if they backed down now. For all the Disciples might have had their positive side, Miska had always found that gang bangers were a little like wild dogs. If you ran, they would chase. They followed Torricone in. The inside of the bar was dark, illuminated by a mix of neon and ultraviolet light. There was a shrine to Santa Muerte, complete with an intricately painted plastic skeleton in a frayed black lace dress nestled among coffin-shaped bottles of spirits.

Even with his tattoos the barman was the fattest looking skeleton that Miska had ever seen. He had a prosthetic lower left arm. His fingers were bladed hooks.

'You sure you're in the right place?' he asked them. Everyone was staring at them. About the one thing the place had going for it was that it was nearly empty. Miska guessed these were the Disciples too lazy to go to the gunfight. The saloon area was a rough L-shape. Teramoto and Kaneda took a seat at a table at the bottom of the L. It was furthest from the door but it allowed them to get their backs to the wall. It was a tactical nightmare: one way in, one way out. 'I think you're lost.'

Torricone ordered five beers and five tequilas. The barman just stared at him.

'I know you, *ese*?' he asked.

'I don't think so,' Torricone said. Miska and Goodluck were flanking the car thief, looking round at the other Disciples, all of whom were still staring at them. She felt like she was at a Halloween party, or in some bizarre horror sense-game. The barman crossed his arms. Miska was impressed he hadn't sliced open his own expansive gut with his finger blades.

'Look, I get it, we walked into the wrong bar. We just want a drink and then we'll be on our own way. We tip well,' she told him.

'You hiding from something?' a woman asked. She looked to be the opposite of the barman, so emaciated her skeleton tattoos looked real. She was only wearing a cropped top and cut-offs. Miska could make out her ribs under the tattooed bones.

'It's a little hot out on the street,' Goodluck said.

'That's what happens when people come up here uninvited,' the woman told him.

'See, you're from off-world,' the barman said, looking at Miska, and then pointed at Torricone. 'But I know I know you, *mano*.'

It could be difficult to tell with Torricone but Miska was pretty sure that he was scared right now.

'Look, do you want us to leave, or are you going to get us a drink?' Miska asked. The barman stared at Torricone a bit longer.

177

'I know I know you …' he said again and then started to get their drinks. Miska sent the bar enough money to appear generous but not enough to cause further suspicion. They headed round the corner but the three of them sat at a different table to Teramoto and Kaneda. If shit went down then Miska didn't want to make them easy targets for the Disciples.

'What are we doing in here?' Teramoto asked over the shared comms link.

'I'm sorry,' Torricone said. 'Things have changed.'

'It's done, we move on,' Miska subvocalised over the link. 'Clearly we can't stay here. Any idea where else we can go?' Torricone didn't answer. He seemed to be wrestling with something.

'No offence, dude,' Goodluck said over the link. 'But you don't seem to have many friends around here.'

'I burned a lot of bridges,' Torricone told them. Miska suspected that the only thing that was keeping them safe was the morphic compound that had changed Torricone's facial features a little. The problem was that the compound was designed to fool image recognition software. People recognised other people in part because of their mannerisms, body language, and their voice. They were very precariously safe, as in off the streets, until someone in here worked out who Torricone was. Miska decided they would stay here for the length of time it took to drink their drinks and review their situation, and then they were off, even if that meant sleeping rough. 'There may be one other place, but it's difficult, let me think on it.'

Miska nodded. She checked the contact lens feeds from the others. Enchi's was dark. Hradisky, Mass and Vido were sat in an automat. Mass was watching their back while Vido looked to be deep in a subvocal comms conversation. Hradisky was looking out through the glass frontage of the automat. Through the Comanchero's eyes she could see the firefight. Tracers rising into the sky towards the assault shuttle. Return fire from the circling Honey Badgers. It looked like a warzone.

'Jesus Christ,' she muttered. The barman brought their drinks over, looked suspiciously at Torricone, and then left again.

'How did they find us?' Teramoto asked.

'Teduzzi dropped a dime on us,' Goodluck said but Torricone was shaking his head.

'The mob own the cops but they don't rat to the FBI,' Torricone told them.

'Who then?' Miska asked. 'Hector?'

'No, he wouldn't do that, he's solid,' Torricone said. He seemed sure.

'Lira or Tina?' Goodluck asked. Torricone didn't say anything.

'Nothing we can do about it now,' Miska said.

'Why an assault shuttle?' Goodluck asked. Miska was coming to the conclusion that the Comanchero OG had a clever head on his shoulders.

Torricone looked a little confused.

'If it was local assets then they would have come in gunships, power armour, or in ground vehicles, like the convoy we saw,' Teramoto said. 'An assault shuttle means a ship.'

It had been bothering Miska as well. The presence of her sister meant that the *Teten* had followed them here. It was the only explanation for the Marshals and the Feds responding so quickly to Teduzzi's tip. Only Raff, presumably his superiors, and people on board the *Hangman's Daughter* had known they were coming to Barney Prime. Miska was betting that not too many of Raff's superiors knew about Operation Lee Marvin because it was so deniable. Nobody wanted what she had done being traced back to them. That said, it was starting to look like she had a leak somewhere. Just for a moment she wondered if her dad had sided with Angela. Her sister had always been the favourite, the good daughter, but Miska knew this was paranoia, held-over sibling rivalry, and a symptom of just how pissed off she was with her dad. Whatever his faults were he would never play his two girls off against each other, particularly not when the stakes were so high.

'Who's Blanca Cofino?' Miska asked Torricone.

'Antonio's niece. When I left she was next in line for the throne.'

'Dominic Cofino?' Teramoto asked. Miska looked over at where he was sat with Kaneda. The young Milliner was in the corner, wedged in next to the Yakuza lieutenant. There was something about Kaneda's body language but Miska didn't have the time to puzzle it out now.

'I know the name,' Torricone said. 'You in contact with Mass and Uncle V?' Miska nodded. 'Ask them,' Torricone suggested. Miska was about to do that when the skeletal woman who had spoken earlier approached their table.

'Push your hood down,' the woman told Torricone. He looked up at her.

'What?' he asked. She moved around until she was stood next to him, far too close. It was clearly meant to intimidate.

'You fucking heard me,' she spat, drool flecking her chin. Miska was pretty sure she was on something.

'Hey,' Goodluck said. 'We just want to have a drink and then we'll be on our way.'

'See, I think you've got a crown of thorns tattooed round your skull,' she said, pressing a finger down on his hood. Torricone moved his head irritably. 'Haven't you, T?' she asked.

'Lady, please, I just want to drink my drink and be on my way,' he told her. She opened her mouth to say something. There was a sickening crunching noise. The point of a bloody, folded steel blade exploded out of her mouth, scraping against her teeth. She spat blood all over Torricone's face and then dropped to the floor, the sword still sticking out of her skull. Teramoto was standing behind her, he'd already released his grip on the sword and was drawing both his SIGs. Miska was moving as well, drawing her own gauss pistol with her right hand, another magazine for it with her left. Torricone and Goodluck were moments behind her. To her boosted reflexes it looked as though they were moving in slow motion. She was aware of Kaneda having moved forward, leaping the bar, pistol in hand. She knew she shouldn't have kept her back to the Disciples but someone at the table had needed to.

She spun to face the gangbangers. Needless to say they were all going for weapons. They too looked as though they were moving in slow motion. Some of them were moving in faster slow motion than others, however. Miska brought the gauss pistol up, crossing her wrists over to provide more support. She felt calm. Her reflexes gave her the most fleeting of microseconds to assess the situation. It was more than enough. She knew who was fastest among the Disciples, who was going to get shot first.

Astonishingly Teramoto fired before her. The hypersonic screams of the bursts from the gauss pistol in each hand filled the air. More astonishingly, he was accurate. Disciples went down. Moving sideways, Miska was firing as well. Controlled three-round bursts. The crosshairs superimposed on the torso of those stripped to the waist. If they wore clothes she assumed that they were armoured and went for the more difficult head-shots. She killed the fastest first and worked her way down.

By moving as far as she could to one side, she had cleared enough space for Torricone and Goodluck to fire as well. She was aware of Kaneda firing long, undisciplined bursts from behind the bar. She saw the fat barman, some kind of fancy shotgun in hand, dance backwards as red pinpricks appeared across his torso.

The ammunition counter in her IVD told her that her pistol was empty. She ejected the magazine, letting it fall to the ground, sliding the spare into the SIG's pistol grip with her left hand and immediately starting to fire again. Her left hand grabbed another vacuum-packed magazine of caseless penetrators from the pouch on her belt but all of the Disciples were down. It was only then she realised that the gang bangers hadn't got off a shot. Miska and her Bastards had been too fast. Their violence too intense. They hadn't hesitated. It seemed that all the virtual training was starting to pay off.

'Shit!' Torricone cried. He seemed to have overcome his pacifist tendencies at last. Wide-eyed, he was holding both his hands to his head. He still had his gun in his right hand. He was clearly appalled at what they had done. Goodluck just looked sad. Kaneda was still pointing his gun at the barman, now out of sight on the other side of the bar. Only Teramoto looked completely calm, almost relaxed.

'Woo!' she cried. 'That was intense.' Nobody said anything, though there was some groaning from the few wounded Disciples among the pile of corpses. 'Reload,' she told them. Teramoto and Goodluck reloaded their pistols, the Yakuza lieutenant doing so with practised ease. 'Kaneda!' Miska shouted. Her voice shook him out of his paralysis and he reloaded his pistol.

'Fuck!' Torricone screamed.

'Keep it together!' Miska snapped at him. He swung around to look at her.

'I fucking live here!' he screamed at her.

'Not any more,' she told him softly. He stared at her.

'The wounded,' Teramoto said. Torricone swung around to face him.

'Leave them,' he ordered. Teramoto looked past Torricone to Miska.

'Get a grip and reload your sidearm, now,' Miska told the car thief. For a minute he looked as though he was about to argue but then he did as he was bid, all the while staring at Miska. 'Now we need to get out of here. I know you had misgivings but you've got to take us wherever you were thinking of, wherever it was that you didn't want to take us,' Miska told him as she reached down to pick up the empty magazine she had dropped. Torricone continued staring at her.

'So you can kill them too?' he demanded.

'Maybe,' Teramoto said as he walked over to the woman he had killed with his *shinobigatana* and removed the short, straight-edged sword from the emaciated woman's head. 'If you walk us into another situation like this.'

Torricone turned on the Yakuza lieutenant.

'Torricone!' Miska snapped. 'I'm not going to tell you again.' He turned back to face her and then spun and walked out of the bar, trying to avoid the blood that was slowly covering the floor.

'Bro!' Miska said turning to Teramoto. 'Where'd you learn to gunfight?' Her father certainly hadn't taught him that. Like most military personal, Gunnery Sergeant Corbin held two-pistol shooting in disdain, despite smartlink technology. Teramoto merely cleaned off his blade and re-sheathed it in the concealed scabbard that ran down the back of his white suit. He did, however, have the slightest smile on his face.

They were using the network of alleys that ran between the larger streets. Miska could see into the houses that lined the alleys. She saw people bathing in the glow of the moving images on their wall screens or holographic projectors. She saw tranced-in sense junkies, zoned-out regular junkies and among it all, worried families trying to go about their business to the seemingly ambient soundtrack of gunfire.

Miska checked the feed from Hradisky, Mass and Vido's contact lenses. She did not like what she saw. It looked like they were sat in the back of a police APC. She opened a comms link to Uncle V.

'What the fuck?' she demanded.

'It's not what it looks like,' he subvocalised back. 'They're friends.'

Deeper and deeper, she thought. Things were becoming more like her dad had predicted as they moved further from the mission objective. She heard the sound of harsh amplified music over engines. Torricone motioned for them to take cover as several vehicles sped past the head of the narrow alley they were in. Disciples. She wondered if they knew about the bodies they had left on the floor of the bar yet.

'Where are you going?' Miska asked Vido. He hesitated.

'I'm not sure,' he said. 'Things are complicated. I'm not trying to be difficult, so please don't blow my head up, but the Feds have roadblocks all over Pueblo Town. Can we talk again when we've managed to get out of here?' Miska was less than happy but she severed the comms link and didn't trigger the N-bombs. Torricone was striding away from them now. He no longer seemed to care about stealth. Miska and the others followed.

Miska certainly hadn't been expecting a church. It was nestled away at the end of a cul-de-sac lined with run-down apartment buildings and surrounded by the canyon cliffs, all in the shadow of the atmosphere processor. The church itself was strangely angular, as though someone hadn't followed the instructions when putting together the modular parts of a prefabricated building.

Miska didn't like it. This entire planet seemed to be made of dead ends. As this thought struck her she realised that three of the lens feeds in her IVD had gone black. Hradisky, Mass and Uncle Vido's.

They were just about at the door of the church. Miska was about to open a comms link to Uncle Vido and demand to know what was going on when the front door opened. The woman standing in the doorway wore jeans, and a black shirt with a white clerical collar. She looked part African American and part Hispanic. She was tall, statuesquely built, handsome, perhaps in her mid-forties, with long black hair so curly it was almost in ringlets cascading down her back – and she looked very, very angry.

'Hi Mom,' Torricone said.

CHAPTER 12

Miska turned to look at Torricone and then back up at the statuesque woman with a face like thunder.

'By mom you mean mother, right? It's a Catholic thing?' Miska asked. Torricone's mom turned to look at her. Miska felt like those brown eyes were burrowing into her skull.

'No,' Torricone said.

Oh shit! Miska thought. She pretty much had a void where some women had maternal instincts but she was reasonably sure that mothers took a dim view of people implanting tiny explosives in their children's skulls and enslaving them. The others didn't seem to quite know where to look. Even Teramoto appeared uncomfortable. Everyone was uncomfortable except for Goodluck, who was staring at Torricone's mum.

'Hello, Mrs Torricone ...' Miska started offering a hand, which was ignored.

'It's Mother,' Torricone said.

'I know she's your mom,' Miska said.

'No, that's the way you address a female priest,' he explained.

'Weird.' Goodluck breathed the word.

'You've brought trouble to my house?' Torricone's mum's voice was little more than a low growl. Goodluck shivered. Torricone's mum produced a shotgun from behind the door but didn't point it at anyone. Teramoto and Kaneda tensed up, hands moving towards pistols. Miska held up her hand and they stopped. Mrs Torricone leaned out, checked all around.

'That noise over by Fourth Street your doing?' she asked, not looking at any of them.

'Yes,' Torricone said. Absurdly, Miska felt a momentary flush of guilt. It wasn't something she was used to. She put it down to some kind of residual response to matriarchal authority.

'Get in, go through the church into the rectory. I'll meet you in the kitchen.' As she said this the door to a freestanding garage next to the oddly shaped church opened, and a four-wheel-drive minibus drove out on autopilot.

'I need to worry about that?' Miska asked, pointing at the minibus. Torricone's mum ignored her, watching the street until the other four had walked past. Finally it was just the two women left.

'You coming in?' Torricone's mum asked. 'Because I'm closing the door one way or another.'

Miska stared at the other woman for a moment or two. Something about her reminded Miska of Angela. Finally she walked past and into the gloom of the church.

The kitchen looked as if it had been furnished from craft shops and second hand emporiums by someone with a degree of taste but not a lot of money. It had a colourful, comfortable, lived-in feel to it. Miska, Teramoto, Kaneda and Goodluck were all sitting at a brightly painted table made of some kind of fibrous

187

plant material. Torricone was perched on the windowsill, leaning against the glass that looked out over a garden. A mix of lawn, flowerbeds and vegetable patches, the garden sloped steeply down towards a small copse of trees with a dirt track running through it. Miska saw the lights of the minibus making its way along the dirt track, stopping among the trees. The minibus's lights went dark.

Clever, Miska thought. Torricone's mum had some kind of escape route set up.

Miska glanced at Torricone. He had a guilty expression on his face, as though his mum had just caught him on the net inside his first virtual porn palace.

'What's your mom's name?' Goodluck asked. There was something strange in his voice.

'Denise,' Torricone said. The temperature seemed to lower as Denise walked into the room.

'Would anybody like some coffee?' she asked. There were muttered assents. Miska nodded. Denise switched on the coffee machine and then slammed Miska's head down on the table, one arm holding her there. For a Roman Catholic priestess she was pretty strong, Miska decided. Then she felt the barrel of a gauss kiss attached to the end of an absurdly large slugthrower pistol against the side of her head.

Chairs scraped against a regolith floor as Teramoto and Kaneda leapt to their feet, drawing down on Denise. Torricone suddenly had his pistol out, levelled at Teramoto. The Yakuza lieutenant shifted the aim of one of his pistols so he was covering Torricone as well. The car thief tensed but he didn't fire.

'Stop pointing your guns at my mom,' Torricone said through gritted teeth.

'Tell her to put her gun down,' Teramoto said evenly. 'You're outgunned and you know it.'

Goodluck whistled, drawing attention to himself. He had his gauss pistol levelled at Kaneda.

'Got your back,' the Comanchero OG told Torricone. Miska was concentrating on not getting shot. She didn't quite understand Goodluck's play. If Torricone's mum shot her then everyone was dead, at least as far as her Bastards knew.

'Thanks, man,' Torricone said. Miska wasn't sure but she suspected that Torricone was a little confused by Goodluck's actions as well.

'Dude, your mom is so hot,' Goodluck whispered. It was pretty much the last thing Miska had expected to hear.

'I'm standing right here,' Denise pointed out.

'What the fuck?' Torricone demanded, glaring at Goodluck.

'I'm just saying,' Goodluck said defensively.

'You guys are always thinking with—' Miska started but Denise banged her head off the table. 'Ow!'

'Nobody needs to get shot here,' Denise told them. 'This young lady's just going to let my son go and then you can all go about your business.'

'You must know it's not that simple,' Miska managed, her face squished against the table.

'Sequestration? Implanted virus?' Denise asked. She didn't sound happy.

'I'm not a monster!' Miska protested and then gave it some thought. 'Well I am, but not that kind of monster.'

'N-bomb?'

Miska tried to nod but it just made the other woman hold her down against the table more tightly.

'With a kill switch,' Miska added. 'Something happens to me, they all die.'

Denise gave this some thought but didn't let Miska up.

'Doesn't sound like any of them stand much of a chance,' she finally said.

'Always better than none. N-bombs, implanted viruses, some skills. You seem very well informed for a priestess.' Then something occurred to her. 'Say, are you single? My dad's single. I mean he's dead and everything but you wouldn't mind a virtual relationship, right? After all it's the—' Denise banged her head off the table again. 'Ow! Seriously, that hurts. I'm being pretty patient here because you're Torricone's mom but you're no match for me, understand?'

'I wouldn't bet on that,' Torricone muttered.

'Disable the N-bomb,' Denise told her.

'Not going to happen,' Miska said. 'And bang my head off the table once more and I'll beat you down in front of your kid here, understand me?'

'Mom,' Torricone said.

'You like being a slave boy?' Denise demanded.

'Yeah, I can't imagine where he would get a taste for matriarchal oppression from,' Teramoto said. He still had his SIGs levelled at Torricone and Denise. They never wavered.

'I could handle some of that oppression,' Goodluck said.

'I'm still in the room,' Denise pointed out.

'Seriously, *mano*!' Torricone snapped.

Miska felt herself being frisked. Her pistol and knife were put on the counter top. Denise put her own pistol down as well and then let go of Miska. Miska bounced to her feet and turned to face Torricone's mum.

'Who the fu—!' she started. It was what Denise had been

waiting for. The kick was fast and powerful enough to put a horse to shame. Denise's foot caught Miska just under the ribcage, lifting her off her feet. She flew through the window, smashing through the glass and landing on the lawn, tumbling a little way down the hill.

Again!

Miska rolled to her feet.

'Motherfucker!' she spat when her implanted self-repair systems had reflated her diaphragm enough for her to talk again. Denise Torricone had just stepped out of the kitchen's back door.

'So I can't kill you,' Denise said. 'Let's try beating you until you let him go.'

'Bring it!' Miska snapped. The four guys had stopped pointing guns at each other and were all peering through the back window at the two women as Denise closed with Miska.

'My mom totally kicked your ass,' Torricone said from where he sat on the toilet in the small shower room. It might have been the happiest she had ever heard him, a badly bruised Miska decided as she tended to her wounds with the church's first aid kit.

'I would have had her if you hadn't stopped the fight,' Miska groused as she held a swellpatch against one of the more extensively bruised parts of her face.

'Sure,' Torricone said.

'Well you've still got a bomb in your head,' she muttered and then turned to look at him. 'You could have stopped that at any time right?'

Torricone raised an eyebrow.

'I don't know if you've noticed, but the women in my life don't tend to listen to a word I say.'

Miska turned back towards the mirror.

'I'm not a woman in your life, just your boss.' Then she took her T-shirt off and examined the roughly foot-sized bruise under her ribs, wincing. Torricone was watching her in the mirror.

'Where'd your mom learn to fight?' she asked. 'She with the Spanish Inquisition or something?'

'Rough neighbourhood,' he told her. Miska turned on him.

'Oh bullshit, she's ex-special forces of some kind,' she snapped.

'Sure you're not just pissed off about getting your ass handed to you by a barrio girl?' he asked, grinning. Miska glared at him, though it was true her pride had taken almost as much of a beating as her body.

'She's used to sorting out any problems herself. You threatened her family and then put her in a situation where there was nothing she could do about it. What'd you expect?' Torricone asked.

Miska turned to glare at him.

'I didn't expect to meet your fucking mother in the first place,' she told him. 'It's not a common feature of black ops.'

'Hey,' he said, 'that ain't right. She's granted us sanctuary. Just be thankful she listened to me, stopped when she did.'

Miska let that sink in.

'Why did you tell her to stop?' she asked more softly.

'I don't want to see anyone get hurt,' he told her, 'even you.'

'Could've fooled me,' she muttered. From her perspective the fight had seemed to go on for quite a long time.

'Okay, well maybe I did want to see you get the beat-down you so richly deserved, but I didn't want my mom to cripple you.'

Miska shook her head and turned away. She packed away the

first aid kit and shoved it roughly back into Torricone's hands. Denise had said that they could stay the night but they were to be gone in the morning. She would drive them to wherever they wanted to go but, the laws of sanctuary notwithstanding, she wasn't going to hide them from the law and the Disciples. She had told them the best thing to do would be to hand themselves over to the *Federales*.

Miska walked out into the hall of the rectory. Teramoto was stood in the doorway to the spare room, closing it. Miska just caught a glimpse of Kaneda sat on the bed. The door to the main bedroom, Denise's, was closed as well. Miska guessed that Goodluck was asleep on the sofa in the lounge. That left Torricone's old room.

'Don't get any ideas,' Miska told him as she went into his room. She wasn't sure what she had expected but the plainness of the room made it look like a monastic cell. There was no decoration other than the crucifix over the bed. The only furniture other than the hard-looking single bed was a small desk/closet/drawers combination and a multi-gym folded up into the wall and ceiling.

'Do you want to slip into your hair shirt? Maybe indulge in some light self-flagellation before bed?' Miska asked, surveying the room. 'Prison must have been a step up in terms of opulence for you.' Torricone made his way past her and lay down on the bed, smiling.

'My room, my bed,' Torricone said. 'You've got the floor. Don't get any ideas.'

'You know who I miss? Uncle Vido, he at least was a gentleman. I've been beaten up! By your mom!'

'Yeah, but you're also the big, tough marine ... well, maybe not big. You should be used to this,' Torricone told her. Miska gave him the finger. 'There are sheets and pillows in the closet.'

Miska shook her head, which made her wince, and then moved over to the closet and started pulling sheets and pillows off the shelves.

'Where are Vido and Mass, anyway?' Torricone asked.

My next job, Miska thought. She opened a comms link to Uncle V. If he didn't answer her then she was just going to blow all three N-bombs in Vido, Mass and Hradisky's heads.

'Okay, I know you're pissed,' Vido started.

'Pissed?' Miska subvocalised. 'I need a terribly compelling reason not to blow the N-bombs.'

'We're with friends ...' Vido started.

'That doesn't reassure me.' Vido and Mass hooking up with their family was the last thing that Miska wanted. It was just as her dad had prophesised. They had taken advantage of the situation.

'Look, you have to admit that things got complicated quickly. We were making it up as we went along. If we hadn't done something then we would have been scooped up by the Feds.'

'So why'd you go dark?' Miska demanded. She could feel Torricone watching her from the bed as she laid sheets out on the floor for herself.

'The people we're with have got security concerns.'

'Who doesn't? For all I know you're biding time while you're trying to get your N-bombs removed.'

'I give you my word we're not. The people we're with want to meet. They could help.'

'Or I walk into a lot of angry Cosa Nostra guns who're insistent on me removing the bombs in your head.'

'They've got bigger problems,' Vido told her.

'Which aren't mine,' Miska replied. She had straightened up

now and was trying hard not to talk out loud. She knew that Vido, Mass and Hradisky were currently a huge threat to the security of the operation.

You don't have an operation. You have an escalating cluster-fuck. The voice in the back of her head sounded like her dad again.

'Please,' Vido said. 'We're down by the coast. Let me send you the address. Meet us here when you can. They just want to talk.'

She was still wondering why she didn't just blow the N-bombs. After all she hadn't hesitated when Enchi had been captured. *Sentimentality?* she wondered. She actually liked Mass and Vido.

'You know how I'll react if this is a set-up, right?'

'Yes,' Vido said. He sounded genuinely relieved. 'Look, you're doing the right thing, I promise ...' Miska cut the comms link and lay down on her makeshift bed on the floor of Torricone's room.

'Everything okay?' Torricone asked from the bed.

'What're you, my second in command?' Miska snapped.

'You know, the slavery thing notwithstanding, you can be a very difficult person to talk to.'

'Your mom just beat me up!' she hissed.

'So you admit it then?'

'Back in Maw City, you know we didn't have sex, right?' *Petty.*

'Of course, the moment you described me as disappointing.'

Miska could hear it in his voice. She knew he was smiling. It only served to infuriate her further.

'Did you kill Vido and the others?' Torricone asked after a little while.

'I killed Enchi,' she told him. *Why did you tell him that?* her inner voice screamed at her. 'The others are still alive. For now.'

'Look, I don't know if it makes any difference to you but Vido Cofino had a reputation for keeping his word, even when it was difficult for him.'

Miska didn't say anything and they lapsed back into silence.

'You've got a lot of people after you,' he said a little while later.

'Jesus Christ, Torricone! What is this, a slumber party? I want to get some sleep!' She heard him roll over and looked up to see him peering down at her.

'There's no happy ending for you. Capture or death is pretty much inevitable.'

Miska sighed.

'Have you considered a career in motivational speaking?' she asked.

'Fuck's sake, Miska, I'm serious.'

'I'm not really a *grow old surrounded by fat grandchildren* kind of person. Now can I get some sleep?'

Torricone rolled back over. Miska decided to check on the others before she went back to sleep, enlarging the contact lens feeds in her IVD.

'Oh,' she said. She wasn't sure why she was surprised but she hadn't realised that Kaneda and Teramoto were lovers. Not giving it much thought, and feeling like a voyeur, she quickly minimised the lens feed and opened Goodluck's. What she saw made her grin, though she minimised that window quickly as well. Seemed like it was a busy night in the ol' church.

'Goodluck is totally boning your mom!' Miska told Torricone with no little glee.

'That motherfucker!'

'Well, yeah.'

Miska wasn't sure what had woken her. She was normally a deep sleeper, though used to being situationally aware the moment she opened her eyes. Now, however, there was just a moment of disorientation while she remembered where she was. She wasn't sure when she had put her hand on the butt of her pistol. She glanced up at the bed. Torricone had gone. She checked the lens feed in her IVD. He was in the kitchen, sat at the table. His mother was in a robe, leaning against the sink. Both of them had mugs of some hot beverage cradled in their hands. Miska knew she should just minimise the feed, that this would be a private moment. Instead she raised the audio so she could hear, convincing herself it was for reasons of operational security.

Not because you're being a nosy bitch, she told herself.

'So she can see and hear this?' Denise asked.

'She's asleep,' Torricone said. His mother replied in Spanish. Miska switched on a translation program.

'Best to assume she can see and hear everything,' Denise had told her son. There was a slight delay in the translation and the voice didn't sound quite right. It was like watching a badly dubbed viz. Torricone looked down at his mug.

'I really am sorry,' he told her.

'What for now? You were sorry when you got caught stealing cars, you were sorry when you killed that guy and got transferred to the *Hangman's Daughter*. I'm betting you were sorry when you got press ganged into her chickenshit army.'

It's not chickenshit, Miska thought.

Torricone looked up at his mother.

'I'm sorry that I'm such a big disappointment to you.'

Denise studied her son. Face impassive.

'I understand what life's like round here but you weren't one of those kids. You had food, a safe place to live, someone to care for you. I'm not naive, I know it can be hard not to grow up a criminal in this world but you're smart, skilled, you could have done anything. It just seemed like such a waste.'

Torricone looked away.

'I was good at what I did.'

'But now you're here.'

'What I was trying to say to you was that I'm sorry I brought this to your door.'

'You can always come here, you know that, no matter what. But you can't stay here, because if the FBI and the Marshals don't work out where you are then the Disciples will.'

'King Skinny won't hurt you,' Torricone said, still staring intently at his cup.

'Maybe, maybe not, but he'd hurt you and your friends. I heard you killed a bunch of Disciples at the Bunker tonight?'

Torricone looked over at his mother again.

'It was self-defence, Mom, I promise you.' He seemed particularly eager that she believed him. Denise held up her hands, motioning him to calm down.

'Relax, I believe you. Did any get away who might have recognised you?' she asked.

'It was quick, Mom. I doubt they could've even got a message out.'

Denise looked sceptical but didn't push the matter.

'She force you to come here?' Denise asked after a while. Torricone shook his head. He'd gone back to staring at his cup. 'You volunteered?'

'It was a chance to get back,' Torricone told her. 'I'm not sure what I was thinking.'

'So you volunteer for these missions?' she asked.

Torricone nodded.

Stop telling her shit! Miska thought. She considered opening the comms link to Torricone but she wanted to see if she could learn anything else.

'Don't volunteer for any more,' Denise told her son. Torricone didn't say anything. 'Mikey, you understand me?' Her voice was sharper. 'You volunteer then they'll say you're culpable. A lot of the sentences of those aboard the *Hangman's Daughter* are being challenged in its absence. The lawyers are claiming that the state cannot provide the requisite level of care for the prisoners, that this so-called Bastard Legion counts as cruel and unusual punishment and is a violation of the prisoners' rights.'

'It's certainly unusual,' Torricone muttered.

'If you can hang on long enough without that crazy bitch getting you killed we should be able to do something about your sentence. It might be a second chance,' she told him. Torricone nodded but he looked unconvinced. Denise sighed. 'Don't try and appease me, boy. You never were very good at lying.'

Torricone sighed and looked out the window.

'I hear you, Mom,' he said.

'But what?' she asked. He didn't say anything. 'You like her, don't you?'

'Oh,' Miska actually said out loud. She hadn't been expecting to hear that. She heard Torricone sigh and then Denise was back in view as he turned to look at his mother.

'Jesus Christ, boy, I thought you had a masochistic taste in women. Now I see it's actually suicidal.'

'Are you supposed to take the Lord's name in vain?' he asked.

Miska was pretty sure that he was trying to change the subject, which was annoying, as she wanted to hear the answer to the question.

Why? she demanded. *It'll just make your complicated life more so.*

'I'm not taking his name in vain, I was actually praying,' Denise told him. Despite herself, and more to the point despite the ass-kicking, Miska was starting to like Torricone's mother.

'She's, I don't know ... just so alone.'

Fuck you! Miska thought fiercely. *I don't need your pity!* Judging by the expression on Denise's face, she wasn't terribly impressed with her son's answer either.

'She's on her own because she's bat-shit crazy!' Denise told him.

You tell him, Denise! Miska thought and then considered what had actually been said. *No ... wait! Fuck you, lady!* She shut down the conversation because she was pretty sure that it was going to make her grumpy. She lay there for a little while, trying to force herself not to think about what she'd just heard. Finally she decided she needed to pee.

Typical, she thought. She could see the glow of the shower-room light under the door. She leaned against the wall and a little while later she heard the toilet quietly flush and the tap run. Then the door opened. Goodluck started when he realised that there was somebody else in the hall.

'Hi,' he said. Miska grinned at him.

'Good night?' she asked him.

'You were watching?' he asked, his tone guarded.

'Caught a glimpse before I realised what I was seeing.'

'That's weird. Torricone know?'

'Captain Oedipus? What do you think?'

'Great,' Goodluck sighed and leaned against the wall. 'It just happened ...'

Miska held up her hands.

'Not my problem,' she told him and went to step past him but caught sight of the tattoo on his chest. She frowned.

'I've seen that symbol before,' she said. 'In some of my dad's old war vizzes. Is that a swastika?'

Goodluck looked down at his own chest. Miska had to admit he was in good shape for a man of his age. She could understand why Denise had found him attractive. Though Miska suspected it was as much because the older woman had an itch that needed scratching as anything else.

'*Svastika*,' Goodluck told her.

'That's what I said.'

'The arms on the one you're thinking of go the other way. This is a symbol of peace in the Hindu, Buddhist and Jainist faiths,' he explained.

'I thought you came from a Voodoo family?'

'Voodoo's not the—' he started. He had the sort of exasperation in his voice that comes from explaining something over and over again. 'I'm not religious.'

'Then why?' she asked.

'The double meaning.' He pointed at the tattoo. 'Peace, yet when I look in the mirror it's a symbol of hatred. It reminds me of the duality of humanity.'

'Oh,' Miska said. 'Cool.' She went to move past him again.

'Peter,' he said. It took Miska a moment to realise that Goodluck was talking about Hradisky.

'What about him?' she asked.

'I know he's a pain in the ass ...'

'He really is.' Miska turned so she was facing Goodluck properly. She had to look up. He really was tall. 'So?'

'It's up to you but you might want to cut him some slack.'

Miska sighed.

'He gets the same rules as everyone. I'm not going to blow his skull bomb because he's a jerk.'

'That kid was born to a junkie, beaten nearly every day by a succession of his mom's pimp boyfriends. He never stood a fucking chance from the day he was born.'

'Everyone's got a hard luck story.' She nodded towards the bathroom. 'Now if you'll excuse me I need to pee.' Goodluck didn't move. Miska looked up at him.

'Really?' she asked.

'He was rehabilitating,' he said. 'Some of us were, before the devil stepped into our life.'

'You both volunteered,' Miska said.

'He volunteered …'

Suddenly it hit Miska.

'You think he's you when you were younger, right? He's your redemption, make up for the bad things you did way back when?' Miska was trying not to scoff. Goodluck was glaring at her. 'That's not how it works. We just do stuff. Some of it's bad, some of it's good. You want to do your pet project a favour just make sure you both do your jobs.'

She shoved him out of the way and reached for the shower-room door. Goodluck took told of her arm. Miska whipped it out of his grip and took a step back. She was angry now and more than happy to deliver a beat-down, if for no other reason than to work her frustrations out on someone.

'Get your fucking hands off me!' she hissed. Goodluck took a step back, hands up.

'Sorry,' he told her. Then he nodded towards the spare room where Teramoto and Kaneda were sleeping.

'You all right with that?' he asked.

'Their business,' Miska said frowning as unease crept into her mind.

'I thought nobody was anybody's bitch any more.'

Miska stared at Goodluck. She wanted to deny it but suddenly so many other things were making sense. She was tempted just to trigger Teramoto's N-bomb. It would save so much hassle but she knew she needed to speak to Kaneda first. She opened up the window with Kaneda's lens feed, expecting to see the inside of his eyelids. Instead she found he was awake and staring at the ceiling.

'Everything okay out here?' Denise, wrapped in a robe, asked from the kitchen doorway.

'Some of us don't want to kill any more,' Goodluck whispered to Miska as he sauntered past her. 'Just a little conversation with the devil,' he told Denise, who was glaring at Miska. The pair of them went back into Denise's bedroom and closed the door behind them. Miska found herself in the dark again.

'Kaneda!' Miska said as the handsome young Bethlehem Milliner walked past the open door to Torricone's room. He wandered back and Miska beckoned him into the room, nodding to Torricone to leave them in peace.

'It's my room,' Torricone protested. Miska glared at him until he left.

'Close the door,' she told Kaneda, who did as he was bid. He looked decidedly uncomfortable. Miska knew the feeling. She had no idea where to start.

'What's this about?' Kaneda asked after several moments of uncomfortable silence.

'You and Teramoto—' she started.

'That's none of your fucking business!' he snapped. Miska couldn't help but glance down at the bound stump of his finger where he had mutilated himself to apologise to her.

'If it's not—' Miska started. 'I mean, he has the power. If he's forcing ...'

Kaneda looked appalled.

'It's not like that. Just stay out of it!' Kaneda snarled and then stormed out of the room. Miska wasn't sure who to believe, Goodluck or Kaneda. She was still tempted to kill Teramoto. She didn't like him, didn't trust him, but she knew he was smart.

She suspected that breakfast was going to be an awkward affair.

Miska sat down at the table and had pancakes accompanied by some kind of synthetic bacon and maple syrup put down in front of her by a begrudging Denise. She wondered if Torricone's mum had spat in it; it didn't seem a very Christian thing to do but then neither did administering a back garden beating. Miska still ached despite her self-repair systems.

Torricone was glaring at Goodluck, who was keeping his head down and tucking into his breakfast. Kaneda was doing the same, though his cheeks were burning red. Miska could feel Teramoto watching her. She knew if she looked up and he was smiling she was going to beat on him, at best.

'What are we doing today?' Goodluck asked her. Miska suspected it was to try and defuse some of the tension.

'Well, once you've finished explaining to Torricone that you're not trying to replace his dad, we're going to go and meet up with the others,' Miska said and smiled. Everyone was staring at her. 'Too soon?' she asked. Maybe Goodluck was right, she thought, maybe the devil was in her.

'Shit!' Denise swore. Miska looked over. The other woman was looking at a thinscreen showing feed from the security lens at the front of the church. A massively muscled figure, covered in skeletal tattoos and bearing a staff that looked like it had been made from human bone, was making his way towards the door of the church. Behind him, parked in the cul-de-sac, was an assortment of customised vehicles all bearing heavily armed Disciples. King Skinny had come to visit.

CHAPTER 13

The distorted light of Barnard's Star shone through the angular
stained-glass windows that depicted the crucifixion and resurrection of Christ. The faint orange light was the only illumi-
nation as Miska and the others headed into the church. Denise
strode between the worn printed pews towards the double
door, shotgun in hand, her son at her side. Miska, Teramoto
and Kaneda made their way, SIGs at the ready, down either
side of the church. They had left Goodluck at the door between the church and the rectory, watching their back in case
the Disciples sent people round behind them. They had a few
things in their favour. The Disciples would have to assault the
building, and her Bastards had better training, just . . . but they
were outnumbered, outgunned and King Skinny could call for
reinforcements any time he wanted.

This was the last thing Miska needed. If the ensuing gunfight
made enough noise then it was bound to attract the attention of
the Marshals, the FBI and her sister.

Miska looked up at the statue of a crucified Christ over the altar. She thought briefly about reconsidering her atheism given the situation but then decided that Christianity was too morbid for her. Besides she'd been in tighter situations, though she had to admit the mission wasn't going well. She signalled Kaneda and Teramoto to shelter behind the pews on either side of the church so they could cover the door. Miska crept along the wall until she was standing to one side of the door and nodded to Denise, who ignored her and opened it anyway.

'Take that heathen piece of shit off church ground before I use it to beat your dumb ass,' Denise told King Skinny. Miska's eyes widened. She was pretty sure that Denise was talking about the staff King Skinny was carrying. She checked the feed from Torricone's lenses. The staff really did look as though it was made from fused human bone. It wasn't an opening gambit that Miska would have used and she wasn't renowned for her diplomacy.

'I think I'm in love,' Goodluck said over the group comms link. Miska kinda knew what he meant. She caught a glimpse of Teramoto hunkered down behind one of the pews. Even he was smiling.

'Okay, keep it quiet unless it's important,' Miska subvocalised over the group comms link. Through Torricone's feed she could see King Skinny standing on the porch. He'd come alone. With the staff, and the blackened bone tattoos that covered all his visible skin, he looked as at home on the church grounds as any demon.

'Mother,' he said. His voice was deep and gravelly. It seemed to fit his appearance. 'Is that how you're going to play me in front of my people?'

'I don't give a fuck about your people,' Denise spat. 'You come here, you come correct, you know that, Pedro.' She sounded genuinely angry, the sort of anger that came from being let down. Through Torricone's feed, Miska saw King Skinny frown as he considered her words. Then, to Miska's astonishment, he turned and walked back down to the open-topped SUV with the throne in the back. The rest of the Disciples watched as their king leaned the staff against his throne and walked back to the church.

'You're pushing him too hard,' Torricone said out of the corner of his mouth. He didn't sound scared, or even nervous, but there was a definite tension in his voice.

'I didn't bring either of you up to be disrespectful,' his mum told him. 'Right is goddamned right.'

She brought both of them up? Miska thought. She wondered how this was going to complicate things.

King Skinny returned to the porch.

'So you going to use that gauge?' he asked, nodding towards the shotgun in Denise's hand. 'Or am I still welcome here?'

'I'm not sure about welcome since you went wrong, boy,' Denise started. King Skinny bristled. 'But this is a church. Try anything in here and I'll blow you out of your socks, understand me?'

Church definitely seems to have become more militant, Miska decided. She was pretty sure they were supposed to have rules about this kind of thing. King Skinny raised his hands and Denise stepped aside to let him in. King Skinny stepped inside the church, the door closing behind him. His eyes seemed to shine in the dim light. Implants of some sort, Miska concluded. The Disciples' king noticed Goodluck first as he looked around, then Teramoto and Kaneda, before turning to look at Miska leaning against the wall by the door.

'Hi,' Miska said brightly. He nodded to her before turning

back to Torricone and opening his arms. Torricone tensed but King Skinny enveloped him in a crushing man-hug.

'I missed you, man,' King Skinny whispered in the car thief's ear before letting him go. 'And I'm sorry.'

'What you sorry for?' Torricone asked.

'I'm sorry we didn't get to the rat before your trial. I'm sorry I didn't realise that you needed protection inside, but most of all I'm sorry for what I've gotta do now.' For what it was worth Miska believed him. She could hear the depth of emotion in the big gang leader's voice. Denise was glaring at King Skinny. She might not be about to kill the gangster but she did look as though she wouldn't have minded beating him for a while. 'You should have joined up, man, we could have ruled this town together. You would have walked into prison a shot-caller.'

'All the bones,' Torricone said pointing at King Skinny's tattoos. 'Not really my thing.'

King Skinny opened his mouth to reply.

'You'd better not threaten my son again in my presence,' Denise warned him. King Skinny held up his hands.

'You know we respect you, leave your church alone.' He nodded towards the statue of Christ. 'I never forgot what you did for me, taking me away from my piece of shit parents, but your son killed a Disciple. Then him and his friends roll into the Bunker last night and dropped a whole lot of bodies. Never mind the fact they got us into a shooting war with the Eff-Bee-I.' He carefully enunciated each of the letters. 'I've gotta do what I've gotta do, you know that, Denise.'

'He's your brother!' Denise spat. Torricone shook his head.

'Not by blood,' King Skinny said quietly but he didn't look at Denise as he said it. For a moment Miska was sure that Torricone's mum was going to hit the gang leader.

'And those pieces of shit are?' she demanded instead, pointing through the door at the Disciples out in the cul-de-sac.

'Mom—' Torricone started.

'Hey, that ain't right,' King Skinny said. Now he was looking at her.

'You going to come in here,' she pointed at the statue of Christ, 'the Lord God looking down on you, and tell me what's right and wrong, boy?' she demanded. Torricone rolled his eyes.

'Can this be made right?' Miska asked. Three pairs of eyes turned to look at her. 'Sorry, this all sounds very family oriented, and a bit religious, so I just thought I'd ask before it escalated any further.'

'And you are?' King Skinny asked. He sounded more amused than anything else.

'Miska Corbin.'

He narrowed his eyes.

'You famous, *chica.*'

'Eh, thanks *chico*. My question?'

'You killed Disciples,' he told her. He sounded sad, as if the whole situation could have been avoided.

'Well, yes . . .' Miska admitted.

'You bring trouble to my town,' the gang leader added. Miska gave this some thought.

'Well . . .' she finally said, 'if I was going to lay the blame for that at any one person's door it would probably be Don Teduzzi's.'

King Skinny's eyes narrowed.

'He dropped a dime on us, Pedro, he brought the FBI here,' Torricone told him.

'That piece of shit!' King Skinny spat. It was the first time Miska had heard him sound genuinely angry. 'Fucking rat bastard!' Denise cuffed him round the head.

210

'Language!' she admonished.

'But you—' King Skinny started. Denise silenced him with a look. Torricone was smiling, shaking his head. Miska actually laughed. King Skinny and Denise turned to glare at her.

'Sorry, it reminded me ... Never mind. Look, we've all got bigger problems. Let's put this down to a bad day and get on with our lives, and if you do catch up with Teduzzi and happen to torture that "fucking rat bastard" to death ...' Miska gave him the thumbs up and grinned.

'Language!' Denise warned her.

'Oh, for fuck's sake,' Miska muttered.

'You want another beat-down?' Denise demanded.

'You come near me and I'm shooting you in your own church,' Miska warned, 'and, y'know, in the legs.'

'Hey!' Torricone and King Skinny said simultaneously.

'Great screaming balls of Christ,' Miska muttered.

'Last warning!' Denise told her.

'You all right, boss?' Teramoto asked over the group comms link. He sounded amused.

'I don't think you guys understand how difficult it is for a marine not to swear, but let's get back to my question?' This last was to King Skinny. The huge gang leader was already shaking his head.

'Sorry, *chica*, too many bodies. I couldn't ignore this if I wanted to, and I don't want to.'

'Oh for f—' Miska started and then noticed Denise glaring at her, '... goodness sake. Neither of us want this. Five of us put down, what, fifteen, sixteen of your guys? Three to one. That's without breaking a sweat. Your guys didn't even get off a shot. I realise your pride's hurting but practicalities? Not to mention Torricone killed in self-defence, as did we,' Miska told him.

Strictly speaking that wasn't true. They might have been able to talk their way out of it but he didn't need to know that. 'Look, we're gone, out of here. You don't need our kind of trouble. Even if you do take us, and that's not the sure thing you might think it is, we'll draw even more federal heat that you don't need.' As she said this she mentally composed a text message to Goodluck and sent it over the comms link. A moment later he disappeared into the rectory. She was pretty sure that King Skinny was keeping them talking as his people sneaked round the back.

'You going to hide behind your mom?' King Skinny asked. 'Let her church get all shot up?' He pointed at Miska and the others. 'You all come out and I'll make it quick. No disrespect. Nothing to the face, open casket at your funeral.' Miska could see Torricone's martyr complex fire up at King Skinny's words. Denise must have seen it as well because she grabbed her son's arm and shook her head. King Skinny just looked at Torricone. 'I'll give you fifteen minutes.' Then he turned and walked out of the church.

Teramoto and Kaneda stood up. The Yakuza lieutenant looked puzzled.

'Anything out back?' Miska asked Goodluck over the group comms link. 'Any movement in the trees at all?'

'Nothing,' Goodluck replied.

'Sure?' Miska asked. Goodluck replied in the affirmative. That was weird, Miska decided, why weren't they taking advantage of this? She gestured towards the door with her thumb. 'Did he just let us go?'

'No,' Denise said. 'He gave us a fifteen minute head start. We need to move now.'

*

'Okay, seriously, nuns?' Torricone asked. They had run out the back of the church, down the sloping garden and into the minibus hidden in the copse of trees.

A few minutes later the four-wheel-drive minibus was making its way through the trash-strewn alleys that ran parallel with the Cypress Road. There was a portable printer in the minibus. Denise had used it to print out five nuns' habits. In the cramped confines of the vehicle Miska and the others were struggling into them.

'Couldn't you have printed monks' habits?' Goodluck asked as he adjusted his wimple.

'Yes,' Denise told him.

Miska had provided Denise with the address that Vido had given her. They were making their way downtown by a very circuitous route.

Miska noticed there was a blinking message icon in her IVD. She ran diagnostics on the message and, deciding it was safe, she opened it. It was a fake ID. It wasn't incredible quality but it would survive a degree of scrutiny.

'Those are your IDs,' Denise told them as she swerved to avoid an actual live chicken. 'We can keep away from a number of the roadblocks this way but sooner or later we're going to have to go through one. Who's got the money?'

'Me,' Miska said as she adjusted her under veil.

'Okay, the police are supporting the FBI with the roadblocks. If you check their AR icons you'll see they all have donation boxes for various police charities.'

'That's where the bribe goes?' Miska asked.

'If you want to get things done around here.' Denise couldn't quite keep the disgust out of her voice. 'Ready?' Denise steered the minibus out onto the eastbound Cypress Road. Behind them was the atmosphere processor. Between the landscaped flora covering it and the internal lights, it looked a little like a huge, pyramid-shaped Christmas tree to Miska. Below them, looking down the terraced hill, they could see the lights and huge holographic adverts of the Strip, the entertainment centre of New Verona.

Directly ahead of them, two police armoured personnel carriers and a number of other vehicles had bottlenecked the road. Armoured police officers were checking each of the vehicles going through the roadblock.

'Waste of time,' Torricone muttered, his features hidden by wimple and veil. 'It's just a toll, they'll let through anyone who pays.'

'Combat exoskeleton, two o'clock,' Kaneda said as the minibus joined the queue of vehicles. Miska checked the position and saw the Honey Badger power armour stood next to one of the police APCs. She magnified her vision. The combat exoskeleton bore the symbol of the Marshal Service, as well as the initials SOG for Special Operations Group, the marshals' equivalent of SWAT. They inched forward car by car as, presumably, each driver bribed the police and was let through. The combat exoskeleton's head was moving all around, watching everyone, but it didn't seem to be particularly scrutinising the minibus.

'You've taken vows of silence, understand me?' Denise said quietly. Miska and the others nodded. The police were almost level with them. They were normal patrol officers but wore body armour. One of them, the overweight one, was carrying a shotgun. The other police officer, a tired-looking middle-aged Asian guy, was carrying a gauss PDW. The fat police officer tapped on the window. The window rolled down.

'Officer?' Denise asked, not doing a terribly good job of keeping the contempt out of her voice.

'ID?' the overweight officer asked. Up close she looked as though she was spilling out of her body armour. All of them concentrated as they sent the officer their IDs. Then the police officer concentrated for a moment. Meanwhile Miska opened a feed to the net to peek sideways. She took a moment to appreciate the subtle defences on the minibus before checking out the rest of the local net architecture. The Honey Bear, like the net representation of most combat exoskeletons, looked like a medieval knight's full suit of armour, though it had a decidedly western look to it, which Miska guessed was a Marshal Service design aesthetic. The two APCs looked like friendly cartoon versions of themselves, and the icons for the two police officers were also friendly-looking cartoon police officers. Miska knew this was designed to aid cooperation; in situations where intimidation was more important, the icons could change to become imposing. There were coin slots in each of the cartoon police officer's heads. Miska sighed. She could see how this would annoy someone like Denise. With a thought Miska sent what she felt was a reasonable bribe to the police officers. She saw the overweight one concentrate for a moment, again.

'Okay, I'm going to need everyone to get out of the car now,' she told them.

'Really officer, is that necessary?' Denise asked. Torricone turned to look at Miska, who rolled her eyes. 'I mean, I'm just taking the sisters down to the beach.'

'Now!' the overweight officer said. She seemed genuinely irritated that the bribe hadn't been high enough. Miska noticed that the officer's net icon had become more ferocious, though it still had the coin slot in its head. The combat exoskeleton's head turned their way. Moments later Miska heard the sound of armoured feet on the pitted blacktop as the Honey Badger made its way towards them. Miska hurriedly topped up the bribe to the two officers.

The minibus fell into shadow as the Honey Badger reached them. The squat power armour was taller than their vehicle. The combat exoskeleton's flight fin had been split in two and folded down across its back. It was carrying a chain-fed fully automatic shotgun. If it turned nasty then there was little they could do against the Honey Badger but Miska decided that the greedy cop was getting shot in the face first on general principle.

'Problems, officer?' an amplified voice asked. Female, so at least it wasn't Special Deputy Castro. The overweight officer was staring at Denise, presumably as she considered the topped-up bribe.

'No,' the officer finally said, though she didn't sound happy. 'You can move on,' she told Denise. Even if the bribe wasn't enough to satisfy the officer, Miska knew that any further action would require effort on her part. Something she didn't seem terribly interested in.

'Hold on,' the Honey Badger said. 'I need you to remove the veils, answer a few questions.' Miska wondered if the nuns had been a mistake. The Honey Badgers were equipped with thermo-graphics. If the Marshal wearing it had thought to use them then she would know that four of them were guys. This wasn't neces-sarily a problem, there were a number of trans nun orders within the Catholic faith, but it might pique the marshal's curiosity.

'I'm not trying to be difficult, officer,' Denise said. 'But these are members of the Order of Poor Clares. They have taken vows of both modesty and silence. Your request violates their right to freedom of worship.'

'They're checked out,' the overweight officer said, sounding exasperated. 'There's not a problem here unless you make one, and if you hassle them they'll just be straight on comms to the cardinal.'

'I hadn't realised there was an APB out on criminal nuns,' the Asian officer said, voice dripping with sarcasm. The Honey Badger's head turned to look at him and then back to the overweight officer. Miska could practically feel waves of contempt radiating out from the combat exoskeleton.

'Move on,' the amplified voice from the Honey Badger told them. It was only after Denise had moved through the road-block and was heading down hill towards the Strip that Miska realised how tense she had been, and relaxed. Beads of sweat were running down her forehead. She saw the other 'nuns' relax, hands moving away from weapons.

'Combat skills, contingency plans, fake IDs, portable printer.' Miska knocked on the minibus's window. 'An armoured four-wheel-drive minibus. Where'd you learn your tradecraft?' she asked Denise.

'Seminary,' the older woman told her.

The crumbling squalor of Pueblo Town had given away to countryside, though they were still in the New Verona City limits. The hills had been sculpted into high-sided terraces. On each of the terraces were rows and rows of genetically modified vines, New Verona wine country. The road sank through the wine country, past mansions in wide open swathes of land-scaped parkland, and then into the city itself. Huge holographic displays offered all sorts of entertainments, gambling, shows, food and drink and other more exotic fare. They passed ornate high-rise hotels, their grandeur imported from another age.

Spotlights stabbed the sky, colourfully illuminated fountains created a sometimes-canopy of water over the road.

The Strip was packed with sports cars and muscle cars, luxury sedans and SUVs, and limousines. The road lit up underneath the vehicles in a colourful display. Above them luxury aircars and other VTOL vehicles flitted between the hotels, clubs and casinos. This was definitely a playground for the rich. Their beaten-up minibus looked particularly out of place. Miska also noticed a heavy police presence, and there was armed security outside most businesses.

'This isn't right,' Torricone said. 'There's nobody in the street. What's with all the extra security?' They were driving through holographic adverts supposedly keyed to their social media profiles. Their fake IDs had them as nuns, so it seemed strange to Miska that they would be driving through splashes of liquid-like holographs advertising lap dancing clubs.

'Dominic Cofino rules with a heavy hand,' Denise told them.

'This the war with the Disciples?' Miska asked.

'Partly,' Denise said. 'And partly his sledgehammer approach to everything.'

'Shame, looks like a nice place,' Teramoto said.

'If you've got the cash,' Goodluck added. Miska wasn't sure that she would have liked it much down here. Maybe with enough money on a drunk with her corps buddies. *Back when you had them.*

'At least with Antonio we could convince ourselves we were just living in a high crime city,' Denise told them.

'And now?' Kaneda asked.

'A military dictatorship.'

*

It was difficult to remember that it was the morning, according to the arbitrary clock of the tidally locked planet. Despite getting some sleep, Miska was finding the static position of the too-large sun a little disorienting. Driving into the banks of steam mist coming in off the sea was almost a relief, though she was already missing the comparatively cool breezes from the atmosphere processor.

Coconut Crab Beach was apparently an upmarket neighbourhood, despite its name, along the rocky coastline just south of the Strip. Miska couldn't see much despite her eyes increasing the ambient light. What little she did see suggested walled compounds masquerading as grand houses from Earth's past. To Miska's mind the high walls and obvious security suggested paranoia and isolation. Some of the automated security systems were less than subtle but she was only catching glimpses of the neighbourhood through the mists.

They were on a winding residential street now. The clifftop properties on the right-hand side of the street looked out over the Steam Sea. They passed a gleaming, parked, police APC and two other parked, remarkably non-descript sedans. Denise glanced at Miska. They were just about at the address that Vido had given them.

'Keep driving,' Miska told her and opened a comms link to Vido. 'We're here, want to tell me why you've got police and others watching the property?'

'Believe me, they're not here for you,' Vido told her. 'Come on in, you're as safe as you're going to get for the time being. You have my word.' He wasn't pleading but Miska could tell that he was eager that she believed him.

Frankly you're running out of options and you've done this to yourself, she thought.

'Okay, turn around as though you've missed the turning. Let's get this over and done with,' Miska told Denise. She drew her SIG and held it down by her leg. This acted as a cue for the others to draw their own gauss pistols. Denise was shaking her head but she turned the minibus around and drove back to the gate. Through the steam mist Miska could just about make out the APC and one of the cars. Its windows were dark, she couldn't see inside. The gate was opening and Denise pulled in. The road dropped away sharply on the other side of the gate, a switchback leading down to a small cove. A beautiful white house that looked like it had come straight out of a history viz nestled in an indent in the cliffs. It had a decorative gabled roof, balconies, and an inviting porch complete with an actual rocking chair. Gunmen and women patrolled the area. Dressed in (presumably) climate-controlled, dark, conservative suits, they were carrying gauss carbines and radiated a degree of competence. There were three identical luxury SUVs parked in front of the house.

'Well it doesn't look like an ambush at least,' Miska said, struggling to remove the nun's habit. Denise brought the minibus to a halt in front of the house as Vido, Mass and Hradisky walked out of it. They were all wearing new, cleanly pressed clothes and looked well rested. The clothes looked odd on Hradisky's junkie frame.

Miska climbed out of the minibus, throwing her wimple back into the vehicle behind her.

'Were you dressed as a nun?' Hradisky asked by way of greeting. The others climbed out of the minibus as well, shedding their disguises.

'Were you all dressed as nuns?' Vido asked, clearly confused. Mass was staring at Denise as she climbed out of the driver's seat. Miska was relieved that she wasn't carrying her shotgun, though her large pistol was still riding her hip.

'That's sacrilegious!' Mass complained.

'She's a priestess,' Miska told him.

'Oh. Sorry, Mother,' Mass said and then crossed himself. Denise ignored him.

'What happened to your face?' Vido asked when he got a good look at Miska's bruised features.

'It's a long story,' Miska muttered.

'Torricone's mom beat her up,' Goodluck told him.

'Cool,' Hradisky said, earning a glare from Miska

'You met Torricone's mom?' Mass asked, confused. Goodluck just pointed at Denise. Mass's eyebrows shot up.

'Really?' He stepped forward. 'Pleasure to meet you, Mother Torricone,' he said and offered his hand. Denise looked at it like it was covered in shit.

'I know who you are,' she said simply. Words like ice. Miska was astonished by Mass's response. His hand dropped to his side and he looked crestfallen.

'Mother Torricone, are you coming in?' Uncle Vido asked carefully. 'Can we offer you some refreshment?'

'I think not,' Denise told the *consigliere*. 'I think I'm going to head back and see if my church has been burned down.' She turned to Torricone and hugged her son fiercely. He returned the embrace. Miska noticed that a woman had come out onto the porch of the picturesque white house. Miska magnified her vision. She was a handsome woman, in her mid-to-late forties. She was slender, tall, and had straight dark hair that matched her equally dark eyes and olive complexion. She wore a very simple black lace dress that had something of widow's weeds about it.

'I'm sorry,' Miska heard Torricone say to his mum. Then Miska was grabbed and slammed against the side of the minibus. Denise was holding her off the ground.

I didn't even hear her, god she's good, Miska thought.

'This isn't over, you understand me?' Denise demanded, flecks of spittle hitting Miska's face. 'I'm going to get my son back, you can decide how hard or easy you want that to go for you.' Everyone tensed. 'He gets hurt or killed doing your bidding and you will live a long life in agony.' The gunmen and women patrolling the area started to take an interest. Miska had the diamond edge of the knife her dad gave her at Denise's throat.

'Put me down now, or I start digging for veins,' Miska told her.

'Ladies—' Vido started.

'Mom,' Torricone said.

'We have an understanding?' Denise hadn't taken her eyes off Miska.

'Sure,' Miska told her. Denise let Miska slide to the ground and opened the door to the minibus. 'You know, I normally expect this kind of macho bullshit from the guys.' Denise just slammed the door behind her.

'Y'know,' Miska said to Torricone as they watched the minibus start its ascent back to the gate, 'I can't make up my mind if I like your mom or not.' Torricone didn't say anything. He just watched his mum drive away.

'Miska,' Vido said. Miska turned around to face the *consigliere*. She might not have been happy with him right now, though their surroundings were definitely an improvement on Pueblo Town, but she found herself pleased to see him and Mass. The jury was out on Hradisky. 'There's someone we'd like you to meet.'

222

Miska followed Vido over to where the woman was waiting on the porch. The others fell in behind her. The gunmen and women were watching them like hawks. Up close the woman wasn't just handsome, she was classically beautiful; there was a restrained elegance to her, a dignity. There was something about her, however, that made Miska think she hadn't had a happy life.

'Miska,' Vido said, 'this is Donna Cofino.'

The woman held out her hand and Miska shook it.

'Blanca Cofino?' Miska asked. The woman nodded. Despite the offer of a hand she didn't look pleased to see Miska. Really not pleased at all.

CHAPTER 14

'I'll be honest, Miss Corbin, I don't think I'm going to like you,' Blanca told her. They were sat in a comfortable sitting room on, in Miska's opinion, over-upholstered sofas. The huge bay window looked out over the steam-shrouded sea, artificially generated waves breaking on the rocky shore.

'Really?' Miska asked. 'I'm actually quite good fun when you get to know me.' She gave the matter a little more thought. 'You're not going to kick me through a window, are you?' Vido was sat next to her, Mass was sitting on the opposite sofa next to Blanca. Teramoto was leaning against the wall close to the door. Torricone was sitting on the windowsill. Hradisky had taken Goodluck and Kaneda to get something to eat in the kitchen. None of Blanca's security people were present.

'It wasn't my intended approach.'

'Did you invite me here just to say you don't like me?' Miska asked. 'Because we have other things we could be doing.'

'Hey,' Mass said, 'show some respect.'

Miska looked over at him. He needed reminding of who was

in command but she didn't want to turn what so far had been one of the more civilised discourses with a local into a pissing match.

'It's fine, Massimo,' Blanca said. 'We have a problem in common,' she told Miska.

'You're here under house arrest, aren't you?' Miska asked. 'The police up in the APC work for Dominic, the guys in the sedan are either wise guys or the FBI.'

'They are my cousin Dominic's people,' Blanca told her. Her accent wasn't colonial American. It sounded as though she had been educated either back on Earth, or in some European colony.

'But he still ratted us out to the Feds,' Miska said.

'Which we don't do,' Mass added.

Now, Miska thought. She turned to look at Mass.

'We?' she asked. 'Forgotten who you're working for?'

Mass opened his mouth to retort but Vido caught his eye and shook his head. It seemed like Mass was just too close to home not to revert to who he'd been. It wasn't surprising really. Vido, however, was a little cannier.

'So cousin Antonio is sick, Dominic steps in for a hard take-over, side-lines the heir apparent,' she pointed at Blanca, 'and you would like us to intervene?'

'Effectively,' Blanca said. The coldness in her tone suggested just how distasteful she found talking to Miska. Miska lay back on the sofa, almost disappearing into the cushions.

'I've neither the time nor the inclination to get involved in a mob war,' she told them. 'If it's all the same to you I'll take my people and be on my way.'

'Where?' Mass asked. Miska turned and looked hard at the

button man. She was more than a little irritated with him right now.

'Well, that's what my local guides are supposed to be working out.'

'Miska,' Uncle Vido said softly, 'Dominic controls the city. And he's doing so much more overtly than Don Antonio did. It's going to be hard to move around under his lidar.'

'Yeah, I'm thinking hard discipline, living off the land, eating cold road kill, that kind of thing. That should be under the lidar enough,' she told them. Vido blanching at this suggestion was reward enough, Miska decided.

'Miss Corbin, as well as a slaver, I understand that you purport to be a mercenary?'

'Huh?' Miska asked, momentarily confused. 'I mean yes, we are, that's kind of the point.'

'Then can we hire you?' Blanca asked.

Miska looked around the room: from Blanca to Uncle Vido next to her on the sofa, and then to Mass.

'Everybody remember who you're working for, what we're doing here, okay?'

'Shortest route from A to B is straight line,' Mass told her.

'I have a question,' Teramoto said. If he was worried about being in the lion's den after arranging for the death of a Cofino associate then he wasn't showing it. Of course, he was still armed.

'Mr Teramoto?' Blanca asked with icy politeness.

'Where do you stand with the Disciples?' the Yakuza lieutenant asked. Miska was aware of Torricone shifting behind her. She was pretty sure that he was paying attention now.

'Going to war with them was a mistake. That said, I don't like how they have been overtly gathering power. If I was assured that they had no interest in the rest of the city then I'm sure we could go back to our previous lucrative arrangement.'

'Where they pay tribute to the princes of the city?' Torricone asked. 'Maybe they're a little tired of your pseudo-Medici bullshit.' Miska had no idea what a Medici was, pseudo or otherwise.

'Watch your fucking mouth!' Mass spat.

'You want to live like a parasite on this city, you can't whine when people push back.'

'Last chance, car thief.' Mass was staring at Torricone, almost shaking with anger.

'Mass, I've got a bomb in my head, do you think I give a shit?'

'Gentlemen.' Blanca may have spoken quietly but Mass lapsed into a brooding silence. Miska glanced behind her. Torricone was staring at Mass but he didn't look as though he was about to push it further. Miska turned back to Blanca.

'You have to show me how to do that,' she said.

'What do you care?' Vido asked Torricone. 'I thought the Disciples wanted you dead.' Miska took a moment to wonder how Vido knew that, but she supposed it was something he could have learned at any point during his incarceration.

'A war profits nobody, particularly those living in the war-zone.'

'Hero of the people now,' Mass scoffed.

'Mass, that's enough,' Blanca and Miska both said at the same time. There was an embarrassed silence in the room. Mass looked down at the carpet, clearly angry.

'What did you have in mind, Mr Torricone?' Blanca asked.

'Autonomy. They buy product from you but no more protection. You don't block civic improvement, or channel the infrastructure investment to already wealthy neighbourhoods. Good for everyone, a wealthier neighbourhood means more money to spend downtown.'

'And in return?' Blanca asked.

'They leave you in peace. King Skinny has no designs on downtown.'

'And his successor?' Blanca asked.

'This Dominic Cofino notwithstanding, you're not a "war in the streets" kind of organisation ...'

'We are when we need to be,' Mass pointed out. Vido made a calming motion with his hands.

'You've got different ways to fight. The Disciples are only a threat on their territory.'

'But you don't speak for them?' Blanca asked.

'No more than you do the Cofino family,' Torricone told her. Mass was on his feet, moving towards Torricone. Miska was moving to intervene.

'Massimo, I won't tell you again.'

Mass froze. He turned to face Blanca.

'He's right,' she continued. 'I am just a widow under house arrest with a powerful name at the moment. I both understand and appreciate the loyalty you've shown me but will you please go and see to your other associates.' Mass looked as though he'd been slapped. Miska actually found herself feeling sorry for him. With a final angry glare at Torricone, he stormed out of the room. Vido was shaking his head. 'Your ideas are in a similar vein to mine but there is nothing I can do from here,' she told Torricone before turning back to Miska.

'I've gotta say that appealing to my better nature probably isn't your best approach because, y'know, fuck the Disciples, quite frankly,' said Miska.

Vido actually blinked, a pained expression on his face. Blanca was staring at her. Then a cold smile crept onto her face.

'Has it occurred to you how much further you could have got in life with just a little tact?' Blanca asked.

'I've got my own mercenary army. Other than a unicorn, it's everything a gal could possibly want,' Miska said and smiled sweetly. Blanca laughed.

'Perhaps I was wrong, I could've grown to like you.' Any trace of a smile disappeared from Blanca's face. 'If you hadn't enslaved members of my family.'

'I'm impressed you haven't threatened me to get Mass and Uncle V back,' Miska told her.

'We discussed the situation,' Vido said. 'She understands that nothing is possible. At the moment.'

'So, you want me to kill your cousin?' Miska asked brightly. Vido winced. 'Too indelicate?'

'That is exactly what I want you to do,' Blanca said. 'Vido hasn't told me what you're doing here but if anyone is operating in this city then they'll need Dominic's support. You remove him, you undermine your opposition.'

'What else are you offering? As you said, we "purport" to be mercenaries.'

'Everything we need to do the job,' Vido told her.

'And then we just walk away at the end of it, no bullshit about Mass and Uncle V here?'

'That is a separate issue,' Blanca said. 'And it's not just Mass and my Uncle Vido. You have other associates of mine on board that ship. Not to mention members of connected families. The next time our paths cross it will not be as allies.'

'But you need me now?' Miska said. She could almost hear the Cosa Nostra matriarch grinding her teeth.

'Miska ...' Vido said. She knew she was rubbing it in. Fact was Blanca was trying to negotiate from a position of strength but ultimately she was helpless and knew it. An idea was starting to form.

'It makes more sense to deal with your cousin,' Miska pointed out. Blanca had a good poker face, Miska decided.

'Then you can blow the bomb in my skull,' Vido said.

'I don't do well with ultimatums, V, you know that.' Miska hadn't taken her eyes off Blanca. 'How much real influence have you got?'

'I still have a lot of friends in this town,' Blanca told her.

'I'm going to give you a list of things I need. Top of the list is going to be setting up an air/sea exclusion zone around the coordinates I provide. That needs to be in play today and it had better look naturalistic as fuck, because whomever we're up against has got a shit-hot hacker working for them.'

'We've hundreds of years of experience in avoiding surveillance,' Vido told her and then winced when he realised he'd used 'we'. Miska glared at him but she was hoping that the Mafia's low-tech, social hacking approach would work in their favour against their enemy's obvious tech advantage.

'Next most important on the list is some top of the line crab surveillance drones, military if you can get them.'

'That can be done.'

'We need to get out of here, quietly,' Miska added.

'There's a boat waiting in the next cove,' Blanca told her.

'We need a base with a workshop where we can work on vehicles. Needs to be a reasonable size, big enough to drive a semi into.' Blanca nodded. 'And I'll need a way to contact Dominic, something that Mass or Uncle V would have known before they went away.'

Vido thought about this for a few moments.

'I can do that,' he finally said before turning to Blanca. 'Do you mind if I have a word with Miska, Donna Cofino?' Blanca turned to face Vido, eyes narrowing. She looked as though she was going to say something but in the end she just nodded, stood up and left the room.

'What the fuck, Vido?' Miska demanded. 'This is exactly what I told you not to do.'

Vido held his hands up.

'Miska, I'm sorry, this wasn't our intent. We were in the wrong part of town.'

Miska pointed at him.

'You just dragged me into a mob war. I've got a good mind to pop your and Mass's N-bombs and abort the mission.'

Vido swallowed. Presumably he knew enough to realise that she was really, really angry.

'Me, not Mass. This is my responsibility.'

'Oh? How fucking noble!' Miska's words dripped scorn.

'Look, there's just some things we don't do. We don't talk to the law and we don't go after each other's families. Dominic's done both.'

That brought Miska up short. *This will complicate things*, she thought.

'Whose family?' Miska asked.

'Blanca's kids. Dominic has a penthouse suite at the Bugsy. He's holding them there. They're my grandniece and nephew. Anna-Marie is sixteen, little Anthony is only nine.'

Miska sighed.

'Has he hurt them?' Miska asked.

Vido was shaking his head.

'He wouldn't dare while Blanca is behaving.'

231

'Appears to be behaving,' Miska said. 'We drove straight past his people, they're parked outside the gate.'

'He saw a priestess and a load of nuns drive in. Blanca's a good Catholic, does a lot of charitable work.'

'Okay, well that's all very sad but not my problem. We're not set up for hostage rescue and even if we were, I wouldn't. They're a fucking nightmare.'

'We hit Dominic, the balance of power shifts, they'll let the kids go because they don't want to face Blanca's wrath.'

'You hope,' Miska said. She wasn't happy about this but Dominic was sounding like an asshole. *Be a badass by all accounts*, she thought, *do what you have to do to get the result you want, but I can never understand why people have to be dicks about these things.*

'I know these people.'

'Why didn't he just kill her?' Miska asked.

'Too overt; that would be war in the streets and she'd win. She's smarter and has more guns. Anybody knew he's got the kids, same thing. He told her he'd kill them if she told anyone. She took a huge risk telling me and I'm taking a bigger risk, telling you.' Something about his words felt raw. He was laying it on the line, begging her to do the right thing.

'He go after your family?' she asked.

'Blanca hid mine and Mass's the moment she realised we were back. Dominic's people went looking, Miska.' He looked old. He sounded frightened. 'Thank you for asking, though.' He leaned forward, face in his hands.

'Have you seen your family yet?' Miska asked. He looked up at her through his fingers and then sat up straight.

'I'm holding true to our bargain. I'll see them once we've done the job here,' he told her and Miska believed him.

232

It was just another complication added to an already complicated operation, Miska thought. Denise smuggling them out of Pueblo Town had enabled them to more thoroughly break contact with the Taskforce hunting them, and her sister. Miska wasn't pleased that Vido and Mass had made contact with their old friends but she was hoping that, with their help, the remaining Bastards would be able to hide from the FBI, the Marshals and Angela while they were on Barney Prime. *If we don't make too much noise.*

Vido was just watching her. Miska sighed.

'Okay we'll kill this asshole, and maybe I can get on with my day.'

The Cosa Nostra may have prided themselves on their low-tech approach but Dominic Cofino's penthouse suite at the Siegel Hotel, affectionately known as the 'Bugsy' locally, was a data fortress. The hotel, an art deco splinter reaching up out of the banks of steam mist in downtown toward the faint light of the orange sun, had pretty good security already. Dominic had obviously had his penthouse, which took up the top three levels of the hotel, data hardened by a security expert who knew what they were doing. Miska was pretty sure she could hack it, eventually, but it would take up more of her time than she was willing to give.

Miska had tranced in and was standing outside the net representation of the hotel, which was basically a neon version of the already heavily stylised architecture. They had exaggerated the hotel's gangster aesthetic in the net. The security programs looked like anachronistic, violin-case carrying hoodlums, straight out of a gangster viz.

Miska herself was in a disguised but naturalistic looking

icon. She didn't think that Dominic would take her seriously in her cartoon form and she was worried that the FBI, or more likely the NSA, would be looking for her image in the net as well. She briefly wondered if she had taken on minor celebrity status yet, given that she had apparently been appearing on the news vizzes.

She walked into the hotel's virtual lobby, which was basically a user-friendly menu for the hotel's various services, as well as access to their virtual entertainments. She paid a little extra for access to one of the more exclusive 'bars'. The bar was basically a virtual hangout with well programmed, tasty, but ultimately useless, alcohol sense-simulation programs. She grimaced as she had to change her icon's appearance to match the bar's dress code. She felt distinctly uncomfortable in the straight, loose dress, newly bobbed hair hidden away under a cloche cap. She wasn't sure about the rouged knees that came with the expensive 'flapper' virtual ensemble, so she cancelled that option.

'Fashion is weird,' she decided. Fortunately in the virtual world her high heels could adjust for how she normally walked, otherwise she would have been staggering around all over the place. She was pretty sure that she hadn't worn heels since the disastrous shitstorm that had been her prom.

Miska made her way through the speakeasy-inspired virtual hangout to the bar and ordered herself a pointless Scotch. She brought her ejection program to the fore in her systems and opened an occulted comms link to the net address that Mass had given her. It took a while for someone to answer, audio only.

'Who is this?' the voice asked. Miska ran it through her voice recognition software. The voice wasn't disguised and it wasn't Dominic Cofino.

'Uncle V's new employer. I speak only to your boss,' Miska subvocalised over the link. She audibly muted the line and listened to the demands, and finally threats, for more information, until finally:

'Who is this?' If the voice was disguised her software couldn't pick it up and it gave a very high probability of it being Cofino.

'You know who this is,' Miska said. 'I'm in some virtual dive called Groucho's in the Bugsy's virtuality. You need to talk to me, somewhere private.'

Either Dominic, or, more likely, someone working for him, pinged her location and she let them.

'I'll be right down.'

Dominic's virtual icon looked like him. Maybe slightly idealised but Miska had seen his picture, he was a good-looking guy. Nice high cheekbones, dark hair swept back down to his neckline, an easy smile and the eyes of a predatory sociopath if you knew what to look for. Miska was too far away to know if the sociopath part had been translated into his icon, somehow she doubted it. More often than not icons were a PR exercise for people like Dominic Cofino. The icon wore a casual lightweight suit, no tie, shirt open at the neck. His appearance in Groucho's was causing something of a stir. He was stopping to talk to people as he made his way towards the bar.

'Idiot,' Miska muttered. He was doubtless being surveilled by the authorities but seemed to enjoy his celebrity status. On the other hand, he had ratted them out. Maybe he had a deal with the FBI and felt protected.

'Hi,' he said as he reached her at the bar. His icon was good but it was clear he wasn't tranced in. He was surface surfing using a trode set. It was what most people who used the net did.

It was only hackers and riggers that tended to have any kind of implanted neural interface beyond smartlinks.

'Drawing enough attention to yourself?' she asked. He sat down on the stool next to her.

'Hey, anybody can claim to be anything in here. You're running a fake social media ID. I've got no idea if you are who you say you are.'

'Happy to prove that somewhere less public,' she said.

'And if it's a trap?' he asked. Miska gave him a look that the technically competent reserve for the technically inept.

'You could take your trode set off?' she suggested. 'I'm the only one in danger here because I'm the only one who's tranced in.' Trancing in was considerably more dangerous than surface surfing but it gave hackers a vast edge in response time. The trade-off was that biofeedback from attack programs could kill.

'We could take a booth?' he said and nodded towards a set of spacious booths against the wall behind them. 'I believe they have enough security to provide the privacy you want.'

Miska nodded, left her drink and walked across the virtual speakeasy followed by Dominic's icon. The air rippled as she stepped into the booth and slid onto the comfortable leather bench that ran around the circular table. Dominic sat down opposite her. His smiling, affable face had gone. Suddenly he looked angry.

'Lady, you'd better be who you fucking claim to be, understand me?'

Miska changed her icon back to her own naturalistic look. It was herself in her battle dress uniform, sans jacket. She slid back on the bench, making herself comfortable, combat boots up on the table, hands behind her head and sent Dominic a data packet.

'Take a moment,' she suggested. 'That should prove I am who I say I am.'

Dominic concentrated for a few moments as he ran through some of the particulars in the data packages. Most of it was POV footage of Vido and Mass she had recorded with her eyes.

'So you're her, huh? The slave lord. You've got a load of my guys on that slave barge of yours, you know that?' he asked.

'Your guys, or Blanca Cofino's guys?' she asked. There was a slight delay while the icon caught up with the signals that Dominic's trode set was receiving from his brain.

'What's that supposed to mean? Blanca Cofino is just a fucking housewife.'

Miska nodded, then sighed theatrically. She took her boots off the table and leaned forward.

'I don't care,' she told him. 'I don't care that in the last round of RICO prosecutions the Feds jailed a lot of people who would have supported Blanca as Antonio's successor, and I don't care about your spin, because I don't care about your war.'

'Hey, you're in our city, bitch!' he hissed.

'Which is presumably why you sent the FBI after me?' Miska asked.

'I'm no fucking rat!' he spat and stood up. Miska gestured for him to calm down.

'Okay, I'm sorry; insulting you wasn't my intention, but you have a problem and I can solve that problem.'

'Yeah? What's my problem,' he demanded.

'Vido Cofino and Massimo Prola think you sold them out to the FBI. The first time, and more recently when Teddy came to see us up in Pueblo Town.'

'I had nothing to do with that,' Dominic said.

'Doesn't matter. Perception is everything.'

'They're the rat motherfuckers who sold out to you!'

Miska frowned.

'You know I put bombs in their heads, right?'

'Then they should have taken their own lives.'

That what you would've done? she managed to resist the urge to ask.

'But they didn't.'

Dominic studied her for a few moments and then sat down again.

'So?' he asked.

'So I need to operate in your city with a minimum of interference from the authorities.'

'I don't like people rocking the boat,' he told her.

'Oh, I'm going to fuck it up some. Gunfire, explosions, that sort of thing – but hey, it just adds to the local flavour, makes the city sound more exciting. Besides you're already at war, what's a few more gunfights? And I'll be gone soon.'

'I'm not hearing what's in this for me.'

'I'm trying to provide you with a solution to your problems,' she told him. He leaned back in the booth, hands behind his head. 'Mass and Vido are problems for you. They know about your operations, your people, even if it's out of date, and worse, they're loyal to Blanca. You let me do my job. Do what you can to keep the FBI off my back, because you don't want Vido and Mass falling into their hands, and on the way out I detonate the bombs I've implanted in their skulls and leave the bodies where you can find them.'

'No deal,' he told her. 'I don't know you. You're asking me to take too much on trust. You want to work here, you turn them over to me.'

Miska tried not to smile.

'After the job,' she told him.

'No way,' he said shaking his head. 'Assuming nothing goes wrong, and frankly I'm foreseeing law enforcement issues, there's no reason why you wouldn't give me the big "fuck you" and be on your way.'

'That leaves me short.'

'Your problem, don't take down scores in my city.'

'I thought this was still Antonio Cofino's city?' she asked and again the barely controlled rage was evident on the icon's features even through the trodes. Miska spent a moment wondering what this asshole must be like in real life.

'You see him sitting here? Fuck that faggot!'

Miska frowned and had to run a search on the epithet.

Wow! Really? Fucking throwback, she thought.

'Fine, that means we set the exchange up quickly. Like tomorrow morning quickly, and you're there,' she told him, standing up.

'I don't do that—' he started.

'No!' she cut him off. She didn't think he was used to that. 'Lack of trust runs both ways. You're there, there's less chance of us walking into an FBI hostage rescue team, and, frankly, if I have to deal with one of your asshole minions like Teduzzi again then I'm sending him back to you in pieces. You're not there, then no exchange, understand me?'

'I don't like this . . .' he started.

'Me neither,' Miska told him. 'The alternative is I drop them both off at the federal building and take my chances with you in the street. See how Uncle V and the Fisherman feel about *omerta* now they're convinced that you've sold them out.'

'I told you, I don't like being threatened,' he growled.

'It's not a threat, it's a simple statement of intent. Why don't

239

we embrace enlightened self-interest instead?' Miska asked. Dominic stared at her for what she suspected he felt was long enough to intimidate her.

'Fine,' she finally said, having had enough of his bullshit, and went to leave.

'Okay, set up the exchange,' he told her.

Miska opened her eyes and smiled. He'd gone for it. Vido had read Dominic correctly when he'd told her how to play him. He was a spoilt little boy on a power trip, with just enough sense of self-preservation to go for her offer. No wonder the likes of Teduzzi were drawn to him. People like Dominic could only ever inherit power, never create it themselves.

Miska was sat in a comfortable chair in an otherwise empty office on a mezzanine floor overlooking the most antiseptically clean looking workshop she'd ever seen. Blanca had really come through for them. The workshop had been set up in a warehouse, big enough for their requirements, on a light industrial estate just to the north of the city, not far from the dig site. The Cofinos had set it up as a place that could be used for the very thing that Miska and the others were using it for. A place to prep work vehicles and weapons for jobs. As the Cofinos had leaned more and more towards drug trafficking and protection, the warehouse had been used less and less. Some of the tools were pretty old but still serviceable. A number of prefab rooms, almost buildings in their own right, had been set up in the warehouse's wide open space: a kitchen/dining/rec area, dorm area, self-contained shower and toilet facilities, a small armourer's workshop, briefing area etc. There was even a pile of sand backed by a large plate of battleship armour pushed against the wall for test firing weapons. In short, everything required when putting together a job.

They had eaten at Blanca's house and then the boat had taken them to the marina at the bottom of the Strip. Miska had arranged for two hire SUVs to be waiting for them and they had driven to the warehouse. The warehouse itself was in a shallow bowl created by some ancient tectonic event in the rocky terrain that surrounded Verona City. There were other businesses in the bowl, mostly fully automated light manufacturing of one kind or another. There were very few people around and Mass, who'd used the place before, had assured them that the security systems in the surrounding microfacturies tended to mind their own business. The surrounding higher ground wasn't good, Miska decided, but she liked that the warehouse was surrounded by a reasonable amount of open ground.

Miska stood up and moved to the door. She sent a text packet to Goodluck, Teramoto and Torricone as she opened the door and took the steps leading down from the mezzanine floor. Mass had been standing guard outside the office. There was no real requirement but Miska felt it was a good idea to get them used to supporting tranced-in members of the team. Down on the main floor of the warehouse Goodluck, Torricone, Kaneda and Hradisky were working on the stolen vehicles that Blanca's people had also provided them with: a muscle car, a pickup truck and four high-performance street racing bikes. Teramoto was sat on the fourth bike, taking his helmet off. He had just returned from dropping the crab amphibious surveillance drones that Blanca had provided them with along the shoreline as close to the dig site as he could get. Vido was walking the perimeter with the gauss carbines that Blanca had provided. She hadn't been able to get any of the heavy weapons that Miska had requested but she had managed to get hold of a shotgun, with some very special loads, and a heavy laser that Kaneda could use as a sniper weapon in a pinch. It wasn't ideal but it would have to do.

As she came down the stairs, Mass just behind her, she saw Goodluck and Torricone receive her message, pause as they read the instructions, and then stand up and turn towards her. Neither of them looked happy. Teramoto was already heading towards her.

'Guys, gather round,' she called. All of them made their way over. Torricone and Goodluck grim-faced, Teramoto as impassive as ever. Vido was last to join them.

'Well?' Vido asked.

'Sorry, Uncle V,' Miska said. He frowned. Miska was aware of Mass cottoning on next to her, he started to move but Teramoto had both SIGs drawn and was covering both the Mafiosi, as were Goodluck and Torricone. Miska hadn't even needed to draw her sidearm.

'What the fuck!' Mass spat.

'It's like you said, Mass,' Miska told the button man, 'shortest route from A to B is a straight line. He may be an asshole but Dominic rules this city. Blanca is a busted flush.'

'You sold us out, you fucking bitch!' Mass screamed. 'You were right, you're going to fucking suffer when I get this bomb out of my head. You will take a long time dying.'

'Maybe,' Miska said, sounding sad, and then turned to Torricone and Goodluck. 'Disarm them, get them down on their knees, smartcuff them and I want them watched until we deliver them, understood?'

Torricone and Goodluck nodded reluctantly.

'Hey!' Hradisky said. 'This ain't right, those guys are okay. They're with us.'

'She does it to us, she'll do it to the rest of you,' Vido told them. She could hear how betrayed he felt in his voice.

'He's right, but what you gonna do? You've all got bombs in your heads,' Miska told them. Then she turned and walked away.

CHAPTER 15

The New Verona Orcs was the Colonial Football League team for New Verona. Their stadium was a little way outside of the city, inland, on the high desert plateau east of the atmosphere processor. In fact, Miska could still see the processor when she looked west towards the ocean, that and the glow of the city. It was hot up on the plateau, much hotter than it was down by the coast; though oddly, for a desert, still humid. The stadium, and more importantly its car park, was completely empty at this time on a Tuesday morning.

Not that a Tuesday morning looks different to any other time of the day or night on a tidally locked planet, Miska mused. From where she stood in the vast deserted car park she couldn't even see the stadium as it was sunk in a deep bowl. All she could see was the curved lip that ran around it.

They had arrived in two SUVs that Torricone had stolen the night before. Miska had hacked their IDs to make their net presence look legit. They would dump them as soon as they were finished here. Blanca had arranged for the stadium's security people to be elsewhere, the lenses switched off. She had also assured them that law enforcement surveillance satellites weren't something that happened over Barney Prime. The FBI would have needed a court order to lace the atmosphere with their own satellites. So unless the U.S.S.S. *Teten* just happened to be overhead, they were probably safe. Of course, Blanca had made these assurances unaware of what Miska had planned for Vido and Mass, both of whom were on their knees on the regolith smartcrete, their hands cuffed behind their backs. Mass had finally stopped shouting. The skin around the corner of his mouth was split and blackening from where Miska, tired of the graphic threats, had cracked him in the mouth. In many ways Vido's silent reproach had been much worse. Teramoto was standing over them both. This may have contributed to their silence. Both the Mafiosi knew that the Yakuza lieutenant wouldn't hesitate to kill them if asked.

Miska was leaning against one of the stolen SUVs. They were parked back to back in case they needed to leave quickly. Hradisky and Torricone, both carrying the Springfield Magnetics gauss carbines that Blanca had provided them with, were standing a little way off. Neither of them was particularly happy about the situation. Miska was pleased that Torricone hadn't started in with his whining hippy bullshit about not killing people, however. It seemed that Cosa Nostra gunmen didn't warrant such consideration.

Miska heard the engines first. Four of them. Performance SUVs, she reckoned. She turned back and looked out towards the car park's gatehouse some five hundred feet behind them. In the orange light the desert looked like a hellish, blackened wasteland. The genetically modified cacti, their spiked, tendril-like limbs waving at the huge, low sun, only added to the alien feel of the environment. The four SUVs were the same civilian version of a military model that Teddy had driven. In fact she was pretty sure one of them was Teddy's vehicle.

Great, Miska thought. The SUVs raced in at high speed. There was an argument for driving at speed in hostile environments. The idea being that anyone following you had to drive equally as fast and therefore would stick out. They'd probably seen it on a viz, or in a sense-game. In a civilian environment a convoy of the same vehicles, driving erratically, just attracted attention.

'Idiots,' Miska muttered to herself. The Mafia SUVs circled the Bastards' own and came to a halt about fifty feet away. They were at an angle to the car park's gatehouse. It wasn't ideal, Miska decided, but it would do. Gunmen and women started climbing out of the SUVs. They carried a mixture of gauss carbines, PDWs and combat shotguns. The apparent militarisation notwithstanding, she was pleased to see that none of them were carrying heavy weapons. She was less pleased to see that Dominic wasn't with them and even less pleased to see that Teduzzi was. She also noticed the gunmen and woman who had come to the garage with the street captain were also present.

'What are you doing?' Miska called to the gunwoman. 'I thought I told you to get another boss.' The woman said nothing but her body language suggested that she was far from comfortable with the current situation.

'Not so funny now the boot's on the other foot, huh?' Teduzzi asked.

'Jesus Christ,' Mass muttered from down on his knees a little way from where Miska stood. Miska looked around, checking that she and the other three Bastards were still armed. Admittedly there were nineteen other gunmen with Teduzzi.

Even so, Miska was coming to the conclusion that she lived in a separate reality to the street boss.

'Teddy, you need to tell me where Dominic is and then not talk, you're not very good at it,' Miska called over the dusty car park. There were a few chuckles from the *soldatos* with him. Even from fifty feet away Miska could see how much this angered Teduzzi.

Don't push him too hard, she told herself, *regardless of how much fun it might be*. She wasn't gunfight adverse, she just had a lot to do at the moment.

'He's not going to waste his time on bullshit like this,' Teddy told her. Miska didn't even bother replying to him.

'Put Mass and Vido back in the SUV, we're out of here,' she told Teramoto.

'On your feet,' Teramoto told their Mafiosi prisoners.

'Go fuck yourself,' Mass told him. Teramoto kicked him in the back, sending him sprawling.

'What the fuck do you think you're doing?' Teduzzi screamed at her. Vido, still cuffed, was struggling to his feet. Mass had rolled over onto his back and was glaring up at Teramoto.

'Get him up,' Miska snapped at Teramoto. The Yakuza lieutenant roughly dragged a furious Mass to his feet.

'You're fucking dead, you hear me,' Mass hissed at Teramoto. 'And you, you backstabbing bitch!' he shouted at Miska, bubbling with helpless rage.

Teramoto grabbed both the Mafiosi and started pushing them towards one of the SUVs.

'Hey stop!' Teduzzi shouted. Miska ignored him. 'Now!' The *soldatos* with Teduzzi started to raise their weapons but Miska and the others had been expecting this. Torricone and Hradisky had carbines at their shoulders, covering the *soldatos* before Teduzzi's people had finished moving. Teramoto was a bit slower. He pushed Mass and Vido back down on their knees and stepped away from them, so they couldn't make a grab for his weapon, then he brought his own carbine up. The *soldatos* may have seemed impressive to another street gang but they were sloppy, undisciplined and Teduzzi was a bad leader, which made them slow.

'You don't stand a chance,' Teduzzi told her. 'We outnumber you four to one.'

'Five to one,' Miska corrected him, 'but that's for us to worry about. You'll be dead.' She made it sound like a simple statement of fact. 'We had an agreement with your boss. He didn't honour his side, we're not honouring ours.'

'He doesn't make agreements! This is our city! You do what you're fucking told, bitch, or you fucking die! Understand me!'

'This guy's dumb enough to start shooting,' Torricone subvocalised over the group comms link.

Shit! Miska thought. With Dominic here this would have been worth the effort, now it was just a waste of time. She wasn't sure if she had underestimated Dominic's desire to get Vido and Mass back, or underestimated the trust he put in incompetent underlings like Teduzzi. She suspected that ol' Teddy spent a lot of time with his tongue up Dominic's ass, telling him what he wanted to hear.

'Okay, just calm down, Teddy,' she told him. *Don't rile him*, she told herself, *twenty guns is still twenty guns*. 'We're going to send Vido and Mass over to you, and then we're going to get into our vehicles and drive away. You tell your boss that I expect him to honour his deal.'

'Fuck you, stupid bitch!' Teddy said. There were a few laughs from some of his people but most of them recognised the seriousness of the situation, even if their idiot boss didn't.

Miska nodded to Teramoto, who moved over to Vido and Mass and dragged them to their feet. On his feet Vido flinched and then turned to stare at Teramoto. Mass turned and spat in the Yakuza lieutenant's face. Teramoto, his expression still impassive, moved back from the two prisoners, wiping the spit off, before shouldering the carbine again.

'Move,' Teramoto told Vido and Mass. With a final look of contempt from Mass, they started making their way towards Teddy and his people. Vido was staggering, his head down. He looked beaten. With a thought Miska sent them a message. She knew that right now the text would appear in their vision, scrolling down the inside of their contact lenses. Vido hesitated for moment but Mass kept walking. Teduzzi ordered two guys out to meet the *consigliere* and the button man.

'Kaneda, you see those guys heading towards Mass and Vido? I need you to take them out when I tell you, acknowledge,' Miska said over the group comms. Kaneda didn't answer. 'I said acknowledge.'

'There's just a chance he doesn't want to kill anyone,' Goodluck told her over a private comms link.

Shit! Miska resisted the urge to squeeze her eyes shut for a moment.

'Ask him if he wants to get us killed, or them,' Miska told Goodluck over the private link. There was no answer. The plan was heading south, fast. The two *soldatos* had reached Vido and Mass, and were leading them back towards Teduzzi's vehicles. Miska waited, sweat beading her skin, more from tension than the humid desert heat. She badly wanted to kill Teduzzi first but he didn't have a gun in his hand. Vido and Mass had reached the vehicles now. Miska picked a victim. Someone who looked like she knew what she was doing. Her smartlink transmitted her choice to everyone else on group comms. The target was now marked in everyone's IVD. Miska saw Hradisky's, Torricone's and Teramoto's marked targets appear but not Kaneda's.

'Now,' Miska breathed over the comms link. At the same time she transmitted the detonation codes to the micro explosives on Vido and Mass's smart cuffs. The memory cable exploded and their hands were free. Vido and Mass started to duck. Miska stroked the trigger of her carbine. Hypersonic screams filled the air as Hradisky, Torricone and Teramoto fired as well, all of them marching forward. Then a bang, the explosion of superheated air, as a line of hard red light connected Kaneda's heavy laser to the gunman who had escorted Vido. There was an explosion of sizzling meat and red steam. The gunman's head was missing, his torso a ruptured mess of splintered ribs as he toppled to the ground. Another red line of light, another explosion of superheated air as Kaneda fired again from under his ghillie suit atop the car park's gatehouse. The gunman who'd been escorting Mass fell to the ground, a red mess.

Vido and Mass, both painted red, drew the gauss pistols that Teramoto had slid into their waistbands at the small of their backs before sending them towards Teduzzi's people. Both of them were firing, three-round burst after three-round burst. It wasn't much of a crossfire but between Miska and her other three Bastards advancing towards Teduzzi, repeatedly firing their carbines, and Vido and Mass already among them, *soldatos* were going down. Another bang, another line of hard red light. A chunk of superheated SUV exploded, the blast knocking one of Teduzzi's gunmen to the ground. The sound of gun and laser fire echoed across the empty desert.

'Reloading,' Kaneda said over the group comms link. The

Tyler Optics heavy laser he was using as a sniper rifle was using a great deal of its battery with each shot to ensure a kill, and so it could be used against the vehicles, which Miska had been pretty sure were armoured.

The *soldatos* were in panic. They might have outnumbered the Bastards but they hadn't expected sniper cover and the sheer violence of the Bastards' attack. Some had stood their ground and fought. They had died first. The rest had scrambled for cover, trying to get behind the vehicles. Miska fired again. Hypersonic rounds sparked off one of the middle SUV's armour, a tracer ricocheting into the air as the gunman she'd been aiming at ducked out of sight. She was aware of Mass taking a shot at Teduzzi as the street captain threw himself between two of the SUVs. The button man missed. Miska had a clear shot but Teddy wasn't a priority as he still wasn't firing himself. Miska shifted aim and fired three thorn-shaped 6.3mm penetrators into the face of a gunwoman shooting across the bonnet of one of the SUVs. They were taking fire now. Miska felt her bike jacket harden as a passing round tugged at her, knocking her off balance. It was the gunman she'd missed. The car park was bathed in hard red light again. Part of the SUV the gunman had been hiding behind exploded and he staggered back. Miska shot him with a three-round burst.

Most of *soldatos* who still lived were hiding behind their vehicles now. Hradisky and Torricone went wide around either side of the parked SUVs, firing. Vido and Mass were crouched behind the middle SUV, by the front and rear wheels respectively. Miska lay down on the ground and started firing under the vehicles. Hypersonic rounds knocked *soldatos'* legs out from under them and then she killed them as they hit the ground. She could see Mass screaming. She knew her rounds were going very close to him. Vido was just very, very still. He looked white with terror. The ammunition counter on her IVD told her that her carbine's sixty-round magazine was about to run dry.

'Reloading,' Miska said over the group comms. She was surrounded by sparks as incoming rounds impacted the printed regolith surface of the car park. She cried out as something hit her leg. The inertial armour on her trousers hardened but her leg still went numb even as she slid the next vacuum-packed magazine of caseless rounds into the carbine. There were warning icons in her IVD but she managed to push herself to her feet and continue limping towards the vehicles.

'Reload—' Hradisky started over the group comms. Then Miska saw him tugged back and he hit the ground.

'Reloading,' Torricone said over group comms. He was hunkered down in front of Teduzzi's lead vehicle. Miska glanced towards Hradisky. His left shoulder was a mess but he had drawn his sidearm and was crawling towards the back of the *soldatos'* rear SUV.

Miska was aware of Mass grabbing a folding knife from the webbing of a fallen *soldato*. He used it to cut through the sling of the man's combat shotgun. Mass took a pistol from the corpse and threw it to Vido, then rolled under the SUV and started firing. Vido popped up and started firing over the vehicle's sloping bonnet, catching a surprised gunwoman in the face.

Teramoto let his carbine drop on its sling and drew both his SIGs, firing three-round bursts from each weapon at anyone who dared to show their head, mostly using them as suppressing fire. He reached the rear SUV, dropped his pistols and threw himself across the bonnet. Torricone was up now, firing across the back of the SUVs. Miska saw the car thief's mouth move as he swore, raising his carbine as Teramoto jumped into his line of fire, sword drawn. Miska couldn't quite believe what she was seeing as the Yakuza lieutenant went to work with his sword on one of the remaining *soldatos*. Mass, now with a pistol in hand, and Vido moved between the SUVs, shouting at the two still-living *soldatos* who were throwing weapons down and raising their hands. Miska limped forward to join them.

'Where's Teduzzi?' Mass bellowed. One of the middle SUVs roared out of line, heading straight towards Miska. She threw herself bodily out of the way. She could already hear gunfire. Feel the pistol rounds whizzing past her to spark uselessly off the SUV's armour. She brought her carbine up and started firing at the back of the SUV as it sped for the gatehouse. She heard another carbine join hers as Torricone fired as well. The hypersonic rounds were making pockmarks in the vehicle's armour, but Miska knew they wouldn't penetrate.

'Kaneda, aim for the engine block,' Miska subvocalised over group comms as her carbine ran dry and she rapidly reloaded the weapon. She could see Kaneda kneeling on the roof of the gatehouse now, the ghillie suit he'd made when they'd arrived in the car park earlier this morning now hanging off his back. She heard the crack of superheated air, saw the red light as lumps of armoured plate were blown off the SUV. Three beams from the laser.

'Reloading,' Kaneda told them over the comms. The SUV was a smoking mess but it was still moving. As it reached the gatehouse Goodluck spun out from behind the building with the shotgun. Miska heard the shot echo over the car park. The force of the blank round that Goodluck had just fired launched the aerofoil grenade that had been attached to the shotgun's barrel. The grenade hit the SUV's front, right-hand-side wheel with less of an explosion, and more of a splash. The grenade gone,

Goodluck continued firing the shotgun. From where Miska was limping back towards their own SUVs she saw the contrails from the rocket engines on the sabot gyrojet micro-missiles the shotgun had just fired.

'Don't waste them,' Miska told Goodluck over the comms. They didn't have very many and along with the laser, the special loads for the Remington shotgun were the closest thing they had to heavy weapons. The smartlink guided micro-missiles hit the SUV, their high-explosive armour-piercing warheads detonating. Then the SUV was wreckage tumbling across the blacktop. Miska reached her own SUV and climbed onto the running board, starting up the vehicle with a thought. An angry looking Mass and a pale, shaken-looking Vido joined her. Miska was more than a little concerned that the *consigliere* was about to have a heart attack. Torricone joined them as well. That left Teramoto and a wounded Hradisky with the prisoners.

'They're alive when we get back,' Mass shouted back to Teramoto. The SUV drove them past the gatehouse where Kaneda was covering the crashed SUV with the heavy laser, and on to the wreckage of Teduzzi's vehicle. It was on its roof, the rear and side pockmarked from Miska and Torricone's fire. Parts of the bonnet still glowed red-hot where Kaneda's laser had superheated and exploded the armour plate. There were chunks missing from the side armour from the HEAP warheads on the gyrojet micro-missiles, but Miska was pretty sure that it was the grenade that Goodluck had fired from the shotgun that had caused the crash. Teduzzi's SUV was equipped with run-flat tyres but that didn't help when a large part of the wheel was missing where the powerful molecular acid in the grenade had eaten it away. The acid was still sizzling, dripping onto the desert floor. Miska hated the weapon, but needs must …

Careful to keep clear of the acid, Mass knocked on the SUV's armoured window.

'Come out and die like a man,' he told Teduzzi. Teduzzi was suspended upside down by the seat's five-point harness. This was unfortunate because he had pissed himself and now it was raining down on him. He was sobbing as he shook his head. Mass turned to look at Miska, who in turn looked at Torricone.

'Hold me,' she told him and let her body drop in what looked like a faint as she tranced in. The net representation of Teduzzi's SUV had excellent civilian-grade electronic security. It was no match for her. The locks were clicking open as she tranced out, back into the real world.

She didn't think Teduzzi was going to give them much trouble but she was still gratified to see that Torricone covered Mass as he dragged the sobbing street captain out of the SUV. Teduzzi curled up in his own filth, crying.

'It's not fair, it's not fair,' he kept whimpering. She was struggling to master her disgust.

'Search him,' she told Mass. The button man did so, removing Teduzzi's sidearm. Then he started slapping Teduzzi's face.

'Look at me, look at me! This is what you get, Teddy.' He punched Teddy in the face.

'Mass,' Miska said quietly. She was a little surprised when Vido kicked a squealing Teduzzi hard. Mass ignored her and hit Teduzzi again. 'Mass,' Miska said a little louder. Vido grabbed Teduzzi by his collar, pulling him up and punching him repeatedly. Miska found herself surprised by the level of rage in the old man. Finally Vido staggered back, out of breath. Mass took over, really laying into the squealing Teduzzi this time. 'Mass!' Miska shouted. This time she got his attention. He turned on her, furious.

'What!' he screamed at her. 'Going to tell me this isn't the way you do things in the marines?' He had drool hanging off his chin. Vido had started kicking Teduzzi again. 'Well fuck you, lady!' He banged his fist off his own chest. 'This is the way I fucking do things! You hear me?'

'I thought you might want your knife,' Miska said, and held up the hooked fishing knife that Mass had printed on board the *Hangman's Daughter*. It was a knife very similar to this one that had earned the Mafia button man his nickname: the Fisherman. Mass stared at Miska and then the knife and snatched it out of her hand. Vido was really going to town on Teduzzi. He let go of the street captain's collar. Teduzzi's face was a pulped mess, but he was still begging for his life, drooling blood down himself, his words little more than a mush. Vido was red-faced, and coated with sweat. He was shaking like a leaf. Miska knew it was the adrenalin. He leaned on Mass, trying to get his breath back.

'I've got this,' Mass told him. Vido nodded. He turned his back on Teduzzi and walked away. Mass stood over the beaten street captain, knife in hand. Miska turned and walked away as well. Torricone followed. They climbed onto the SUV's running board and started back towards Teramoto, Hradisky and the prisoners, stopping to pick up Kaneda and Goodluck on the way. That was when the screams started behind them.

CHAPTER 16

Teduzzi was still screaming as the SUV came to a halt by Teramoto where he stood over both the prisoners, though judging by the moaning a few of the other *soldatos* hadn't quite succumbed to their wounds yet. Hradisky was on his feet, pain etched across his taut features. Miska stepped off the SUV's running board and opened the vehicle's boot to retrieve the first aid kit. She threw it to Torricone, who went to attend to Hradisky's shoulder. Vido climbed unsteadily off the running boards.

'You okay, Uncle V?' Miska asked.

He was still red-faced, bathed in sweat and shaking like a leaf. He looked up at her but didn't say anything.

'First gunfight?' she asked.

Vido nodded.

'Hell of an age to start,' Hradisky managed through gritted teeth. Torricone had sprayed the shoulder wound with an anaesthetic and was applying a cleaning solution to it.

'What shall we do with them?' Teramoto asked, his sword

still dripping with blood. It was becoming clear to Miska that the Yakuza lieutenant not only relished combat but that he was a one-man killing machine. It didn't matter. She didn't like the obvious power Teramoto displayed over Kaneda. She had been thinking on it since her conversation with Goodluck, and had decided the Yakuza lieutenant had to die on this job. She couldn't blow his skull, he hadn't been caught doing anything to publicly warrant that, but she'd had enough of his games, his manipulations and whatever the fuck he was doing to Kaneda. It would be a stray round somewhere, before he could do any more damage, undermine her further.

Friendly fire, she thought.

'We let them live, they go running to Dominic, he'll work out that I was never going to hand you and Mass over. It won't take much for him to work out that we were doing Blanca's bidding and then her kids are dead,' Miska subvocalised over the group link, but Vido was already shaking his head as she finished.

'No, they're not going to go running to Dominic, are you, Cecilia, Paul?' he asked.

'We're sorry, Vido,' the woman, Cecilia, said. She was the same gunwoman who had accompanied Teduzzi to Hector's garage. 'Dominic's the boss now. We have to follow orders. He said that you turned rat.' Cecilia nodded towards Miska.

'I really don't think I can express how little I care about the Mafia,' Miska said, yawning. It had already been a long day, though she had to admit that she had enjoyed the gunfight.

'There will be little pain, I promise,' Teramoto said, raising his sword, but Vido held up his hand. The *consigliere*, despite the shaking, despite how tired and haggard he looked, was still managing to radiate anger.

'You know better.' He pointed between Paul and Cecilia.

'You both do. Antonio Cofino is your boss. You follow his orders. Including the one where he made his niece, Blanca, his successor.'

'You weren't here! She stepped down!' Paul protested. He must have sounded a little too uppity for Teramoto, Miska thought, because he laid the bloodied blade of his sword on the man's shoulder.

'It's all right,' Vido told Teramoto. The Yakuza lieutenant nodded and removed the blade. Vido looked down at Paul again. 'Blanca was forced to stand down. Dominic ratted all of us out. He was the reason we got sent away, the reason the FBI were able to make the RICO charges stick.' Both Paul and Cecilia stared at Vido.

'Bullshit,' Paul said. Vido took a step forward and both the *soldatos* shrank back.

'Who the fuck am I?' Vido demanded. Age, physical state, the shaking, none of it seemed to matter. These people were afraid of Vido.

'Sorry, Uncle V,' Cecilia said, Paul was nodding.

'He also dropped a dime on us,' Torricone told them. He was using a flesh knitter on Hradisky's wound. 'Sent the FBI looking as soon as we arrived on-world.'

Cecilia and Paul turned back to Vido.

'It's all true,' he told them. 'If he turned on us, then he'll turn on you.'

Miska took a moment to check on the others. The screaming had stopped and Mass was walking back across the car park towards them. Goodluck was watching their back; she was pleased that someone was. Kaneda was leaning against one of their SUVs. He was still shaking. He looked like he could do with a cry but he'd done well, Miska decided. He'd come through in the end. His sniping had probably been the definitive factor in their victory.

'We need to speed this up,' Miska said. She knew they had until a car went past the stadium and saw the wreckage before the authorities were called and that meant the FBI, the Marshals and her sister.

'You want to live, want to take the bodies of your friends home?' Vido asked them. Paul and Cecilia nodded. 'Then you go to Blanca and beg her forgiveness, and then you do whatever she tells you to do to make amends, understand me? Because if you go to Dominic' —both the *soldatos* shrank away as Vido leaned forward— 'then you're just another rat, and you know what happens to rats, right?'

Miska watched them both blanch. It wasn't how she would have handled it but they were definitely scared and she was convinced that they hadn't known what Dominic had done.

'Let's go,' Vido said and walked back towards the SUVs. Teramoto was wiping his sword clean.

'Hey,' Miska said. The two *soldatos'* heads jerked around towards her. 'Look around,' she told them. Their friends' bodies were islands of dead flesh among the sea of red that was leaking out of them. 'Dominic's pissed us off. Ask yourselves how long you think he's going to be around for.' Then she followed Vido. Teramoto fell in behind her. Mass had almost reached them, both his hands red and dripping.

The SUVs that they had stolen had taken more than a few rounds. One of them wasn't handling properly and Torricone had to nurse it back to the underground car park in a land train stop where they had parked the two rental vehicles. Miska had spoofed the tracker on both vehicles and according to the

260

rental agency they were both parked down by one of the surfing beaches.

They had headed back to the warehouse in silence. All of them had seen the FBI's assault shuttle shoot by overhead, heading in the opposite direction, towards the scene of the crime.

I wonder if she's blaming me for every gunfight that happens in New Verona? Miska asked herself. Though in fairness this one really had been her doing. *Omerta* notwithstanding, the surviving *soldatos* owed her nothing. She hoped that they managed to get away before the Feds and her sister turned up.

Miska had ridden with Teramoto, Kaneda and the two Hard Luck Comancheros. Kaneda seemed to have got control of himself but he was still very quiet. Mass and Vido had chosen not to be in the same vehicle as her.

She had checked her leg. She reckoned she had caught a ricochet, rather than a direct shot. It looked like a painful bone bruise. She wrapped a medgel around it to stimulate healing. Other than that, Hradisky's shoulder, and a cut on Teramoto's cheek from a near miss, they had got off pretty lightly for the number of guns they had been facing, Miska decided as they pulled into the warehouse after Torricone's SUV.

She was climbing out of the SUV when Mass hit her in the face. The surprise and her hurt leg both contributed to her hitting the ground. He stood over her, bloody handed, face a mask of rage. Miska kicked out from the ground. It took a lot of self-control not to aim for his knee. Her foot caught Mass just under the chin, staggering him. Miska swept his legs out from under him and the button man hit the painted concrete floor hard. Staying low, she covered the distance to him quickly, sliding her lower leg across his throat and putting her weight on it. He tried to grab her. She locked up one arm, painfully, and knelt on the other with her free leg, which made her wince in pain.

'You wanna die, Mafia boy?' she demanded. She was angry, but more with herself for being taken off-guard like that. 'I won't blow your skull. I'll just choke you to death.'

'Miska!' Vido shouted. She took her eyes off Mass just long enough to look up at Vido. The Bastards were all standing around, staring at her. Vido was shaking his head. Miska looked back down at the button man.

'I'm going to get off you now. You try and hit me again and I'll cripple you, understand me?'

Mass just glared at her. She moved off him carefully and stood up, rubbing her jaw. Mass stood up as well, his expression a mixture of fury and wariness.

'Take it easy, Mass,' Vido said softly.

'Fuck's sake, Mass, that really hurt,' Miska told him. She was pretty sure that if hadn't been for her subcutaneous armour and reinforced skull his punch would have broken, if not powdered, her jaw.

'Yeah?' Mass asked. 'Good!'

'What the fuck, Miska?' Vido demanded. 'We thought we were going to die.'

Miska managed to calm herself down.

'Well, maybe next time you'll think about that before you get us caught up in a mob war,' Miska told them.

'Why didn't you let us in on the plan?' Mass demanded.

'What can I say? I'm a fan of method acting.'

Mass gaped at her. Vido put a hand on his shoulder just in case. Mass pointed at her.

'You do something like that to me again and you'll have to kill me, you understand?'

Miska started to bristle again but then forced herself to be calm.

'I'll put you in harm's way. I'll get you killed for money. I'll kill you myself if you step out of line, but I won't sell you out.'

'What about Enchi?' Kaneda asked. Miska turned to look at the young Bethlehem Milliner.

'I didn't sell him out,' she told them simply. 'Now, we've got work to do.' She limped away looking for some place quiet to trance in.

The Master of Puppets, aka Hugo Kidston. Miska was impressed despite herself – she hadn't given Raff much to go on, just the sports car. The file had been waiting for her in one of the dead letter boxes when she'd tranced in. She was now reviewing it in one of her secure sanctums that she'd designed to look like a cartoon house.

A number of the windows orbiting where she was sprawled out on a beanbag showed footage from the submersible crab surveillance drones that Teramoto had released to spy on the offshore dig site. It was still ongoing. They hadn't tried to move anything yet. If they had found something then the crabs hadn't picked up on it. She also had windows open from the contact lenses' feeds. She realised that morale was low, a number of them were pretty pissed with her and she wanted to see them coming if they decided to do something about it.

Kidston was a mercenary drone rigger, hence his nickname, with a reputation for completing his jobs no matter what. It went some way towards explaining why the marine archaeo-logical dig was so heavily automated. One of the reasons that he was so good at his job, apparently, was because he was a chimera. It was a practice that had started some hundred and fifty years ago during the war with the alien Them. The war had been going so badly that every human was needed. This included the differently abled. Subject to conscription, they had been hooked up to various war machines from mechs to starships via direct neural interface. In effect the war machines became their bodies. The practice had stopped after the war.

Kidston had revived it. A surgical addict and mechanophile, a psyche report suggested that Kidston was obsessed with becoming a machine. To this end he had arranged to become a quadruple amputee. He lived in a protein-bath-filled, womb-like, mechanical cradle that he plugged into his customised vehicles. He was rumoured to use illegal neural forking technology to puppet master his army of drones.

Raff suspected that the Master of Puppets was on Barney Prime. He also suspected that he was working for Mars. Miska was less sure about this. The CIA were prone to seeing Reds wherever they looked. Except the MoP was top-dollar. You had to be seriously moneyed to hire him, and he had the reputation and ability to command such a high price. His suspected list of employers included multi-billionaires, mega-corps, some of the larger cartels and, of course, governments. He was exactly the sort of contractor Mars would use as a deniable asset.

Raff had also looked into Miska's suspicion about hacker support for whomever they were up against. He'd found nothing. She briefly wondered if it was the NSA but if Raff was right, if Martian Intelligence was behind this, supporting Kidston with a hacker, then it would also explain the trace that was put on her search program. It had certainly been that level of sophistication.

Miska did not like how this was starting to feel. With the best will in the worlds, her band of criminals were no match for a specialist Intelligence-trained hacker from a nation-state with considerably higher technology than she currently had access to, and an independent contractor with the MoP's resources and abilities.

She transferred Raff's file – it had already been sanitised, there was no evidence of where it had come from – and sent it to the rest of the Bastards. At least if they were fighting drones Torricone might be able to keep his hippy bullshit in check.

'Miska?' Torricone asked over a private comms link. Miska groaned, he had that plaintive tone in his voice. She could see through his contact lens feed that he was working on the pickup truck. Both the muscle car and the pickup truck were armoured, apparently it was a pretty common option for vehicles in New Verona. Even the concertinaed crash cowls on the bikes were armoured. The sunroofs on the pickup and muscle car were made from kinetic-force-deadening ballistic glass. Torricone and the others were modifying them to use the sunroofs as shields for ad-hoc firing positions.

'What?' she demanded accepting the comms link.

'Hector ...' he started.

'There's nothing I can do about it. He knew the risks when he took money from shady people like us. If he sticks to the story about us threatening his family then he should be okay. The only thing I could do is throw more money at the problem but if the Feds traced it he'd be in even more trouble.'

She was about to sever the link when she thought of something else and added Vido to the conversation, waking him up as she did so. Both he and Mass had been exhausted and neither of them knew much about vehicles. They had left Teramoto on guard.

'Vido, I know you're pissed off and exhausted but I need you to get in contact with Blanca.'

'We didn't get Dominic,' Vido pointed out.

'Work in progress. Tell her he's on the list and we will get him, Vido, I promise you.'

'What do you want from her?' Vido sounded more curious than anything.

'I need her to live up to her side of the bargain, clear the way for when we move and I want you to make sure that the no-fly, no-sail zone is up and running around the dig.'

'She'll do what she said she would,' Vido told Miska. 'For now. But if you don't live up to your side of the bargain then I'm with Mass, you're going to have to kill me.'

'You need to remember who you work for now,' Miska told him. *And if you keep on having to remind them of that then your command is ineffective*, a voice that sounded not unlike her father told her. 'When we go, you're here working comms. Liaise with Blanca's people to keep the police off our back, find out what you can about what the Feds are up to.'

'Understood,' Vido said somewhat begrudgingly.

'Torricone, I want you to put Blanca in touch with King Skinny,' Miska told him.

'You remember the Disciples want me dead, right?' Torricone asked. Miska wasn't sure but she thought the car thief sounded amused.

'Oh bullshit, King Skinny doesn't want to kill you,' Miska scoffed. 'He's just backed into a corner. That's why he let us go. Besides, I'm not asking you to walk into their clubhouse, just put a call through. Get the ball rolling. Maybe Blanca might want to hire some muscle.'

'You good with this, Vido?' Torricone asked. There was a moment or two of silence.

'It'll need handling carefully, but let's see where it goes,' the *consigliere* finally said. 'Let's talk about it.'

Miska left them to it.

'Miska-*sama*?' Teramoto asked over a direct comms link a little while later. Miska had been reviewing the routes from the warehouse to the archaeological dig. His voice sounded, well, it sounded not-Teramoto-like. He sounded concerned.

Frightened? Miska wondered but dismissed it.

'Yeah?' she asked.

'This Kidston.' He was being far more hesitant than Miska was used to him being.

'What? You know him?' Miska couldn't help sounding surprised. For all his intimidating manner and white linen suits, Teramoto wasn't far removed from a street thug. The MoP operated at a different level altogether.

'I don't know,' he told her. Miska just waited, her cartoon icon sitting on a cartoon beanbag in her cartoon sanctum house. 'There was a girl,' he finally said.

Not how I thought this story would start, Miska decided.

'This was back when I rode with the Thunder Tribes,' he continued. He meant the *bōsōzoku* bike gangs like the Bethlehem Milliners. Proving grounds for the Yakuza. 'We all knew she was a rich girl, rebelling against her parents, but we liked her, she was popular.'

He stopped again as though he was struggling to tell her the rest.

Is he upset? Miska wondered. It must have cost him to tell her this, unless it was just another manipulation, a game of some kind. Then she remembered how he had reacted to the sleek black sportscar they had seen when they had come up from the dive.

'What happened to her?' Miska asked.

'A bike wreck. She was riding bit— pillion through the tunnels and the rider lost it. He survived. She didn't.'

'Tunnel racing?' Miska asked. She knew that one of the main pastimes of the Shirow City *bōsōzoku* was to terrorise road users by holding illegal street races through Lalande 2's tunnel-road system.

'Yes,' Teramoto told her simply.

'How rich was her dad?' Miska asked.

'We didn't find out until after she had died, when private security contractors turned us away from the funeral, but he was rich, own-part-of-the-planet rich.'

Which put him in the bracket of those who could afford the MoP. Only the best for his dead daughter.

'What happened?' she asked.

'We heard stories first: phantom car in deserted tunnels. Then accidents.'

'Members of your gang start dying?' she asked. Teramoto did not answer. 'Shigeru?' Miska wasn't sure she'd ever used his first name while speaking to him before.

'There's a reason my generation of Bethlehem Milliners rose through the ranks so quickly, why we were so ruthless,' he finally told her. She noticed that he hadn't directly mentioned the Scorpion Rain Society, the Yakuza organisation he belonged to that dominated organised crime in Shirow City and much of the Japanese Colony on Lalande 2. 'We had nothing to lose.'

'He went after your families, your loved ones, the people you cared about?' Miska asked. Teramoto didn't say anything for a while. He didn't need to.

'It was some months after she died. There had been rumours that we had been under surveillance, we had thought the police.'

Instead he had been working out how to hurt you the worst, Miska thought.

'All car and bike accidents, all hit and runs, the tunnel lenses not working for one reason or another. I checked the file you sent us, Kidston was thought to have been on Lalande 2 fifteen years ago.' He was quiet again but didn't sever the comms link. Miska didn't really know what to say. She felt more than a little absurd having a conversation like this inside her cartoon world. 'I thought I saw the car once. Sleek, fast, expensive, silent. There one minute and gone the next.' Something about the way he said it made Miska think it had scared him.

'What was her name?' Miska asked, though she had no idea why.

'Miyuki,' Teramoto finally said, 'She was one of those people that everyone just ...'

The comms link went quiet. Then Teramoto severed it. Miska resisted the urge to check his whereabouts on the warehouse's surveillance lenses. She suspected he needed a moment.

'Something's happening.'

Miska opened her eyes. She was slightly disconcerted to see Teramoto standing over her, particularly as she had decided that he was going to die in the not too dim and distant future. She had decided to get some sleep while she could. Her Bastards had things in hand and she wasn't much use on the mechanical side of things.

Miska sat up and increased the size of the windows showing the feeds from the crab drones in her IVD.

'Oh,' she said, scratching her hair. It wasn't quite what she had expected. The crab drones showed various surface and sub-surface perspectives of a tube that had grown out of one of the warehouse-sized prefabricated habitats on the ocean floor. Miska shared the feed to the rest of the Bastards' contact lenses over group comms.

'Meet me in the briefing room,' she told everyone as she stood up. She'd been sleeping on the floor of the office on the mezzanine so she could get away from the noise in the workshop below.

The tube had grown out of the sea and up onto dry land. It had a flat bottom. It continued growing up the beach, flattening the terrain in its path as it reached for the coastal highway.

'That's nanotech, right?' she asked Teramoto as they both made their way down the stairs. Even nanotechnology that wasn't weaponised, or used for human augmentation, was heavily restricted. She saw the others making their way towards the briefing room, except for Vido who had already made it his office.

'A city this corrupt, I don't doubt for a second that whoever is behind this has all their permits in order,' Teramoto said from behind her. 'Also, you are searching for your father's murderer.' It hadn't been what Miska has expected him to say. She stopped on the bottom step and turned to look at him. The Yakuza lieutenant's face was as impassive as ever.

'Now why would you say that?' she asked dangerously. As far as she knew it wasn't common knowledge.

'I may be able to help, but I will need time,' he told her.

'In return for what?' she demanded. He just smiled and gestured towards the briefing room. Miska didn't budge.

'You should know I lose my otherwise sunny and cheerful demeanour when it comes to this subject. What do you know?'

'Let's just say I'm pursuing a line of enquiry,' he told her.

'Don't fuck around!' she snapped. Heads turned their way. 'Tell me what you know, now,' she said more quietly.

'Please, just leave it with me for the time being.' Then he smiled. Miska wondered if he would tell her if she gut-shot him and threatened to leave him to bleed out in agony. Teramoto pushed gently past her and made for the briefing room. He'd baited his hook and got the reaction he wanted.

Damn! This changes everything! Her friendly fire idea wasn't going to work now. He had to be kept alive.

Miska walked across the warehouse and into the briefing room. The thinscreens that covered most of the wall were already showing the crab drone footage.

'So they're taking it out by road,' Mass said as he sat down in one of the chairs.

'Because the no-fly, no-sail zone has worked,' Vido pointed out.

'But they've not got any vehicles at the dig site,' Torricone said.

'Because we've forced them to make this shit up as they go along,' Miska added, smiling.

'Which is what we're doing,' Goodluck said.

'So what are we looking at?' Hradisky asked. He still looked a little pale and was in obvious pain but working on the vehicles seemed to have improved his attitude.

'An up-armoured civilian ground vehicle, anything up to about the size of a semi-truck, judging by the size of the tunnel,' Miska told them. 'Presumably armed with whatever Barney Prime's reasonably lax weapons laws will let them get away with – and we should expect a few less-than-legal surprises.'

'We got enough firepower for your plan?' Mass asked. 'Such as it is.'

'Sure,' she told them. They looked unconvinced. She wasn't entirely sure herself. 'Look, if we're hopelessly outgunned and there's no chance, I'll abort, we'll head back to the *Daughter*. We can kill Dominic on the way out of town and then maybe play a hand or two of Blackjack.' There were a few chuckles. 'Until then, we stay on-plan. Where are we on the vehicles?'

'We've attached clips for the weapons, and modded the sunroofs,' Goodluck told her. 'They'll stop some rounds but I wouldn't want that to be all there was between me and sustained fire, particularly not from electromagnetics.'

'Mass drivers and railguns illegal for civilian use on this world?' she asked Vido.

'Of course,' he told her. There were a few more laughs from the off-worlders. The gun laws were lax but even their carbines were illegal. They'd been modified for hypervelocity and full automatic fire. The pistols they had brought with them were also illegal due to their adjustable velocity and full automatic capabilities. Kaneda's heavy laser was apparently a legal hunting weapon, though Miska couldn't imagine anything that would require such a weapon to hunt on a world with no indigenous fauna. The laser had, however, been modified to an illegal power setting, hence the drain on its civilian battery.

'We've not had time to race-tune the engines,' Torricone told her. He sounded disappointed. 'But the vehicles will run and soak up some punishment.'

'The bikes are going to be exposed,' Kaneda surprised everyone by saying.

'You and Teramoto are our scout snipers,' Miska told them. 'Teramoto, you'll be going ahead of us.' The Yakuza lieutenant nodded. 'Kaneda, I want you to hold back, you're our ace in the hole. I'll be forward observing for you. I call a target, you hit it.

Chances are you'll be shooting at weapon mounts and comms gear.' Kaneda nodded as well.

'Rules of engagement?' Torricone asked.

Here we go, Miska thought. 'It shoots at you, shoot back. If it's got a gun, shoot that as well. If it's a drone, shoot that too.'

'Police?' Torricone asked. Miska took a deep breath.

'As far as I can tell they're just another criminal gang,' Miska said.

'They're not going to be a problem,' Vido assured the car thief.

'Feds?' Torricone asked.

'Fuck's sake,' Miska snapped, 'I thought we were past all this. Can't we just agree to shoot people who are shooting at us? Seriously, it's what they're paid to do. They know the risks. They're not going to get angry, well okay they are, but it's their job.'

'That's the point. They're just people doing their job,' Torricone said.

'Fuck that,' Mass said crossing his arms. 'Fed gets in my way he's getting shot.'

'Won't do much good if they're in a combat exo,' Goodluck pointed out.

'What about your sister?' Torricone asked. Then Miska saw it. Torricone didn't give a shit about the Feds or the police, just like he hadn't given a shit about the Cofino *soldatos*. They weren't the innocent victims of circumstances that the car thief's complicated moral code had decided the miners on Faigroe Station had been. This was some misguided concern for her. She wasn't sure whether she was touched or even more irritated.

'You see my sister coming, you have my permission to try and surrender quickly enough before she kills you,' she told them.

273

'And then you blow the N-bomb in our head?' Kaneda asked. Miska's head dropped. She squeezed her eyes shut and rubbed the bridge of her nose.

'I killed Enchi,' she said, opening her eyes again and looking up. 'It was operational security. He knew too much. At this late date if we get caught we're screwed anyway, the mission's off, so surrender. I promise I won't blow your head up.' *Because I'll be dead anyway*, she didn't tell them. To be honest, she didn't want to shoot at the Feds. Torricone was right, they were just doing their job and serving the same master that she was, in theory anyway. At the same time, she wasn't going to end up on some prison barge, so she was going to shoot at them just enough to commit suicide.

'Your promise doesn't mean sh—' Kaneda started.

'That's enough,' Teramoto said and Kaneda subsided into a brooding silence.

'What about what we know about the *Daughter*?' Goodluck asked.

'Trust me, you don't know enough to be a threat,' Miska assured him. 'That said, any surrendering before the complete failure of the mission will result in instantaneous skull rupture.' She smiled sweetly. There were groans from around the table.

'We've got friends on the force—' Vido started.

'You mean you own them,' Torricone said. Miska caught the irritation as it flickered across Vido's face.

'—any 911 calls shouldn't get near the Feds,' the *consigliere* finished.

'Okay.' Miska clapped her hands. 'Vido runs comms and interference for us back here.' Vido nodded. 'Goodluck drives the muscle car, Mass is his shooter.' Mass and Goodluck bumped fists. 'Torricone drives the pickup. Hradisky, you good to shoot?'

'I was hoping for a bike, but yeah I can shoot,' the young Hardluck Comanchero told her.

'I'm with you guys initially,' she told Hradisky and Torricone. For some reason this made them grin. 'Teramoto and Kaneda are on the bikes.' Teramoto nodded.

'Uh, boss,' Hradisky said, nodding at the screen. She followed his eyes.

'That's a big truck,' she admitted.

CHAPTER 17

The black top disappeared under the wheels of the high-performance pickup truck as they followed the snaking coastal highway. Miska knew that the truck's sensors were sending information to Torricone's contact lenses, forming a three-dimensional map of the road ahead, enabling him to drive at ridiculous speed into the steam clouds seeping in off the ocean. The light of the omnipresent too-close sun seeped into the hot mist, permeating it with its strange orange glow. The muscle car, driven by Goodluck, was ahead of them, creating eddies in the mist with its passing. Miska was in the back of the pickup truck, kneeling down in the cargo bed, holding onto the roll bar. She had the large battery for the laser cutter strapped to her back. Her Springfield Magnetics gauss carbine was slung securely down her front.

Hradisky was kneeling down next to her, his carbine held to port in one hand. The full-face visor on his crash helmet was pushed up. He had a fierce grin on his face. All of them were wearing crash helmets and bike body armour over their, mercifully climate-controlled, inertial armoured clothes. There were two more carbines clipped to the back of the truck's cab, along with the Remington combat shotgun. There was already an aerofoil acid grenade affixed to the shotgun's barrel. The remaining rounds in the tubular magazine consisted of half their remaining sabot gyrojet micro-missiles. Kaneda was trailing behind them, the crash cowl still up on the sleek, low, long bike, so he could get his hair in the wind. To Miska's eyes it looked like he was chomping at the bit. He wanted to throttle the machine and speed past them like Teramoto had. The Yakuza lieutenant had gone ahead of them, ostensibly to get eyes on the target.

Miska checked the footage from the crab drones. The tunnel was still there but the robot truck had yet to emerge from it. Miska checked the feed from Teramoto's lenses. His head was inches from the ground as he leaned in low to a corner, the bike moving at terrifying, exhilarating speeds on the winding road. Teramoto righted the bike as he came to a straight and poured more speed on. A four-wheel-drive van, black in colour with blacked-out windows, passed Teramoto's bike going in the other direction. The rock walls were a blur in the feed as Teramoto glanced behind him, to look at the van. Then he opened a window in the IVD on his contact lens. It showed feed from the bike's rear-facing camera as the van receded into the distance behind them.

'I thought the road was closed,' Teramoto said over the group comms.

'It is, the police have closed the road ahead of you guys and behind you,' Vido said from the briefing room back in the warehouse where he was coordinating with Blanca, the authorities, and a number of his own contacts. 'There are probably a few vehicles who got through before they closed the road.'

'You see the roof of that van?' Teramoto asked. Miska had, there had been lot of comms gear on top of the vehicle.

'What of it?' Hradisky asked next to her.

'Teramoto thinks it might be this Master of Puppets,' Torricone said over the group comms.

'Take it out?' Mass asked as their little convoy slewed around a piece of headland, waves splashing against the rocks below them. It was an appealing idea and it could save them a lot of hassle. With a thought Miska brought up the initial footage of the robot truck that was carrying their target. It was a heavy duty, twenty-six-wheeler semi-trailer truck. If it was armed then the weapons were concealed. Judging by the number of wheels, however, it was capable of carrying a lot of weight, particularly on a planet like Barney Prime that only had .75G. That either meant what it was picking up was very heavy or the truck was armoured. Possibly both. They pretty much had nothing that they could touch it with. Maybe the aerofoil acid grenades, but she couldn't see them doing enough damage to even eat through the armour. The aerodynamic, sloping cab of the track had a black bubble of thick, presumably armoured, glass that would contain the vehicle's dumb AI autopilot as well as the protected comms system through which it could accept orders from the Master of Puppets. That would be the weak spot. It wasn't much of a weak spot. There were also two pannier-like structures protruding slightly from the tractor unit. Miska wasn't entirely sure what their purpose was. She suspected weapon systems, but whatever they turned out to be she couldn't see them being good for her side.

'Can't risk it,' she finally said. 'Could be just some poor civvies on their way home from a day at the beach.' Besides, if it was the MoP she suspected that his personal transport, which would be ferrying his cradle, would be very heavily armed and armoured. The job could be over before it started. Unless ... 'Kaneda, when the van goes past I want you to break off and follow it, keep a good way back but make sure he knows you're following. I want to see what he does.'

'Sure it's a good idea to get rid of the sniper and one of the few heavyish weapons we've got?' Goodluck asked from the driver's seat of the muscle car.

'Boss, I would like to be involved ...' Kaneda started.

'You will follow orders,' Teramoto said over the group comms. There was no answer from Kaneda. Miska glanced behind her at the bike. Kaneda was leaning left and right as they made their way through a particularly windy bit of road between the rock, before they were out on the ocean side again.

'Kaneda?' Teramoto's voice was a low growl.

'Understood,' came Kaneda's begrudging answer. Miska looked forward again to see the van approaching them. She suspected that it was supposed to look non-descript but there was something in the bull bar, the raised suspension, the adjustable tyres and the suite of comms gear on the roof that suggested it was more than it seemed.

'Sucker should've worked from an aircar,' Miska muttered to herself. Then there wouldn't have been much they could do. Kaneda let it go by, put some distance behind them, then he slammed on his brakes, spinning the bike round a hundred-and-eighty-degrees in a cloud of smoking tyres. He accelerated so quickly after the van that the bike's front wheel came off the road as he popped a power wheelie.

'Here we go,' Teramoto said over the group comms. Miska wasn't sure but she thought that she detected a degree of excitement in the Yakuza lieutenant's voice. Miska checked his feed.

It was strange, the entrance to the tunnel was so close to the water line that it looked as though the massive robot truck was emerging from the water. It drove up onto the newly laid temporary road and across the beach towards the coastal highway.

'Teramoto, I want you to keep going until you're out of sight and then turn back and come up behind it,' Miska told him over group comms.

'Understood,' Teramoto answered. He definitely sounded excited. Miska wasn't sure if she was surprised or disappointed that he actually had real human emotions.

The truck had reached the highway and turned right, heading towards Verona City. It was presumably making for the spaceport, or one of the electromagnetic catapults used for launching cargo into low orbit. It also meant it was heading towards them.

'Everyone ready?' she asked and received affirmatives over the group comms. She saw visors being snapped down. They rounded another headland and about half a mile ahead they could see the semi snaking its way towards them. Miska knelt down. She tugged Hradisky down as well before peeking sideways into the net. It was as she had thought. The semi was an isolated system. It didn't show up in the net. The Master of Puppets would be in contact with it via a tight-beam uplink. *So much for the easy way*, Miska thought but she had known that it wasn't going to be that simple.

'Keep your weapon out of sight,' she told Hradisky. If the robot truck was armed then it would have to have some pretty stringent ROE programmed into it to stop it from blowing away passing civilians. Miska watched the truck getting closer and closer. She wondered when she had started smiling. All the job was missing was some raucous old-time rock music to act as accompaniment, but it might have got in the way of comms.

She checked the feed from Teramoto's lenses. He was skidding sideways down the blacktop, bleeding off speed before heading back along the road after the truck.

'Close as possible, T,' Miska told Torricone. He didn't answer.

'He's running,' Kaneda said over the comms link. Miska checked Kaneda's lens feed. The van was increasing speed, trying to pull away from the bike.

'Kaneda, I want you to find some high ground and take out the comms gear on top of the van, okay? Just the comms gear, in case we're wrong, then wait for us to come to you and do what you can,' Miska told him.

'There's an elevated viewpoint, just over half a mile ahead of you,' Vido told Kaneda.

Nice, Miska thought. Vido was working for a living.

'Understood,' Kaneda said. Miska minimised all the feeds in her IVD. She would need all her concentration. They were nearly parallel with the truck now, as they disappeared into another bank of steam. The truck's power plant was very quiet. Miska held onto the roll bar tightly, helped by the tiny molecular hooks on her gloves, kneepads and the soles of her boots. Ahead of them Goodluck passed the semi, slewed the muscle car onto the other side of the road and braked hard, spinning the car round in a bootlegger turn. The semi whispered past them like a ghost in the humid mist, leaving spiralling eddies in its wake. Miska was slammed forward as Torricone braked the pickup hard, starting the turn while still parallel with the semi. The pickup slewed round and narrowly missed clipping the robot truck. Tyres smoking, the pickup leapt forward after the robot vehicle. The muscle car emerged out of the mist and tyre smoke behind them. The armoured sunroof on the passenger side of the car was open and Miska could see Mass, carbine in hand, covering the semi. Next to her Hradisky was doing the same. Miska didn't bring up her carbine yet, she just watched.

'Kaneda is engaged,' Vido said over the group comms. Miska was aware of red flashes coming from the minimised window in her IVD but she couldn't allow herself to be distracted.

'Reloading,' Kaneda said over group comms.

'Difficult to be sure,' Vido said, 'but the comms suite on top of that van looks like slag; good shooting, young man.' Miska hoped so. If they had cut off the comms between the MoP and the semi then the robot truck would have to use its own autonomous systems. They would be considerably less efficient than a neurally interfaced rigger and they would have various safety guidelines to avoid collateral damage.

'I'm pointing north, waiting for you guys,' Kaneda said. 'Call your targets.'

Torricone was rapidly gaining on the semi. The robot truck had increased speed but such a bulky vehicle could only go so fast on roads like this.

'Why isn't it firing?' Mass asked over group comms. It was a good question, Miska decided.

'Maybe it's unarmed,' Hradisky suggested with a degree of optimism that Miska didn't feel.

'It's drawing you in,' Vido said. She suspected he was right.

'Keep the chatter down,' Miska told them. The muscle car and the pickup were side by side now as they closed with the semi; Miska was still waiting for some lethal countermeasure to present itself.

'I don't like this,' Torricone said over a private comms link to Miska as he kept the pickup bull-bar-to-bumper with the semi. Miska didn't either. It felt like a trap.

'I'm going for it,' she told them. Miska ran over the pickup's cab, down the windscreen and over the bonnet and then, at close to seventy miles an hour, she leapt for the rear of the semi's trailer. The molecular hooks found purchase, the gloves and the soles of her boots gripped the trailer's rear door as the semi started to weave from side to side to shake her off. Between the carbine and the laser cutter, with its bulky battery, she felt weighed down, but slowly she started to climb. She was still waiting for the other shoe to drop.

Miska poked her helmeted head over the lip of the truck's curving roof. It looked clear. She reached a hand over and with no little difficulty, she managed to pull herself up on to the roof. The slipstream almost tore her off but the hooks held. Then the other shoe dropped. The concealed turret flipped over. She had a moment to take in the gauss minigun, the six barrels already rotated up to speed. It was only a short burst and it fired the same 6.3mm caseless rounds the carbines fired, but then a short burst from a minigun was about twenty rounds.

The carbine strapped across her chest ceased to exist. Not all of the twenty rounds hit her, but those that did ripped through her hardening inertial armour. They had been slowed down enough that Miska's own subdermal armour stopped them before they shredded her internal organs. The force of the electromagnetically driven projectiles tore her off the roof of the trailer. It had happened so quickly but now, in the air, everything seemed to slow down. She registered the pain in her chest from the repeated tiny hammer blows, she knew she was never going to breathe again. She was sailing over the top of the pickup in slow motion. She couldn't make sense of the black smoke coming from all six of the vehicle's wheels, the widening gap between the pickup and the truck. It took a moment to work out that Torricone was braking hard, trying to catch her. Then suddenly the pickup's cargo bed was rushing up to meet her. She hit it hard. Bounced, hit the tailgate, her helmeted head just touching the speeding blacktop before she was dragged back into the truck.

'I've got you,' Hradisky said, arms wrapped around her as he dragged her back over the cargo bed to hunker behind the pickup's cab. She felt nauseous and she could see light in her vision, either that or too many warning icons from her implanted medical systems. She couldn't quite understand what was happening. It looked like parts of the pickup truck were being eaten. Then she realised that breathing was an issue. Panic as she tried to draw air in and couldn't. She started to thrash around. Hradisky had to hold her down.

'Easy!' the Comanchero shouted.

'Kaneda, they're almost with you, just about to round the headland to your south,' Vido said over comms.

'We need to abort,' Torricone said. Even though she couldn't breathe and she knew that breath was somehow important to life, his voice still annoyed her.

'Not unless she's dead,' Mass said.

Not dead, Miska tried to say as words started to make sense again, though she'd still need to be able to breathe to make her own. She was forcing herself to calm down. To try and make sense of all the icons she was seeing in her IVD.

'Targets?' Kaneda asked.

'Two miniguns, they're mounted on rails on the roof of the semi, they're moving around a lot,' Teramoto said.

Miska was sitting with her back against the cab of the truck and looking out over the tailgate she could see Teramoto's bike, the crash cowl pulled over, speeding towards them. She managed to suck in a ragged breath as her internal air supply finally managed to reflate her battered diaphragm.

'Don't abort!' she shouted over group comms. She enlarged Teramoto's contact lens feed. The lens feed was, in turn, receiving footage from the Yakuza lieutenant's bike's forward lens, because the cowl blocked his view. There were two rail-mounted pop-up turrets on the roof of the semi's trailer. They were pouring fire down on the muscle car and the pickup. The armour on both vehicles was covered in hundreds of pockmarks. Miska knew there was only so long they could stand up to such sustained fire. She minimised Torricone's feed and partially enlarged Kaneda's. He had dragged three picnic tables together and was lying down on them, sighting down his Tyler Optics heavy laser. There were crosshairs in his lens feed from the laser's smartlink. He was aiming at the road that curved around the headland.

Miska grabbed the Remington combat shotgun from its clips.

'Teramoto, hold back, don't get any closer to the truck,' she said over the comms link. He didn't answer but when she enlarged his lens feed she noticed that he had stopped accelerating. Miska used the feed from his lens for targeting information and then fed it to the micro-missiles in the shotgun. 'When Kaneda shoots, he's going to draw fire from at least one of the turrets,' she started.

'Wait, what?' Kaneda asked.

'Mass, I want you to draw fire from the other turret,' she continued.

'I hate this plan,' Mass said. Miska took that as an affirmative. From Kaneda's feed she saw the truck come around the headland. The young Bethlehem Milliner shifted target. The angry red line of hard light reached out across the coastal landscape three times in quick succession. Suddenly there were tracers flying towards him, the lenses showing frantic movement from Kaneda's point-of-view. Miska minimised the feed and then popped up from behind the pickup's cab in time to see Mass duck back down into the muscle car as the semi's other minigun poured fire down on it. Miska brought the shotgun to her shoulder, and the smartlinked weapon overlaid a crosshair where it thought the aerofoil grenade might land. The ballistics weren't a sure thing with such a weapon. The minigun stopped firing and six spinning barrels turned towards her. Miska squeezed the shotgun's trigger. Then she ducked down behind the truck's cab and fired the shotgun four further times out of the back of the pickup, roughly in the direction of Teramoto's bike. The sabots fell away, the gyrojet motors ignited and the missiles, guided by the targeting information she'd taken from Teramoto's bike's lens footage, guided them back over the pickup. There were four explosions as the micro-missile's HEAP warheads exploded in the turret, and then it was quiet except for the four vehicles' humming power plants.

Miska risked peeking over the pickup's cab. The turret she'd hit with the acid grenade and the four micro-missiles was a mess. She couldn't see the other one but she was pretty sure that Kaneda had taken it out. The armour on both the pickup and the muscle car looked like the surface of a particularly meteor-attracting moon, more pockmarked hole than actual armour. Mass was sat up in the passenger seat, carbine aimed at the semi.

'Ow,' he said.

'You get tagged?' Miska asked as she opened Kaneda's lens feed.

'Ricochet, knocked the wind out of me, but the armour held

up. Something caught Goodluck as well, scored up his helmet, rang his bell, but he'll live.'

'Comes from driving with the sunroof up,' the OG said. He sounded like he was enjoying himself.

'Kaneda, are you okay?' Teramoto asked over group comms. Miska couldn't be sure but she thought she heard concern in his voice. She checked the feed. Kaneda was lying some distance away from the wreckage of the picnic tables.

'I got tagged as well but I'm okay. Laser's gone, though,' Kaneda told them.

Shit! Miska thought. That wasn't great news. She handed the shotgun to Hradisky.

'Reload that, just the micro-missiles, don't fire it unless I tell you to,' she told him. He nodded and started removing the sabot shotgun shells from the receiver-mounted shotshell holder, sliding them into the weapon's tubular magazine. 'Kaneda, if your bike's still functional see if you can get in front of the semi but stay well ahead, we'll call you if we need anything.'

'Understood,' Kaneda replied. She wasn't sure if he sounded relieved or disappointed.

'Torricone, get me bumper to bumper with that bitch,' she said and felt the car thief accelerate the pickup towards the rear of the semi. Goodluck dropped the muscle car back a little, giving him space to manoeuvre. Torricone tried to pull around the semi but the long vehicle was fishtailing. One hit from the trailer would put the pickup either into the ocean or the rock wall.

Yay! Miska thought, *a long walk for me*. She grabbed one of the carbines from the clips on the back of the pickup's cab and slung it down her front. This time she didn't wait for the pickup to get right up to the truck. She ran down the bonnet and leapt, trying for height, just as the semi fishtailed. Straight away Miska realised she'd made a mistake. She hit the trailer at a difficult angle, scrabbling for purchase and sliding down the truck. The toe of one boot just touched the blacktop, kicking her leg up into the air. Miska screamed. The hooks on her right glove caught and she was hanging off the rear left corner of the truck trying to keep her legs up. Then suddenly the rock wall was coming at her as the robot truck tried to scrape her off. She kicked up with a leg. The sole of her right boot connected with the rear of the truck and the hooks held. She let go with her glove, swung round the rear corner of the truck just as it hit the cliff-side with enough force to powder rock. Her helmet just scraped the blacktop again as she found herself hanging upside down by one boot from the back of the truck.

Why is this happening to me? she wondered, taking the most fleeting moment to examine the decisions she'd made in her life. Even though she was swinging backward and forward, even through the spiderweb of cracks in the pickup truck's windscreen, she could still make out the appalled expression on Torricone's face. The semi was fishtailing even more violently now, trying to shake her off.

'Fuck's sake! Cut me a break!' she screamed.

'Er … Miska, are you all right?' Vido asked.

'Oh, I'm perfectly fine, you fucking moron!' she answered. Later it would occur to her that people didn't talk to Vido Cofino like that, particularly not around these parts. She managed to connect the other boot to the rear of the truck. With a scream she grabbed her legs and bent double at the waist, pulling her head up. This was made all the more difficult by the carbine strapped to her front and the heavy battery strapped to her back.

Great, now what do I do? she wondered. At least the truck had stopped fishtailing.

'Jesus Christ!' Mass said over group comms. With an impending sense of foreboding Miska partially enlarged the feed from his lenses in her IVD. The two pannier-like structures on the cab had opened. Two armed bike drones unfolded, wheels already spinning as they dropped to the road.

'Well shit,' Miska said.

CHAPTER 18

Miska heard the hypersonic scream of gauss PDWs being fired. She was peripherally aware of Mass returning fire. Heard the squeal of tyres as one of the bike drones braked hard. It appeared on her right. The drone looked exactly like a motorcycle but there was a thick armoured carapace where the seat and rider should be. It had a swivel-mounted pod containing a hopper-fed PDW on either side, where the handlebars should be. They were already firing. Rounds sparked off the semi's thick armour and Miska cried out again as some of them hit but were stopped by her inertial armour. The impacts still hurt like hammer blows. She heard the roar of the muscle car's engine as Goodluck made the vehicle surge forward. His bull bar hit the bike drone hard, crushing it against the rear corner of the semi, pushing it under. The muscle car lurched into the air accompanied by the angry screech of twisted metal as the bike drone went down and Goodluck ran it over and left it spinning on its side of the blacktop.

Miska managed to bend her legs and wrap her arms around

them, hugging her knees, effectively crouched at a ninety-degree angle stuck to the semi's rear doors.

'I have made poor choices,' she managed to mutter before letting go of her legs and putting her palms down against the doors. She could hear more firing from Mass in the muscle car and Hradisky in the pickup truck's cargo bed. Surprisingly, she heard both bike drones return fire.

'Ah, shit!' Hradisky cried. Miska worked her hands up the doors until she was in a safer and more comfortable position before risking a glance behind her. Her visor spider-webbed as a round hit it. 'Fuck!' The thorn-shaped penetrator was lodged in the visor. She flipped it up and was surprised to see that the bike drone Goodluck had run over was back up, battered but still functional. Torricone looked as if he was trying to put the pickup between her and the rear bike drone. Hradisky was in the pickup's cab now, firing his carbine out of the rear window. The other bike drone popped out on the left-hand side of the truck. One of the PDW pods was firing at her. The other was unloading at near point-blank range into the passenger side windows on the pickup. Miska screamed again, the impacts face-planting her into the back of the semi. Her inertial armour held out but she knew there was only so much more punishment it could take.

There was a grinding noise as Torricone sandwiched the bike drone between the cliff wall on the left-hand side of the highway and the pickup. Sparks flew. Miska forced herself to climb. Torricone pulled away from the cliff, the bike drone spinning across the blacktop, but it righted itself and came after the convoy. The bike drones split their pods between firing at the vehicles and firing at Miska. She reached the lip to the roof, pulling herself past the wreckage of one of the pop-up turrets, feeling like every inch of her body was being massaged by flying hammers.

'Cease fire,' Teramoto shouted over the comms link. Miska pulled herself over the lip and lay flat on the roof. The curve of it didn't provide her with much cover but it was better than nothing. From her vantage point she could see Teramoto's bike, the crash cowl pulled down, speeding towards them. 'Slow down, stop them getting by you.' The bike drones had noticed him as well. Both of the pods on one of the drones inverted themselves to fire at Teramoto's bike. It looked as though it had been wreathed in sparks.

'Goodluck, can you drop behind us, act as the blocking car?' Torricone asked. Goodluck answered by braking slightly and falling behind the pickup, weaving from side to side to stop the bike drones from getting by and to soak up the incoming fire.

Miska pushed herself up into a crouch and watched one of the most insane things she'd ever seen as she readied her carbine. Teramoto's bike drew level with the rear bike drone. The crash cowl drew back. The Yakuza lieutenant had his short, straight *shinobigatana* sword in hand. He rammed the sword through the drone's front wheel, destroying it. The drone tumbled forward, hitting the blacktop hard and bouncing high into the air. Somehow Teramoto still had hold of his sword. He went after the other drone, swerving hard to avoid the wreckage of the one he'd just killed as it bounced off the blacktop.

'Jesus!' Mass said over the group comms. The remaining drone sped away from the sword-wielding lunatic on the bike. It accelerated so hard its front wheel came off the ground.

'Shit!' Goodluck shouted as the drone made it past the muscle car.

'Crush it between us!' Torricone shouted but the drone

swerved suddenly to one side and tried to speed past. Hradisky fired an acid grenade from the shotgun at near point-black range into the drone.

Too close! Miska thought.

'Ah, fuck!' Hradisky screamed, falling back into the truck bed, his crash helmet smoking, but the drone was smoking as well as the acid ate its way through the armour. It had made it past the pickup, though. That gave Miska a clear shot. On one knee, getting buffeted by the semi's slipstream, she put as many rounds as she could from half the carbine's magazine into its acid-damaged armour.

'Out of the way,' Teramoto said over the comms link. The pickup and the muscle car moved out of the bike's way. Miska stopped firing as Teramoto came up behind the drone, which tipped down low, close to the road, and went under the truck. The truck fishtailed, trying to hit Teramoto with the trailer and knock him into the ocean. Teramoto followed the drone, leaning in low, the blacktop inches away from his face as he went under the semi as well. Miska crossed the top of the trailer and knelt down again as the drone bike appeared on the other side of the truck, righting itself. She sighted and emptied the rest of the magazine from the carbine into the drone bike. It seemed to wiggle and then bounce off the semi and the rocks as it became fast-moving wreckage. Teramoto accelerated hard, the crash cowl closing as parts of the drone bounced off his bike, making it wobble dangerously. The semi tried to crush the bike against the cliff-side but Teramoto shot out in front of the robot vehicle.

Miska was on her feet, head down, making her way against the slipstream as she struggled up the semi's aerodynamically curved roof. She reloaded the carbine. She reached the apex of the roof. The hooks on her boots notwithstanding, she felt like she was going to be torn off the roof by the slipstream. Looking down the trailer's slope she could see the cab. At first she thought that the trailer was disintegrating when the holes started appearing in the front half of its roof. They looked like strangely regularly shaped sinkholes in the armour, falling away like quicksand. Then she realised it was some sort of nanotech application. She guessed this was the illegal surprise she'd half been expecting.

'Eh, boss,' Mass said, 'there's something odd happening to the side of the truck.'

'This side as well,' Torricone said. Miska had the butt of her carbine nestled in her shoulder now. The holes in the armour were starting to look like some kind of hive structure.

'Mass, Hradisky, I want you covering either side of the truck, anything comes out of—'

She saw the first insectile, mechanical leg appear over the edge of one of the holes. Then there were spider drones, long, needle-like mandibles dripping venom, scuttling towards her. Miska started firing burst after burst. She heard Mass and Hradisky firing as well. She wasn't sure how many there were but it looked like a lot. One scuttled over the side of the lorry next to her. She only just caught its movement in the corner of her vision. She swung and fired a three-round burst and it ceased to be. Another came over the side but exploded as Mass shot it, but another one had got closer while her concentration had been elsewhere. She was moving backwards now, firing, shifting aim, firing again. 'Guys, they can't get behind me.'

'Miska, one's just gone on to the roof behind you,' Torricone said.

'Two on this side,' Mass added.

What'd I just say? Miska was moving backwards faster now, as the scuttling drones closed in on her. She spun to face back. One of the drones was in the air as it pounced at her. She shot that first. Another took to the air, and she caught that with a three-round burst, then she destroyed the third as it crouched to leap. She swung back to find more trying to flank her. She all but ran backwards, still trying not to get blown off the truck. She was shooting them out of the air. Wired reflexes, instinct honed through training, years of experience, and smartlink technology were the only things keeping her alive.

'Fuck! It's on the car!' Mass's voice came over group comms.

Shit! Miska was about to run out of trailer and she would be damned before she leapt back onto the pickup. She risked glancing behind her. There were spider drones all over the front of the pickup. Hradisky was firing at them from the cargo bed. Torricone was driving one-handed. He had his SIG in his free hand, a spider drone crushed up against the passenger window as he fired repeatedly into it.

She swung back around, fired three more bursts and her carbine ran dry. She let the weapon drop on its sling. Two of the drones were close enough to leap at her. Fast drawing her GP-992 with one hand, a spare magazine for the weapon with her other, she fired. One of the leaping spider drones exploded in mid-air. Miska stepped to one side and the other flew past her.

That can be Hradisky's problem, she decided as she continued firing bursts from the SIG. She knew she was about to be overrun, literally, but she really didn't want to retreat. She watched the number on the ammo counter in her IVD get smaller and smaller. She ejected a magazine from the pistol, slid another one home straight away and started firing again but the spider drones used that time to close in on her.

'Hradisky, unless you're about to die, get the shotgun ready!' she shouted over group comms, desperately hoping that their situation had improved.

One of the spider drones landed on her. She ripped it off and flung it away. Another got kicked away. A third bit her legs but her armour hardened and its hypodermic mandibles didn't breach skin. A fourth attacked and she felt mandibles scrape her subdermal armour before she stamped on it and then shot it. The pistol's magazine ran dry again and she touched it to the smartgrip holster, which sucked the weapon into it.

'Hradisky, now!' Miska sent the targeting info to the shotgun.

A spider drone leapt at her face. She caught it, bore it to the roof of the truck and boosted muscle drove the synthetic diamond edge of her combat knife through its metal and plastic guts. She heard the shotgun firing in rapid succession. It seemed to take an age until she saw the contrails from the gyrojet motors as the micro-missiles hit the spider drones, catching many of them mid-leap. The HEAP warheads went off. Multiple explosions buffeted Miska, shrapnel tore at her, but she managed to keep her balance on the roof. She looked around. There didn't seem to be any more of the horrible things. One side of her face was bleeding. With her visor up a bit of shrapnel had made it inside the helmet, narrowly missing her eye.

'Clear?' she ventured.

'Clear,' Hradisky said.

There was a burst of gauss carbine fire.

'Clear,' Mass added.

Miska reloaded the carbine, then the pistol, and started walking back up the sloping roof of the trailer with some purpose. She stepped over the hexagonal holes in the roof, checking for more of the drones as she did so. There was no movement inside the technological hive structure. Miska was sick of this semi and sick of this so-called Master of Puppets. She suspected that he wasn't controlling the drones otherwise everything would have been that much more difficult. If she had been right about tight-beam communication then Kaneda had probably cut off comms. The robot vehicle and the other drones had been acting autonomously, which had been bad enough. Once again Kaneda had proven his worth.

Miska crawled from the trailer onto the roof of the tractor unit's cab and slid down onto the smooth black bubble of tinted, armoured glass that covered much of the front of the vehicle. The semi was still weaving from side to side but the motion was almost comforting now.

'Teramoto, you got eyes on me?' Miska asked. He was ahead of the robot vehicle.

'I'm watching you,' he replied.

Anchoring herself with one gloved hand and the pads on both knees, Miska unhooked the laser cutter. The strobing red beam started to cut through the glass. It took a while to get through the armoured material but eventually Miska used the molecular hooks on her glove to pull out a sizeable panel of the thick glass. She found herself looking at the tight-beam uplink dish, which she knew would be connected to the dumb AI's solid state CPU. Miska smiled. She used the soles of her boots and the pad on her knees to clamp herself over the hole she'd made. She pulled her electronics tool kit from one of the pouches she'd clipped to the bike jacket and used it to attach two data clamps, each with wireless transceivers, to the connection from the uplink to the CPU. She checked the connection and peeked sideways into the net. They were no longer locked out of the robot vehicle's systems. In the area's rather sparse netscape it looked like a western style stagecoach, mixed with armoured cars. Eight black stallions, all with burning eyes and flaming hooves, pulled the stagecoach.

'Cool,' Miska decided. This Master of Puppets might be a jerk when it came to setting up death traps but she liked his aesthetics. 'Teramoto, come and get me.' She turned around carefully until she was sat on the cab's sloping front, held on by the pads on both gloves. Teramoto was braking. It looked as though his bike was reversing towards the front of the truck. The rear wheel of the bike was almost touching the front of the semi when Teramoto accelerated again, just keeping ahead of the robot vehicle. The pockmarked crash cowl folded back and she could see him bent low over the bike. Miska pushed herself up and ran down the front of the semi and then leapt into the air. She landed on the seat just behind Teramoto. The bike swerved hard but Teramoto fought the wobbling vehicle and finally managed to get it under control. Miska's boots adhered themselves to the passenger footrest, her hands adhered to Teramoto's shoulders and then she collapsed on the Yakuza lieutenant's back as she tranced in.

In the net Teramoto's bike was a perfectly rendered animation of a classic bike design from the manufacturer's history. Miska was standing on the back of the bike in her comically angry cartoon icon, looking at the horses and the stagecoach. She frowned. The stagecoach had a driver. He was a tall, thin, cadaverous-looking gentleman, wearing a tailed frockcoat, vest, bowtie and stovepipe hat. He smiled at her, letting her see a mouthful of particularly sharp and pointy-looking teeth. He raised his hat to her and Miska realised he didn't have any eyelids. Miska was pretty sure it was another hacker's icon.

So where did you come from? she wondered. It was clear that he'd gained entry to the truck's systems by its still-functioning tight-beam uplink. Kaneda had taken out the tight-beam uplink on the Master of Puppet's van, so that ruled the MoP out. It was also highly unlikely that the MoP was a master drone rigger *and* a master hacker. This suggested that there was someone other than the MoP involved. She thought back to the subtle trace that had been run on her search program when they'd first discovered the facility. Was this the hacker? With the level of skill and technology involved, could this coachman be the MoP's Martian Intelligence handler as Raff had suspected? The coachman stood up in the driver's box, a whip held easily in one hand. The running lamps either side of him were burning like hell itself.

'You don't want it, and can't have it,' he called across to her. He sounded very reasonable, almost pleasant. Miska wanted to agree with him.

'Ever wonder why your life isn't easy?' she asked him. He shrugged amiably.

'The choices we make,' he suggested. Miska just nodded and then sent a command to the semi's CPU to switch off the tight-beam uplink. The whip lashed out as lightning, and the command was destroyed. Miska leapt into the air, her club held high. The whip lashed out again and again. Umbrellas appeared all around her, each one blocking a lash of the lightning whip and then disappearing. She landed on the yoke between the two lines of flame-eyed stallions. She rammed her club down onto the yoke. Her attack programs manifested as cartoon shockwaves. The coachman's electric lash flicked out and caught her. It was agony. She screamed out loud. She knew that back in the real world her body would be bucking around on the bike, blood seeping from her ears as a result of the biofeedback. The shockwaves caught the coachman and he stumbled backwards. While he was distracted, Miska slapped one of her black-furred, sneaky worms onto the flank of the closest galloping stallion. Then she started leaping from horse to horse as she made her way towards the coachman. He was standing in the driver's box again, spinning the lightning whip around him. Miska leapt into the air, club held high above her head in a two-handed grip. She was going to hammer this fucker into the ground like a nail.

The whip caught her as she fell. Suddenly she was dressed in energy. Tendrils of the electricity crept out, trying to violate her systems, force their way into her integral computer and then her neural interface and, despite her high spec defences, they were slowly succeeding. The hacker was not only good but he was packing state of the art, military grade software. Miska knew that she would really be thrashing around behind Teramoto now. She hoped he didn't dump the bike.

The only thing she had going in her favour was the coach-man's overconfidence.

Her fuzzy black worm had snuck from horse to horse – they represented the robot vehicle's control systems for the power drive – crept around the CPU, which she knew the coachman would be monitoring carefully, and switched off the uplink. The coachman simply disappeared as the sneaky worm isolated the semi's system again, with the exception of the wireless transceiver that Miska had added. Miska landed in the driver's box. She dropped worms liberally all over the stagecoach. It had excellent intrusion countermeasures in its own right but with a generous application of her club she was able to subdue them as well and take control of the vehicle.

'Are you all right?' Teramoto asked over a private comms link. Miska opened a window so she could see Teramoto's bike.

Then, using the feed from the truck's rear lens, she opened another window to the real world. The muscle car and the pickup looked badly damaged but they were still running and somehow everyone was still alive.

'I'm good,' she told them over the group comms. She knew that she was going to have one hell of a headache when she tranced out, but they'd done it. Stolen whatever was in the back of the robot truck. She hoped it was worth it.

CHAPTER 19

Miska watched from the net as the battle-damaged robot truck drove into the warehouse behind Teramoto's bike. The crash cowl on the bike slid down and Miska saw her own limp form adhered to the Yakuza lieutenant. She didn't like how she looked clinging to Teramoto like that. She saw Kaneda's bike was already there. He was waiting for them. He had replaced his lost laser with one of the Springfield Magnetics gauss carbines. Vido came out of the briefing room. He was carrying one of the carbines as well. The muscle car and the pickup, their armour covered in hundreds, possibly thousands, of holes, parked either side of the truck. Miska was pleased to see Torricone, Hradisky, Mass and Goodluck climb out of their vehicles and take up positions around the semi. Miska tranced out, returning to her meat and a white-knife migraine.

'Ow fuck!' She almost slid off the bike. With a thought she flooded her system with painkillers. She tried to stand up but her foot almost went out from under her and she had to steady herself against the bike. She suspected she'd broken something in her foot when she'd bounced it off the blacktop while hanging off the semi's trailer. She just hadn't noticed with all the adrenalin flooding her system. She experimented with putting weight on it, and it held, though it hurt. The painkillers were reducing both her problems to a dull ache. Teramoto was just watching her. Miska was grateful that he hadn't offered her help, or asked her if she was okay. She slid the heavy battery off her back and lay the laser cutter on the floor as she hobbled towards the truck.

'We get to see what all the fuss was about?' Mass asked over group comms. Miska had to smile at the curiosity in his tone.

'Man, that was a rush!' Hradisky shouted. He was on the other side of the semi. Goodluck was smiling but shaking his head. She could also see Torricone. He didn't look happy at all. Miska thought about getting him to admit that he'd enjoyed the job but she knew she had to remind them that they were still working without ruining their victory.

'Vido,' she asked over group comms, 'what's the story with the cops?' They had turned off the coastal highway and up into wine country using what back roads they could. Thanks to Blanca's influence, the cops had known to be elsewhere. Subtle manipulation of the local traffic systems meant they'd passed very few other vehicles on their way back to the warehouse and once they had reached the industrial estate, most of that traffic had been automated.

'They're responding now but they're not going to be looking for us for a good long time, unless someone with more clout makes them. So the quicker we deal with Dominic, the better,' Vido told her.

'One thing at a time,' she said. 'Vido, keep monitoring comms. As soon as we know what we're dealing with, we'll need to start making arrangements with Blanca to get it off-world.'

'Dominic will need to be dealt with before that ...' Vido started.

Miska had reached the front of the semi. She turned to look at the *consigliere*. He just raised his hands and leaned against the wall of the briefing area. Miska climbed up the tractor unit's cab. It was a lot easier to do now that the vehicle wasn't travelling at seventy miles per hour. She was a little suspicious that there were no lenses or sensors in the trailer that would allow her to see the contents. She was hoping the holes created by the spider drones would let her get eyes on the contents of the trailer.

'Kaneda, Teramoto, I want you walking a perimeter, keep an eye on the security lenses. Mass, Torricone, Hradisky and Goodluck, just cover me,' she told them. Despite the pain in her foot she'd managed to scramble back onto the roof. She brought the carbine up to her shoulder, covering the regular hexagonal holes in the truck. She magnified her vision, not wanting to get too close to the holes in case the Master of Puppets had left any more surprises for them. It was some kind of machine hive. She broadcast what her eyes were seeing over group comms.

'Looks like a tech honeycomb,' Goodluck said. There was a degree of disgust in his voice.

'Nanotech?' Torricone asked.

'The process that made the holes in the trailer's armour probably was,' Miska told them. All nanotech was heavily restricted but material-based nanotech was the easiest to access. 'The rest of it looks like standard tech, though it's a weird set-up.' Despite all the machinery implanted in her own meat, she was finding something creepy about machines designed to imitate arachnid and insect life. She ducked down, to get a closer look into the holes.

'Careful,' Mass said, uneasy. Miska magnified her vision but all she could see was more machinery for the spider drones. She straightened up and made her way gingerly across the holes towards the back of the trailer.

'Looks like we're going to have to do this the hard way,' Miska told the others as she crested the curving apex of the roof and started walking down the still intact back part of the trailer. 'Goodluck, Hradisky, I want you to cover the rear doors, Torr—' Two enormous cuboid hammerheads exploded through the roof, narrowly missing her. She caught a glimpse of something armoured, mechanical and brutal-looking bursting out of the back half of the trailer, before the impact on the roof sent her flying.

She landed on the pickup truck's bonnet. The suspension cushioned some of the blow, as did her bike armour. Her spine didn't snap thanks to her bones being reinforced. It still hurt. A lot. She would have screamed but breathing was an issue yet again. She was aware of the hypersonic screams as her Bastards opened fire on the thing crouched among the wreckage of the rear part of the semi's trailer.

No! she tried to scream. She'd only caught a glimpse of it but she was pretty sure she knew what it was. She managed to roll off the pickup and onto all fours on the floor. Hypersonic roaring. It looked like the pickup truck had just folded in half as railgun rounds destroyed it.

'Run!' she screamed over comms as the ability to breathe returned. With a thought she switched on the warehouse's sprinklers. 'Take cover, hoods up!' The muscle car exploded, then the bikes were tumbling across the warehouse, eaten away by railgun fire in mid-air. She could see the briefing room. Vido had disappeared inside it. Kaneda was firing at the war droid stood in the wreckage of the trailer.

No! Miska thought. The carbine rounds would do nothing against the droid's military grade armour. She saw Teramoto sprinting towards the briefing room. His crash helmet split open, there was a spray of red, he ran a few more faltering steps and then collapsed to the ground.

What the fuck! Miska still wasn't quite sure what she had just seen. Kaneda folded back into the briefing room. Miska made it to the kitchen area and threw herself into it just as railgun rounds tore through the flimsy internal walls and suddenly appliances, kitchen furniture and foodstuffs were flying through the air. Miska just lay on the floor and hoped one of the large calibre rounds didn't tag her. At best she'd lose a limb, more likely she'd be dead. The firing stopped. Miska dared to look up. She found a terrified-looking Torricone and Hradisky staring back at her. Both of them were covered in splattered foodstuff. She was as well.

Hradisky mouthed the words: 'What the fuck?' at her. She signalled him to remain where he was. She moved to one of the impact holes in the wall of the kitchen and peeked through. The war droid was a squat, six-limbed, armoured behemoth. It was about the same size as, and comparable in power to, a light mech, but it was either being rigged as a drone, or more likely it was operating autonomously. Its front two limbs ended in pneumatically powered hammerheads. It had a combination missile launcher and 20mm Retributor railgun mounted on its back. It was crouched half on, half off the trailer. Something about its posture reminded Miska of an animal protecting its young. She could see the edge of something in the trailer, the cargo, but couldn't make out what it was.

'Why isn't it killing us?' Torricone subvocalised over group comms.

'I think it got Teramoto,' Goodluck subvocalised back. Miska shifted position a little. She could see the Yakuza lieutenant lying face down in a pool of expanding blood. She checked his biometrics in her IVD. He was dead and he hadn't been killed by the war droid. If he'd taken a hit from the Retributor his body parts would have been scattered all over the warehouse.

'It can't see us,' Miska said over group comms. With walls between it and them its lenses and lidar would be all but useless. It would have thermographics but between the coolant systems built into their inertial armour, and the sprinklers, they would appear close to ambient temperature. The only way it could find them was by actively looking for them and it seemed that it had been programmed to protect the truck's payload. 'Just don't move around and don't make a noise.'

'It took out the vehicles,' Vido said over comms. He would be watching what was happening on the thinscreens via the warehouse's internal security lenses. 'Teramoto looks dead.'

Yeah, because Kaneda shot him! She was sure of it. Miska wondered if Vido had seen that.

'He's dead,' she subvocalised.

'So now what do we do?' Mass asked. It was a good question.

'We got anything that'll touch it?' Goodluck asked. Miska checked the feed from his lens. He was hiding in the dorm area, the water from the sprinklers cascading down on him.

'No,' Miska answered. No heavy weapons, no plasma guns. *Fuck my life!* The best she could think to do was try and extract without getting anyone else killed. The mission was over. They'd failed. Except something that Vido had said kept nagging at her. The war droid had taken out the vehicles. It was trying to keep them here. Miska frowned and then peeked sideways into the net. She had assumed that the war droid would be an isolated

307

system, or at the very least using a tight-beam uplink to prevent hacking, but there it was in the middle of the warehouse's anachronistic virtual rendering, an iron, beast-like, clockwork golem standing among the virtual wreckage of the stagecoach. Tiny clockwork insects were growing out of its skin, the virtual representation of the virus scampering towards the warehouse's systems as the war droid attempted to suborn them. Neon light shot from an anachronistic spinning communications dish on the virtual representation of the war droid's back as it transmitted to any local comms device that would listen.

In the real world Miska collapsed face-first into a mass of chopped tomatoes as she tranced in. *Fuck!* The war droid was telling the Master of Puppets and god knew who else where they were.

Miska wasted no time as she appeared in her cartoon battle-form in the net. She leapt into the air, club held high, dropping worms in her wake. Her fuzzy worms went after the war droid's virus. An ancient-looking ack-ack gun grew out of the clockwork golem's back and started firing attack programs at her in the form of explosive flak. Her protective software manifested all around her as umbrella shields.

Angry cartoon Miska landed on the golem and she started pounding on it with her club. Acid-green fuzzy worms dropped out of her pockets and started burrowing into the golem. The seek-and-destroy virus was going straight for the war droid's CPU. Meanwhile, Miska distracted the war droid with the blunt force trauma of her less than subtle club attack program.

'Miska!' It was Torricone over group comms. She didn't want to be distracted but she risked opening a window to accept the feed from security lenses in the warehouse and the kitchen area. The war droid was stomping across the warehouse floor towards the kitchen. She was touched by the 'loyalty' her Bastards showed when they opened up, pointlessly, on the droid from different parts of the warehouse. Or perhaps they were just worried about the N-bombs in their heads going off if she got smushed. Fortunately the returning Retributor fire from the war droid seemed mostly suppressing in nature. The electromagnetically driven 20mm rounds were eating away at the soft internal walls, forcing her Bastards to take cover.

The war droid burst through the wall of the kitchen. Miska saw her impending death as though it were happening in a viz. The war droid picked up her limp body, even as she pounded on its virtual representation. It drew back one of its pneumatic sledgehammer fists. Cartoon Miska grimaced. She wondered if she would actually see her death before her brain shut down.

Torricone was pouring fire from his carbine onto the war droid. He was doing little more than creating sparks and rico-chet, but the thought was there. Hradisky fired the remaining four micro-missiles from the shotgun at the war droid. It saved Miska's life. Not because the exploding HEAP warheads did much in the way of damage but because the war droid, or who-ever was piloting it, momentarily thought that Hradisky was a threat. The war droid threw Miska at Hradisky with enough force to knock them both through the kitchen's flimsy internal wall. Its turret turned the Retributor towards them to turn them into a smear across the cratered warehouse floor.

One of cartoon Miska's little green worms made it through the war droid's intrusion countermeasures and into its CPU. The acid-green worm ate the war droid's operating system. The war droid froze, the ruins of the kitchen raining down around it.

Miska sent her worms after the comms messages that the

droid had got off. It was a waste of time, she knew that, but she had to try. She was about to trance out when she looked up and saw a clockwork owl watching her from a perch on part of the stagecoach's torn armoured plate. The bird hopped off its perch and disappeared into the stagecoach. Miska stared at it for a moment. Frankly, unless it was attacking them she didn't have time to investigate it at the moment.

Miska opened her eyes, back in her aching meat, and drew in a ragged breath.

'Fuck!' she howled as she rolled off Hradisky and sat up. 'This is really intense! Anybody else finding this intense?'

'Yes,' Hradisky gasped. Miska looked down at him. Hradisky was on his back. He seemed to be struggling to breathe.

'Oh shit, you okay?' Miska asked. Torricone ran over to them, the water from the sprinklers slowly washing off all the various foodstuff and powdered plaster dust that he was covered in. Hradisky was pointing at his chest. 'T, get the med kit, he might have a busted rib, hook up a medpak to it, see what you can do,' Miska told Torricone. He just nodded and ran for the med kit. Mass, Goodluck and Kaneda had emerged from their various hiding places, carbines at the ready, still pointing at the inert war droid. 'Don't worry, it's dead,' she reassured them. 'Vido, keep your eye on the external lenses, the war droid got off a message. We should be expecting company.'

'Understood,' Vido replied, all business, but she could hear a degree of shakiness in his voice.

'Boss,' Mass called. He was standing by Teramoto's body. 'I'm no expert but I don't think this was a railgun round.'

Miska turned to look at Kaneda. He looked pale, shaken, scared shitless. She had no idea if it was the fight, or what he'd done.

'He ran right into my line of fire,' Kaneda offered. Mass gaped at him.

'Friendly fire?' he demanded. 'A-fucking-gain!'

'We don't have time for this,' Miska told them.

'We'll deal with this when we get back to the *Daughter*, understand me private?' Mass demanded.

'Yes, corporal,' Kaneda said, staring at the floor. Torricone came running back with the med kit and knelt down next to Hradisky.

'Mass, I want you and Kaneda walking the perimeter. Kaneda, watch your fucking fields of fire because if you tag anyone else I will blow up your head with a thought, understand me?'

'Yes, boss,' Kaneda said in a small voice. Miska knew that she would have to deal with this later. If he had done it on purpose she couldn't really blame him. She would have done it herself if Teramoto hadn't intimated he knew something about her father's death.

'Torricone, join Mass and Kaneda when you're done. Hradisky, once he's finished playing nurse join V in the briefing area,' Miska continued as she limped towards the semi's mostly destroyed trailer. 'Goodluck, you're with me.' The Comanchero OG joined her, carbine at the ready.

'I think if the devil drove a truck it would be this one,' Goodluck muttered.

'Certainly seems to have no end of tricks,' Miska said, and then over group comms: 'Uncle V, no bullshit, we need to move quickly. If possible, we need to get a heavy lift transport, probably with two cargo exoskeletons to be on the safe side, if not a truck with the same, but we need to move now.'

'I'll see what I can do,' Vido said. He didn't sound entirely confident. They had asked a lot of Blanca, after all.

Limping a bit Miska raised her own carbine as they approached the partially destroyed trailer.

'Miska,' Goodluck said quietly. She followed his eyes and saw the strange, black, root-like structures. They looked like they had grown through the truck's armour, the wheel arches and wheels and into the warehouse's concrete floor. There they were starting to branch out. The roots looked as though they were made of some kind of soapstone-like rock. Something about them made her think that the root-like structures were tech of some kind. She felt Goodluck staring at her. She just shook her head.

'How're we going to move it if it's taken root?' the Comanchero OG asked.

'We've still got a laser cutter,' Miska said, shrugging. 'Fuck it, it's not my alien artefact.' Now Goodluck was staring at her. Miska moved round, carbine at the ready, so she could get a better view of the contents of the trailer. It looked like a slab of soapstone, with a raised frame running around it. The frame was made of the same material as the slab but was shaped like tightly packed ribs.

'What …?' Goodluck started.

'I've no idea,' Miska said but as she was staring at it the image got fuzzier, as though there was some kind of interference. She felt a tug towards the object.

'This isn't right,' Goodluck whispered. Miska tended to agree. Her head was beginning to hurt again, like a hot knife was being thrust into it.

'Boss,' Vido said over group comms. Miska used it as an excuse to turn away from the object. The pain in her head lessened but her skin was itching. 'I think we've got company.' He shared the warehouse's external lens feed with her. Miska could see a six-wheeled vehicle parked on the slope that ran down into the bowl that formed the light industrial park. It looked for all the world like a passenger coach, except there were no windows. She knew it would be armoured, probably six-wheel drive, and she was pretty sure it was either being piloted or controlled by the Master of Puppets. He must have been close when he'd received the war droid's message. She looked sideways into the net but his battle-bus was an isolated system, it had no net presence.

'Uh guys,' Mass asked, 'where's Teramoto's body?'

CHAPTER 20

Miska turned back to look at where Teramoto had lain. Mass was stood over a bloodstain but there was no body.

'And what the fuck is that?' Mass added. The root structure they had seen growing from the artefact ran like veins through the floor to the bloodstain.

'When did that happen?' Goodluck asked, his voice laden with superstitious dread.

'Uncle V, run the footage from the internal lenses back. What's going on?' Miska asked. Then, through the external security lens feed, she saw that the MoP's battle-bus had split open. Soldier drones, humanoid droids not dissimilar to the guard droids on board the *Hangman's Daughter*, were unfolding from extending cargo racks. 'Shit!' She started striding towards the door of the warehouse, Goodluck falling in next to her.

'Why didn't you just use drones?' he asked.

'Because they can be hacked,' she told him. She left out that they were expensive to maintain and replace, and none of them had murdered her father.

'Nothing,' Vido said. He sounded badly spooked.

'Torricone, Mass, Kaneda, get up on the roof. You shoot anything you find up there,' Miska told them. Torricone and Mass started moving. 'What do you mean nothing?' she asked Vido as she opened the front door to the warehouse just wide enough for her and Goodluck to fire through. She could see the drones moving down the steep slope next to the road and onto the loading area of one of the automated microfactories. They moved tactically, like soldiers, but exactly like soldiers. They were working from a program. They would be easy to predict. She lifted the carbine to her shoulder, the smartlink crosshairs in her IVD adjusted for range, settling over the featureless metal face of one of the soldier drones. She stroked the trigger, firing a three-round burst. The droid collapsed forward. She shifted target and fired again.

'One minute he's there, the next he's not,' Vido said. He didn't sound that far from panic himself. This was bad news. That meant someone had hacked and then spoofed the warehouse's systems, apparently without triggering any warnings at all. Miska fired again and another droid dropped. With a thought she uploaded a diagnostic program from her implanted computer, through her neural interface, into the warehouse's systems to see what it could find. There was little else that she could do.

She could hear firing from the roof as Torricone, Mass and Kaneda joined the fight. Goodluck was firing as well but he just seemed to be causing little explosions of earth.

'If you can't aim for shit, at least use the smartlink,' Miska told him.

'I am,' he said. He sounded shit-scared. Miska turned round to look at him. He was shaking.

315

'Goodluck, get up on the roof with the others. Keep your head down but I want you watching their backs, checking the other three sides of the building, got that?'

He nodded. He was coated in sweat.

'I'm sorry,' he told her and fled. Miska fired again. Four of the droids were moving behind one of the microfacturies, presumably to flank them. Now three of them were trying to do that. She ducked back behind the door as she saw tracers coming her way.

'Vido, Hradisky, find cover in there, make sure you can see as much of the interior as possible. Keep your heads on a swivel because I don't know what happened to Teramoto. V, you're running comms on the run, okay?' Both of them answered in the affirmative, both of them sounded shaken. She was taking a lot of fire now. The droids might be predictable but they were fearless. They could walk into fire and still shoot straight. She closed and locked the warehouse door and then she too started running for the stairs to the mezzanine floor and the roof. Hradisky and Vido had emerged from the briefing room and taken up position behind bits of wrecked muscle car and pickup respectively. They hadn't needed to be told to keep away from the artefact.

'Can we use that?' Vido asked, pointing at the war droid standing stock-still in the ruins of the kitchen.

'No,' Miska told him, 'I trashed the operating system.' It gave her an idea, though. A really good idea but it was one that she really, really didn't want to initiate. She composed a message and sent it. Then, as she scrambled up the stairs to the mezzanine, she had a really bad idea. She composed an addendum to the original message and sent that as well.

'Any idea on transpo, V?' Miska asked.

316

'We can't ask Blanca's people to walk into this,' Vido answered. Miska sighed, he was right.

'Okay, cancel it, but tell Blanca we may have to get arrested to get out of this. If she wants us to deal with Dominic, and we're still the best chance she's got, then she could do with a contingency for getting us out.'

'I'll tell her,' Vido replied. Judging by his tone he didn't hold out much hope for Blanca's response.

'You know anybody who'd snitch us out to Dominic?' Miska asked Vido over a private comms link. He didn't answer immediately.

'Yes,' he finally said, warily.

'Arrange for them to find out where we are but tell them we're gone in thirty minutes,' she said.

'Miska …'

'Just fucking do it!' she snapped.

Miska had reached the ladder from the mezzanine floor to the roof hatch. As she climbed it, holes appearing in the walls of the warehouse, the fierce sodium glow of the industrial park's lights shining through, she wondered where the fuck Teramoto had got to. She had checked his biometrics. They were still flatlined. His lens feed had gone dark.

Miska climbed up onto the roof. Kaneda, Torricone and Mass were firing east, out over the front of the warehouse, towards where the droids had been advancing from the coach. They ducked behind the lip at the edge of the roof as they received withering return fire. Goodluck was firing long panicky bursts to the south. Miska watched as a round tugged at the shoulder of his bike armour and he fell back onto the roof.

'Torricone, take the north, Mass the west, Kaneda stay

where you are. They're droids, give them a chance and they will not miss. You fire a three-round burst, head if you can, chest if you can't. Then you duck down, move, pop up and fire again. Even if you think you've got a second shot, you do not take it. Keep the movements as random as possible,' she told them over group comms. Mass and Torricone were already moving as she reached the east facing lip of the roof. Kaneda was ducking down. The position that he'd just fired from was getting hit by a lot of incoming fire. Miska went down on one knee. Crosshairs centred on the head of a droid and she stroked the trigger. The droid went down. She ducked behind the lip and moved. Kaneda popped up and took two single shots rather than a three-round burst. *Whatever works*, she thought as she popped up, firing again. 'I'm a roving shooter, you get into trouble you call for me. Now call out what you got,' she said over group comms.

'West quadrant, zero tangos,' Mass told her. Tangos being targets.

'North quadrant, zer— four tangos trying to stealth us,' Torricone told her before starting to fire.

'Eh ... Miska ...' Goodluck said.

'You got this?' Miska asked Kaneda. He looked pale, almost sickly, but he nodded. Miska crouched down and ran across the roof to the south quadrant. She enlarged Goodluck's lens feed to see what was going on but he was moving along behind the lip. She reached the lip and took a knee, peering down towards the ground. Six droids were making a run for the wall. She dropped one of them, ignored her own advice and tried for a second but the return fire forced her to duck behind the lip. She crawled along behind it as Goodluck popped up and fired. She saw him walk a sloppy seven-round burst in on another droid. He got tagged again in the return fire, this time in the arm, and fell back.

'Goddamnit Goodluck! You're staying up too long,' she told him. 'You okay?'

'Just glanced the arm,' he told her, sounding pained. Miska guessed that hardening inertial armour had deflected the round. She popped up again but the droids had reached the wall. She pointed straight down and fired, dropping one with three rounds straight through the top of its head. Another had been attaching a frame charge to the wall.

'V, Hradisky, about a quarter of the way down the south wall from the west corner, you're about to receive guests, frame charge ...' It blew. The warehouse shook. She enlarged Vido's contact lens feed. He was staggering about a little but she caught a glimpse of the hole in the wall. Hradisky was firing. The droid coming through the hole in the wall staggered backwards and then toppled over. Vido got his act together and put a three-round burst into the next one.

'Boss!' Kaneda cried over the comms link. She started to move towards the eastern lip of the roof.

'Miska!' it was Vido, panicked. She checked his feed. She couldn't quite believe what she was seeing. Teramoto, sword in one hand, had lifted Hradisky off the ground by his head. Teramoto looked larger, and his back now had a pronounced hunch.

'Shit! Anyone not currently engaged, help Kaneda!' she shouted over group comms and ran for the hatch to the roof.

Miska landed on the mezzanine floor, moved quickly around the office. She took a moment to try and understand the scene. Teramoto's fingers had grown through Hradisky's face. The dead Yakuza lieutenant's mouth was open unnaturally wide, his throat bulging as what looked like a thick, black swarm of flies surged out of him and into Hradisky's equally distended mouth and swollen throat. The transformed Teramoto was holding Hradisky between himself and Vido. The *consigliere* was trying to get a clear shot. Miska triggered Teramoto's N-bomb with a thought, but nothing happened. She levelled her carbine at Teramoto but caught movement to the south. She shifted and fired, taking out one of the droids coming through the hole in the wall. She moved to the side and knelt down, rounds impacting all around her, and fired again, taking out the second droid. She swung her carbine back. Hradisky was lying on the floor, spine bent close to snapping as he spasmed violently. She just caught Vido disappearing into the briefing room. *Fair enough*, she decided.

Teramoto was sprinting towards her. She had time for a quick shot. She saw matter spray from the back of his head but it didn't seem to slow him. He leapt into the air and landed in front of her, swinging his sword. She managed to get the carbine in the way. The folded steel of Teramoto's *shinobigatana* cut through her weapon. Miska backed away, her left hand hitting the quick release on the sling, letting the remnants of the now-useless carbine drop away. Her right drew the SIG Sauer GP-992 gauss pistol. She got off a burst before Teramoto slapped it out of her grip. Her hand went numb. He grabbed her around the neck.

She felt his fingers grow newly sharp, long nails trying to push through her subdermal armour. He lifted her into the air. His back looked like a hive. Flies were crawling all over it. She felt a wave of revulsion. Her knife was in her hand now. She rammed it up into his wrist. He howled. It didn't sound right. It was modulated somehow. She sawed the knife round and he dropped her. Teramoto raised his sword. Miska leapt into the air and buried her knife in his skull to the hilt. Teramoto became very still. He stared at her. He looked very angry. Miska found herself resisting the bizarre urge to apologise.

'Miska, move!' Vido shouted. He had emerged from the briefing room fumbling with the Remington combat shotgun. Teramoto tore the knife from his head and threw it at Vido. Vido fired the shotgun. Miska threw herself back. The knife hit Vido with sufficient force to send him flying. The aerofoil acid grenade hit Teramoto and exploded. Miska howled as a splash caught her cheek. She tried to crawl away from the pain but it followed her. She saw her SIG on the floor, however. She grabbed it and rolled over. Teramoto was a blackened, screaming mess. She emptied the entire magazine from the gauss pistol into him. He barely seemed to notice. He did turn and run into the office. Miska clambered to her feet, cheek smoking, and rapidly reloaded the SIG. She swung around into the doorway of the office. There was a Teramoto-sized hole in the opposite wall. Miska turned and raced down the stairs. She looked under the mezzanine floor but she couldn't see a thing. *Where the fuck'd he go?* She glanced over at where the artefact lay on the semi's trailer. She heard a moan, swung round and almost shot Vido as he sat up.

'You okay?' she asked. He stared at her as if she was a moron for a moment and then managed to push himself to his feet.

'The armour stopped it, but you know when people say they're too old for something, but they don't really mean it?' he asked. She nodded. Her cheek was still smoking. It hurt a lot. 'Well, I really mean it. What the fuck is going on?'

She didn't have a good answer but she had a sneaking feeling that they were in here with an alien.

'You think our message got through to Dominic?' she asked,

changing the subject as she approached Hradisky, gauss pistol levelled at him. She only just caught Vido's shrug.

'You're hoping that he comes here in force and they wipe each other out?' he asked.

Miska grimaced. Hradisky was a mess. She didn't have to check his biometrics to realise he was dead. Patches of skin and flesh were missing. It looked like it had been eaten by some kind of necrotising virus. Flies were buzzing around his corpse. She leaned down and caught one. She magnified the view. The fly was a machine. Some kind of nanobot, she suspected. She didn't know much about nanotechnology but she suspected the fly was pretty sophisticated and had originated with the artefact. Vido was staring at her. She crushed the nanobot, and picked up Hradisky's gauss carbine, running a diagnostic on the weapon as she attached it to her sling before retrieving her knife. She could still hear firing from the roof.

'How many more acid grenades have we got?' she asked. Vido held up two fingers.

'Put two blanks in the shotgun, keep one of the grenades on the end of it, only to be used on Teramoto unless I say otherwise.'

Vido nodded and started sliding the blank rounds into the shotgun's tubular magazine.

The big eastern double door blew in. Miska turned instinctively away from the blast. She turned back almost immediately, shrapnel bouncing off her armour. Her carbine was up. She was marching towards the wreck of the pickup, rapidly firing bursts from her weapon. She was aware of Vido diving for cover. Miska knelt down behind the wreckage, still firing. Something hard caught her on the side, spinning her around. A 6.3mm penetrator had beaten the inertial armour and lodged in her subdermal armour, and she felt blood running hot and wet down her arm. She swung around. There were more droids coming through the existing hole in the south wall. She was firing as incoming rounds sparked off the wreckage. Vido was firing as well.

'We need you all down here, we're about to be overrun!' Miska shouted over group comms and fired again. One of the soldier drones made a run for cover but Miska cut it down, and then turned her attention back to the breach, trying not to think about how the other drones would be consolidating their position outside. Then Torricone and Kaneda were firing from the mezzanine floor, providing cover for Mass and Goodluck as they made their way down the steps onto the warehouse floor. Then Mass and Goodluck returned the favour. There was another explosion and a hole appeared in the north wall. Torricone and Goodluck both moved to cover, firing at the northern breach.

'Kaneda, Torricone, you've got the southern breach. Vido, you're with me on the eastern,' Miska told them as they found cover and resumed firing but she knew, as she reloaded her carbine, it was just a matter of time now. She raised her weapon again but at least two drones had made it to cover inside the warehouse. Part of her felt a degree of satisfaction that the MoP would end up with the cursed artefact.

The war droid exploded back to life. She swung around and almost fired. Goodluck did just that.

'No!' Miska shouted over comms. 'Concentrate on the soldier drones!' Mass cried out and fell back behind the tool chest he'd been using as cover, moments later Torricone cried out as he was hit as well. The war droid staggered forward and collapsed. It managed to push itself to its feet and stagger around, careening into the semi and bits of wreckage. It looked drunk, the twin pneumatic hammer arms spinning round like a child playing at being a jetcopter. The hammer limbs still managed to catch two of the soldier drones, though, battering them into the wall.

Miska exchanged fire with one of the soldier drones hunkering down behind the corner of the semi's trailer. It fired back and kept firing right up until the war droid kicked the back of the semi and sent it sliding into the wall, crushing the drone. Another lost its head to a pneumatic hammer blow as the war droid's new operating system managed to get its act together. Then the railgun started firing. Soldier drones were torn apart. Powdered regolith concrete filled the air like smoke as the war droid moved among the soldier droids, shooting them, smashing them with its hammers, stamping on them and pulling them apart. It still looked more than a little uncoordinated, however. Miska and the others had stopped firing. The war droid loomed out of the concrete dust over Miska.

'Worst idea ever!' a familiar voice snapped over group comms.

'Hi Dad,' Miska said.

CHAPTER 21

'I thought it was a pretty good idea,' Mass ventured. The war droid's head turned to look at the button man. Mass held his ground.

'Gunny,' her dad said, or rather the copy of her dad's program, the one used in the construct, the one that she'd downloaded into the hole in the war droid's CPU left by the destroyed operating system, said.

'Gunny,' Mass reluctantly added.

It was funny, the war droid may have been a mass of armour plate, servos, weapons and sensors, but somehow it still seemed to be radiating the same kind of disapproval that her dad was capable of in person. Well virtual person anyway.

It had taken a while for her message to reach the *Hangman's Daughter* where it was hiding deeper in-system, and then for her dad's electronic ghost, a sizeable program, to be sent back.

'I meant the other idea.' The war droid's head, actually its main sensor platform, turned to look at Miska.

'Did you do it?' she asked, voice brittle. This wasn't the time to start rehashing old arguments. The mission might be a total clusterfuck but it was a total clusterfuck that she was still in charge of. Her dad didn't answer. 'Gunny?'

'I did it,' he said over group comms. He knew enough not to argue now, but she knew that this topic would be revisited.

'What other idea?' Vido asked. Torricone was watching her.

'Does it matter?' Mass asked. 'Gunny here goes and destroys everything and we take this artefact out of here, go and kill Dominic and we're good, right?'

'Teramoto,' Vido said simply. Only Miska was pretty sure that whatever it was wasn't Teramoto any more.

'Well this looks perfectly fucking awful. Sitrep?' Gunny said.

'Pete!' Goodluck was suddenly running to where Teramoto had thrown Hradisky's body. Miska was on her feet, sprinting to intercept. She didn't bother trying to explain it to him. She just barged into Goodluck's side and sent him flying.

'Are you out of your fucking mind?' Goodluck howled. He started bringing his carbine round to point at her but found himself looking down the barrel of the war droid's Retributor.

'Don't be stupid, son,' Gunny said over group comms. Miska had one hand on her carbine, the other in the air.

'Easy, Goodluck,' Miska.

'Look at the body,' Vido told Goodluck. The Comanchero managed to calm down enough to look at Hradisky's corpse. Miska glanced at it as well. She could see the tiny fly-nanobots crawling in and out of the necrotic lesions on his pale flesh. Goodluck just stared.

'What happened?' Gunny asked.

'Teramoto got killed,' Vido said. He glanced at Kaneda but didn't elaborate. 'The artefact did something to him. He's

326

running around doing that to people and refusing to succumb to gunfire and acid.'

'Well, let's try it with a bigger gun,' Gunny said. It was macho nonsense, everyone knew it, but their training sergeant was with them and talking tough seemed to make them feel a bit better.

'You!' Goodluck's voice rang out across the warehouse. He had his arm outstretched, finger pointing at Miska. 'You did this!' There were tears in his eyes.

'Tell it to someone with a conscience,' Miska muttered. Now they were all staring at her.

'I think you're the devil,' Goodluck said quietly.

'Decide whether or not you want to live,' Miska told him and then turned away. 'Fall in around Gunny, we're getting him up to speed, and then we're coming up with a plan. You keep your eyes out for Teramoto. You see him, you call out and Gunny deals with him.' All but Goodluck answered with an affirmative – but even he moved to form a loose perimeter around the war droid, facing outward covering the breaches in the warehouse walls, looking for whatever Teramoto had become.

Miska briefed her dad as they moved across the warehouse, the war droid in the centre of them. They walked past the wreckage of the semi. The artefact's roots were still growing into the concrete.

Fuck it, she decided. The artefact was no longer her priority. If she could get it, she would, she would take the laser cutter to the root structure, but getting the remaining Bastards out was now the priority.

The Bastards moved out of the war droid's way, covering Gunny's back as he cracked open the door and peeked out of the warehouse. The night air was filled with hypersonic screaming as the soldier drones opened fire. The war droid was wreathed in sparks. The gauss carbines the soldier drones were carrying didn't have anything like the power needed to pierce the larger droid's armour. Miska checked the lens feed from the war droid. The soldier drones had taken up positions all around the warehouse. Then they stopped firing as one. Apparently the Master of Puppets had realised there was nothing they could do to the war droid. The battle-bus was still parked on the slope, in plain view, and that was a mistake.

'Well?' her dad asked.

'Pull back,' Miska told the Bastards. They fell back deeper into the warehouse in a rough circle, backs to each other, covering all three-hundred-and-sixty degrees. Miska was aware of Goodluck's brooding presence. The Comanchero kept glancing towards where his gang-brother lay, the flies buzzing around the corpse. 'Go for it,' Miska told her dad. Fire shot out from the missile launcher on the war droid's back-mounted turret. From the feed she watched as the missiles shot over the loading bay towards the battle-bus. The war droid was sliding the warehouse door shut. Flashes of red and the missiles exploded as the battle-bus's point defence laser took them out mid-flight.

'Back!' Gunny shouted over group comms. Miska's audio filters cut out her hearing as a deafening ripping noise filled the air. Railguns firing so rapidly that the individual hypersonic bangs became one long roar of thunder. Holes appeared in the warehouse's door. The war droid juddered as the railgun rounds hit its armour, cratering it, some of them at least penetrating. The war droid almost collapsed but managed to scuttle backwards. Something bigger than a railgun round punched through the door and made a furrow in the concrete floor. Miska triggered the sprinklers again. There was an odd delay but then they came on. The water wouldn't mask the war droid's heat signature completely but it couldn't hurt.

'A twin Retributor mount and an eighty-millimetre mass driver,' her dad told them. The furrow in the floor was glowing from the friction-generated heat of the mass driver shell.

'Those are definitely illegal, even in New Verona,' Vido said weakly.

'We should call the police,' Mass suggested. It got a few weak laughs.

'So?' Gunny asked. Miska glanced at the firing range with the battleship armour backdrop. The war droid's sensor head followed her eyes. 'I can't carry that.'

'Not all of it,' she mused, 'but we've still got a laser cutter.' They had all moved back into position around the war droid. It felt safer. 'Use the cover to close with the battle-bus ...'

'And it moves,' Torricone pointed out. 'I mean it has wheels.' He was right. Miska knew he was right.

'Yeah, okay. We walk out of here, Gunny provides cover, the Master of Puppets gets the artefact.' She could hear sighs of audible relief. Miska caught movement out of the corner of her eye as Hradisky sat up, flies crawling in and out of necrotic wounds. Miska sent the code to detonate the moving corpse's N-bomb. Nothing happened. The war droid's turret turned to point at it. Miska started to tell her dad to destroy Hradisky's body.

'No!' Goodluck had his carbine pointed at her. The war droid's Retributor twitched round to point at the Comanchero OG.

'Vido,' Miska said over a private comms link to the *consigliere*. He lowered his carbine, sweeping it to one side and letting it hang there, before unslinging the combat shotgun with the acid grenade on the end of the barrel and starting to bring it up.

'Don't you do that!' Goodluck cried. Vido hesitated, looking at Miska.

'It's not him, *mano*, you know that,' Torricone said quietly. Hradisky's body lurched to its feet like something out of an old time horror viz. Miska was relieved that it wasn't moving like Teramoto, not yet anyway.

'You want another one of those things in here?' Mass asked.

'Listen to them, lower the carbine,' Gunny said over group comms. 'There's nothing you can do here.'

'Goodluck, I like you but I will kill you if you don't lower your weapon,' Miska told him. He had tears running down his face. It wasn't just gang brotherhood, friendship, Miska knew that Goodluck had loaded his own hopes of redemption on Hradisky's rehabilitation.

'He's just upset,' Torricone said, 'nobody has to die.' He sounded almost desperate, like he needed someone, anyone to listen to reason. Hradisky started to lurch towards Goodluck, arms outstretched, a pained, pleading expression on his face. Miska new it was a trap, a masquerade.

'You know she'll kill you,' Kaneda told Goodluck. The Comanchero just nodded. Miska was pretty sure he didn't care any more.

'Miska, please,' Torricone pleaded.

'He hasn't lowered his weapon,' Miska said. 'Vido.'

Vido brought the shotgun up to his shoulder.

'No!' Goodluck screamed. He swung round towards the *consigliere*. Miska triggered the N-bomb in his head at the same time as her dad fired a three-round burst from the war droid's Retributor. Goodluck's body came apart and scattered

330

itself across the warehouse floor. Vido squeezed the trigger on the shotgun. Miska stepped back quickly as the acid grenade exploded against Hradisky's corpse. The rest of the Bastards scattered out of the splash radius. She heard Mass cursing. Kaneda shrugged off his smoking bike jacket and let it fall to the ground. Hradisky was letting out an inhuman screaming noise as the molecular acid ate away at his body. Gunny put him out of his misery with another burst from the Retributor. Miska looked at the mess that had been Goodluck. It was a waste, a stupid fucking waste that hadn't needed to happen. That was when she realised that she could hear gunfire from outside. Long, undisciplined automatic fire, instead of the short controlled bursts of the MoP's soldier drones.

'Dominic's people?' Mass asked. Miska hoped so. She hoped they'd come mob-handed and blundered into the drones.

'Fuck this, we're out of here,' Miska announced.

'What are you doing, son?' her dad asked over group comms. Miska had no idea what he was talking about until she turned around to find herself looking down the barrel of Torricone's carbine. The war droid's Retributor was already pointing at him.

'T, we know how this ends,' Mass pointed out.

'Please, Michael,' Vido said.

'He's right, isn't he?' Torricone said quietly. They could hear shouting and even screams intermingled with the gunfire outside. 'Everything you touch becomes corrupted, just more pain, suffering and death. You're like a fucking virus.'

Miska was surprised how much that hurt. She was also surprised that she hadn't triggered the N-bomb in his head.

'Did we kill any innocent people?' she asked. 'Everyone out there chose to pick up a gun.'

'That supposed to be a justification?' Torricone asked.

'I don't need a justification—' Miska started.

'I know, we've got bombs in our head.' He nodded towards the smear on the floor that had been Hradisky. 'We're starting not to care.'

'Do you want to die now, Michael?' she asked, hoping that nobody noticed her voice crack just a little. She didn't know if she could send the codes to detonate his head bomb but she did know that her father would kill him if he didn't lower his weapon. Torricone was shaking his head.

'I wish I had the courage of my convictions.' He lowered the carbine. There was a collective sigh of relief. Miska felt it as well. 'But I'm not doing this shit any more,' the car thief told her.

Someone landed behind Torricone. His eyes went wide. The tip of a sword burst out of his chest and he spat blood down himself. Teramoto was at his shoulder, nuzzling against his neck in an obscene parody of a lover. Miska was moving, bringing her carbine up. Suddenly the normally crystal clear clarity of her IVD was filled with distortion. The image of Teramoto pushing a sword through Torricone's chest froze and blinked off. Miska tranced in. Involuntarily.

It was a perfect one-to-one simulation, indistinguishable from reality, total sensory immersion, total verisimilitude. She could smell the night blossoming flowers, taste the salt spray in the air. She was stood on a rocky outcrop among what appeared to be the ruins of a temple under a sky of black velvet interspersed with pinpricks of light. Vines grew up around pillars and a crumbling statue of what Miska suspected had once been a beautiful woman. She was wearing a simple dress of a type that Miska was convinced she'd seen in some viz about Earth's history. The outcrop looked down on a sandy bay. There was a town of ancient-looking white stucco buildings, illuminated by braziers and flickering torches nestled in the bay.

'Okay,' she said, sounding much calmer than she felt. She'd just seen Teramoto run Torricone through. She knew Torricone was dead. He couldn't survive a wound like that. Her cheeks were wet. She wiped away the tears angrily. This virtual construct was too good. Her artificial eyes couldn't cry in the real world. Then she noticed the owl watching her from a fallen, vine-covered column.

'Who are you? What am I doing here?' she demanded.

'It's an owl,' a woman's voice said. Miska turned back to look at the statue.

'Okay who are—'

'You do not have the time.' The statue hadn't moved but the voice definitely seemed to be emanating from it. 'I have contracted time in here as much as I can, but it is still passing in your world. One of the weapons platforms that orbits Barnard's Prime has been suborned. We have launched a kinetic kill weapon at your coordinates.' Miska's eyes went wide. 'Pavor cannot be allowed to escape. You have mere seconds to reach the artefact, or you will all die. We can save your love.'

'He's not my ... What's ...'

Miska opened her eyes. She was still falling. She landed in a crouch, palms on the floor. Teramoto slid the sword out of Torricone's chest, still holding him up. One of the war droid's pneumatic hammer hands hit Teramoto really hard. He went flying through the air. Torricone staggered forward, still drooling blood down himself. Miska was on her feet racing towards him. The others were beginning to react now. Kaneda first, screaming, as he fired at Teramoto, Mass joining in. Vido was struggling with the shotgun, trying to affix the last acid grenade to the barrel while shaking. Miska caught Torricone. Somehow Teramoto was back up, racing towards the mezzanine, railgun rounds kicking up the concrete floor behind him as her dad fired the war droid's Retributor.

Teramoto ran under the mezzanine and moments later it collapsed as railgun rounds cut through its supports. The war droid launched another missile. Boosted muscles meant that Miska was strong enough to scoop Torricone up into her arms. He was still alive, just. The blast from the missile's explosion knocked her down onto one knee. A piece of shrapnel opened up the side of her head.

'Get to the artefact now!' Miska screamed over group comms.

'You've got to be—' Mass started, real dread in his voice.

'The N-bombs go off in anyone not at the artefact in the next five seconds!'

Miska ran towards the semi's ruined trailer, carrying Torricone. Vido, Kaneda and Mass followed. The war droid was keeping pace with them, its turret scanning all around, looking for the thing wearing Teramoto's body. Torricone spasmed in Miska's arms, getting ready to breathe his last. Kaneda ran past her. He reached the back of the semi-trailer and turned around to cover them. Teramoto was perched on top of a remaining part of the trailer's roof, looking down on Kaneda like a predator ready to pounce. Railgun rounds hit the trailer but Teramoto was gone again. Kaneda turned to look up but the black roots reached out from the artefact, grabbed him and dragged him screaming into it. His passing through didn't even make a ripple on the artefact's surface and he was gone. Again there was that distortion in the air and Miska felt the artefact somehow pull at her. She faltered for a moment but forced herself to move on. She all but threw Torricone onto it. Roots grew around him and he was enveloped.

She turned back to check on Mass and Vido. The war droid was firing its Retributor into a corner of the warehouse at a racing figure. Mass and Vido were staring at the artefact with naked, abject terror. Mass was shaking his head. Vido crossed himself.

'Die here, now, or take your chances,' she told them. 'Suicide is a sin.' They looked at each other. 'No time.'

Vido moved first. He was climbing into the trailer when the roots grew around him. Mass was screaming out the Lord's Prayer as he was sucked in. Miska turned to follow, trying to ignore her own sense of supernatural dread. Teramoto was standing on the back of the trailer, dripping sword in hand, between her and the artefact.

'Bitch,' he told her. He jumped off the trailer and strode towards her. Miska was thrown into shadow as she raised her carbine. Her dad the war droid stepped over her and swung one of his hammer limbs. Teramoto rolled out of the way. The hammer knocked a huge gouge out of the concrete. Miska ran for the artefact and dived for it, spinning in mid-air so she could see behind her. She landed on the alien device. The thick, viscous roots grew around her. She could see Teramoto running towards her, his face a mask of fury, the war droid right behind him. She gave Teramoto the finger. The roots grew around the finger. The world seemed to tilt. And then it was gone ...

... replaced by total blackness and white, searing, agony, as though every iota of her form had been pierced. She felt as though she was being taken apart cell by cell, atom by atom, while being forced to somehow understand the experience. She tried to flail away from the pain, with no idea if her intention was being translated into actual physical movement.

Then light, the surface of a dim world. She had no idea how she was receiving this sensory information. She was somehow just aware of it. A vista of standing-stone-like structures analogous to servers, composite trees with solar panels for leaves trying to leach energy from a cold, fading, somehow-caged sun, a pentagonal net stretched around the world, technology and landscape indistinguishable from each other.

Suffering for eternity and then the sensory overload of birth and the pain of light as she was vomited back into ...

... the real world. She was curled up in a ball on bare rock in a huge crater next to the artefact.

'Freeze!'

'Don't move!'

'Lose the weapons!'

Jeez, she thought, *which one is it?*

It took her a moment to realise that she wasn't in pain any more. From anything. Her foot, any of the hits she'd taken. She reached up to touch her face. The acid scar was gone.

Torricone! She forced herself to open her eyes. They polarised under the harsh glare of the searchlights. Torricone was there, sitting up, hands in the air. He looked fine, no trace of his impalement. If anything he looked relieved. The others were there as well.

'It's okay, guys, we know the drill,' Mass said, though his voice was shaky. Vido looked as though he was about to weep with relief. Kaneda was just staring around, mouth wide open.

FBI Hostage Rescue Team members, pointing weapons at them, surrounded Miska and her surviving Bastards. Honey Badger combat exoskeletons circled them in the air. Miska checked the clock in her IVD. It was synchronising with the local net. They'd lost four hours. It had seemed much longer. According to her GPS they were still in exactly the same place. The bowl that the light industrial estate had been in was now a crater. Miska prayed that the kinetic javelin had got Teramoto. It disturbed her that they, whoever 'they' were, felt such an action necessary.

She could hear the HRT members talking:

'Where did they come from?'

'Did they just come out of that thing?'

Clearly they were rattled enough that it was affecting their discipline.

'What have you done now?' a familiar voice asked.

Miska sagged. She realised that she was shaking. Then she looked up. Angela was stood over her, little more than a silhouette against the searchlights. Her arms crossed.

'Hey Sis,' Miska said, more cheerfully than she felt.

CHAPTER 22

'You caused a tectonic event!' Angela shouted at her. Miska felt this was a little unfair.

'That wasn't me,' she pointed out. They had been disarmed, searched and cuffed, and were now being marched out of the crater by the HRT members, with close air support from the Honey Badgers. What Miska didn't see was any of the Marshal Service SOG combat exoskeletons. This looked to be an all-FBI affair. They were being marched towards an APC parked next to an assault shuttle.

'Do you think I'm mad?' It was out of her mouth before she'd even thought about it. Torricone, Mass and Vido all turned to look at her. Kaneda just kept trudging towards the APC.

'Really want me to answer that?' Angela asked.

'I didn't have anything like the time to hack Strategic Space and Air Command.'

'Then who did?' Angela demanded. It was a good question; Miska didn't know. The statue of the woman had mentioned someone called Pavor. It meant nothing to her. They reached the APC. Miska and her Bastards were pushed down onto their knees. A tech ran a Geiger counter over them. Another took a blood sample. Miska could see some kind of quarantine tent being set up by people dressed in hostile environment suits. She couldn't help but think that particular horse had bolted. She had to smile at how uneasy the HRT members looked upon seeing all the precautions being taken after they'd been crawling over the kinetic harpoon's impact crater.

'Miska!' Angela snapped. Miska looked back up at her sister, only now realising that she'd been saying something.

'What?' Miska asked. Angela opened her mouth. 'No wait, I'm guessing that it's another lecture on how irresponsible I am? What are you whining about? You got a shiny new alien artefact that without us would've fallen into Mars's hands.' She wasn't sure she believed that but she was enjoying the look on her sister's face. Angela opened her mouth again. 'Seriously,' Miska started before her sister could speak, 'it's been a really long day. Could we go to jail, please?' She was aware of Mass and Vido nodding.

'Yes, please,' Vido said. 'A nice long comfortable life sentence in a quiet ultramax; that seems like bliss.'

'Hey, you guys wanted to come,' Miska pointed out.

'We made a mistake,' Mass said. Torricone was staring at her. Miska couldn't read his expression. Kaneda was just looking at the ground.

'You guys will be lucky if you don't end up dissected in some laboratory!' Angela spat.

'Hey!' Miska shouted. Angela's head twitched round to stare down at her little sister. 'Leave them alone. It's me you're angry with.'

'Is it too soon to ask to speak with my lawyer?' Mass asked.

Angela kicked him over. Miska, hands cuffed behind her back, head down, charged her sister. Angela stepped to one side and, with a touch, sent Miska flying. Miska rolled onto her back and saw her sister raise a boot to stomp her.

'Captain Corbin!' Angela froze. Miska moved her head until she could see a tall, solid-looking man with the kind of clean-cut chiselled features that she was starting to suspect came as standard when you joined the FBI. He was wearing the same armour as the rest of the HRT members but he looked older. Miska also suspected that he dyed his hair.

'SAC,' Angela said, addressing the man. Miska knew it stood for Special Agent in Charge, of the FBI part of the operation anyway, but she couldn't help but laugh. She was starting to suspect she was borderline hysterical. Mass and Vido burst out laughing as well. Even Torricone smiled.

'Captain Corbin, the disgraceful display I have just witnessed notwithstanding, you are to assist me in securing the area until the USSAF First Contact team get here,' he told her.

Angela turned to face the Special Agent in Charge.

'That's not my remit.' Her finger stabbed out towards Miska, who had to try hard not to flinch. 'I'm on secondment, the Marshals deputised me to put a stop to this crazy bitch—'

'Hey!' Miska protested. The SAC gave Miska a look of distinct disgust.

'We have our orders, Captain. I've arranged for transport for our prisoners.'

'Where are the Marshals?' Angela demanded.

'Castro and his team are on their way back from New Erebus as we speak, but they're still three hours out.'

'Well, let's wait,' Angela said.

'We can handle a prisoner transport I think, Captain.' Then he turned away as though the matter was resolved.

'SAC!' Angela shouted after him. He spun around, face like thunder. 'You need to send six of the Honey Badgers with the transport.'

'I'm sending back one of the APCs with four of the HRT members, and I'm not even supposed to spare that many. My orders are to use all available assets to secure this area. If you don't like those orders I suggest you take it up with the Colonial Department of Defence and Department of Justice.' He took a step towards her, 'After you've done what you're fucking told!' The orders made sense. Whatever Miska had done, it paled in comparison with securing an apparently active piece of hitherto unknown alien tech. 'Now I suggest you un-bunch your panties and we can get on with our day.'

'Wow,' Miska said. Few people had the balls to talk to her sister like that. Angela looked even more borderline apoplectic than normal. This made Miska happy. 'It's okay, Sis, we promise not to escape,' Miska lied. Angela backhanded Miska hard enough to send her sprawling. 'Ow,' Miska told the dirt.

'You Corbin girls have real anger management problems, don't you?' Mass said, taking his life in his hands.

'Captain Corbin! I don't care if she is related to you, you can't—' the SAC started.

'Shut the fuck up!' Angela screamed at him. Suddenly it got very quiet around the crater and everyone was looking their way. Angela pointed at Miska, who was trying to push herself back onto her knees using her head. 'Listen to me, you little pencil-necked prick! Anything happens to my prisoner and I'm holding you personally responsible. Think about that.'

'Are you threat—' the SAC started.

'Go about your business before I cripple you and see if your second in command is more competent,' Angela snapped. The SAC went a funny colour before doing a quick about-face and stomping off. Miska had the feeling that some subordinate was in for a rough time.

'Nice guy, not too bright though,' Miska offered. The look Angela gave her suggested that her older sister would have cheerfully strangled her, right there and then. Miska just smiled.

Miska was quite pleased that her head had stopped ringing. They were in the back of one of the FBI armoured personnel carriers, heading back to holding cells in the federal building in New Verona.

Miska had caught a glimpse of other prisoners before they had been loaded into the APC. Maybe about a dozen men and women. She suspected they were all that remained of Dominic's people. They looked shell-shocked. They must have been quite far back to avoid the kinetic javelin's impact.

'Y'know, I think I quite like your sister,' Mass said. He was sitting between Vido and Torricone on the opposite bench in the back of the APC. Kaneda, still quiet but radiating a palpable sense of relief, was sitting next to her. There were two HRT team members by the door watching them.

'Yeah?' Miska asked. 'Well she didn't hit—' The impact sent her flying the short distance across the APC to collide painfully with Torricone. Her world was tilting again. Miska couldn't quite work out what was going on. Then she realised the APC had been hit, hard, and was rolling. Somebody fell on her as the APC came to a stop on its roof. Her head was ringing again.

'Fuck's sake!' she snapped. 'Get off me! Move!' She crawled out from under Uncle Vido. She could see the two HRT

342

members in a pile by the APC's rear door. They were starting to move. She lay on her back, and brought her wrists under her feet, stepping through her cuffed arms. The first HRT member was up, bringing her weapon to bear on Miska. Miska put her hands on the ground and kicked out and up with her right leg. Her boot caught the woman just under the chin with enough force to momentarily crush her windpipe and cut off her oxygen. Miska knew this would only work if HRT members weren't as well augmented as special forces. The other HRT member was trying to get up as well. He had his back to Miska. She hooked her cuffed wrists over his head, using the smart cable to blood-strangle him – crushing the veins in his neck to cut off the blood flow.

'Erm, is this a you'll-blow-up-our-heads-if-we-don't-help, situation?' Vido asked. 'Because we'd quite like to go to jail.'

'Now!' Miska shouted. She could hear shouting from outside. Kaneda and Mass crawled over the roof of the now-upside-down APC to help restrain the two HRT members until they passed out. Behind her Miska was aware of intense heat from a glowing rectangle that had appeared in the rear bulkhead of the APC. The thermite frame charge cut its way through the armour plate, dripping molten metal into the armoured vehicle. The rectangle of metal was pulled out of the bulkhead and King Skinny peeked in.

'Hello, everyone,' he said and chuckled.

The Disciples had used a cargo mech, basically a walking crane that they had probably stolen from the spaceport, to knock the APC over. They had abandoned the low loader that they'd used to transport the mech, on the side of the road at the intersection where they had ambushed the APC. The four FBI agents hadn't

343

been treated gently but they were all still alive. Miska was quite pleased that it was a rescue rather than a kidnapping. It seemed that Blanca had indeed reached out to the Disciples.

Miska cracked the lock on the APC's locker and they had retrieved their weapons. She wasn't too bothered about most of them but she liked the SIG GP-992, and the knife that her dad had given her had sentimental value. On the other hand, if she was going to live up to her word then she was going to have to attend a family reunion. She took the carbine as well. She couldn't imagine Mass and Vido's families being terribly happy about what she'd done to the two Mafiosi.

The small convoy of Disciple vehicles pulled into the courtyard of the brown stucco compound out in the desert. Some of Blanca's people were waiting for them at the door to the house.

Miska held back a little. She let the others go ahead of her. She could hear the sound of their reunion. The tears. She knew this was a mistake. She was a practical girl but she didn't want to see this. Despite what people thought, she wasn't dead inside. She knew she would have to wrench them away from their families again.

You could leave them here, she thought, but she knew it would have a knock-on effect. *You could walk away.* Now her little voice was starting to sound like Torricone. *This is too hard. Too much cost for too little gain.*

Even as she thought it she felt herself harden. She'd never walked away from anything because it was difficult in her life.

She concentrated and sent a message that included her current whereabouts.

*

344

They had been given a chance to shower. Clean clothes laid out for them. Miska felt like she could have slept for a week, as she walked through the open French windows onto a patio, but she knew they were up against a clock. The Marshals and the FBI would be looking for them. The patio looked out over an exquisitely landscaped garden, sprinklers providing the extra moisture the modified plants needed. An extensive feast had been laid out on a banquet table on the lawn. It was pretty much being ignored. Miska guessed there were at least four generations of family surrounding Vido, maybe about twenty people, and enough tears that Blanca could have switched off the sprinklers. Mass's family was smaller – a formidable look-ing dark-haired woman with too much make-up on, and three reasonably fat kids. There was an older looking guy with them as well. A fading tough guy who Miska suspected was Mass's father. Suddenly a number of things made sense.

Miska hadn't meant to draw attention to herself but she was really hungry and the buffet was being criminally ignored. She started gathering a plate of food, ignoring the odd hysterical shriek and threat. Vido and Mass tried to calm the two families down. She was aware that the old guy with Mass's family was staring at her as though he had known what to do with people like her back in the old days.

She grabbed a beer and took her plate back into the house. She passed Blanca on the patio. Still dressed in black, the desert wind tugging at her dress, she was just watching the reunion. She looked lonely.

Miska saw Kaneda sat in the lounge, his carbine between his legs. Miska went and sat down next to him. He looked up.

'You should eat something,' she told him. He just watched

her, his expression as hard to read as Teramoto's had been. 'Did you do it on purpose?'

He considered the question.

'I don't know,' he finally said. He seemed to wrestle with something. 'Back on the ship, if the Milliners or the Scorpion Rain Society think I did it—'

'I'll have a word with the others, tell them to keep it to themselves. You know Vido and Mass will try and use it to get influence over you, right?'

'I've had enough of that,' he said through gritted teeth.

'Teramoto was looking into something …' Miska started. She wasn't sure how to proceed. She didn't want to give too much away.

'About your father?' Kaneda asked. Miska had to force herself not to react.

'Yes,' she told him. 'You know anything about that?'

Kaneda shook his head. Miska suppressed her disappointment.

'But I can see if I can find something out,' he told her and stood up. 'I'm going to get something to eat.'

Miska nodded at the stump of his little finger. It seemed that it hadn't been healed when the artefact had taken them wherever it had taken them.

'We'll get that fixed when we get back,' she told him.

'I don't think so,' Kaneda told her and walked out, nodding to Blanca as she came into the lounge.

'He's very young,' she said, watching Kaneda walk towards the buffet.

'He did good,' Miska told her.

'How long have you got?' she asked.

'Not long. It's not the police who're after us. The FBI, the

Marshals will actually come looking. Have a story prepared. We coerced you, bombs in family members' heads, that sort of thing.'

'I won't have to use too much imagination.' Blanca walked over to one of the other sofas, her heels clicking on the marble, and sat down.

'Dominic? My children?' she asked. Miska knew how much this was costing the other woman. It was clear that she had been used to wielding power. Dominic had stolen that from her and now she was forced to rely on someone who, at best, could be described as a wild card. Miska checked the messages in her IVD and smiled.

'It's in hand,' she told Donna Cofino, just as she heard the sounds of the *Little Jimmy*'s engines overhead. Blanca's security people came running. 'I'd keep your people on a tight leash if I were you.'

The *Little Jimmy*'s wings elongated, unsheathing two impellers as the stealth ship circled over the house and came in to land on the back lawn. Miska had come out onto the patio to watch. She found herself standing next to King Skinny.

'Thank you for getting Donna Blanca and myself talking,' he told her. Miska shrugged as the *Little Jimmy*'s three landing struts sank deep into the lawn. 'Torricone, he cannot come back here.' Miska turned to look at the gang leader. 'I'll have to kill him. I won't like it but I'll have no choice.'

'Do you know how little I care about your petty gang bull-shit?' she asked and turned back to look at the stealth ship. The ramp was coming down.

'I think you care about him,' King Skinny said quietly. Miska tried to ignore the gang leader. Tried to ignore the prickling feeling that his words were forcing her to examine. Then the Ultra walked out of the *Little Jimmy*, holding hands with a very serious-looking boy of about nine or ten years. There was an attractive teenaged girl a few steps behind; she was clearly her mother's daughter. In his free hand the Ultra carried a cool box.

'Antonio! Anna!' Blanca cried and rushed forward to hug them, tears in all of their eyes. The Ultra took a few discreet steps back. Miska walked down the steps onto the lawn. Vido was staring at the Ultra in abject horror.

'The Ultra? The fucking Ultra! You sent that sick bastard—' Mass started. Miska silenced him with a look.

Blanca looked up from hugging her children at the serial killer.

'Thank you, thank you!'

The Ultra simply bowed his beautiful head. His alabaster skin reminded Miska of the statue of the woman she'd seen in the perfect virtual construct.

'They saw and heard nothing, Donna Cofino,' the prolific serial killer told the Mafia Donna.

'Dominic?' Miska asked as she reached the group. The Ultra just held up the cooler and then laid it on the lawn as if making a votive offering to Blanca. Miska nodded and allowed herself a smile before turning to Mass.

'Mass,' she said, 'five minutes and we are gone.' Mass sagged but nodded. The complaints, shrieked insults and threats started again. 'Good work,' she told the Ultra as she passed him. He just smiled.

The coolness of the *Little Jimmy*'s interior felt like escape.

CHAPTER 23

FOUR WEEKS LATER

Waterloo Station was a modular station that had been assembled to act as a staging area for the mercenary forces fighting the proxy war down on the jungle moon that orbited the vast gas giant. They could dock there and then both sides of the conflict could bid for their services. Mercenaries of various genders could be drinking together one night and then, depending on how the bidding went, murdering each other with one-generation-old weapons down on the surface the next day. It was pretty much a mercenary/military contractors-only conflict. To Miska, it felt like a massive, very expensive, strategy game being played out with real blood. She wasn't even sure what the fighting was about; as far as she could tell all the real resources were in the gas giant's cloud mines. On the other hand it was a job, and more to the point, a job where the US Marshal Service and the FBI had no jurisdiction. Not that that would stop bounty hunters and angry sisters.

Miska had started checking via the net the moment the *Hangman's Daughter* had decelerated into the system. She had known what to look for, and how to avoid being found by countermeasures. That was why she was making her way through one of the main hotel streets in the station. She had her head down, she was in her BDUs, and was wearing a shemagh, sunglasses and a forage cap to help disguise her appearance. By now the other mercenary companies would know that the infamous *Hangman's Daughter* had docked. She knew there would be people looking to make a point at the expense of her and her Bastards but she didn't have the time to deal with that right now. She glanced up at the transparent ceiling, subjectively looking down on the surprisingly bright swirling colours of the gas giant.

Miska had already booked a room in the hotel, so she just ignored the automated reception and caught the elevator up to the fourth floor. She walked into her room, opened the French windows to the balcony, swung over them and dropped down onto the balcony below. Landing, she drew her SIG and used her smartlink connection to the weapon to drop the velocity to subsonic. With her other hand, she connected a lock burner to the French windows. The door clicked open and she stepped into the dark room. The figure on the bed was reaching for a pistol on the bedside table. Miska squeezed the SIG's trigger twice, burying two of the 4.7mm rounds silently into the pillow next to the figure.

'Don't!' she ordered. He froze. Miska crossed to the bed and knelt down on it. She jammed the barrel of her pistol underneath his chin. It might have been unprofessional, but then she was still angry.

'What the fuck, Raff?' she demanded. He'd booked into the

hotel using the cover of a war correspondent; work he might have actually done once, before the CIA had recruited him.

'I sense you're angry,' he said.

'What was that thing you sent us after?' she demanded and jabbed him with the pistol again.

'Ow! You mean the alien artefact that I told you was an alien artefact and you didn't believe me?'

'Some fucking warning of its capabilities would have been nice!' Miska spat.

'We didn't know!' he protested. 'Alien!'

She looked down at him, frowned, but holstered the pistol and then pushed him off the bed with her boot in a fit of general pique.

'Fuck's sake, Miska,' Raff said, climbing to his feet.

'What is it? And don't fucking bullshit me!'

'We don't know,' he told her. 'We've found a few things like it. They have certain similar characteristics, they're all very old, they're all seemingly indestructible, but each does different things. Some of them create odd temporal effects, others seem to break down probabilities in some way and some just fuck with physics in a manner we don't understand.'

'And let me guess, the Company's Directorate of Science and Technology wanted their very own?' she asked.

'Better it went to Mars?' he countered.

'Sure it was them?'

'As sure as we get in this business.'

Miska was quiet for a moment, trying to digest what Raff had told her.

'I'm serious, Miska, we told you what we knew.'

'You said they were old. How old?'

'Thirteen-point-seven billion years, give-or-take.'

351

Miska made her impressed face.

'That's old,' she admitted.

'Miska, it's the age of the universe.'

That got her attention.

'I think the one on Barney Prime was a portal,' she told him. 'I think we went somewhere else. Some kind of machine world, and I mean an actual world that consisted entirely of tech.' She was struggling to properly express herself. What she had seen had been an absence of nature, as though it had never existed, as though something else had evolved. 'It also managed to inject Teramoto's body with some kind of weird nanotech.'

Raff was just watching her.

'You okay?' he finally said.

'Don't fucking start,' she warned. He held his hands up.

'Okay, fine, but I need an after-action report, as detailed as possible, with any relevant footage,' he told her. She just nodded.

'The Master of Puppets?' she asked.

'That battle-bus of his may as well have been an APC. It survived the blast but rolled. There was some kind of escape vehicle inside.'

'So the fucker lived?' Miska asked.

Raff nodded.

'Who's Pavor?' she asked.

Raff looked mystified. 'I've no idea,' he told her.

'Well, I've been doing a little bit of research of my own. It seems that Pavor is the Romanised name of a Greek god,' she told Raff. She could see the same discomfort at the mention of gods that she'd had when she'd discovered this – the same creeping dread.

'Which one?' Raff asked reluctantly.

'Phobos,' she told him, 'It means fear. Twin brother of Deimos, which means terror, sons of Ares, which is of course the Greek name for—'

'Mars,' Raff finished.

Phobos and Deimos were both satellites of the Red Planet back in the Sol system.

'What the fuck is going on, Raff? Did a Small God possess one of my people? Was that why the orbital weapons platform was hacked so easily?'

Raff looked appalled.

'Miska ... I don't know. Did the kinetic javelin kill him, it?'

'I fucking hope so, but tell your people to keep an eye out for the artist previously known as Teramoto Shigeru, and don't fuck around. If they see him. I'd recommend a particle beam weapon.' She swung her boots off the bed and stood up. 'You pay us half what you owe for this, understand me?'

'Miska ... I'm not sure I can square that with the bosses. You failed ...'

And she was marching towards him. He backed away from her wrath and into the corner of the room by the door.

'What do you mean we fucking failed?' she demanded. 'Where is it now?'

'I don't know, best guess would be USSAF, maybe the DOE,' he said, meaning the Department of Energy. 'Or ...'

'Or?' she demanded.

'Well, your sister was there ...'

'She was after me.'

'That doesn't mean Black Chamber wouldn't take advantage of the situation.'

That made a degree of sense. Black Chamber was reputed to be the NSA's blacker-than-black covert operations unit.

'So we, as in America, have the artefact, we kept it out of Martian hands. That was the point of the exercise, wasn't it? So the mission succeeded. So we get fucking paid and I don't kneecap you.'

'It's not that simple—' he started. Of course it wasn't. Keeping it out of Martian hands had been one of the objectives, but there had been easier ways to do that. The FBI could have closed down the dig and confiscated the artefact but this had been an interagency pissing contest, empire building. The CIA had wanted access to the artefact, hence the incredibly illegal long shot of a mission that they'd sent the ultimate deniable assets on.

'We get paid and you hook us up to the slush fund as agreed, or I'll need a new case officer. Think about what happened to the last guy who screwed us over.'

Raff stared at her, appalled.

'You wouldn't dare,' he managed. Miska just looked at him. Finally he nodded weakly. She didn't have to open the door into his face as she left the room but she was pissed off and feeling petty.

Miska's virtual representation was sat up on the roof of the command centre's tower looking out over Camp Reisman. In the distance she could see mechs moving among the trees. By all accounts, the conflict below on the jungle moon was a mech-heavy one, despite the difficulty of the terrain.

'How're they doing, Gunny?' she asked. She'd been aware of her dad standing just behind her for a few moments now. The electronic ghost of Gunnery Sergeant Jonathan Corbin, USMC retired, took a few steps forward, sat down next to his daughter and handed her a pointless virtual beer.

'It's a work in progress,' he told her. 'Mass seems to have taken to it. I think he likes the feeling of power.'

'Well, he embraced the Wraiths when we hit Faigroe Station,' Miska said. 'I'm surprised any of the Barney Prime veterans are interested in volunteering any more.'

'Kaneda's still practising his sniping, he's getting good. He's also started teaching himself to shoot ambidextrously,' her dad told her. That got Miska's attention. She turned to look at her dad's craggy features.

'Like Teramoto?' she asked. He nodded and she looked back over the camp.

'He's good, I mean, it's movie bullshit, not real shooting ...'

'You didn't see Teramoto, Dad. The guy was a one-man street-fighting slaughterhouse, you would have approved.'

He sighed.

'I doubt that, somehow.'

'Is this the lecture?' she asked. They'd been tip-toeing around each other since she'd returned from Barney Prime. 'Going to tell me you told me so?'

'No, I was going to apologise,' he said.

She turned to stare at him.

'Wow, I guess this is the day the galaxy starts spinning backwards, right? I should have played the lottery.'

Her dad rolled his eyes.

'Going behind your back and speaking to Torricone was messed up and unprofessional. I shouldn't have done that.'

'No, you shouldn't have. It undermined me, made him think I was out of control.'

'Even if you were?'

'Even if I was,' she muttered reluctantly.

'I reviewed all the footage. It was an extreme situation but two of your crew pulled weapons on you. That's a problem, Miska.'

'I know,' she said. 'I can't see Torricone volunteering to come out with us again. He came the first time because I made him, he went to Barney Prime to see his mum, who I still think you should date, y'know, now that Goodluck's dead.' She turned to look at him again. 'Too soon?'

'Torricone's requested medical training from the doctor,' her dad told her. 'Said that he won't carry a weapon for us. Goddamned hippy.'

Miska wasn't sure how she felt about that. At least he was still in the game.

'What about Vido?' she asked, to change the subject.

'He told me that another mission like that one will kill him, and I tend to agree. He said that he can be more use to us logistically, and possibly in terms of intelligence and strategy.'

'What do you think?' she asked.

'I think you're asking me what I think so you can pretend that you actually listen to your old dad,' he told her. Miska cast a rueful glance her dad's way. There was just the slightest smile on his face. 'Yeah, he's a good choice, he may need the rank to go with it.'

'Okay,' she agreed.

'Which brings me to ...'

'I'm sorry Dad, you were right, I was wrong,' she told him. 'I never should have taken the mission and I shouldn't have conducted it the way I did. I should've listened to you.'

He didn't say anything for a while.

'I don't want to undermine you. I understand and respect your abilities Miska, I really do. You are an extraordinary warrior ...' he started. She knew the *but* was coming, but even so

356

the praise made her heart soar. '... but even you have to admit you're pretty damn reckless. The way it stands at the moment, if I was alive, and operational, there is no chance in hell I'd have you on my team.' The soaring stopped and she crashed and burned. She felt like crying and then she was furious at herself for feeling like that. The worst of it was that she knew he was right.

'I was operational for twenty years, and already more people have died under your command than ever died under mine,' he told her. Now she was really feeling like shit. 'If you want me to keep doing this then all I ask is that you listen to me. Take advice. All good commanders listen to their subordinates. You were SF, you must know this.' He was right, she did. 'Your drive, my caution, we can get things done.'

She forced herself to look at him. Then she nodded. Her dad studied her for a moment. She guessed he was trying to decide if she meant it or not. He seemed satisfied and looked away again. He took a sip from his beer and then grimaced as he saw two of the mechs in the distance collide. Miska had to smile as she heard him muttering obscenities under his breath. Then he lapsed into silence. It looked as though he was wrestling with something.

'Spit it out,' she told him.

'The Ultra,' he said simply. She knew the rest of it. Giving him access to the *Little Jimmy* had been a foolish risk. Not to mention now Mass, Vido, Torricone and Kaneda all knew of the existence of her main escape route if things turned bad.

'I know,' she told him.

'I get that you were desperate,' he said, 'but he's an alien shaped like a man, and smart. Don't let it in.' She was pretty sure that her dad calling him an alien was hyperbole.

357

'I understand, I even agree, but I'm going to let him form his Nightmare Squad,' she told her dad.

'After you just—'

'Wait, hear me out. You see the footage of Phobos?' Phobos was how they were referring to whatever had possessed Teramoto's body. Her dad nodded. 'That's why. We're also rebuilding Skirov.' He looked as though he wanted to object but she was starting to suspect that he actually saw her point. He took another sip from his beer.

'You saw your sister, then?'

'Yep,' Miska took a sip from her own pointless beer, 'and she's still a bitch.'

Her dad's face fell.

'Miska, what've I told you about talking about your sister like that?'

ABOUT GOLLANCZ

Gollancz is the oldest SF publishing imprint in the world. Since being founded in 1927 Gollancz has continued to publish a focused selection of bestselling and award-winning authors. The front-list includes **Ben Aaronovitch**, **Joe Abercrombie**, **Charlaine Harris**, **Joanne Harris**, **Joe Hill**, **Alastair Reynolds**, **Patrick Rothfuss**, **Nalini Singh** and **Brandon Sanderson**.

As one of the largest Science Fiction and Fantasy imprints in the UK it is no surprise we have one of the most extensive backlists in the world. Find high-quality SF on Gateway written by such authors as **Philip K. Dick**, **Ursula Le Guin**, **Connie Willis**, **Sir Arthur C. Clarke**, **Pat Cadigan**, **Michael Moorcock** and **George R.R. Martin**.

We also have a strand of publishing in translation, which includes French, Polish and Russian authors. Gollancz is home to more award-winning authors than any other imprint, with names including **Aliette de Bodard**, **M. John Harrison**, **Paul McAuley**, **Sarah Pinborough**, **Pierre Pevel**, **Justina Robson** and many more.

The SF Gateway
*More than 3,000 classic, rare and previously
out-of-print SF novels at your fingertips.*
www.sfgateway.com

The Gollancz Blog
*Bringing you news from our worlds to yours. Stories,
interviews, articles and exclusive extracts just for you!*
www.gollancz.co.uk

GOLLANCZ
LONDON